GEIST

Realms and Realities Series

C.L. Merklinger

Copyright © 2024 by C.L. Merklinger

All rights reserved. No part of this publication may be reproduced, distributed, or transmitted in any form or by any means, including photocopying, recording, or other electronic or mechanical methods, without the prior written permission of the publisher.

This is a work of fiction. Unless otherwise indicated, all the names, characters, businesses, places, events and incidents in this book are either the product of the author's imagination or used in a fictitious manner. Any resemblance to actual persons, living or dead, or actual events is purely coincidental.

ACKNOWLEDGEMENTS

MY EDITOR - JENNIA D'LIMA

For a wonderful experience and amazing guidance.

MORBID PODCAST

For keeping this Weirdo Brain completely weird.

MARYLAND WRITERS ASSOCIATION

For Your Support

THE WRITERS IN THE SCRIBE SYNDICATE

PARK BOOKS MD

For taking a Chance on an Indie Author

JAMES MONTGOMERY

For being my fellow creative and amazing Chef

GEIST

German for a ghost or spirit; also referred to as a poltergeist. Typically, non-malevolent…typically…

CHAPTERS

PROLOGUE
CHAPTER ONE - ON THE ROAD AGAIN
CHAPTER TWO - JONESBOROUGH
CHAPTER THREE - RELAX
CHAPTER FOUR - HERE'S BENJI
CHAPTER FIVE - EXPLORERS
CHAPTER SIX - TO GIGI'S HOUSE WE GO
CHAPTER SEVEN - HEADSTONES AND MINDFUCKS
CHAPTER EIGHT - LEARNING CURVE
CHAPTER NINE - BISCUITS AND BEAGLE EARS
CHAPTER TEN - HISTORY LESSONS
CHAPTER ELEVEN - FOOD AND FOND FAREWELLS
CHAPTER TWELVE -HOME AGAIN~HOME AGAIN
CHAPTER THIRTEEN - THE BREAKFAST CLUB
CHAPTER FOURTEEN-HER VERY OWN JAKE RYAN
CHAPTER FIFTEEN - HELPING HANDS
CHAPTER SIXTEEN DISCOMBOBULATED
CHAPTER SEVENTEEN - WHAT'S A BESTIE FOR
CHAPTER EIGHTEEN - DOUBLE DATE
CHAPTER NINETEEN - ODDS, ENDS AND KUCHEN

CHAPTER TWENTY - NEW DO, NEW YOU
CHAPTER TWENTY-ONE - NEW CHAPTERS
CHAPTER TWENTY-TWO - PREPARATIONS
CHAPTER TWENTY-THREE - ROAD WEARY AND PUT AWAY WET
CHAPTER TWENTY-FOUR - A NEW DAWN A NEW DAY
CHAPTER TWENTY-FIVE - MOVING DAY
CHAPTER TWENTY-SIX - HELL OF A DAY
CHAPTER TWENTY-SEVEN - MARGARET FUCKING COBB
CHAPTER TWENTY-EIGHT - FUN AND GAMES
CHAPTER TWENTY-NINE - CHANCE ENCOUNTER
CHAPTER THIRTY - WHO'S THE NEW GUY
CHAPTER THIRTY-ONE - THE FASCINATING WORLD OF GHOSTS
CHAPTER THIRTY-TWO - THE BITCH IS BACK
CHAPTER THIRTY-THREE - HALLOWEEN
CHAPTER THIRTY-FOUR - CHANNELING THEIR INNER SCOOBIES
CHAPTER THIRTY-FIVE - SUCK IT! MR COBB
EPILOGUE

PROLOGUE

IN THE QUIET SOLITUDE OF her home, Margaret tended to the fire, a necessity during these winter months in Eastern Tennessee. As she added two small logs to the flames, the winds blew hard against the walls, bringing a biting chill that she could not stay ahead of. The roof, burdened by the weight of the freshly fallen snow, let out a groan as if to seek empathy. Through the small opening in the frosted window, she saw a figure just over the pond in the distance. A lone female, bundled in layers approached at a snail's pace, hindered by the depth of the snow and the winds pushing through the holler. This woman, *this* woman was no ordinary woman. To Margaret's dismay, her husband Elias had been carrying on an affair with this beauty. Quite successfully, in fact, until the women's paths crossed one day. That fateful day when Elias had found out Betsy was with child was when the pair decided to join forces and seek reparations for the grief he had caused not only the both of them but the community as a whole. Elias was not only a philanderer; he was also a con man, a fraud. Swindling locals out of their hard-earned wages. He had a reputation - a reputation that would bring him to his end.

As the last of those thoughts left her mind, Margaret looked out again; Betsy had made her way to the front path leading toward the home. Opening the door a crack, allowing the crisp cold air and a small swirl of snow to enter, Margaret said, "Hurry, please. I'm struggling as it is to keep the chill out of this home."

Picking up her pace, Betsy entered through the front door, immediately taking a deep breath, as if inhaling the warmth the room provided. Shutting the door, Margaret turned to assist her guest with her coat, placing it on a hook near the fire to aid in drying out the heavy fabric.

Maneuvering herself to the fire, Betsy reached her hands out and feverishly began to rub them together. Watching Betsy perform this task, Margaret admired Betsy's beauty and youth. Although she could not fathom what her treacherous husband had done to Betsy, she could see where the temptation had lay. Betsy's long, thick blonde hair, plump, smooth skin, and otherworldly-blue eyes were in stark contrast to Margaret's plain features. Their physiques could also not have been more in contrast. Time and life events had not yet taken hold of Betsy, and all her assets were still set where God had placed them. No longer the svelte beauty she had once been, Margaret did, however, possess a quick wit and a resourceful mind, as well as the talents given to her as a witch.

"Today we end his evil ways," Betsy said solemnly, turning away from the fire. Her doe-like eyes caught the flicker of the flame, causing Margaret to get lost in them for just a moment.

"Why…yes. My dear, I mean, *our dear* Elias will be brought to atone for the sins he committed against us, God, and the others in this community. Did you bring the items we spoke of? Lay them before me, quickly."

Reaching in her dress pockets, Betsy retrieved a small velvet pouch. Placing it on the large wooden table, she then pulled out the brooch Elias had given her as a token of his love and adoration. Setting it down, she continued to remove a ribbon and a small paper envelope containing arsenic.

Margaret retrieved two tea cups and saucers from the small cupboard and placed them with Betsy's items. Adding a few small spoons and a tea strainer to each tea cup, she instructed Betsy to put on an apron and add the arsenic to the cup to the far right. Mindful to not touch the poison, Betsy used the corners of the apron to cover her hands as she tore a small corner of the envelope to create the tiniest of openings. Leaning the pouch over the lip of the tea-cup, she gave it several taps, then replaced the strainer on top. Folding the envelope, she placed it back into the pouch and then her pocket.

Margaret heated a kettle of water and placed small spoonfuls of tea leaves into the strainers on top of the cups. Knowing that Elias would not be able to refuse a hot cup of tea upon his return in this cold weather, the pair sat and waited quietly, patient for their fraudster to arrive.

Just as the sun was set to disappear over the tree line, a horse was heard neighing. Margaret instructed Betsy to take her coat from the hook and disappear to the back room and remain out of sight until Margaret signaled. Obeying, Betsy retreated behind the curtain that separated the main space from the pantry to the rear of the kitchen. No sooner than she had, the sound of boots approaching the front door was quickly followed by Elias' large silhouette appearing in the open door.

"Please, Elias! Shut the door!" Margaret scolded as she stood to help her husband with his coat and hat. Seating him, she knelt before him and assisted in the removal of his boots. Setting them by the fire, she retrieved the kettle and slowly poured the hot water over the tea leaves. "My dear, you must be frozen solid. Here, let's have some tea to warm you up, and you can tell me of your day." As the pair sipped their tea, Elias regaled her with his tale of how the previous year he had convinced a gentleman in Roanoke to give Elias controlling interest in the land his farm sat on. In exchange, Elias promised assistance in distributing the crops to aid the failing farm. A promise Elias had not kept. The farm failed, as Elias had planned, and the income from the land would now surely bring them enough fortune to get through the next winter months. Listening in disgust, Margaret dutifully praised her husband and his ingenuity until the effects of the poison took hold.

At first, Elias fidgeted with his collar and ran his hands through his hair, complaining that the room suddenly got hot. Standing, he said "Margaret, I…don't feel…" and leaned forward toward the fire and began retching. Calling to his wife for help, he knelt and continued to vomit and convulse. Standing behind Elias, Margaret said "Elias, you don't feel well, my sweet? I wish I could be of some help, but you see, I cannot. Nor can your dear Betsy." And with that, Elias turned his head to see Betsy reveal herself from behind the curtain. Unable to talk through the vomitous retches, Elias doubled over again in pain.

"Quickly, Betsy, bring me the items I've placed on the stool as well as the brooch." Obeying the instructions, Betsy joined her side. "Now lay the brooch near Elias. There, on the floor." Again, Betsy did as she was told and then returned to Margaret's side. "Place your hand in mine," Margaret instructed as she wrapped a ribbon around their hands, binding them to each other. Betsy, distracted by Elias's obvious pain, missed the next set of instructions and was quickly brought back to reality with a slight slap to her cheek by Margaret's free hand. "Girl! You must focus now! We have but one chance to make this work, and I'll not let this poor excuse of a man get away so easily with death and death alone. You hear me, Elias?" Margaret spat at her husband. "Your transgressions shall be yours to carry with you through eternity."

Unable to keep himself up on his knees, Elias fell to his side, still retching, although no further elements expelled from his orifices. Raising her and Betsy's intertwined hands in the air, she instructed the young beauty to repeat her words with conviction. "We, the women you have wronged, seek vengeance and retribution for your evil ways. You shall no longer lie, cheat, and steal from those around you, Elias Cobb. We summon the forces of darkness to banish you, to live forever in limbo inside this tiny prison. We command you, Hecate, to send this wretched soul to suffer forever within the bowels of this token he gave so willingly to his mistress." As Betsy finished repeating the last of the words Margaret had said, the room darkened, and the brooch began to emit a soft light as it rattled against the hearth-stone. And with one final cry of pain, Elias took his last breath, and a soft mist of light exited the top of Elias' head and into the brooch. The room silenced, and without hesitation, Margaret snatched up the brooch and pinned it to the delicate lace dress, which adorned a small doll she had made in anticipation of this day.

CHAPTER ONE
ON THE ROAD AGAIN

STANDING ON THE BOW of a small sailboat, the clear water beneath her, Charlie noticed the silhouettes of three dolphin fins in the distance as the came into focus. She smiled, remembering what her mom had said about dolphins and how they were considered a good omen when you were at sea. Watching the dorsal fins bob in and out of the water, shortening the distance between themselves and the boat, she sprawled out on a towel and slipped on her headphones. Relaxing as the breeze blew across her warm skin, she became increasingly aware of a huge change in the breeze's velocity. Leaning up in an attempt to see what may be going on, she heard an alarmingly loud horn in the distance. *Funny, I don't remember seeing any other boats.* Again, the horn sounded, louder this time. Almost immediately, it sounded again. Snapping forward, Charlie barely had time to register a train approaching from the driver's side. The breeze from her open window swirled around her head one final time before they came to a complete stop in front of the train tracks.

"Welcome to the land of the living, sleepyhead," Jared teased as he looked over at her. "Looks like we may be here for a hot minute. This train seems to have no end in sight."

Charlie nodded and sat upright in the bucket seat as Jared reached over and wiped the small pool of drool that had formed on her left cheek. "There, much better," he said as he winked.

"Thanks," Charlie said with a half-smile. Yawning, she asked, "So, where are we?"

"Approximately two hours from our destination. The last sign I saw placed us near Roanoke, Virginia. I took this exit figuring we could stretch and get some gas," Jared said, increasing his volume a bit as the train's wheels let out a screech on the rails as it passed.

Charlie reached down by her feet and pulled up a warm bottle of Coke she had stashed earlier. Tapping the cap gently, she reached in the glove box and pulled out her rusty, key-shaped bottle opener. With slight pressure, she released the seal on the cap and heard the all too familiar fizz releasing from its confines. Satisfied there would be no foam over, she took a long swig. Gasping as the bubbles hit the back of her throat, Charlie managed to choke out, "Want some?" as she gestured with the bottle toward Jared.

"No thanks, I'll hold off for something a bit colder," Jared said, nodding to his left to signal that the train was coming to an end. "So, after that nap, I'd say you're glad we decided to split the driving, huh?" Charlie nodded. "Yeah, I didn't realize how long of a drive twelve hours really was. When we stop, let's take a look at the map again, then I can take over the last stint if you want."

"Well, if there's a payphone, I should call my aunt Tilde to give her an updated arrival time," Jared replied. The pair had realized early on during their escapades that mobile phones weren't very "mobile" unless they were willing to pay exorbitant usage rates to use one.

Staring out her window, Charlie watched as they passed through the rural route. Their travels this summer had exposed her to a plethora of home styles that she just didn't see in the Rochester, New York area. Here, the range of home styles was more prevalent than anywhere they had driven through so far. From small ranch-style houses and cape cods to log cabins and historical beauties, no two homes were alike. Homemade signs for fresh eggs and free wood were commonplace. So, it seemed, were abandoned vehicles of all makes and models.

Taking the last swig of her Coke, Charlie looked over at Jared and smiled. The wind was assisting his hair in a wild dance, exposing his chiseled jawline. The sun had been good for his skin tone. Charlie envied his ability to tan. His olive skin glowed with no effort other than just being. Charlie, however, had two modes-pale and burnt. This vacation, however, she managed to gain enough freckles to make it look like she was tan…ish. With summer soon coming to an end, she knew it would fade fast and she would be her normal ghostly self by mid-September.

The clicking of the turn signal snapped her out of her introspection,and she looked up to see a small gas station straight out of a horror movie. The well-worn building was split into two sides-a small glass-encased general store on one half and what Charlie assumed was a repair shop on the other. Two pumps sat out front, and as Jared pulled in, a bell dinged, alerting the attendant inside that they had arrived. A slight man in oil-coated coveralls pushed through the door and shuffled toward them as they slid out of the car and stretched. Closing in on them, Charlie could see his skin was worn from what she would gather was too much sun, drinking, or smoking. The latter was confirmed by the raspy "howdy folks" as he arrived at the pumps.

"What can I get for y'all today?" he asked.

"We need a fill up, please, and a few items from inside, too," Jared replied as Charlie squinted to read the oil-smudged name tag on his coveralls. *Smitty.*

"G'hed and take a look-see," Smitty stated, waving his left hand toward the store while the right one loosened the gas cap. Charlie nodded and shyly asked if there happened to be a restroom she could use. Smitty bobbed his head and said, "Look up on the counter next to the register; there's a key. Toilet's around the backside. Mind the low tree limbs as you head out back, though; they can be a bit ornery."

Jared and Charlie began their walk toward the store as Smitty slid the nozzle into Juicy. Opening the door, another bell jingled, and Jared guided Charlie in. Scanning the room, Charlie made a beeline for the register and spotted the key Smitty had mentioned. It was attached to a monkey wrench with a metal chain. *Kitschy,* she thought. Charlie grabbed it and excused herself as Jared slid open a cooler and began looking at the contents.

Confounded by the sheer size of the key and its companion, Charlie snuck a peek over at Smitty as he yelped across the parking lot to her, "See ya found it!" Turning the corner of the building, Charlie took time to gather her wits about her; the area surrounding the building's exterior was in just as rough shape as the building itself. Overgrown grass, unruly trees, and bushes with thorns created a semi-treacherous path. Narrowly escaping the teeth of one of the vines, she saw dozens of empty soda and beer bottles lining the ground in front of her. Gingerly hopscotching between them, she reached her destination. A large steel door with a hand painted warning-*Paying Customers Only-See Smitty for Key*-stood ominously before her. Sliding the key in the lock, she turned it and heard the latch release. The sharp, pungent odor hit her within seconds. Like a crypt being opened after centuries, the small room emitted a rotten and stale stench from its bowels. Holding back a retch, Charlie reached blindly around the corner in search of the light switch. Wishing she had a sleeve long enough to cover her fingers, she felt around for the grimy nubbin and flicked it upward, engaging the most horrendous fluorescent light she had ever seen. Squinting against the harshness, she took a few steps forward, her shoes sticking and then releasing from the putty-colored tile. Finishing her task as quickly as she could, she debated whether washing her hands would create more germs than simply exiting the tiny petri dish. Her brain convinced her that anything else would be better than attempting to wash in the rusty sink. She turned to back out of the door, not wanting to touch the handle, and about jumped out of her skin as Smitty softly asked her if she was finding everything to her liking. Unable to hold back the loudest **Fuck** she had ever verbalized, Charlie grabbed her chest and, in the process, dropped the key.

"I got that for you, missy," Smitty interjected as he bent down to grab the lunk of a keychain.

"Thh...thhhaaank you. You surprised me, is all," Charlie said before making swift work of the obstacle course back to the front.

With Smitty in tow, she could feel her heart in her throat. Smitty, once again, beat her to the punch, grazing her hand as she reached to open the front door.

"Ladies first," he said with a smile that showed off his shoe-pegged, yellowed teeth.

"Hey! Charlie! You'll never guess what I found!" Jared yelled from the back.

Not remotely in a guessing mood, Charlie looked up to see Jared holding up two bottles marked "Double Cola." As if seeing the confusion on Charlie's face, Jared proceeded with a brief history lesson. "You don't see these anymore, especially in New York. These here are genuine Tennessee relics. Straight from Chattanooga! I promise you'll love it!"

With his head akin to a bobble head, Smitty fervently nodded up and down in agreement. "I tell you what, now. That there is some of the best fizzy you'll ever taste. Guaranteed."

And with that, Jared armed himself with two more bottles and added them to the growing pile next to the register. "Anything you want to grab?" he asked Charlie.

Knowing she had to find something to at least rinse her hands with, Charlie stalked the shelves, looking for the needle in a haystack. "No Phisohex, I'm guessing?" Charlie asked, trying not to sound totally stuck up.

"Welp, gosh, no, I don't reckon I've heard of that, missy. Apologies," Smitty slid out with his Southern drawl. "What's it akin to?" he asked.

Just as she was about to answer, Charlie saw a small, familiar brown bottle of hydrogen peroxide. "Nevermind, this will do," she said a bit too loudly. Jared tilted his head in the universal sign for "are you ok?"
Giving a nod, Charlie added the bottle to their pile as Smitty did some quick math and punched the keys on the well-worn register. "That there with your gas'll be eighteen twenty-three."

Handing Smitty a twenty, Jared said, "Keep the change" as he swept up their haul in his arms.

"Mighty obliged," Smitty slurred. "Y'all have a great day now, ya hear?"

The pair waved goodbye as they swiftly maneuvered to Juicy.

"I've to pee like a racehorse," Jared said, ducking his head into the driver's side to set down the items. "But based on your reaction, I'm thinking I can wait."

Charlie said, "Wise move" as she leaned out the passenger door and squirted copious amounts of hydrogen peroxide over her hands.

"Hey, I almost forgot! I gotta call Aunt Tilde,'" Jared exclaimed. "Do me a favor and look at the map. I'd like to do the rest of the trip on back roads, if possible. Can you see if that's a go?"

Nodding, Charlie scooped up the map from between the seats and began to research.

A few minutes later, the driver's side door opened, and Jared informed Charlie that Aunt Tilde was "tickled pink" that they were arriving early. "Did you find our route?"

Charlie confirmed with a head bob as Jared reached up to crank the convertible top. "Well, that's perfect timing," he said as he exited the vehicle. He lifted the top up and over before tucking it in and engaging the clips. "Don't forget the cover," Charlie sounded off from over her shoulder.

"Aye-aye, captain," Jared joked as he completed securing the snaps on the cover. Re-situating himself in the driver's seat, he placed his hand on Charlie's knee and said, "Next stop, Jonesborough."

CHAPTER TWO
JONESBOROUGH

CHUGGING DOWN THE MOUNTAIN ROADS with the wind in their hair, Charlie and Jared marveled at the various sights before them. Brighton was a small town but not as small as some of the towns they were passing through. Charlie swore several times that some of them began and ended before she could blink.

"We're getting close," Jared said, turning in her direction. Even after spending a whole summer together, Charlie still had butterflies whenever she looked into his eyes. "As a matter of fact, we're about to head into Piney Flats. My best friend from high school, Benji, still lives there. Plan is to visit him tomorrow," Jared stated with an affirmative nod.

Looking ahead, Charlie could see the sign for Piney Flats. Like most of the small towns they had passed through, it was listed as "historic." The sign contained a brief history and stated that the "village" was a result of the railroad system and was established soon thereafter in 1854. Almost immediately, the railroad's lasting presence was confirmed as Juicy bounced over the tracks. Situated a quarter mile on the left was a tiny building that had been the official post office, seemingly abandoned now. A quick right- hand turn past the school and Jared announced they were heading into the town he grew up in and their final destination - Jonesborough.

Peering ahead, Charlie saw what could only truly be described as a fairy-tale town. A long row of quaint, brick buildings were filled with local artisan shops and historical stops, bakeries and coffee shops dotted throughout. An old marquee came into focus as they neared the end of Main Street. The Jackson Theatre promised locals a taste of Broadway.

"That theater used to be an old casket factory, believe it or not! Just went through a renovation in the last year or so. We should check it out if we have time. Another left ahead and then we'll be there," Jared announced.

Charlie could feel the butterflies forming in her stomach. *Why on earth are you nervous*, she thought. But she already knew the answer to that question. She and Jared had spent the whole summer together, and their relationship had moved along at a rapid pace. It mattered a lot to her that his family accepted and, more importantly, liked her. Charlie, deep in her thoughts, didn't realize that the car had stopped.

"Here we are! Chez Cooper," Jared announced with a dramatic swoop of his hand.

Charlie looked up to see the most wonderful farmhouse. Grand in size, it sat on a slight hill. Happiness immediately flooded Charlie's heart. With its buttercream siding, green tin roof, and large front porch, the home was beyond impressive. Stepping out of the car, Charlie stood, mouth agape, as she focused on the details. A clock-tower-like structure separated the two sides of the house. Shaker siding capped the peaks on the far side of the home, and brick chimneys dotted the roofline. She was so enthralled with the house she barely registered the chatter between Jared and his aunt Tilde until she felt his hand on hers.

"Charlie, let me introduce you to Aunt Tilde," Jared softly said. But before Charlie could acknowledge him, Tilde came in for a bear hug.

"Oh, Charlie! I'm so glad to meet you! Jared has said tons about you, but honey, his words don't do you justice! Step back and let me look at you!"

Unable to get in a word, Charlie felt like she was on display, like a prized cow at the county fair. Tilde circled her twice, eyeing up and down.

"My, you're such a pretty thing, honey," Tilde said with a smile.

Charlie felt herself blush as Jared stepped in and said, "Ok, Aunt Tilde…enough of that. I'm sure Charlie would love to get inside and maybe have some of your famous pink lemonade?"

"Of course she would; where are my manners? Charlie, honey, follow me. Jared and my husband, Arthur here, will get your things." A heavy-set man made his way down past Tilde and said a quick "Hello," then followed Jared to the car as Tilde swooped Charlie up the path to the house.

"Have a seat," Tilde said, pointing to the line of wicker chairs along the length of the front porch. "I'll be back in a jiffy."

Charlie sat and watched the guys tackle the tiny bit of luggage they had been making do with all summer. She giggled at the sight of their attempts to accomplish the noble gesture. Due to Juicy's size, they really didn't have much, but what they were missing in quantity they made up for in weight. As the men made their way up to the front porch, Charlie could see poor Arthur's face turning various shades of red. Jared winked as they walked past and through the front door.

Charlie scanned her surroundings and heard the jingle of glassware approaching the front door. Hopping up, she made it to the screened door just in time to open it for Tilde, who was carrying a large tray filled to the brim.

Thanking Charlie, Tilde maneuvered to the small table between the chairs and placed the tray down on it, causing a clatter followed by an expletive or two. She smiled and apologized to Charlie. Charlie smiled in return and let her know it was alright.

"So, I bet you're plum worn out from your drive. How far was it again?" But before Charlie could answer, Tilde continued. "I can't even fathom being in a car for more than twenty minutes with Arthur. I think we'd kill each other. My nerves can't handle his unique style of driving. Bless his heart." Handing Charlie a glass of lemonade, she continued on with her soliloquy, only stopping long enough to take a small breath. Just as she was gearing up for another, the calvary came through the front door.

Taking a seat next to Charlie, Jared leaned in and mouthed *How's it going?* Charlie winked and quickly smiled at Tilde, who had poured a glass for Jared and shifted her questions to him.

"Honey, sit, take a sip or two of your lemonade. Let the kids fill us in on their trip down," Arthur said in his booming, yet gregarious voice.

"Of course, what was I thinking?" Tilde said with a slight flush to her face. "Go on, now. We're all ears."

For the next hour, give or take, Jared and Charlie regaled them with their adventures so far. Conversation flowed equally between them, and before they knew it, dusk arrived with its friendly precursors - cicadas.

"Well, time sure has flown!" Tilde said. "How about you two go freshen up? I've dinner all set to cooking, and that will give me time to get the cornbread in the oven."

"Sounds great," Jared said, standing and grabbing the tray from the table. "Let me get these in for you." Carrying the tray, he used his foot to flick the screen door open, holding it open for Charlie to enter.

Passing through, Charlie was in awe. The large center room was enormous. She could see a room to her left, which appeared to be a library. Straight ahead of her was a large cased opening that took you to the kitchen with a beautiful wooden staircase on the left side leading to the upstairs. To her right was a gorgeous brick fireplace with floor-to-ceiling bookcases flanking its sides. This room had a cozy home feel to it with its oversized furniture and knick-knacks. She looked at the photos lining the stairwell as she and Jared made their way to the second level.

"We have you in the tower room," Charlie heard Tilde state. "It's got a special treat that I'll let Jared show you." Winking, she excused herself and said to "holler" if they needed anything.

"Phew," Charlie said, collapsing on the king-sized bed, that let out a loud squeak as the coils bounced back under her weight. A few more squeaks followed as Jared joined her. "Shhhhh!" she scolded. "Tilde might think we're up here fooling around." She giggled, turning her face toward Jared's.

"Who says we aren't?" Jared teased as he leaned in for a kiss. "But seriously, dinner's gonna be soon. How about I show you the coolest thing about this room and we save this for later," he said in a sultry tone that sent chills down Charlie's spine.

"You got a deal," Charlie said, sitting up on the edge of the mattress. He stood and crossed the room to an oddly shaped door. Holding his hand out, he blurted, "Up and at 'em."

Charlie stood and joined Jared as he turned the knob to the mysterious door. A slow creak sounded, followed by instructions to watch her head.

Entering, a spiral staircase appeared before them. Ascending the steps around several curves, they reached the landing at the top, where the most beautiful oval stained-glass window was housed. Its primary colors glowed as the beginning of the full moon shone through the patterns in the glass. With a gentle push, the window pivoted open. Sliding one leg out and then the next, Jared assisted Charlie onto a small Juliet balcony. From this vantage point, they looked down on Main Street. To their right, they could see the Washington County courthouse clock tower.

A few dozen people walked up and down the streets, likely taking advantage of the August evening's cooled down temps.

"Soooo cool," Charlie said, hip checking Jared. "This was your view all through middle and high school?"

"Yep. I used to come up here with my sketchbook and chalks and sketch out whatever scene played out before me."

They stood for a few more minutes, holding hands, Charlie's head firmly planted on Jared's shoulder. Then, bolting upright, Charlie let out a panicked yelp.

"Fuck! I have to call my dad and let him know we got here ok. With all the fanfare, it totally slipped my mind."

"Of course," Jared replied. "There's a phone in Aunt Tilde's room. I'm sure she wouldn't mind you using it. Let's get back in so you have time to call before dinner."

Swiveling the window open, Jared held it for Charlie as she entered, leaving Charlie to make her call. Four rings later, her dad answered.

"Bauman residence," Dale said.

"Hey, Dad!" Charlie said.

"Hiya, Charlie bear. How's the trip going?"

"We finally made it to Jonesborough. Crazy long drive, but things went smoothly."

"How did Juicy do? She holding up ok?" he asked.

"Yeah, so far so good. Wasn't sure she would be able to handle the wear and tear in all the heat, but we've kept the A/C to a minimum, which I think helps. How are things there at home?"

"Well it's only been two days since we last talked, but things are going well. Still sorting, packing and purging. Speaking of, you're still planning on stopping by on your way back east, right?"

"That's the plan. Jared has some things he wants to make sure he crosses off his list this visit. That will dictate the timing a bit."

"Great. Yeah, I'd love a couple sets of hands here. My real estate agent is on my back to get the house listed. I still can't believe I let your grandparents talk me into this," he said with a slight chuckle.

Charlie snickered, knowing very well that her dad couldn't be talked into anything he wasn't already open to, even though Grandpa Walter was one A-1 salesman. She continued the conversation, and just as she was about to go into details on Jonesborough thus far, Tilde called up to them that dinner was served.

"Hey, Dad. Gotta go. Dinner's ready. Can I call you the day after tomorrow?"

"Sure thing, Charlie. Oh! I almost forgot; you got some mail from Cornell. Would you like me to open it for you? Probably just class stuff. I can let you know what's what next time we talk."

Charlie agreed, and they said their goodbyes. Laying the handset on the cradle, Charlie got up, found Jared, and asked where the bathroom was, as she needed to wash her hands. Making a left out of the room, Jared guided her two doors down the hall and ushered her into the guest bath.

"I'll wait here. I washed up earlier when I brought the luggage in," he said.

A minute later, the pair descended the stairs and made a sharp left into the kitchen. Charlie's eyes widened at its size. The layout was beyond impressive with a huge island between the eating area and main space. Cabinets galore, with glass fronts, displayed all of Tilde's kitchenware beautifully. A fancy stove, wall ovens, and a ginormous double-door fridge completed the workspace. Knowing a bit about older homes, she assumed a renovation had to have happened and decided to hold that question for dinner conversation, if topics ran low.

As they approached the large farmhouse-style table, Jared pulled out Charlie's seat and said, "After you, madam." Unable to hold back a chuckle, Charlie slid into her seat and scootched it forward as Jared joined to her immediate left. Tilde was the lone soldier across from them, with Arthur proudly seated at the head of the table.

Eyeballing everything on the table, Charlie gawked. Before her sat the biggest bowl of fried chicken she had ever seen, with an equally big bowl stacked high with corn on the cob. An array of sides was scattered around the table: baked beans, potato salad, summer salad, mac and cheese, green beans, coleslaw, and of course the corn bread, shaped appropriately like ears of corn.

"Smells amazing!" Jared said.

"Help yourself," Tilde replied.

Taking turns loading up their plates and passing the sides, Tilde asked Charlie if she wanted more lemonade or sweet tea with her meal. Before she could answer, Jared shot a warning regarding the sweet tea.

"This isn't just *any* sweet tea, babe. This is the sweet tea to end all sweet teas. It comes with a warning from the American Dental Association," Jared teased.

"Hush now, Jared," Tilde said with a toothy smile. "These here are all real and no worse for the wear." She finished with a tap tap to her front teeth.

Laughing, Charlie held her glass out for Arthur to fill with tea. "Thank you," Charlie said, nodding in Arthur's direction.

"Welcome there, honey," he replied.

Man of few words, Charlie thought.

Plates piled high, they bounced the conversation back and forth, stopping only long enough for a healthy bite or two. Jared, who had no issues talking with his mouth full, filled them in on their travels so far. "We headed out right after finals and made our way to Watkins Glen for some hiking. Got to see the most beautiful waterfalls I've ever seen."

Charlie interjected with, "There's this spot where you can walk behind the falls and watch the water cascade past you. It's totally awesome!"

"We have a place or two not too far y'all should check out," Arthur said.

"Oh, my, yes! Laurel Falls! You have to go! And if you have time, maybe Sill Branch or Coon Den Falls too. This time of year, they're great spots for a hike and a dip," Tilde said with a wink.

Helping herself to another piece of fried chicken, Charlie said "Sounds like fun!"

"Where'd y'all head to next?" Tilde asked.

Charlie took over and explained their stop in Boston to visit a friend of hers who had moved to attend Harvard. "From there, we went to Brooklyn to visit some friends of Jared's. Made a day or so of it in New York City. Saw a really off-off Broadway show," she finished, giving Jared a knowing look.

"New York City? I've always wanted to go! Arthur promises me we'll get there one day," Tilde expressed wistfully.

"I'm sure you will," Jared said softly to his aunt. "When you do, I have plenty of recommendations."

They wrapped up their travel details with their last leg down to Jonesborough, replete with Smitty and his gas station of horrors. Small talk continued throughout the meal until everyone had their fill. Tilde stood to start clearing the table, and Charlie offered her services.

"Of course, darlin'. I'd love the company," Tilde answered.

Eyeing Jared with the universal signal for let's make ourselves scarce, Arthur cleared his throat and nodded toward the living room.

"Go ahead," Tilde said. "Us girls got this. We'll join you in a bit for some dessert."

Hands full, Charlie followed Tilde until the table was empty. Entering the kitchen with the last round, Tilde gestured for Charlie to sit.

"Have a seat; I'll wash, and you can dry for me as we go," she told Charlie.

Charlie nodded and settled on a stool at the counter as Tilde tossed her a tea towel.

"Tell me about yourself. Jared's pretty tight lipped about his personal life. We don't really know much about you," Tilde said.

"Well, I'm from a town just outside of Rochester, New York, called Brighton. Only child. Born and raised in the same house, which my dad has decided to sell this year after my mom's death."

"Oh, yes, honey. My condolences. Jared did mention that to us. If you don't mind me prying, how did she pass?"

Charlie looked down at her hands, currently twisting the towel within inches of its life. Taking a breath, she started slowly. "How much did Jared tell you?"

"Not much t'all. Just that she passed suddenly. Oh dear, was it the cancer?"

"No," Charlie quickly stated. "She died in her sleep and it wasn't natural by any means. Let me ask you this, Tilde, do you believe in the paranormal?"

"You mean like ghosts and demons and such? Well, I guess anyone religious would have to believe in spiritual beings, but I've never been one to believe in *those* things, in *that* way. I'm of the see-it-to-believe-it crowd myself. I know Jared has always been a firm believer in those things ever since he was a child. Also, I've plenty of friends who swear they've experienced things. Why do you ask?"

With a slight sputter, Charlie began, "That's how she died. A spirit not at rest, or content with how she passed, decided they wanted her life, her energy, and so they took it. That's how I met Jared, actually. He helped me solve the mystery. We became close while researching my mom's old journals in an attempt to figure out what happened to her. Had to get a psychic involved and used some *magic* of sorts to vanquish the entity. It was… a lot."

Tilde, who had been listening intently, finally spoke. "My goodness, dear, that must have been a terrifying and emotional experience for you," she said, giving Charlie a pat on the hand. "I'm glad Jared was there to help you get that all sorted out, and again, I'm so sorry you lost your mama. You and Jared have that in common, you know? Losing a mana." Seeing the look on Charlie's face, she immediately knew that Charlie did NOT know. "Oh my, I've done it again," she said, sighing. This time, she pulled a stool up across from Charlie and stated, "I'm about to tell you what happened, but you have to agree that you'll be surprised when he finally does tell you."

Charlie didn't like the way this was heading, but before she could accept or object, Tilde continued.

"Jared's mom was my sister. My baby sister by five years. Holly was a spitfire. Always wanting something more. This small place wasn't big enough for her and her dreams. But, as fate would have it, she met Ben in high school and love took precedence over her dreams. They married young. Had Jared, then his sisters Emily, Karina, and Ann. Life was good for a bit. Then she got sick. And with the stress of four children and a sick wife, Ben left. Not so much as a note. Just up and left. Holly and the kids moved in with my first husband, Chuck, and me shortly after. We made her as comfortable as we could, but she only lasted another year before passing. Jared was only seven, the girls much younger. Chuck and I stepped in, but parenthood proved to be too much for him, and we separated by the time Jared was eight. Unable to raise all four on my own, the girls went to my older brother Craig's to live with him and his family. I raised Jared on my own for a bit until I met Arthur. We bought this place from Arthur's grandma after we married. Been here since. Despite everything, Jared turned out to be quite a wonderful young man." She sniffled and cleared her throat. "Well, that's enough of that! Let's get to these dishes."

Charlie, still in shock over Jared's story, began drying the dishes in a robotic state until she almost dropped one of the glasses, which quickly snapped her back to reality. Shaking her head in an attempt to refocus, she cleared her throat and used the opportunity to ask about the house.

"So, this house was Arthur's grandma's, huh?"

Tilde nodded. "Sure was, but it had been in the family since it was built in 1887. Mostly it is as it was, but we've made some updates here and there."

"I noticed," Charlie said. "This kitchen was one of them, correct?"

"Uh huh. The original kitchen was over where the dining table is now. Tiny, tiny space. No room at all to properly cook these days. The only thing we kept was his grandma's beautiful oven and the buffet which we moved over to the opposite wall. The space we're in now was the original great room and the room the men are in was the receiving room. Remind me to show you photos sometime, why don't ya."

Accepting the offer with a nod, Charlie realized she had fallen behind on her drying duties. Picking up the pace, the duo finished their task soon thereafter. Setting her dish rag on the faucet, Tilde slipped over to the archway between the rooms.

"You men save room for dessert?" she bellowed.

A synchronous "Yes!" echoed its way to the kitchen.

Making her way to the icebox, Tilde pulled out a huge layer cake encased in the classic yellow Tupperware cake keeper. Charlie knew it well.

"Charlie, hon, can you be a doll and reach up in the sideboard and grab four dessert plates for me?"

Charlie maneuvered back to the counter with the plates as Tilde sliced into the cake, exposing, not one, not two, but four layers of golden cake separated by the creamiest chocolate icing she'd ever seen.

Placing a slice on each plate, Tilde then turned and scooped up forks for each of them, and with Charlie's assistance, delivered the goodies to the living room.

"Quick show of hands, please," Tilde said. "Milk or coffee?" With a unanimous vote for milk, she soon returned with a large bottle and four glasses.

Noshing on the decadence that was the cake, the group continued with their conversations until the grandfather clock in the study chimed eleven.

"Wow! Time flies, now, doesn't it?" Tilde said exuberantly. "Y'all have to be plumb worn out."

Nodding in agreement, Jared turned to Charlie and asked if she was ready to head up.

"Yes, please," Charlie answered while stifling a yawn.

"Charlie, I'm very glad you're here with our Jared," Tilde started "I've got you all set up with the guest bath. Extra towels are in the hall closet if you need them. Jared, you know where to find them." Giving Charlie a hug goodnight, Tilde moved on to Jared and whispered, "I think you hooked yourself a good one here."

"Thank you, Aunt Tilde. Good night, Uncle Arthur," Jared said as he patted his uncle on the back. "See you in the morning."

Shutting the door behind them, Jared and Charlie collapsed in unison on the bed.

"I'm too tired to shower, but man do I need it," Charlie said with a sigh.

"How about we relax here for a bit, then you can go ahead in," Jared said softly while simultaneously cuddling up to Charlie, who mustered a meek "mmm hmmm."

CHAPTER THREE
RELAX

THE SOUND OF JARED snoring snapped Charlie out of her slumber. She quickly realized they had never made it to the shower. Exhaustion from their travels had overtaken them, and they had fallen asleep fully clothed on top of the covers.

Her eyes adjusted to the dimly lit room and she looked out the far window to see the sun peeking over the horizon in the distance. Thirst hit her like a freight train. She instinctively reached over to the nightstand for a glass of water, only to have the rapid realization that this wasn't her dorm room and no such glass existed. Moaning softly, she sat up and slid off the bed to not release the squeaks of the springs.

Shuffling across the oak wood floors, she maneuvered her way out the door and down to the hall bath. The room was lit by a nightlight to the left of the sink. As she stood in front of the mirror, she snickered to herself at the state of her hair. Since starting the trip she had foregone any visits to salons in an attempt to let her hair grow out, but all she had truly accomplished was forming massive rat nests that, unless confined by a ponytail, could not be tamed.

Turning the water on, she flashed her teeth to her reflection, and with the absence of a toothbrush, used a finger to scrub the film that had coated them during the night. Running her tongue over them, she was satisfied with the end result. Since no cups were in sight, she tilted her head to the side, grabbed her hair over her shoulder and began slurping at the cold water escaping the faucet. Satiated, she released her locks and splashed cold water on her face. Grabbing a hand towel, she sat on the toilet to pee, killing two birds with one stone.

Charlie walked back to the bedroom wishing she had remembered to pack her slippers to shield her toes from the chill of the wood floors. She took extra care when she sat back down on the edge of the mattress. Unfortunately, said mattress alerted Jared to her presence, and she heard a soft moan followed by a heavy hand to her back. Letting herself fall on the pillow, Charlie was immediately encased by Jared's arms.

"Hey there," he said. "What time is it?"

Charlie looked around the room for a clock but couldn't find one anywhere. Setting her gaze instead on the far window, she said "Well, the sun's about to pop through the trees. My guess is, about five-thirty to six?"

Rolling slightly toward Jared, she caught him playing possum. His eyes were closed a little too tight, hidden behind several tendrils of hair. Charlie guided the hairs behind Jared's ears. As she finished, she caught one gorgeous blue eye peering at her in the dim daylight. Leaning forward, Jared gave her a delicate kiss on the lips, sending a shiver down Charlie's spine that escaped through her toes.

Releasing from each other's embrace, they heard a rooster crow in the distance, and the pair broke out in laughter at the timing.

"So, what do you want to do today, Charlie?" Jared asked. Not waiting for an answer, he continued. "I mean, I know you wanted to explore some, but I was hoping we could go visit Benji and maybe coax him to go out with us."

Charlie leaned up on her elbows and replied "This is your town, so I'll defer to you if that's ok. I'm up for whatever, honestly. I do need to see if your aunt will let me give Ramona a buzz today. I promise to keep it short. I haven't checked in since Boston, and I know she's dying to hear what we've been up to. After that, I'm all yours!"

"I'm sure Aunt Tilde won't mind" Jared started to say, but before he could finish, there was a rap at the door.

"Mornin', sunshines! Don't mean to pry, but I heard y'all stirring and figured I'd let you know breakfast will be ready shortly. G'head and get y'selves decent and hop on down in, say, thirty minutes?"

"Sure thing, Aunt Tilde," Jared replied, his voice just a tad too loud.

With what she knew was a mortified look on her face, Charlie asked, "Do you think she *heard* heard us?"

"Well, you're quite a firecracker, Charlie," Jared teased.

Burying her face in the pillow, Charlie let out a long groan.

"See! That's what I'm talking about," Jared said, belly laughing as he reached for Charlie's hand. "But seriously, I think we're fine. Uncle Arthur is a serious snorer, and Aunt Tilde sleeps with cotton stuffed in her ears. I promise."

Sitting upright, Jared spun his legs over the edge of the bed. The sun had completely risen, and the room glowed with hues of oranges, dust dancing between the beams of light.

"You wanna shower first?" he asked.

Charlie shook her head, followed by, "You go ahead. I'm going to work on my to-do list for when we get to Rochester."

Jared grabbed his shorts from the floor and slid them on before cracking the door open just enough to make sure the coast was clear.

Charlie watched him exit the room, then threw on a pair of undies and Jared's T-shirt, which had puddled at her end of the bed. With a long stretch, she maneuvered over to her bags, grabbed her backpack, and ascended the stairs to the tower. She crawled out the window and sat criss-cross applesauce against the far railing, where she had a full view of downtown and the clock tower. The air hadn't had a chance to get thick yet, and as Charlie inhaled, she took in the most wonderful smell of the crepe myrtles that dominated the landscaping up and down the street. A slight breeze carried another waft up to her; she couldn't help thinking how they smelled like lilacs, her mom's favorite flower. Closing her eyes, she inhaled again, fading into a memory of her mom visiting the botanical gardens in Rochester.

It was hard to believe, even several months later, that her mom was gone. Charlie's experiences over the past year were mind blowing, to put it mildly. A natural death would have been hard in and of itself, but finding out that her mother was stolen from her added another layer of pain. Even with help from Jared, the Master, and Marcus, the circumstances surrounding her mom's death were tragic. Charlie still struggled daily with it all. Most of all, she struggled with the knowledge that her mother, Birdie, would want her to forgive Astrid for taking her life. That should make it easier to reconcile, but it didn't. Charlie still had waves of loathing and resentment that plagued her thoughts. At moments, they were all consuming. Charlie had grown to have some semblance of peace with regards to Astrid. She had placed herself in Astrid's shoes. She thought about how she would have felt losing her mother at such a young age and then her life. While she couldn't completely reconcile herself with Astrid's actions, she had come to accept that there had been a greater power pushing her. She thought of the good Astrid would be doing now that she was under the guiding light of the Master again. However, the thought of the bigger picture, and how many others in the world were exposed to tragedy and loss at the hands of those inhabiting the other realms, really had a profound effect on her. So much so that she had actually made the decision to change her focus at school. Not completely, of course, as that would negate her efforts to date. But she was willing to take this, her junior year, and devote at least the first semester to study more non-traditional topics.

The chirp of a song-bird snapped Charlie out of her thoughts. Giving her head a quick shake to expel the cobwebs, she reached into her bag and pulled out a pen and pad of paper. Flipping to an open page, she quickly scribbled *Rochester* at the top with a doodle or two, and then a bold *TO-DO* centered underneath. Pausing slightly, Charlie continued to work on her list and was so deep into the task at hand she didn't hear Jared sneak his head through the window.

"Watcha doing?" he blurted, startling Charlie so badly her pen flew out of her hand and plummeted to certain death below.

"What the hell! Jared," she exclaimed as she grabbed her chest. "That was one of my fave pens!"

Jared winked and blew her a kiss. "The shower is free if you want to go head down."

"Thanks," Charlie said as she gathered up her stuff.

The pair descended the stairs, and Jared promised to go rescue the pen and check on the status of breakfast while she showered.

The hot water beat down on her back, relieving some of her tension. Charlie wished she had more time to enjoy it. To help speed up the process, she chose not to shampoo her hair. She shut off the water and stepped out to dry off. A quick flicker of the lights made her cast her gaze to the steamed-over mirror where a message lay before her. Instinct and a little tinge of PTSD made her heart skip a beat until she saw the non-threatening message in front of her, a simple "HI C" followed by the letter "M." Charlie inhaled a sigh of relief and said, "Heya, Marcus" into the ether. Ever since they took on Astrid and the Dark Magician, Marcus popped in from time to time to let Charlie know he was watching over her. Like Astrid was to Birdie, Marcus was to her. Unlike Astrid, Marcus understood his role and embraced what it meant to be a "guardian." He was not plagued by the desires and jealousies that had driven Astrid to the dark side.

Dashing back to the bedroom to get dressed, Charlie threw on a pair of pale blue running shorts and a tank. She twisted her hair up and secured it with a clip. She chose a pair of Keds, slipped them on, and made her way down the stairs. The undeniable smell of french toast and bacon greeted her about halfway down. She rounded the corner and saw Jared and Arthur seated at the island as Tilde fluttered about, whirling and flipping the spatula.

Charlie greeted the group with a chipper "Good morning" as Tilde spun around with a cup of coffee in her hand. Charlie accepted the mug and giggled at Tilde's apron, which had *Sweet, Sassy, and Southern* scrawled across it in a fun cursive font and the cutest cartoon chicken Charlie had ever seen.

"Sugar and cream are in front of Jared there," Tilde said, flicking the spatula in his general direction.

"Smells delicious," Charlie said as she doctored up her coffee and gave Jared a peck on the cheek.

"Have a seat. We're doing informal this morning," Tilde informed the group, setting down a giant dish of butter and syrup. Charlie smiled as she saw the syrup was her grandma Eleanor's go to-Log Cabin.

"I have sausage and bacon going. Who wants what?" Tilde asked.

A cacophony of meat names filled Tilde's ears. "Whoa, whoa there, y'all. Not all at once," she said with a belly laugh. She pointed to each of them and gathered their choices in a more orderly fashion. Serving up the rest of the items, she handed everyone their plates and said, "Dig in."

"What about grace?" Arthur interjected.

"Honey, I don't think we're going to impose that on our guests this morning. Heck, we don't even know if Charlie here is religious or what? Am I right?" Tilde asked, turning toward Charlie.

"Ummm. Well. Thank you for the consideration, but I guess I consider myself *spiritual* more than religious. I definitely believe there is something, especially after all that happened last year." Jared reached his hand under the counter and gave her leg a squeeze in a show of solidarity.

Finishing up her food and second cup of coffee, Charlie asked Tilde if it would be ok if she made another long-distance call and promised to keep it short.

"Honey, of course you can!" Tilde said.

With a heartfelt thank you, Charlie excused herself from the group, assuring Jared she wouldn't be long. Taking the steps two at a time, Charlie reached the landing and realized she had neglected to pay attention earlier to which door was the master bedroom. *Use your powers of deduction, Charlie,* she thought to herself. Knowing which door was her and Jared's room and which was the bathroom, she was left with three others, not including the obvious closets. Channeling her inner Goldilocks, she tried the first one-too small; the second-a craft room; and finally, the third...*just right!* Snickering at her comedic prowess, Charlie picked up the phone, carried it over to sit on the window box, and began to dial Ramona's number. She spun the rotary dial round and round as she glanced outside just in time to see a squirrel sneak off with a snack. *Mr. Squirrel, we both have snacking in common,* she thought to herself. Stifling a giggle, she heard, "Lorenzano residence." Taking a guess that the pre-pubescent cracked voice was Ramona's brother Tony, Charlie said a quick "Hi," then asked for Ramona. A muffled sound resonated from the other end, followed by an immediate, "Hey! Butt-face, it's for you!"

Moments like these made Charlie a bit envious that she didn't have brothers or sisters to taunt. Ramona pretended to despise being a big sister, but deep down, Charlie knew Ramona wouldn't trade her brothers for the world.

Twirling the phone cord, Charlie smiled when she heard Ramona pick up "Ok, knucklehead, now hang up!" Ramona said, scolding her brother. A curt slam of the phone contrasted with Ramona's soft greeting of "Hello?"

"Heya, bestie! What's up?" And with that, the flood-gates opened with what could only be a Guiness World Record as Ramona began the run on sentence to end all run on sentences. Charlie attempted to keep up. She got "What took you so long," "Where have you been," "I cut my hair, lopped it, actually," and a few other sporadic anecdotes. Taking advantage of Ramona's need to breathe, Charlie quickly slipped in "Ramona! Slow down." Ramona inhaled and Charlie continued. "I don't have long 'cause this is long distance. Let me answer some of these before I forget what you asked. We're in Tennessee, arrived yesterday. Sorry I didn't call from Brooklyn. We got all wrapped up in the visit and time flew."

The conversation continued at a normal pace from that moment on with tales of dating and family drama on Ramona's side. Trip details and Jared info from Charlie, culminating in the one item Charlie had actually called for. "Hey! We're gonna be in Rochester soon and wanted to make sure you're around. I want you to meet Jared and play some catch up. You down?"

Ramona laughed and said, "Make sure I'm around? Where would I *possibly* go? I live an extremely boring life here, Charlie." With the window of soliloquy back open, Charlie sat back and listened. Glancing at her watch, Charlie saw she had gone well over her intended time limit.

"Hey girlie, I gotta go. But I'll touch base when we get to Dad's. Ok?"

"Sure thing! Can't wait to see you! It's been way too long," Ramona lamented.

Hanging up the handset, Charlie maneuvered it back to its original resting spot. She descended the stairs and heard laughter coming from the kitchen. She cleared her throat loud enough to announce her presence just before rounding the corner.

"Shhh...she's coming," Tilde kidded, winking at Charlie as she sauntered into the kitchen.

"How'd it go?" Jared asked.

"Good! We played a quick round of catch up and got us all set to meet when we visit my dad," Charlie answered. "Thank you again, Tilde, for the use of the phone. Let me know if the damages are too much, and I promise to handle them."

"Honey, I'm sure it's not all that," Tilde said with a smile. "I'm all cleaned up here and have a few things to get started on. Jared has a key in case we miss each other today. Enjoy your day, and we'll see you tonight!" Tilde said, setting her apron on the hook, grabbing her bag and heading out the back door to the garage.

CHAPTER FOUR
HERE'S BENJI

"SO! LET'S GET THIS PARTY started!" Jared said. "Benji should be up by now. We can swing by for a visit and set some plans as we go? You may want to either change your shoes or bring a spare in case we go hiking. Those Keds won't do you much good out in these woods."

Charlie ran back upstairs and grabbed her Nikes, a light jacket, *just in case,* and her bag. She gave a quick shout down to Jared to see if he needed anything, and with his "no", she made her way down and out to the front porch.

The temperature had increased exponentially since she was out earlier, as had the humidity. Charlie was glad she hadn't bothered to wash her hair as it would end up a sweaty mess soon enough. Opening the passenger door, she slid in as Jared released the top. It was definitely a top-down kind of day, especially since Juicy's A/C was flakey at best. She eyeballed her boyfriend as he performed this task. He looked particularly yummy today in his shorts and form-fitting Cornell T-shirt.

Jared hopped in and gave Charlie a quick peck, then said, "Before I forget, madam, a little gift for you," handing her the pen he had resurrected from its traumatic fate.

"Why, thank you." Charlie giggled, batting her eyes. She placed the pen in her bag as Jared put Juicy in gear, and the pair headed downhill toward Main Street. Like the drive into

Jonesborough, Charlie was just as enamored with this path to Benji's. Historic homes of all styles dotted the streets. One even resembled the Addams' Family house with its mansard roof.

———⋄—※—⋄———

Making the turn out of Jonesborough proper, Jared made a conscious decision to take Charlie down the backroads. It was longer but definitely more scenic. Crossing over the Watauga River, he gave Charlie a mini history lesson.

"...In 1772, the Watauga Association established the first independent government in what we now know as Tennessee..." he started.

Charlie tried hard to stay interested as he continued his lesson but was fading in and out of focus.

"...and the Watauga Purchase in 1775 was negotiated between the Watauga Association and the Cherokee. It was one of the earliest recorded land deals between European settlers and Native Americans and eventually led..."

That was the last thing Charlie heard. She had chosen instead to turn her attention to the views. It wasn't Jared's fault. She had never been one to enjoy history.

Crossing over the water, Jared finished his story and took a sharp right toward Huffman Hollow Road, winding around the hills until he brought Juicy to a slow. Jared pointed out the places he used to hang out with Benji and others when they were growing up.

Charlie noted that the houses were fewer and farther between out this way, and based on their condition alone, seemed older than most of what she had seen so far. As that thought made its way through her brain, Jared said, "And here we are."

Taking a slow turn at a small dilapidated red mailbox, the dingy numbers barely visible, Juicy gave a slight bounce and groan as they went from paved road to pea gravel and eventually just plain old dirt. The long driveway snaked under a canopy of trees. The temperature had dropped what felt like ten degrees, but the humidity didn't budge.

"Wow, he really lives off the beaten path, huh?" Charlie asked, astonished.

"Yeah, great place to ride dirt bikes, though. Especially—" Before he could finish his statement, Juicy finished it for him as she convulsed over a very large pothole.

"That didn't sound good." Charlie frowned.

"No, it didn't," Jared said. "His house isn't much further; I'll take a peek when we get there to make sure we didn't knock something loose."

A chill ran over Charlie. *Odd*, she thought. It was way too warm out and there was absolutely no wind. Completely *dead* air was what came to mind.

Jared pointed out spots in the woods where "this happened" or "so-and-so broke some body part." He was wrapping up a story about Benji shooting a wolf with a BB gun in an attempt to save their friend Carla when Benji's house came into view.

Red in color—well, *rust,* actually—it was a decent-sized farmhouse-style home with a small covered area over the front door. She could see where the original structure had been and where someone had added on to it. *"Franken-House,"* Charlie murmured. Despite its obvious age, the house was in pretty good shape, and the area around it was well kept. Off to the right, set off in some brush, were a few abandoned vehicles and a tractor. Charlie was startled from her introspection as Jared honked the horn to announce their arrival.

Pulling Juicy parallel to the front of the home, Jared leaned in for a quick kiss, then exited the driver's seat. Charlie watched as he knelt on the ground and assessed Juicy's undercarriage. "Everything looks ok to me," he said, giving a thumbs up. "When we go to leave, we can look for any dark spots in the dirt. Make sure we didn't crack anything open on that pothole." Standing up, he brushed off the gravel that had pressed into his knee caps, leaving behind a dozen or so red indentations.

Charlie opened the passenger door and was about to exit, when she heard a holler come from inside the home. Jared howled back and proceeded to walk toward the door. The screen door gave a creak, then a slam, and Charlie saw Benji. Taller than Jared by five inches or so, and with long gangly arms and legs, he had bright red hair cut into a mullet that surrounded his skinny oval face and more freckles than Charlie had ever seen on one individual.

"Jared, buddy!" Benji called out in a definitive Southern drawl. "How ya been?"

The duo clapped a hug on each other as Charlie joined Jared's side. The hug lingered while Charlie finished assessing Benji—green eyes, no visible tattoos, and wearing jorts and a Black Sabbath T-shirt. Releasing their hug, Jared placed his arm around Charlie and introduced her to Benji.

"Soooo, you're the infamous Charlie?" Benji questioned, giving her a quick up and down. "I've heard a lot 'bout ya. Some crazy shit that went down with your mom, huh?"

"Uh, yeah, sure was," Charlie replied, nervously sliding her left hand into Jared's rear pocket.

"Well, heck! I wanna hear the full story for sure!" Benji said. Turning his back to the pair, he continued. "But first, let me get y'all a drink and give you a proper tour of this palace. Follow me!"

The two walked toward the house, Jared stepping ahead to grab the screen door.

"Hey, man! That's my job," Benji teased. "Ladies first," he finished with a swoop of his arm.

Charlie thanked both Jared and Benji, stepping over the threshold and into the foyer. A weird combination of wood, smoke, and Renuzit filled Charlie's nostrils. Allowing her eyes to adjust to the change in lighting, she took in her immediate surroundings. The foyer was similar to her parents' home in New York, small with an off-center staircase leading upstairs. A long hallway running the depth of the house led to a large room in the back. To her right was a room that seemed to have no defined purpose. There were couches, chairs, and a wall of empty shelves but no TV or much of anything else. Closed pocket doors and a large hutch-like piece of furniture blocked it. To her left was a coat rack and a narrow door situated to its right.

Benji moved past them and turned his back away, continuing his tour guide impression. "This used to be my maw maw and pop pop's house. That front room was their reading room. This down here is where all the real fun happens." Spinning quickly on his heels, he entered the large back room. Spanning the full length of the house, the room was a three-in-one. To the far left was a living room, housing a wood stove, a large couch, and two cushy chairs. An absurdly large television was positioned kitty-corner in the room.

Right in front of them was a small circular dining table, circa the nineteen-fifties, with a well-worn, goldenrod Formica top, with silver trim and lots of coffee stains. To the right was the small kitchen. Again, goldenrod was the theme.

Benji pointed to a closed door off the far side of the kitchen. "That's my room. Used to be Maw Maw and Pop Pop's, but after they passed, I moved down here. No tour, though; kind of a mess." He winked. "Have a seat. What can I get you?"

Charlie and Jared both accepted a Coke while Benji flipped a tab on a beer. Sitting down at the table, Jared said, "How you been, man? Still over at ETSU?"

"Yep. Keep changing focus though; who knows when I'll actually graduate."

"Charlie here is kind of doing the same. Tell him, Charlie," Jared said, taking a gulp of his Coke.

"So, yeah. Everything that happened with my mom has me rethinking my life path at the moment. I decided to switch gears and take a semester or two of exploratory classes to help me learn and hopefully fully process what happened."

"Whoa! That's cool! So, go ahead now, tell me what happened," Benji chided.

With a deep breath, Charlie went through the events.

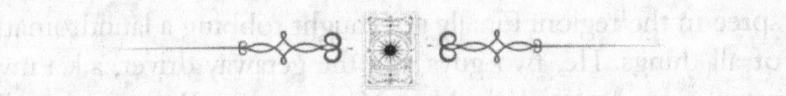

"Holy shitballs! Ok, my mind is officially blown! That means you're kind of a believer now, right? And you have your very own personal watcher?" Benji said. Not waiting for an actual answer, he quickly stood up and said, "Well, ok! Let's finish this tour, and then I'll take you to our very own haunted house!" He rubbed his hands and gave a Vincent Price chuckle.

"Dude, I wouldn't say haunted, but yeah, it's pretty gnarly," Jared said.

"But hey, how's about after the upstairs tour, we go for lunch, then come back for a hike around the property and, um…the house."

"Sure thing, bro!" Benji said, scooting back the chair with a screech. Charlie could feel the noise in her teeth. Benji led the way up the stairs and showed Charlie pictures of his maw maw and pop pop, along with several of his school photos that were taken over the years.

"If you don't mind me asking, if your maw maw and pop pop raised you, what happened to your parents?"

"Nope, don't mind. They're actually serving time here in good old Tennessee. When I was about five, my dad decided he was made for a life of crime and gave up his bricklaying job to join a bunch of locals who went on a small robbery spree in the region. Finally got caught robbing a laundromat, of all things. He, two guys and the getaway driver, a.k.a my mom, were arrested. So Maw Maw and Pop Pop raised me." Changing the subject back to the tour, he continued. "Three bedrooms up here. All unused. Mostly junk. Bathroom down there and the attic access over there. Nothing much," he said matter-of-factly. "Now let's go eat! You thinking what I'm thinking, Jared?"

"Heck yeah! Best burgers in the area!" Jared said.

CHAPTER FIVE
EXPLORERS

SURVIVING THE THIRD PASS over Benji's driveway, Juicy came to a stop. They exited the vehicle, and Benji made a mad dash inside. Jared grabbed Charlie by the arm, spun her around, and pressed his body to hers, pinning her to the side of the car.

"So," he said, planting a kiss on her, "whatcha think so far?"

"Of?" Charlie teased. "I mean, lunch was great, the kiss was mediocre…" She laughed so hard she couldn't continue her mockery.

"Of Benji, ya goof," Jared said.

"Oh! Well, he's definitely interesting. Got a lot of energy. But he seems like a good guy. I can see how you two have remained friends all these years."

Their conversation was interrupted by a slushing of ice as Benji walked out the front door with a Playmate in one hand and a boombox in the other.

"All right, y'all, let's get this exploration going! Anyone need to relieve themselves before we head out?"

Jared and Charlie shook their heads, but Charlie decided she was going to need to switch shoes. Based on what she saw around her, she wasn't willing to sacrifice her white Keds.

Popping them off, she tossed them onto the front floorboards and grabbed her backup sneakers. To save some time, she took the lazy way out and slid her feet directly in, avoiding the lace-up process.

With a thumbs up from Charlie, Benji pressed the play button on his boombox and Warrant's *"Cherry Pie"* belted out as he led the way around the side of the house to a path of sorts.

The trio wove their way through the brush, chatting and singing along to Benji's rock mixtape. Charlie took in her surroundings and felt a sudden twinge of lightheadedness.

A strange tingling sensation washed over her. Charlie's surroundings shifted to a shadowy room. The air was thick with the scent of burning herbs and aged wood. Candles flickered and cast long shadows on the rustic walls. A woman stood at a table covered with dried herbs, vials, and unknown artifacts. She mixed and measured various ingredients, then moved to the fire. Charlie watched in awe as the woman recited incantations under her breath. Rhythmic. Each word resonated within Charlie. She felt herself inhale, and her breath caught in her throat. The woman turned toward Charlie; she bore her mother's face. "Mom," Charlie heard herself say. "Mom, I miss you." She continued to look at the woman, afraid she would lose sight of her mother if she looked away. Tears welled up, and Charlie instinctively reached out to caress her mother's face, but her hand passed right through. Again, she attempted, and again she failed. The vision began to blur and fade...

Charlie was snapped back to reality when Benji said, "Yo! Did you hear me? I said we need to be on sticker bush alert going forward. Oh, and chiggers, too."

"Chiggers?!" Charlie exclaimed incredulously. "He's making that up, right?" she asked, looking directly at Jared.

"Nope, they're the real deal around here, and chances are we're all gonna be covered in them tonight," Jared replied.

"Covered? Them? What exactly is a chigger, Jared?"

Benji fielded this question. "Chiggers are tiny little fuckers. They hang out in these weeds here and love to sink themselves into our skin. Almost invisible, these little shits hurt like hell. Jared knows what I'm talking about," he said as he laughed. "As a matter of fact, he knows exactly what to do to get rid of them. You're in good hands."

Charlie shivered, questioning her decision to wear shorts today.

"We got skeeters and 'no see ums,' too, but the chiggers, they're no joke," Benji continued. Clicking his tongue, he switched gears and became tour guide again. "Over there, about two hundred yards or so, is my family plot. We can hit it on the way back. Pretty much all my relatives are buried there. And up ahead is where we're gonna explore. There's a small pond over yonder with a footbridge that leads to Elias

Cobb's old house. He was like my super-duper great grandpa back in the 1700s."

Charlie nodded, took Jared's hand, and allowed herself to be distracted by Ratt—the band, not the rodent—in an attempt to forget about the chiggers. Up ahead, she could see the "pond" that Benji mentioned. It was not at all what Charlie thought it would look like. This pond resembled more of a lake, as far as she was concerned. At least ten football fields long and four wide, the body of water was unbelievably beautiful and impressive. Gone was the image she had of a slimy, frog- ridden muck. There was a walking bridge over the narrow end, and hanging from the largest oak tree she had ever seen was a tire swing.

Jared noticed Charlie's gaze and said, "Oh, you wanna try it, don't ya?"

Benji chimed in with, "Yeah! Let's go, guys! We have time for a dip. The water temp should be perfect, having had all summer to warm up."

Before Charlie could answer, Benji ran ahead, tossed the cooler and boombox with wild abandon into the dirt, and yelled like Tarzan as he leapt on the tire and swung out to the center of the water. Letting go with a howl, he kerplunked and was quickly swallowed by the splash he created.

Grabbing Charlie's hand tighter, Jared broke into a trot, dragging her behind him, only letting go so he could repeat Benji's performance. Jared, however, was not so graceful.

Charlie winced at witnessing Jared's very painful looking belly flop. She removed her shoes and walked over to dip her toe in. "Hey! None of that now, ya hear?!" Benji yelled across the pond. "Just run and jump. That swing has been there forever. Totally safe."

Dragging her toes across the top of the water, Charlie pirouetted and ran about fifteen feet to the opposite side of the tire and began her charge. Screeching as the tire swung out high over the water, she released and did a front tuck into the water below. Charlie could hear the cheers from under the water. She came up and announced, "And that, boys, is how it's done."

They laughed and swam for another hour. After the music had stopped, Benji climbed out and flipped the tape, doing an interpretive dance to "Welcome to the Jungle." He slipped open the Playmate and asked Jared and Charlie if they were ready for a beer. A resounding *yes* shot out over the splashing, and they rose out of the water. Shaking themselves free of the excess water, they each grabbed a can and sat down next to Benji on a fallen tree.

"This is very cool," Charlie said. "I bet you're out here a lot, huh?"

"Actually, not so much anymore. I'm not big on being out here alone. Kinda gives me the creeps."

Unable to register that sentiment, Charlie just said, "Oh, that's a shame."

"You'll see what I mean soon enough," Benji declared, giving Jared a knowing look.

Jared nodded and said, "Yeah, this place, well *that* place over the hill" —he pointed across the pond— "has quite a history."

Charlie looked over at the hill and wondered what this house looked like and why they felt this way. But, again, any old house was going to set off those kind of vibes, wasn't it?

With the aid of the sun, the group had dried out for the most part by the time they finished their beers. Gathering up their shoes, Benji let them know he was going to leave the cooler and boombox there. "No sense in carrying this shit all that way. 'Sides, it will distract from the creepy vibes if we do," he said, ending with a cackle. "Seriously, though. Follow me." And they began their walk over the bridge.

CHAPTER SIX
TO GIGI'S HOUSE WE GO

ONCE ON THE OTHER SIDE, it was a short hike up the hill and slightly down again. Looking up, Charlie saw the house before them. She wasn't sure how, but the house seemed to be leering at them, judging them. The windows on the second floor resembled eyes. Very off putting for sure.

The house, although not large, loomed over the area around it. Charlie could tell the house had been added onto, as the first level and second weren't quite a match. This house, Charlie decided, had a soul, and as she got closer, she could feel its pain. *Odd,* she thought; why would she even have that thought to begin with? She had never assigned human emotions to a building before, so why now?

Something, though, however you sliced it, was wrong with this house. She just knew it. She was so enthralled with it, she had actually missed everything that Benji had said since they had laid eyes on it.

"Hey, Benji. Sorry, but I totally spaced. Can you go over that again?"

Benji let out a laugh. "It's ok, Charlie. The house seems to have that effect on some people. I was saying that this house was built by Elias sometime in the 1700s for himself and his wife Margaret, or as my maw maw called her, Gigi. Rumor has it, the original design was simple, mostly due to the nefarious ways Elias came about the materials. The cottage was not built with materials purchased or bartered for. Instead, he resorted to theft, targeting the local farmers struggling to sustain their own livelihoods. The stolen materials allowed Elias to build his home without incurring personal costs. It was also rumored that the land had been acquired via unscrupulous methods. It's always been said that because of this, the land and the house are cursed. But who knows, really."

Benji finished up his tale just as they reached the front of the house. With very little effort, Benji pushed open the front door. Stepping up onto the porch, Charlie could feel the boards shift under their weight. Giving a silent wish that it would hold long enough for them to enter, Charlie breathed a sigh of relief.

"It's been a while since anyone's been in here," Benji announced, swatting away cobweb after cobweb. Jared gestured for Charlie to move ahead of them as Benji walked into the living room. "This whole first floor used to be one large area. Here, where the fireplace is, was the kitchen and eating area. The space we came in was the living area. The bedroom is behind that wall. Not much to it, as you can see. The second level was added years later by Elias' wife, Margaret."

Charlie stood, admiring all the wood and stone. Simple construction for sure, but she could see how it was a home once.

"So, this wall wasn't here, correct?" Charlie asked, pointing to the long wall across from them.

"Nope, follow me. I'll show you," Benji said, walking back toward the front door. Making a right at the stairs, he showed them the door that would have been the access to the only bedroom at the time. He then gestured to an opening in front of them. "Take this, remove that wall, and there ya go!"

Charlie nodded and looked at the space. A tiny kitchen with maybe four cabinets and absolutely no counter space lay before her. There was an old, small oven and cooktop and one of those really old fridges, wooden with iron handles, like on *Little House on the Prairie*. Touching it, she confirmed, "Ice box, right?"

"Yep, a good old-fashioned ice box. Put a block of ice in here, straw and sawdust here, and it kept the bare minimum cold."

In the opposite corner was a teeny-tiny wood stove. Charlie couldn't get over the layers of dust covering everything in sight. "When was the last time someone lived here?" she asked.

"My guess would be the late 1800s," Benji replied. "Hey, we better get upstairs while we still have daylight."

The trio made their way up the bizarre stairway. It gave Charlie serious fun house vibes.

"What's with these stairs?" she asked.

"Ya know, I'm not really sure, but some say these were added later. The second story originally only had a ladder going up to it."

Once at the top, Charlie was in awe at the space's enormous size.
"This is huge! Looks like this was supposed to be an attic…am I right?"

"Well, it was used as a bedroom for a while. But I think their son Thomas made it storage space after Margaret died."

"Look at all these cool things," Jared said, walking around and yanking covers off various items as he went. "This mirror is rad!"

"So is this chair in the corner," Charlie said. "And this trunk." Kneeling in front of it, she used one of the covers Jared had tossed to remove the inch of dust that enveloped it. "Can I open it?" she asked.

"Be my guest" Benji said "Who knows what, if anything, is even still in there."

Lifting the lid, a haunting creak echoed in the open space. Propping it open with a stick Jared handed her, Charlie peered in. There was a stack of books, some clothing that had seen better days, and tons of dead moths. A few pouches of small trinkets were tucked in the corners and something wrapped in a cloth that looked to be a scarf.

Charlie carefully lifted the wrapped item out of the trunk, laid it on the floor, and gently unwrapped it. Dust that had gathered over the years, plumed up in a small cloud, causing Charlie to choke. Letting out a deep cough, she peered down and saw a doll staring back at her. It had the sweetest face with tiny black eyes, which she assumed were marbles. They sat deep in the sockets and the cherub cheeks were dusted with the prettiest pink blusher. The teeniest little lips pursed as if to give Charlie a kiss. Dirty blonde hair, tightly curled, flowed to the shoulders in stark contrast to the royal blue velvet dress with lace trim around the collar and waist. Charlie ran her fingers over the velvet and landed on a brooch, which seemed out of place due in part to its size. It was not in proportion to the doll at all. Charlie guessed it had been fastened on after her creation.

"Well, *that's* not creepy at all," Jared said, rolling his eyes. "Leave it to you to discover something that weird."

Charlie nodded her acknowledgement. She was too entranced by this cutie to form actual words. She heard the guys shuffling as she examined the doll further, oblivious to the conversation going on around her.

"Earth to Charlie," Jared said, plucking the doll from her hands.

"Oh, hey. Yeah. Sorry. What's up?" she asked.

"What's up is you and this crazy doll," Jared replied, wrapping the doll back up in the scarf.

"Guys," Benji said. "Feel free to keep anything you find here. This stuff is just going to rot away if it isn't rescued."

"I'm assuming this doll goes in the keep pile, huh, Charlie?" Jared teased.

"Totally, and I think I'm going to want these too," Charlie said, handing Jared a short stack of books from the pile and a tiny pouch. Closing the lid, Charlie stood and joined Benji, who was elbow deep in a stack of old papers.

"This stuff ...whose is it?" Charlie asked.

"I've no way of knowing for sure. I'd say mostly Margaret's. My maw maw and pop pop never lived here. It's been vacant for at least a hundred-fifty years."

"Anyone need a mink stole?" Jared asked. "Looks like he still has some teeth," he said, finishing with a snarl.

Giving Jared the gag me face, Charlie watched as he flung the carcass around his neck, sending a plume of dust flying up around his head.

"Serves you right." Charlie giggled. She meandered around the attic in an attempt to find something to carry her treasures in. She snatched up a small crate and placed her items securely inside. "There, easier to carry back," she said, proud of herself.

"If we're all done rummaging, we can go ahead and start out. Should give us some time to swing by the graveyard if you still want to go," Benji offered.

Jared and Charlie confirmed they did, and the trio left the house and made their way back over the footbridge.

Benji gathered up his cooler and boombox, but not before grabbing a beer for the walk. Winding through the brush, Charlie had a deja vu moment as the cemetery came into view.

CHAPTER SEVEN
HEADSTONES AND MINDFUCKS

SMALL IN OVERALL SIZE, there were dozens of headstones dotted about. No two seemed to be alike. As she got closer, she read the headstones that were still legible.

Staring down a row of headstones, Charlie noticed one in particular with a miniature fence around it. She made her way between the rows; the headstone was for an infant. How sad, she thought, to lose a child so young. She deduced from the headstones surrounding it that this was all one family. The mother outlived each of her family members. She thought back to her mom's funeral and how she had wished her mom was given the chance to achieve this goal. With a deep sigh, Charlie moved to the next row when she heard Jared yell, "Guys! Come check this out!"

Benji, who was a few steps ahead of Charlie, stopped dead in his tracks. "Jared, dude…"

Jared, standing across the graveyard in front of a meager headstone that read "Elias Cobb," nodded. "I know…we've been back here hundreds of times since we were kids, and I don't ever remember seeing this one."

"Well, in our defense, it was buried under this huge pile of sticker bushes and debris."

Charlie leaned in between the guys to see what the fuss was about. A simple headstone sat at their feet. After years of neglect, it was lying flat on the ground. "Elias Cobb. Born November 8, 1764 Presumed Dead December 1801."

"Presumed dead?" Charlie questioned. "How is that even a thing? And why is he over here, separated from the others?"

"All great questions there, Charlie," Benji said, sounding bewildered. "He's the one I told you who built the house we were just in. The only family rumors were that he up and left his wife. I'm not sure what this headstone is insinuating."

The threesome stared at the headstone. A breeze seemingly came from nowhere, sending chills up and down Charlie's spine. Shivering, she leaned in closer to Jared to share some of his body heat. Almost in unison, Charlie felt what she thought was Jared's hand on her shoulder; and heard a voice. *Charlie, dear, it's Marcus. Open your mind. Relax and see if you can feel what is happening here.*

Not wanting to alarm Jared or explain herself to Benji, Charlie closed her eyes and took a deep breath. Listening to Marcus guide her, her world disappeared, a mist taking its place. Then the faces of two women talking nervously came into focus. One was more flustered than the other, who seemed to be older in years than the first. *Focus, Charlie. Let's see if you can **hear** them*, Marcus continued. Attempting to dial in on the voices, Charlie instead picked up on the surroundings. Crickets chirping, frogs trilling, and a...a...moan? No, not a moan, a wail. She waited. There it was again. Still outside of her immediate earshot. Then—gone. Marcus, the women—everything. In its place, she saw Jared and Benji horseplaying over in the main graveyard area. Shaking her head, Charlie looked down one final time at the aging stone and sighed. "Here, Elias, let me at least straighten you up," she said, tipping the stone to a somewhat upright position.

Marcus had been working with her since the ordeal with Astrid in the spring to help her understand their world. The otherside. The paranormal. She had wanted to use his help to understand what happened, and where her mom and Astrid landed after everything settled. Marcus and the Master believed Charlie was born with a "special gift" and that she was foreseen to be a beacon of light and hope to those seeking help. Both in her world and theirs. Whatever that meant. She was still getting used to Marcus just popping in on her. It was never scheduled and not always convenient. Over the past several months, she hadn't felt like she'd been much of a student. There had not been much progress with regards to her abilities but Marcus had been the ever-present cheerleader.

Turning, Charlie saw Tweedle Dee and Tweedle Dum mock wrestling in the distance. *Boys,* she thought, and began her walk over when something caught her eye in the moonlight. A flash. Kneeling, she dug around the leaves and layers of dirt. She was about to give up, chalking the gleam up to a firefly, when her fingertip snagged something. Pushing the item from side to side to release it from its earthen tomb, Charlie successfully plucked it from the ground. She placed it in her opposite hand; it was metal and round in shape. However, due to the layers of crustiness, she couldn't see what it actually was. *Nothing spit won't fix,* she thought and gave an overzealous hock into her hand. Swishing it around,

she began to make out some details. Raised ivy patterns covered the top. Fervently polishing it on her shorts, she brought it back up for further examination. This time, she saw it was, in fact, a button. Old, for sure. Running it through one more spit rinse, Charlie thanked her grandpa Walter for his teachings and placed her find in her pocket to share with Jared later.
With a quick spring up, she turned on her heels and joined Jared and Benji.

"Anyone else getting hungry?" Benji asked. "I'm thinking it's burger time."

In agreement, the group started on their way back to Benji's house.
Charlie looked ahead at the path. Fireflies flickered like tiny sparklers on the Fourth of July. Spiderwebs danced in the beams of light. Charlie shifted the crate from her right hip to her left. It wasn't necessarily heavy, but it was a tad cumbersome.

Reaching their destination, Benji took his items inside while Charlie and Jared slid the crate into the small area behind the front seats. At that moment, exhaustion hit Charlie. She wasn't sure how she was going to manage a cookout, but knowing how important it was to Jared, she reached down on the floorboard and rescued one of the bottles of Double Cola they had gotten at Smitty's. She crossed in front of Juicy and bellowed to Jared, "Hey! I need a caffeine boost. Could you do me a huge favor and get me a cup of ice for this?" and held up the bottle like a trophy.

"Sure thing. I was heading in to help Benji with stuff for the BBQ anyways. I'll grab you some."

Eyeballing the choices in front of her, she deduced that the safest bet would be the orange and blue striped chair. It was only missing *one* center strap. Sliding the chair closer to the grill area, she carefully sat down, grimacing as the remaining straps gave way a little too much for her comfort level. Leaning her head back, she looked up at the night sky. The early stars were starting to appear, and the sky's purples and pinks were fading into hues of blues and blacks. She got lost in her thoughts as a rogue firefly or two zig zagged their way in and out of her field of vision.

Charlie watched as they danced in the night sky and let herself drift into a cherished memory.

It was a warm summer night like this one. She was young, and her mother was vibrant and full of laughter. They had wandered out into her mom's garden, each carrying a jar with holes punched in the lids. The smell of summer moved through the air, and the chirp of frogs rang out. "Look, Charlie," her mother had said. "They're like little bits of magic." Charlie giggled, reaching her small hand out to catch one. Her mom had shown her how to catch them the year prior using the cupping technique. They spent hours out in the garden, catching and releasing the delicate flying stars. With their jars filled, the fireflies created tiny glowing lanterns that illuminated their faces as they told story after story. It was that night her mom taught her the firefly song: "I'm a little firefly, dark and bright. You'll see me appear on a warm summer night…"

Laughter filled Charlie's ears. Realizing she was singing out loud, Charlie floundered to give the guys an explanation for what they had witnessed. But alas, the duo would not cut her any slack. This would be one of those stories for the ages, the kind you tell your grandchildren.

Jared sat next to Charlie, patted her leg, and consoled her by saying "You're officially one of the gang now."

"Thanks," Charlie said, feeling her cheeks warm.

"So, Benji here is gracing us with his world-famous burgers tonight!" Jared announced.
"Yeah, I could tell you the secret recipe, but then I'd have to kill you," Benji said with a chuckle. "All kidding aside, though, my secret is to add the cheese to the center. Keeps the cheese from burning and dripping all over the place." Pressing the burgers down with his metal spatula, he stated that the key to a perfect burger was the grill marks. Pressing again, juices sizzled on the flames below and filled the air with the aroma of freshly burnt meat.

The three traded banter as the burgers cooked. With a nod, Benji gave a simultaneous thumbs up to Jared. That seemed to be the cue for them to dig in. Grabbing three paper plates, Jared plopped a bun on each one and carried them over to Benji, presenting them for burger placement. Jared handed Charlie hers. She walked over to the larger cooler to top off her burger. *Benji is actually well prepared,* she thought. Ketchup, mustard, pickles, onions, and mayo. Grabbing a bag of Doritos on her way back, Charlie sat down and watched Jared stack his burger as she popped open the bag.

Sitting down, Benji kept the grill open as the coals burned out and provided some light.

"So, Charlie. That doll! Quite an interesting find. I wish I was able to tell you more about it and whose it was," Benji said.

"Yeah, it sucks there's no one to ask," Jared replied.

"Well, I mean, I could ask my dad next time I visit him in jail. I don't visit often, but it would give us something else to talk about other than what he had for breakfast that day."

"That'd be awesome! Thank you. This burger, by the way, delish!" Charlie said.

Benji took a bow from his chair and laughed. "What are y'alls plans while you're here?"

Jared filled Benji in on the plans to visit the falls the next day. "You're more than welcome to join us if you want."

"I'll keep it in mind, for sure," Benji replied.

The party continued well into the wee hours until a grizzly yawn from Charlie burst their bubble.

"Sounds like Charlie here is up past her bedtime," Benji joked.

"Yeah, man. It's been a long day. I think we're gonna jet," Jared said.

"Totally get it! Be safe driving back, dude," Benji said, planting a bro hug on Jared. A quick peck on Charlie's cheek and they said their goodbyes for the evening.

Exhausted from the day, Jared and Charlie spent most of the drive back to Tilde's in silence. Only the sound of crickets and tree frogs could be heard over the summer air flowing through their hair. Opting to bring the box of finds in the next day, the pair quietly entered the house so as to not wake Tilde and Arthur. They successfully made it past the creaky screen door and the squeaky stairs. They both agreed that even though showers were desperately needed, they would hold off until morning since the guest bath was directly across from the master bedroom. It was then that Charlie was bolted out of her daze by the thought of chiggers.

"Jared, we can't go to bed without that chigger check. I wouldn't be able to sleep! If we can't shower, can we at least strip down in the bathroom and give a quick once over?"

Jared agreed they could do a quick check. A few minutes later and the coast was clear. Not a chigger in sight.

Sliding into bed, sleep came quickly for both Charlie and Jared.

CHAPTER EIGHT
LEARNING CURVE

WAKING AGAIN, AND WITH no real sense of time, Charlie squinted as the sun beamed across the room. She looked to her side and saw Jared still sound asleep. Slowly sitting up to not wake him, she grabbed her journal from the side table.

She made notes from her experiences the day before, and tried to get a sense if anyone else was up. She needed a shower badly; she could definitely smell herself. That was never a good thing. Opening the door a crack, a welcoming waft of fresh air and coffee hit her. *Yes!* Dropping her clothes to the bathroom floor, Charlie messed with her hair as the hot water made its way up through the pipes. She was pretty sure she was ready for a change in the style. Holding it up so it fell just below her ears, she thought maybe a bob would be the next move. Putting a pin in that idea, she released her hair and let it fall on her shoulders. The steamed mirror was her ready, set, go cue that the shower was hot enough. Stepping in and out from under the almost too hot stream of water, she decided scalding was a small price to pay for the intense relaxation she was feeling, so she fully committed to the heat.

Soaping up her hair, she closed her eyes and thought about her "lesson" with Marcus the night before. Inhaling the hot, wet air around her, she focused on the sound of the water to visually bring herself back to the graveyard. Charlie played back the mental video and saw the two women. Just as she had thought the prior night, one was definitely more mature than the other. Not a mother/daughter age difference but perhaps sisters? Focusing on their energy, Charlie could feel the energy frequency the younger woman was emitting. Nervousness? Agitation? No. Fear. It was fear. But why? Charlie saw nothing this woman should be afraid of. The older woman wasn't a threatening presence that Charlie could see. As a matter of fact, she seemed to be very focused on her task.

Taking another deep breath, Charlie attempted to zone in on their conversation, but, as usual, the voices came across sounding like Charlie Brown's teacher. What she could hear was the same wail. A sound that definitely was not coming from either woman. Zooming in with her vision as a director would with his camera, Charlie targeted the area below the women's waists. Trees, bushes, and snow. Lots of snow! And then Charlie saw it. Blood. A trail of droplets circling the area around the women's feet. Charlie immediately got cold, ice cold. This is a first, she thought. She had never been able to feel these visions before. How…odd.

A loud clank startled her out of the vision, and Charlie realized she wasn't feeling cold from the vision; icy water now rained down upon her. How long had she been in there? Quickly feeling her hair to make sure there wasn't any lingering shampoo, she shut the water off and grabbed her towel. She was shivering so hard her teeth chattered. Drying off, she wrapped her hair with one of the smaller towels on the rack. The water had run cold for so long that the steam had retreated from the mirror, and Charlie saw that her lips had actually turned blue. Taking a deep breath, she released a small sigh that caused her lips to quiver. She knew the lost time was from her vision and not at all like what had happened between her mom and Astrid. It was unnerving. In the dozen or so practices with Marcus, she had never fully lost sense of time or space. Charlie gave herself a quick admonition for attempting this without Marcus present. *Serves you right, dufus.*

Giving her teeth a thorough brush, Charlie walked back down the hallway and into the room where Jared was just waking up.

"Morning," he groaned.

"M…m…morning," Charlie chattered. She quickly climbed between the sheets to vampire any and all body heat Jared was willing to give up.

"Good grief! Why are you an ice cube?!" he blurted.

"I…I…ran out…of …ho…ho...hot water," Charlie replied.

Shaking his head, Jared said, "This house has one of the largest water heaters known to man. Damn thing must be broken if it couldn't cover your shower. I'll tell Uncle Arthur when we go down." As he finished that statement, the realization he wasn't going to get a shower any time soon seemed to kick in. "Of course it happened on the one day I smell like Oscar the Grouch."

Gaining some warmth, Charlie retorted, "It's not broken. I just lost track of time is all. You should be good to shower in a few." With the feeling back in her toes and fingers, Charlie slipped out to get dressed.

"What do you mean you lost track of time? Should I be concerned? Was it Astrid? Has she gone back to her old tricks?"

"No, no, babe. Not at all! I tried to go back to a vision Marcus showed me last night and I got sucked in and lost track of time."

"Marcus? Last night? When?"

Charlie filled him in on the visit she had when they found Elias' headstone.

"Man, I knew he popped in on you, but that…" Jared started.

Charlie nodded. Teeth still chattering, she said, "Yeah, I think maybe I need to set some boundaries. Can you have boundaries with your guardian angel?" she asked, looking up. "Either way, it's totally my fault for trying this alone."

"Did you see anything more?" Jared asked.

Sitting up on the edge of the bed, Charlie wrapped a blanket around herself and replayed the new scene for him.

"Interesting. Never a dull moment with you, that's for sure," he said. "Well, I don't know about you, but I need coffee. How about we go down, have a cup, and I'll leave you to chat with Aunt Tilde and Uncle Arthur while I shower? We won't mention any of this, ok?" Jared finished as he slipped into shorts and a tee. Charlie nodded, and the pair made a beeline for the kitchen.

CHAPTER NINE
BISCUITS AND BEAGLE EARS

THE DUO MADE QUICK WORK of their coffees and plopped on the couch in the family room, joining Tilde and Arthur. Tilde was amidst a puzzle, and Arthur had his face buried in a detective novel. "Figured you needed to sleep in," Tilde finally said, breaking the silence. "Heard you come in late," she finished with a wink.

"Of course you did," Jared joked. "I've never been able to sneak in the house…ever," he said with a chuckle.

Arthur guffawed, saying, "Don't know what made you ever think it was possible. This lady here has the ears of a beagle."

"Enough." Tilde swatted at him. "I'm just blessed with good hearing s'all. You two ready for some eats? I'm going to finish up the edges of my puzzle and head in to make breakfast."

Charlie leaned into Jared and whispered, "I thought you said she slept through *anything*…"

Tilde snapped the last connecting piece into place and turned toward Charlie. "Making sausage, biscuits, and gravy. I could use a second pair of hands."

Charlie accepted and followed Tilde to the kitchen. Jared trailed behind, veering off for another cup of coffee while announcing his plans to go shower. "Hey, before you go, can you top me off, too?" Charlie asked, handing him her mug. With a quick kiss, Jared completed his task, handed over the coffee, and took off for shower time.

"Alright, Charlie. Let's get cooking!" Tilde said, handing Charlie her very own apron. Slipping it over her head, Charlie looked down to see *Kiss the Chef* and an image of a very rotund Italian man, replete with a large white chef's hat.

"So, like I said. Sausage, biscuits, and gravy. I'll get you started with the biscuits, then I'll tackle the sausage and gravy. Everything should time out perfectly that way," Tilde said with a flourish and a smile.

To Charlie's surprise, "biscuit making" was not the version she was used to. No pop-fresh cans in sight. She was instead given a recipe card with an actual recipe on it.

"Um, Tilde, I've never baked anything real in my life," Charlie said, feeling panicked.

"Oh, honey. Then biscuits are exactly the thing to cut your teeth on. Metaphorically speakin', of course. Nothing more simple. I promise. Just follow these here instructions step by step and you'll be broken in in no time," Tilde stated, giving Charlie a pat on the shoulder. "Everything you need, utensil wise, will be in that cupboard and drawer over there. I'll grab the ingredients for you. Set you up right here at the island. Ok darlin'?" Tilde asked.

Carefully reading the steps, Charlie did feel a bit better with what she had to do. Pretty simple, she thought. Attempting the first step, however, she was faced with failure in the form of butter. About halfway through "cutting" the butter sticks she had been provided, Charlie heard laughter coming from Tilde. "Bless your heart, Charlie," she said, shaking her head and handing Charlie the pastry cutter. "Use this. You'll want the butter to be in tiny bits before adding it to the flour. Make sure it's not too soft before you do, though. Here. Let's pop these in the freezer for a minute or two to stiffen them up," she said, taking the butter and setting it on the top shelf in the freezer. "Why don't you come over this way and give this sausage a crumble?" Charlie began to break apart the sausage in the cast iron pan when Tilde asked, "So, your mama; did she cook with you at all?"

"Oh, yes! Well…maybe it wasn't as much cooking as heating up. Don't get me wrong, she made great dinners. She just usually stuck to things that could be made in a crock pot or casserole dish," Charlie answered.

"Some of the best meals come from crock pots," Tilde said. " I'm lucky in that my family has always been avid cooks and bakers. Most of my recipes have been passed down. I even have some of Benji's maw maw's recipes she shared over the years. Don't worry, Charlie; if you want to, I can make you a certified Southern goddess in no time. Now. That butter won't cut itself!" she finished, nodding toward the freezer.

Grabbing the frozen butter, Charlie continued with her biscuit tasks and was surprised at how fast she had the dough ready. "What's next?" Charlie asked shyly.

"Well, that mat rolled up in the drawer, roll it out, sprinkle some flour on it to help keep the dough from sticking, and begin to roll. Try to keep it about a half inch thick."

Charlie did as she was instructed and proceeded to roll out the dough. Using the biscuit cutter, she formed a dozen perfect circles. Carefully placing them on the cooking sheet, she slid them into the oven. Tilde set a timer and called Charlie over to observe the gravy making process. "The key," she started, "is the bits on the bottom of the pan. That's where all the flavor is going to come from. We scrape that up real good, then add the butter and the rest of the ingredients. Cooked sausage goes in last, and then we let it simmer."

With both of their tasks accomplished, the pair sat down to enjoy the rest of their coffee. Taking a long sip, Charlie heard footsteps bounding down the stairs, and then Jared's face popped into view.

"Smells amazing! When's chow time? I'm starving!" he said, rubbing his belly.

"Soon enough," Tilde said.

"Ok, well, I'm going to run to the car and grab the box for you, Charlie," he said, turning toward the front door.

"Box?" Tilde asked. Charlie explained their archeological dig in the attic over at the abandoned house and promised to show Tilde when Jared got back.

"Ohhh, I love a good treasure find," Tilde said with a smile. The screen door creaked, and moments later, Jared appeared with the box in hand. "Where can I set it?" he asked.

"How 'bout on the coffee table in the family room? I gotta get these biscuits out and give them a butterin', then I'll join you for show-and- tell while they set up," Tilde said.

They joined Arthur, still secured in the pages of his book. "So, little backstory here," Jared started. "You know that old abandoned farmhouse on Benji's land? Well, he took us for a tour and let Charlie have free reign of the picks in the attic. She's got some interesting stuff," he said with a wink.

Giving Jared an elbow to the ribs, Charlie smiled as she began sorting through the items again. Even more impressed with her treasures in the daylight, she said, "I picked these out of an old trunk," and handed the stack of books to Tilde. "I'm pretty sure these are diaries or journals. I didn't get to spend time with them last night, so I'm not one hundred percent positive."

"Do you mind if I crack one open?" Tilde asked

"Sure, go ahead," Charlie said. Tilde grabbed a tissue from her apron pocket and dusted off the cover of the first book. "Why, what a beautiful binding," she said. They all looked down at the deep royal blue leather-bound book. Carefully opening it, it cracked as the leather gave way. "Probably the first time it's been open in decades," Tilde said. The pages, browned with age, certainly had seen better days.

"Definitely some sort of journal," Charlie whispered in excitement. "Can you tell the year?"

"Not yet." Tilde responded. Flipping the pages delicately she finally found a reference to the year—1799. "Just about a hundred-and-ninety years old! Wow!" Jared said.

"It's in a woman's handwriting, too. But I'm going to let you explore that more, Charlie. It's your find, after all. What else you got?"

Emptying the pouch on the table, Charlie began sorting the items. She had been on the right track the night before with her guess. It seemed to be a mix of lower-end jewelry and other trinkets. "Ring, thimble, pin, string, and a button!" A button she immediately recognized. The raised ivy pattern matched the button she had placed…where? Jumping up, she excused herself and ran up the stairs. In her wake, she could hear Jared ask, "You ok, Charlie? What's wrong?"

In the bedroom, she scoured the floor for her clothes from the night before. Charlie then remembered she had left them on the bathroom floor after the chigger check. From down the hall, Jared asked again if she was ok. "Be right there" was all she could muster in her quest to find the other button. Finding her shorts under Jared's clothes, she reached in her pocket and pulled out the button she had spit cleaned the prior evening. "Gotcha," she said. Hopping down the stairs she plopped back into place to the obvious bewilderment of everyone, including Arthur, who had actually looked up from his book.

"What's the deal, Charlie?" Jared asked.

"The deal is *this*," Charlie began. "*This* button I just found mixed in with the trinkets from the pouch" —she set the button front and center— "and *this* button I found last night buried in muck by Elias' headstone." She laid the twin next to its mate.

"Whoa, those are cool," Jared said. "They look like buttons to a coat from way back," he hypothesized.

"*Or*," Tilde started, plucking the buttons up in her plump fingers, "maybe boots? I'm no seamstress, but they just seem to be an odd size for a coat."

"Well, Tilde, my mom *was* a seamstress, and I believe you may be correct! Not necessarily about them being boot buttons, but they're definitely the wrong size for a coat."

"You know," Tilde suggested, "you could take these items down to the historical society on Main Street and see if they could help you out. Just a thought."

"Oh! Could we?" Charlie turned toward Jared. "Maybe on our way out today?"

"Sure. Let's see if there's anything else we may want to bring," he offered.

The last item to be unveiled was the doll. Charlie laid her down on the table and began to unwrap her. In this light, Charlie could see her hair was in desperate need of a comb, but the dress seemed to be in excellent shape. "Isn't she sweet?" Tilde said, looking over the doll. Running her finger over the lace trim of the dress, she noticed the brooch. "Oh, what's this? This is definitely an add on," she said, lifting the doll for a closer look. "You may want to take this brooch in with you! It's quite impressive."

Agreeing that she would, Charlie placed the buttons in the small satchel and carefully removed the brooch from the dress. Upon doing so, she felt a surge through her fingertips. Not electricity, exactly. More like energy moving through her. Negative energy. This was a first. Charlie had never felt energy like this before. Not even from objects surrounding Astrid last spring. Unsure how to process what happened without alarming those around her, Charlie made a note to ask Marcus the next time he popped in. Maybe it was nothing, but it was probably something. Setting the brooch in the satchel with the buttons, she cinched up the opening and re-wrapped the doll as Jared's belly let out a growl to end all growls. "Ok, we get it!" he said, giving his stomach a pat. "Can we please go eat?" he asked, sounding way too much like a two-year-old.

"Why of course, darlin'!" Tilde said. And with that, the whole lot of them made their way to the dining table.

Bellies full, Jared and Arthur thanked Tilde and Charlie for their contributions, offering to clean up. Tilde excused herself back to her puzzle while Charlie decided to use the time to call her dad. Carrying the box of goodies up with her, Charlie set them at the foot of the bed and headed to use the phone again.

Dialing her dad, Charlie sank into the window seat while it rang. Looking out the window, she could see it was going to be yet another gorgeous day so she unlatched the lock and slid the window open. A burst of fresh air blew through as Charlie heard the comforting "Bauman residence."

"Hey, Dad!" Charlie began. "I didn't wake you, did I?"

"Heck, no. With everything going on around here, I'm lucky if I get to sleep till eight anymore. How are you, kiddo? How's your time going in Tennessee?"

Charlie filled her dad in on what had been going on since their arrival: The dish on Tilde and Arthur and the house. Her and Jared's visit with Benji. The cool items she had found. She left out the shower episode, however. She did not want her dad to worry or ask questions that she couldn't answer yet. Dale reconfirmed the approximate day he could expect her and Jared, reminding her that although he knew they were sharing a bed on the road, he would have the guest room set up for Jared when they got to the house. "Your dad's still an old fuddy duddy, I know," Dale said. "But you're my baby girl, and it's my job to make sure things are on the up and up, no matter how quickly society is changing."

Charlie agreed that was fine. She mentioned that she was going to want a day for just her and Ramona, and could her dad maybe think up something for him and Jared to get into for a bit that day. He promised he would come up with something, but before he could continue, the doorbell sounded on his end. "Hey, Charlie. I've got to get that. Claudia, my real estate agent, is here to do another walk through to make sure I'm progressing on my 'homework.' It's like she wants to sell this place or something," he said with a snicker. Charlie said her goodbyes as the doorbell rang again.

"See you soon, Dad. Love you."

"Love you too, Charlie bear," he replied.

Charlie headed back downstairs to see if she could get a plan of action together with Jared. Turning the corner to the kitchen, she stopped dead in her tracks. Standing at the sink in the silliest apron she had ever seen was Jared, holding a dish in one hand and a towel in the other. He beamed a huge smile at her and said, "You like what you see?" Charlie couldn't stop laughing as she said she never thought he'd have a better set than her, referring to the well-endowed female figure printed on the apron that made Jared look like a French maid. "Aunt Tilde loves her apron collection, that's for sure. Here, help me finish these," he said, tossing her a dry towel. Stepping to his side, Charlie grabbed a bowl and began drying.

"So, you get a hold of your dad?" Jared asked.

"Sure did. Got some things brewing for our visit. Oh, by the way— you'll be crashing in the guest room," Charlie said with a wink.

"Ahhhh," Jared said. "But of course."

"What are we doing today?" Charlie asked.

"I was thinking we'd go down to get those pieces looked at and then head over to the falls for a bit? Then just see where the wind blows us? Sound ok?" Jared asked.

"Totally!" Charlie said, smiling back. With the last of the silverware dried and put away, they headed up to change for the day.

CHAPTER TEN
HISTORY LESSONS

SAYING THEIR GOODBYES to Tilde and Arthur, Charlie and Jared decided to get some exercise and walk down to the historical society. Jared gave Charlie a complete lowdown on who was who, who lived where, and what escapades occurred on which lots. The beauty, variety, and age of the homes excited Charlie. She couldn't put her finger on it, but she felt connected even though she had never been here before. Reaching the bottom of the hill, they turned right onto Main Street. Pointing to the left side of the street, Jared said, "Where we're going is just up ahead." As they crossed, Charlie got a phenomenal view of the courthouse with its impressive clock tower.

Jared held the door for Charlie, and the pair walked into the foyer and over to the help desk to see who, if anyone, could help them. The woman sitting behind the desk, whose nameplate deemed her as Ethel, proudly greeted them. "Welcome to the Jonesborough Historical Society. How may we help you today?"

Jared and Charlie introduced themselves and stated that they were looking for help figuring out the origins of some historical items they had found. Perking up, Ethel said, "Why, of course we can help with that!" Picking up the phone, she pressed a square button on her phone set, turning it red. A few seconds later, she announced to the person on the other end, "We have two visitors who would like to meet with you." Hanging up the handset, she politely told Jared and Charlie to have a seat and Lowell would be up in just a moment to meet with them. Turning toward the seats, Charlie was more interested in what she saw on the wall before her than the idea of sitting. Walking over, she stopped to see a row of framed family tree sketches. She skimmed over the names and saw one that caught her attention—Elias Cobb. Next to his name was a woman's name, Margaret, and under them was the name of their child, Thomas. *Odd,* Charlie thought. Based on Margaret's birthdate and the child's, Margaret would have been thirty-eight when she had him. Just as she was about to show Jared, a man arrived at the desk with Ethel.

Ethel introduced Jared and Charlie to Lowell and informed them they would be in good hands. With a nod, Charlie gave Lowell a quick once over. Shorter than Jared, but not short in a man's world. Definitely not in shape. He reminded Charlie of Buford T. Justice from *Smokey and the Bandit*, down to the creepy little mustache crawling across his lip. Lowell extended his hand and gave each of them a firm yet damp handshake. Charlie hoped her grimace was not easily discernible. Sliding her hand in her pocket to discreetly wipe off the moisture, she shared why they were there to meet with him. "We went to visit one of Jared's friends, whose family is over in Piney Flats."

Lowell nodded. "Yep, know it well."

"Great," Charlie continued. "Well, we were taken to an old abandoned farmhouse and allowed to go on a treasure hunt of sorts. I found some things and brought them back home with me. We were going through them this morning and wondered if maybe someone here could help us with what they would have been used for and maybe a time frame."

Beaming, Lowell folded his hands together and began to rub them. "I would love to! Here, let's go back to my desk and have a looksee." He guided them down a hallway and past more historical displays. Charlie poked Jared as they walked and mouthed that she wanted to be sure to look at all the stuff before they left. Jared nodded, and the trio entered the coolest little office Charlie had seen in a long time. Floor-to-ceiling cherry shelves on the far side sat behind a large secretary desk. A burgundy and brass-studded chair sat prominently between the two. Taking his place in said chair, Lowell guided Charlie and Jared to take a seat in a pair of smaller, matching chairs. Setting the pouch on the desk, Charlie looked around to get an idea of what else Lowell had going on. Artifacts lined the shelves, along with hundreds of encyclopedias and historical books. Clearing his throat, Lowell set his gaze on the pouch. Jared nudged Charlie out of her daze, and she quickly reached forward to untie the pouch.

"Sorry. I was just admiring your office. These three items are what we were wondering about," she said, setting the items in a line before Lowell. As Lowell picked up the buttons, Charlie stated how they had originally thought they were from a coat, but because of the shape and size, thought maybe they served another purpose. Placing the buttons in front of him on his blotter, Lowell slid open a drawer and pulled out a magnifying glass. He lifted one of the buttons up to view it beneath the glass.

"Why, yes. I see what you mean. Definitely not a button that would be used on any functioning overcoat, but perhaps a handsome waistcoat. To be boot buttons, they would have to be manufactured in the 1800s, as side-button boots weren't a thing until later in that century." Flipping over the button, Lowell homed in on the underside. "Ok, here we have a clue. See this?" he said, sliding the magnifying glass and button over to Charlie. "Look at the shape and construction of the button for me." Charlie looked and saw a curved piece of metal rising from the center. "That's a shank," Lowell explained. "Shanks like that with a hole drilled in the center make this a piece from the 1700s. The other clue is the material. This button is definitely brass. Caked up for sure, but once she's polished up, she's going to be a beauty. My guess is this is a waistcoat button from the mid-1700s."

"Thank you!" Charlie said, handing the glass and button to Jared to take a look.

"Now, what's this?" Lowell said, plucking the brooch up and holding it eye level. "This is a fine piece also. Let's see what we've got." Taking the magnifying glass back, he emitted a few uh huhs and mm hmms and fine fine before he set the items down and stood to face his bookshelf. He maneuvered his head back and forth and up and down in an obvious search for something in particular. With a flourished, "Aha!" Lowell swiped a book down and sat back down with it. "Let's take a look, why don't we? I've an idea about this piece." Running his finger through the index pages, he eventually flipped open to a page that displayed a brooch similar in shape, although way more ordinary than the piece Charlie had brought.

He turned the book around to face Jared and Charlie. "This," he said, "is what is called a witch's heart. It originated in Scotland in the seventeenth century, and this picture shows one of the earliest designs when it was known as a Luckenbooth, named after the booths in the jewelry quarter in Edinburgh. These pieces were originally designed as talismans to protect loved ones. Over time, Luckenbooth migrated to the name witch's heart. You can see the bottom of the heart turns to the right, so when it's worn, it points to the human heart. Eventually, they were worn for their 'magical' properties. Think warding off evil spirits or protecting a loved one. They were often pinned to baby blankets for protection. As we headed into the eighteenth century, they became more of a symbol of love and less of a talisman. What you have here is a phenomenal piece, definitely from the same era as the buttons. This piece, however, is sterling silver, and this blue center is made of blue glass. The flower set in the blue glass is made of what was called paste diamonds. Think of it as the first cubic zirconias. This piece would have more than likely been a replica of an original, more expensive piece and created for everyday wear so as to not lose the one of true value. Where was it again that you found this?"

Charlie explained that it was pinned to a doll she had found in the attic of Elias Cobb's old house over in Piney Flats. With that news, Lowell quickly set the piece down and said, "Well then, I see," with an evident change in his demeanor. Confused, Charlie asked if something was wrong. "No, no, dear, nothing wrong. I just forgot I have a meeting soon with a local professor and noticed the time. I'm sorry to have to rush you out. I hope I answered your questions to your liking?"

Charlie said, "Of course," but before she could continue, Lowell had slid the pieces back into the pouch and stood up, stating, "Then why don't you follow me back to the front." Lowell turned as Charlie looked over at Jared, who was giving her a *what the fuck* look. Shaking her head, she mouthed "weird," and the pair followed Lowell back to the lobby.

Lowell said his goodbyes and handed off the pouch to Charlie, then exited toward another long hallway. Ethel said, "Hope you were able to get some answers." Charlie nodded and asked if they could meander around and look at the artifacts and other items on display. "Of course, dear," Ethel replied. "Let me know if I can help with any questions you may have."

Taking Jared by the hand, Charlie led him over to the tapestry she had seen earlier on the wall. "Look! Elias Cobb," she stated, pointing to his spot on the family tree. "Sure is," Jared said. "I'm sure you did the math on that too, huh?" he finished with a nod toward the piece.

"Yep. I may be wrong, but didn't women back then tend to have their children young? She was like forty, and even by today's standards, that's pushing the envelope."

Jared concurred and said, "Maybe Benji can be of some help, but based on his lack of knowledge yesterday, we may have to do our own detective work. Why don't we see what else they got here?"

As the pair made their way around the open foyer, Charlie asked if Jared thought Lowell's behavior was at all odd. "I mean, I mentioned Elias, and he went from Mr. Historian to secret agent almost instantly."

"Yeah, I did notice. Maybe Elias wasn't well liked around here. Let's add it to our detective list." He winked.

Not much else piqued their interest. They did find some cool older photos with the types of coats Lowell said the buttons had come from, but nothing to tie them to any one person.

"Let's jet then," Jared said "The falls are awaiting. You're going to love it! I promise. But let me stop at the payphone outside and see if Benji is up and maybe wants to join us for lunch later."

Charlie had been to several falls before, from Letchworth to Niagara, but there was something about these falls that she loved. They resembled the Watkins Glen Falls but on a much smaller scale. Exploring a bit, the weather allowed for them to take a quick dip. After about an hour of swimming, they sat on some rocks to dry off. Charlie's stomach reminded her of swimming's effect on her appetite. "Let's go get you some grub," Jared said, looking at his watch. "Benji should be there soon, also."

Charlie and Jared walked in to find Benji propped up by a window three booths back. As they took their seats, Benji let them know he took the liberty of ordering a round of beers but held off on the food, even though he was starving.

"Well, I know you already know what you want," Jared teased Benji. "You've never been very adventurous when it comes to your food choices."

"Au contraire, mon buddy. I've expanded my horizons. I believe you will be quite surprised," Benji said with a chuckle.

The trio examined the menus as the waitress set a beer glass and a pitcher on the table.

"What can I get ya?" she asked.

"I'll have the mushroom Swiss burger, fries, and an order of mozzarella sticks," Charlie said.

"Double bacon cheddar for me," Jared replied.

"Chili mac crunch burger for this guy," Benji said.

"Whoa! You weren't kidding!" Jared said "Charlie, this guy always got the grown-up version of a kids' burger. Plain and dried out. Color me surprised," he finished, giving the table a slap.

"Fries all the way around?" the waitress asked.

They all confirmed, and she turned to get the order in.

"So, how you guys doing today?" Benji asked.

"We went to the historical society. Wanted to get those items Charlie snagged looked at," Jared said.

"Yeah. We had a bit of a kooky guy helping us. Lowell. He knows his stuff for sure. But he got really weirded out when we mentioned Elias. Any reason why?" Charlie asked.

"Gosh, not really. I mean, like I told you, he had a reputation for being kind of a dick. If you want, I can dig around some next time I pay a prison visit to my dad. See if he knows anything," Benji said.

"Really? That would be super cool if you could," she said.

"Oh, Charlie, ask him about Margaret and the baby, too," Jared prodded.

"Oh, right! We saw this family tree type thing, and it showed that Elias and Margaret had a son. But based on the dates, we were a little confused. Do you know if she had a baby late in her thirties? We were thinking that was kind of late in age back then," Charlie said.

"Hunh," Benji said. "I know for sure there was a kid. Thomas. I can add it to the *ask my dad* pile for you. If you need a quicker answer, there's gotta be documents around somewhere."

Charlie nodded as the smell of burgers and fries wafted her direction. The trio continued their small talk, and after finishing up their lunch, stood to say their goodbyes.

"Jared, man, a pleasure as always. Don't stay away so long this time," Benji said, going in for a hug.

"I won't, I promise. And heck, you gotta come for a visit sometime," Jared replied.

"I think I'll keep my toes where it's a bit warmer, if you don't mind," Benji teased. "Hey, Charlie! Pleasure meeting you. Keep this guy on the straight and narrow, please. Good luck with all the new adventures, too," he said.

Charlie gave a quick hug and promised she would.

CHAPTER ELEVEN
FOOD AND FOND FAREWELLS

RETURNING TO THE HOUSE, the pair walked into yet another Tilde dinner that did not disappoint. The delectable smell of meatloaf wafted through the air.

Charlie excused herself for a shower since she and Jared had taken on another couple falls after lunch and she was smelling pretty ripe.

Jared passed Charlie on the stairs when she finished, gave her a kiss, and said, "Tag, you're it."

Charlie joined Tilde and Arthur, filling them in on Lowell and all that came with that visit.

They enjoyed the last meal of the visit, and as the sun dipped below the horizon, it cast a warm glow across the living room. Tilde announced she had one more surprise for them. "G'head now and have a seat out in the living room with Arthur. I'll be quick, I promise," she said, shooing them out of the kitchen.

Within minutes, the scent of freshly baked cookies filled the air, followed by Tilde carrying a tray of milk their way. "Here ya go. Take these and I'll be right back with some ooey, gooey goodness to dunk with," she said with a huge, toothy smile.

The group enjoyed their dessert and conversation, then Jared announced that he and Charlie were going to head up for the night. "We need to leave early if we want to stay on track."

"Of course, honey," Tilde said, giving them each a kiss and hug. "Sleep well. We'll see you off in the morning."

"Oh, and Aunt Tilde…no breakfast for us, ok?" Jared said. Tilde nodded as the pair made their way up to bed.

Morning came way too fast for their liking. Charlie and Jared groaned as they gathered their stuff and made their way down the stairs. Not surprising, Tilde greeted them with coffees for the road.

"Drive safe, honey," Tilde said, dishing out hugs and kisses.

Arthur reached out his hand for the obligatory goodbye handshake, and the pair waved as the kids drove Juicy toward Main Street. If you listened closely, a slight sniffle could be heard from Tilde's porch.

CHAPTER TWELVE
HOME AGAIN~ HOME AGAIN

PULLING UP TO CHARLIE'S neighborhood, the street lights led the way. As they drove toward their destination, Charlie filled Jared in on the neighborhood gossip as she remembered it from her last visit. She was about to relive the ongoing battle with the Miller's RV, but a hitch caught in her throat as she saw the for-sale sign ominously placed front and center of her home. This was more than a for-sale sign; it told a tale—the tale of her mother's death and her father's heartbreak. The tale of being forced to head into the next chapter of his life. She knew he was selling the home. She knew he would be moving back to Ohio. She knew her mom would not be coming back. All these things she *knew*. That didn't mean any of it hurt any less. This was her childhood home, her *only* home, and although it would never be the home it once was, it did hold all her memories. For this reason, she ached. Jared reached out his hand to hers and gave it a squeeze.

"Go ahead and pull up into the driveway," Charlie instructed. "Stop at the second bay door next to the Jeep. Dad told me he's using the garage to store the boxes he's packed up until I get a chance to decide what we will be keeping and letting go of." The last two words were said with a heavy sigh and lingered in the air.

Jared nodded and pulled up to the right of her dad's Jeep. One final squeeze of her hand and he let go. Charlie opened her door and stepped out just as her dad exited through the back door.

"Hey there, Charlie bear!" he said, walking toward her with open arms. Giving his daughter a big bear hug, he stepped back and extended his hand to Jared, who had made his way around the back of Juicy. "Hey, Jared. Glad you both made it back ok. How was the drive?"

"Long, but good, sir," Jared said.

"Hey, Dad. Before I forget, I really would like you to give Juicy a once over while we're here. She's being temperamental."

Jared nodded. "A bit more than temperamental," he added.

"Of course we can," Dale said. "Anything I can help you guys carry in?" Following Jared, Dale loaded up, and the pair began their journey toward the house. "It's amazing how light you guys can travel."

"Actually, what you have are Charlie's newly acquired tchotchkes. Our clothes are all in the two bags here," Jared said, patting the straps of the duffels.

"Well, then. Even more impressive," Dale said with a chuckle.

They entered the sunroom, and Dale asked if they wanted to go up and get settled first. Heading to the front staircase, Charlie said, "Nope. Let's set everything down here. If I go anywhere near a bed, I'm done for the night." Jared agreed but urged Charlie to take the box with her to the kitchen to share with her dad.

"Anyone have an appetite?" Dale asked. "I've packed most of my kitchen stuff up, but thanks to Irene, I have plenty of food to reheat."

Ignoring the reference to a new female, Charlie replied, "I could eat. Whatcha got?" She poked her head into the fridge.

"There should be some stew, pot pie, lasagna and—" But before Dale could finish, Charlie grabbed the large platter and said, "You had me at lasagna," and laughed as Jared came into the kitchen.

"Did I hear lasagna?" he exclaimed.

"Sure did!" Charlie chirped as she slid the blue and white Corelle dish into the microwave.

Turning back toward the fridge, she reached in and grabbed two Cokes and set them on the island. "You going to join us, Dad?"

Shaking his head, Dale explained he had already eaten, but if they wanted to exchange the Cokes for beer, he would indulge with them. Not needing a second prod, Charlie returned the Cokes to the fridge and pulled out three Genny Cream Ales.

Charlie handed Jared one for himself and one for her dad. Jared joined Dale at the table.

Charlie grabbed paper plates and plasticware from the drawer and dropped them off as the ding of the microwave announced its job was complete. Charlie slipped two dish towels around her hands, reached in, and carried the piping hot lasagna over. "Did you keep out any spatulas or are we making due with these?" she asked, holding up two forks.

"I kept a few things over in the drawer to the right of the stove," Dale said. "I'll grab it for you." Handing Charlie the spatula, Dale continued. "We have a lot of catching up to do. How's about we keep the conversation light tonight, and you and I can delve into the house stuff tomorrow at some point?"

Charlie nodded as she served up a plate to Jared and then one to herself. As they ate, Dale filled them in on the neighborhood goings on, and Jared filled Dale in on pieces of their trip that weren't already discussed in phone calls.

Stomach full, Charlie tossed the plates and other items in the trash and set the lasagna pan to soak. She grabbed another beer for each of them and joined Jared and her dad in the living room.

"Whatcha got in the box?" Dale asked.

Charlie told him about the day trip to the house on Benji's property and the stint in the attic. Reaching to slide the box toward her, she said, "And the result is what's in the box.

There were a lot of cool things up there, but these spoke to me, I guess you could say." She repeated her show-and-tell she had performed for Tilde, ending with the pouch of trinkets. "Originally, Jared and I were confused as to what this button was for, and we also wanted to get a handle on the brooch's age. We went to the historical society in Jonesborough to see if anyone could help us. A really kooky man, Lowell, helped narrow down the button's use. We were thinking they came from an overcoat or boots, but he thinks it was for a waistcoat. The brooch has an interesting background also," she stated, giving Jared the *I'm not ready to tell him everything yet* look. Jared winked back in acknowledgement, and Charlie moved on to the books. "These seem like they could be cool. I'm hoping to get to scope these out while I'm here," she said.

"These are neat," Dale said, pointing to the button and brooch. "But that doll. She's creepy," he finished with a nervous chuckle. "If you need help with any research, you know your grandpa would jump at the chance." A not-so-subtle yawn escaped Dale's lips.

"Sorry, haven't been sleeping well, add a beer or two, and voila! How about we get you set up for the night?" Dale said. Dale guided them to the guest bedroom upstairs at the end of the hall. "Here's where you'll be, Jared. Charlie's room is back down the hall. I'll let you complete the tour, Charlie. Time for me to hit the hay," he finished with a hug.

Jared set his duffel at the foot of the bed and followed Charlie back down the hall to her room.

"Cool overlook," Jared said, gesturing to the oculus.

"Yeah, it's my favorite thing about the house. I haven't seen one anywhere else," Charlie said with a sigh. Reaching her door, Jared laughed out loud at the signs—"Beware," "No Boys Allowed," and a few small posters of Duran Duran and Culture Club. Charlie elbowed him in the ribs as she opened the door. "Here she is! The place that spawned the girl you know today."

Dropping the duffel to the floor, Jared said, "Impressive. Girly, but impressive. This carpet is killer!"

"Squish your toes," Charlie dared. The two stood facing each other, simultaneously squeezing their toes in and out of the carpet's lush fibers.

"It's like a massage for your feet," Jared said.

"Here's where I found my mom's journals," Charlie said, walking over to the window seat. Sliding her stuff to the side, she lifted the lid and pointed down into the well. "Seems like a lifetime ago," she said wistfully.

"Sure does," Jared concurred.

Charlie let the lid fall into place, and Jared came in for a hug. Standing for a moment to let the power of the hug sink in, Charlie took a deep breath and continued with the tour. "Let me show you the bathroom. We can check out the attic and the rest of the house tomorrow," she said.

While Jared took the first shot at the shower, Charlie sorted through her duffel to separate out the laundry for the morning. With that organized, she took the box of goodies over to the window seat. Placing the doll against a pillow, she set the trinkets and journals on her nightstand. A light knock on the doorframe let her know that Jared had finished up. Following him back down the hallway, Charlie couldn't help but notice how amazing he smelled and how his hair, when wet, fell perfectly over his left eye. It definitely made her curse her dad for being old school on the sleeping arrangements; she could have gone for a little one on one time for sure. Shaking the thought out of her head, she let Jared know if he wanted to sort out his duffel, she was planning on laundry in the morning. *There*, she thought. *Laundry—the perfect mood killer*. She chuckled to herself as Jared cocked his head to the side as if he was attempting to read her mind. Before he could tap into it, she leaned in and gave him a kiss goodnight. A soft moan escaped his lips.

"And now you know," Charlie taunted with a wink.

Her shower completed, Charlie snuggled up in her bed and felt a sense of peace that she hadn't felt in a while. With everything that happened with Astrid and then the traveling, she had never had a chance to settle. Leaning her head back against the wall, she inhaled and took in the smells that came with home. She was going to miss this place. She would no longer have it to come back to. A place to feel cozy and calm in. Sure, her dad would have a place in Ohio, but it wouldn't be the same. Her eyes welled up with tears; she bit her lip and allowed the pain to overtake the heartache. A few more deep breaths and she realized that she wasn't as tired as she had thought she was. Flicking on her nightstand light, she reached over and grabbed one of the books from the stack.

Outside of her initial perusal with Tilde, she had not had a chance to assess them as a whole. The first was smaller, and had grown aged and crackled through the years. Realizing she should have probably cleaned it off before setting it onto her bed, she improvised by taking the case off one of her extra pillows. Carefully wiping the dust off the cover, she focused her attention back on the book. Unfortunately, upon lifting the cover, the first few pages stuck together. In fear of damaging them further, Charlie opted to skip ahead. The handwriting was unmistakably feminine. She flipped through further to see if she could gather names or places to help ascertain who this particular book had belonged to.

With nothing standing out, Charlie figured the name might be on the pages that were stuck together, which would make sense since it was a journal. Setting it back on the nightstand, she moved onto the next in the stack. This one was in much better shape overall, due in part to the leather strap-style binding that housed it. Fingering the strap she noticed it had seen better days as it was dry and cracked. Following it around to a reddish brown "button" with the initials E.C. engraved on it, she unwound the cord and repeated the dusting process. Charlie flipped open the cover and exposed the pages within. Immediately, she could see this was not a journal but a business ledger of sorts. The pages documented business ideas, transactional notes, and cash flow. She found written accounts of Elias' dealings with locals in Jonesborough and Piney Flats to as far out as Roanoke, Virginia, and Paducah, Kentucky. Skimming over the text and endless numbers, the sleepy bug hit Charlie hard. Deciding to release her curiosity for the night, she gave in to the desire to sleep. She placed the ledger to the side with the first book, wiped her fingers on the pillow case, and tossed it to the floor. Clicking her light off, she slid under her layers of blankets and fell fast asleep.

Marcus watched intently as Charlie perused the stack of books she had found. Being her *guardian angel* was an assignment he had taken on with both enthusiasm and trepidation. Charlie would be his first charge on his own. This excited him, but with the excitement came worry. The knowledge that Charlie's life was not going to be an easy one sat heavy. Her foreseen gifts would bring her joy, yes. But they would also bring her immense sorrow and pain. She would be destined to achieve greatness and be a guiding force for hundreds to come, but this would come at a price. This knowledge weighed on his heart.

Charlie, being human, had the power of free thinking and choice, which made her path a hard one to predict. The best he could do was keep an eye on her and guide her within his limits and protect her from those in the Dark Realm seeking to claim her as their own. Before closing his window on her world for the night, Marcus recited a small blessing of protection, for she was about to open herself to a force she was completely unprepared for.

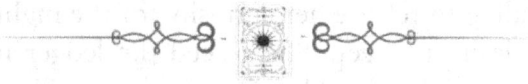

Standing alone in the dark, Charlie shivered. Squinting to see through the din she could faintly make out a light in the distance. Thinking she should check the light out, she realized she was already in motion, yet not actually moving. Floating...she was floating. As the distant light grew closer and closer, so did the shape of a cottage. Odd, she thought; the cottage seemed to be secluded with no trees or wildlife, or external light to illuminate its facade. Unsure as to what was happening, Charlie could only describe what she was experiencing as being summoned. The house was summoning her.

She drew closer and closer to the cottage, and a sound began to grow both in and around her. Muffled at first, it grew louder and more ominous with her approach. She knew this sound intimately. It was her own heart-beat. Filling her ears, it crescendoed to a thunderous and deafening resonance, then a piercing "HELP ME" echoed, followed by a flash of intense light...then...complete darkness.

Charlie bolted upright in bed. Her heart racing, she could feel beads of sweat trailing down her temple. Taking a deep breath, she peered around her room. Realization hit her with a wave of relief. It was just a dream. Swinging her covers off, she placed her feet flat on the ground and scrunched her toes into the carpet beneath them. Satisfied she was indeed awake, Charlie glanced out her windows and saw it was still o'dark thirty. The moon shone down on the juniper trees just outside, casting dancing shadows on her window seat. Standing up, she decided to go relieve herself, rinse the sweat off her face, and grab a glass of water. She set foot out into the hallway and chuckled as the sounds of dueling snores made their way along the corridor, and carefully descended the steps so as to not wake anyone. She avoided the squeaky step and shuffled to the kitchen, cursing herself for not putting on socks or slippers as her feet turned to ice with every step.

Futilely searching for a glass, Charlie gave up, figuring her dad must have packed them. She opened the fridge and pulled out a single serve orange juice box. "Beggars can't be choosers," she whispered to herself. Charlie cracked open the paper spout and took a swig and meandered her way back up the stairs and into bed.

"Wake up, sleepy head," echoed in Charlie's head. Thinking it was a dream, she moaned and rolled to her other side. No sooner did she do so, she felt kisses fall upon her cheek, forehead, and finally her neck. "Wakey, wakey, eggs and bakey," Jared taunted with a final kiss on her lips.

Charlie rolled onto her back and slowly opened her eyes, looking up to see Jared's face surrounded by a mess of his luscious locks and a golden halo of morning sunlight. A quiver ran down to her toes. It was hard to believe that a year ago she had never really had a guy in her life who was more than a mere friend, and now she was being woken up by this gorgeous specimen of a man. Charlie knew where her attraction lay with regards to Jared, but she was still amazed that *he* found *her* interesting. While he had made it clear early on in their relationship that he had a few sexual encounters, he had also made it clear he was picky about who he chose to be in a relationship with and how he felt toward her. She just found it hard to see in herself what he saw. She knew she had come a long way since the gangly teen years, braces and all, but she still struggled a bit with her confidence. Especially when it came to men.

"Earth to Charlie, come in, Charlie," Jared teased, waving his hand in front of her face.

"Oh sorry, babe. Good morning. Guess I got lost in thought. Restless night's sleep. How about you?"

"Slept like a log," Jared replied.

"A log being sawed in half," Charlie said, giving a snort. "I woke up to get water, and between you and my dad...good lord!"

"Ok, ok, enough. Up and at 'em, girlie," Jared said, pulling the covers from Charlie's body.

With a whimper worthy of any pouty five-year-old, Charlie got up and threw on her fuzzy robe and slippers. The pair walked down to the kitchen. Ecstatic that her dad had kept the coffee maker out for their visit, she let out a mini *whoo hoo*. Padding her way over to the pantry to grab some coffee and filters, Charlie watched as Jared took a seat at the table. She reached up and grabbed the supplies from the shelf as he said, "I can see why you're going to miss this place. Even with half the stuff gone, it still feels like a home. While Aunt Tilde did her best, I always felt like I was visiting her house. It never felt quite like *home*. Silly, I know. I feel guilty every time I think about it. She and Uncle Arthur did so much for me and my sisters, but I think not having both my parents changed things. Your mom and dad really put a lot of energy into this place to make it a home," he finished, placing his head in his hands and pushing his hair back from his face.

Spinning around to flick the brew button, Charlie turned back to Jared and said, "I don't think it's silly at all. You had a home with your mom. At least, your heart believes that. Moving in with Tilde, no matter how homey it is, doesn't replace the feeling of *home* that your mom provided you." Spinning back around to search for coffee mugs, she continued. "This is home because it's where my mom and dad loved me together. It's where I felt safe, content, and happy. I know my dad has found a new house, and he will fill it with a lot of what was in this place, but without Mom and the rest of it, it will never be *home*." Snatching two coffee mugs, Charlie finished and turned to see Dale walking through the archway.

He looked at her with sadness, and Charlie quickly jumped to reword her sentiment, but Dale jumped in ahead of her and assured her that she wasn't wrong. "This will always be your home; I know that, Charlie. Just like Mom and Dad's will always be my home. But I'll try hard to make it a place where you feel loved and safe and happy. I promise," he finished quietly, choking back tears.

Charlie nodded in acknowledgement.

"Charlie and I were about to have some coffee. You want any?" Jared asked Dale.

"I think I'm going to stick with orange juice this morning. Thank you though," Dale said.

Charlie said, "About that...I had a late-night snack attack and couldn't find a water glass, so I may have snagged your last orange juice."

"Oh!" Dale exclaimed. "Well, you know what, it's probably for the best, because I'm bare bones here. How's about we cancel the beverages and go find ourselves a proper breakfast? Thinking Macedon Hills? Bit of a drive, but well worth it. Whatcha think?"

"I defer to Charlie," Jared said with eyes as big as saucers.

"Let's go," she said. "Jared may be deferring to me, but I can see the look in his eyes," she finished with a chuckle. "We'll get dressed and meet you back down here in, say, ten minutes?"

Dale concurred, and the team made a beeline up the stairs.

CHAPTER THIRTEEN
THE BREAKFAST CLUB

"SO, THIS IS BRIGHTON? Correct?" Jared asked as they drove out of the neighborhood in the Jeep.

"Yep. It's a suburb of Rochester, as is the town we're headed to. We're a bit closer to the city itself here, but Macedon is pure country. You'll see what I mean the closer we get."

Dale's description of Macedon couldn't have been more accurate. Although they traveled on a main road, there was expansive farmland in the distance. They had left behind most of the commercial rigamarole about ten minutes prior, and the only sign of commercialism was local small businesses dotted about, the restaurant being one of them. They pulled into the parking lot and made their way inside. They were greeted by the waitress/hostess and seated promptly. Deciding on coffee and orange juice for the table, they buried their faces in the plastic-covered menus.

"What do you recommend?" Jared asked.

He heard "pancakes" from Charlie and "Western omelet" from Dale and laughed.

"Honestly, you can't go wrong with anything here," Dale said. "But whatever you do decide on, you have to get the home fries as a side."

The waitress returned with the drinks and took their orders. Dale got the Western omelet, Charlie ordered pancakes with whipped cream and chocolate chips, and Jared opted for the big breakfast. It was the best of all worlds—scrambled eggs, sausage, bacon, pancakes, and home fries with toast or a biscuit. He was steered toward the biscuit and took the advice. They added that she might as well keep the coffee flowing, too.

Dale took a sip of his orange juice and asked what the plans were for the day. Charlie looked at Jared and said, "Well, I was hoping to get Jared over to finally meet Ramona and play some catch-up for a bit. Then we can shoot back to the house and help you with packing and sorting if that's ok?"

"Sounds like a plan," Dale said. "Oh, and Jared, you're in for quite a treat with Ramona," he continued with a chuckle and a wink.

"So I've heard," Jared replied. "I've caught glimpses of her personality via the many calls she and Charlie have had."

"I'm going to have to spend some one-on-one time with her while I'm here. I figured you two could manage to find something to get into during that time?"

"I'm sure we can work something out," Dale said, nodding toward Jared. "So, you haven't had a chance to look at the mail you received from Cornell. But it looks like all your classes are set, and I sent the deposit and first month's rent over to your new landlord. Can you please check and make sure your roommates have done the same when you get a chance? I would hate for you to have any hiccups when it comes time to move in."

"Sure thing, Dad. Thank you for taking care of that. I'll give Heather and Scarlett a ring later today and double check their side of things. So, you saw my new schedule for this year so far, huh? You ok with my decision to switch things up a bit?" Charlie asked sheepishly.

"Well, you know me. I think you need to stay on track. However, I do understand how what happened with your mom has raised some questions and a desire to learn more about the world beyond ours. As long as you can circle back around, I'll be fine. You have too much of me in you to go fully off course," Dale said with a warm smile.

"Thanks, Dad. I really need to do this, and it helps that you're on board," Charlie replied.

The trio reviewed what Dale had accomplished so far, and what to expect from their gathering later in the day. They wrapped that up since breakfast had made its way to their table.

"So, you're moving to Ohio, correct?" Jared asked Dale.

"Yes, I am. Not too far from my parents in Chagrin Falls. The house is much more fitting for a bachelor with a college student than what I have now. Bausch and Lombe has agreed to a traveling research slash sales position, which means I'll be out and about and even back here to headquarters from time to time. Definitely will be an adjustment. But no more than the adjustments I've had to make since Birdie passed," he finished with a sigh.

Jared nodded as Charlie reached across the table to pat her dad's hand. "I don't think I've told you," Charlie said, "Jared lost his mom, too. He and his sisters were raised by relatives—the folks we stayed with when we were in Jonesborough raised Jared."

"Ah, yes! You mentioned them last night during show-and-tell. Please, tell me more about your visit," Dale encouraged.

Charlie and Jared batted tales back and forth while the group finished up their breakfasts. With the check paid, they hopped back in the Jeep and headed back to Brighton.

As promised, Charlie quickly called Heather and Scarlett to confirm the rental details and coordinate arrival dates and the move in party. Hanging up, she dialed Ramona.

"Lorenzano residence," Ramona chimed.

"Hey, bestie," Charlie said. "You ready for us to head over?"

"The fact that you aren't here already hurts my feelings, Charlie," Ramona teased. "Get your asses over here now! I need to finally meet this dream-boat." They hung up, and Charlie and Jared headed out the door, promising to not be too long.

CHAPTER FOURTEEN
HER VERY OWN JAKE RYAN

JARED AND CHARLIE DROVE Juicy over to Ramona's house. Charlie reminded Jared of a few need-to-know points. "Ramona will accost you. She's a hugger and a flirt. If her mom is there, you're in for a treat. Her brothers will, more than likely, be out trolling the neighborhoods on their bikes, so we won't have to deal with them. The first topic of conversation will most definitely be us. But believe you me, Ramona will swing it over to her so fast you'll swear you got whiplash."

"Thanks for the heads up," Jared said. "I think I'll let you two guide the conversation and I'll just sit back and look pretty. Ok?" He gave his signature smirk that melted Charlie's heart every time.

Pulling onto Ramona's street, Charlie gave him a brief history that was not unlike his and Benji's. It included tales of games of tag, jump roping contests, dodgeball, and other activities.

"That house right there is Ramona's," Charlie said, pointing ahead at a classic colonial brick home. "Park on the street," she instructed. "It looks like Mr. L isn't home yet. and we definitely do not want to block him from his own driveway," she said with a chuckle.

Jared slid in parallel to the front of the house, and the two made their way up the slate-stone path to the front door.

Before Charlie could knock, it swung open, and Ramona immediately wrapped herself around her friend, almost knocking her and Jared to the ground. With an *oomph* and a *Good grief, Ramona,* Charlie regained her footing and pried Ramona off. Charlie turned to introduce Jared, but Ramona was already on it.

"Soooooo, this must be your Jake Ryan!?" she sang. "I'm Ramona, the bestie! Glad to finally meet you, Jared," she finished with a complete up and down perusal. "Sorry for the near miss there."

"Uh, yeah. Wow! That's cool. Who's Jake Ryan?" Jared asked.

Ramona stood aside and ushered the pair into the house, explaining to Jared that Jake Ryan was Charlie's first celebrity crush. "Molly Ringwald's hunk in *Sixteen Candles*. The handsome guy who was seemingly just out of her reach," she finished with a wink.

"Don't mind her," Charlie said to Jared with a slight elbow to Ramona's side. "She sometimes speaks before she thinks."

"Sometimes?" Ramona cackled. "I'd say almost, most definitely, one hundred percent." Laughing, she guided them to the family room. "Can I get you anything? Coke, water, tea, something stronger?"

"Cokes are fine," Charlie said. Before sitting down next to Jared on the couch, she asked, "Need help with that?"

"Nope. Got it. You two just sit there and stay cute. I'll be back in a jiffy."

"Wow," Jared said. "You tried to prepare me…but wow!"

"Yeah, she's special. She'll calm down once the novelty wears off. I promise," Charlie replied.

"And what's with the plastic?" Jared asked, giving a quick wiggle on the couch, creating a plastic concerto.

Charlie laughed hard at the sound and Jared's face when he made it. "Those are slip covers. They're on everything that Mrs. Lorenzano wants to protect. I don't get it either."

"It's a good thing the air conditioning is on, otherwise you may have had to peel me off the couch when we left," he said.

Charlie laughed again at that thought as Ramona entered the room and asked, "What's so funny?"

"Your mom's proclivity for plastic," Charlie said with a chuckle.

"Oh, yeah," Ramona said, rolling her eyes. "It's like she doesn't trust anyone to not mess up her prized possessions. If I never see plastic anything when I move out, it won't be soon enough," Ramona said, handing Charlie and Jared their Cokes.

"So! Tell me all about yourself, Jared! I want to know everything," Ramona said.

"Everything?" Jared asked, looking toward Charlie as if for guidance.

"Yep. Start from the beginning," Ramona said firmly.

Jared started with the basics—name, rank, and serial number—then moved on to more generic topics. Ramona looked back at Charlie to give her gestures of approval. The last -hubba hubba- eyebrow raise made Charlie choke on her drink.

"You ok, Charlie?" Jared asked, oblivious to what had been going on.

"Yeah, went down the wrong tube, I guess," Charlie explained, giving Ramona the stink eye.

The group continued their conversation, which ran the gamut between Charlie's new school path to Ramona's indecisive life path, and finally ended up circling back around to Ramona's still steady relationship with Eric. "I was thinking we could double date while you're here! You know, hang as a group before you head back to college and forget I exist again?" Ramona teased.

"As if you would ever let me forget about you, Ramona the brat," Charlie chastised. "But yeah, let's do it. We have stuff with Dad tonight, and I was hoping you and I could have some one-on-one time tomorrow. Wanna shoot for tomorrow night?" Charlie finished, looking at Jared for approval.

"Ok. I'll see what works for Eric, and you and I can settle it up tomorrow when we hang. What are *you* doing tomorrow while we have girl time?" Ramona asked Jared.

"Dale and I are going to hang out. Not sure what the plans are officially," Jared answered.

"Where's your mom?" Charlie asked Ramona. "I figured she'd be here since I see her car."

"Oh, she's over at the Schwartz's house. She plays spades with a few of the moms on the street every now and then. Dad's still at work, and the knuckleheads are out terrorizing someone else for a change. You guys in any kind of a rush?"

"Nope, we're all yours until about three or so," Charlie said.

"Wanna finish these up and walk over to the second show theater to see a matinee? I've been wanting to see *Pet Sematary*, and Eric refused to see it with me when it came out, but I'm too scared to see it alone."

Charlie looked to Jared for his vote, and with the nod, Ramona called the movie line to confirm the time. The group began their walk through the neighborhood.

"Charlie and I use this short-cut all the time," Ramona said. "It's a little tricky when you get closer to the shopping plaza, but this dirt path takes you directly there." She ducked under a low tree limb. "What's your favorite type of movie, Jared?"

"I'm kind of all over the place, but I would say comedies and psychological thrillers interest me the most," Jared answered.

"Well, Charlie and I love our John Hughes, but horror is our thang. Just wish we weren't so chicken shit," Ramona said, laughing.

"I figured from her collection of VHS tapes that was going to be the answer," Jared joked.

"And here we are!" Ramona erupted. "We just have to squeeze through this fence down here and head around the corner."

They secured their tickets, entered the old theater, and made a right directly to the concession stand. One jumbo buttered popcorn and three Cokes later, they settled into their seats. Ramona sat to Charlie's right, with Jared to Charlie's left.

"Looks like we may be the only ones taking advantage of the early showing," Jared said.

Leaning in toward Charlie, Ramona gave her soft whisper of approval just as the lights dimmed and the animated hot dog and popcorn began their dance on the screen.

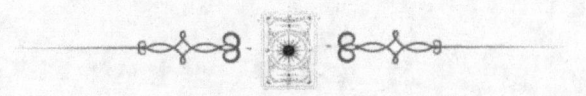

The credits rolled, and Charlie, Jared, and Ramona stood up, stretched in unison, and left the theater.

"Well, that was terrifying. I'll never look at a toddler or a cat the same way again," Charlie said.

"I'm not going to sleep tonight," Ramona sputtered.

Jared snickered at the pair and looked down at his watch. "Tell me why you insist on watching horror movies if they cause you such anxiety?" He looked at the girls, who performed a synchronized shrug, and continued. "Hey, Charlie, we should think about heading back if we're going to help your dad. I think we're going to need some daylight out in the garage."

Charlie acknowledged his statement as they exited the front doors of the theater into the mid-afternoon sun. "There's your daylight," Charlie said, squinting behind her raised forearm.

On the short walk back, they talked about the movie some more and the plans for the next day, confirming Ramona would reach out once she had a chance to talk to Eric.

With a hug goodbye, Ramona waved as Juicy circled around the cul-de-sac and out of her field of vision.

CHAPTER FIFTEEN
HELPING HANDS

"HEY, POPS," CHARLIE SAID as she entered the back door into the sunroom. "Your helping hands are here." When there wasn't an immediate answer, Charlie figured he might be up in the attic. "No time like the present to show you the creepiest room in the house," she said to Jared, grabbing his hand.

As they approached the door, Charlie's suspicion about her dad being in the attic was confirmed by the cursing that echoed down the stairwell.

"Hey, Dad! We're back! Coming up!" Charlie announced in an effort to not startle him.

"Definitely full-blown attic vibes up here. This is where you found that secret journal of Astrid's, right?"

"Yep. Right over there. It was tucked in a box. My guess is that she had hidden a bunch of stuff up here, or should I say, she had my mom hide a bunch of stuff up here in one of her trance takeovers."

"Hey, you two! Ready to get your hands dirty?" Dale asked.

"Sure are! Where do we start?" Charlie replied.

"I've already started over there in the corner. How's about you take a peek inside and decide if there's anything you want to keep? I'll mark them trash and donate after you go through them. Jared, if you could be our muscle and get them downstairs into separate stacks?"

"Will do, Mr. Bauman," Jared said, giving a short salute.

"Let's cut that Mr. Bauman out now; call me Dale. I insist," Dale said.

"Will do, Dale," Jared corrected.

Dale continued his front-line duties as Charlie went through each box and began to set aside items she wanted to keep. With Jared criss-crossed next to her, she made it known how hard this was to choose. "I feel like I'm condemning memories of my mom to death. I hate that we have to choose. Like this here," she started, holding up an example "This was a project she and I worked on together when I was a little kid. She was teaching me how to sew. I had gotten the basics down, but she wanted me to learn some advanced hand stitches, so she had me make this stuffed elephant."

"Ummmm. Elephant?" Jared questioned with a hint of disbelief. "If you had asked me what I thought it was, I would have said a one-armed monkey. Who ever saw an elephant that skinny or that brown?" He chuckled, grabbing it from Charlie's hand and making it dance.

"Hey! I was a kid. Imagination and shit," she said, rolling her eyes. Grabbing it back, she gave it a quick hug and placed it in the trash box with a heavy sigh.

"You'll always have your memories, Charlie. This," he said, circling his arms, "this is just stuff for the most part. It's ok to let some of it go."

They worked their way around the attic, and it was Dale who noticed the sun was starting to set through the gable vent at the end of the dormer. "Guys, you want to take ten or twenty and head to the garage while we still have some daylight?"

"Got it! I'll take these boxes down and meet you out there," Jared said.

While Dale went out back, Charlie grabbed a few Cokes from the fridge and the bag of Doritos from the pantry. She loved that her dad had taken time to get a few provisions for her visit. Carrying them out back, Jared, who had gone out the front and wound up around back with Dale, was already scoping things out in the garage. Charlie handed each a Coke, and tore open the Dorito bag and set it on one of the side shelves in the garage. "Ok, what's the plan here?" she asked.

"All of this is mostly stuff from my office, the living room, and kitchen areas. I packed and marked the essentials I'll be taking with me to Ohio, but again, I need you to help me decide what is donation worthy and what's trash. I'm assuming most of this won't interest you in the least bit, Charlie bear," Dale finished. Before Charlie could ask about her mother's studio, Dale said, "You and Jared will have free reign of Birdie's studio tomorrow if you like. I have what I need, and I know that most of that is super special to you," he said with a nod and a wink.

Charlie mouthed *thank you,* and the gang made their way through the garage with paper squares Dale had prepared, and markers and tape. The furniture was easy. With the exception of a small bookcase, a lamp, and her mom's footstool from the family room, Charlie couldn't take most of it where she was going, so the majority was labeled donate. The boxes were just as easy, as Charlie had no need for most of the kitchen appliances, plates, and other cookware. She didn't even bother with the two boxes that came from her dad's office. She knew if he wasn't taking it there was a reason.

With a total sense of accomplishment, Jared and Charlie leaned back on the workbench and finished the last of their Cokes. Jared nudged Charlie to walk out with him to watch as the sunset fell behind the horizon.

"How does pizza sound?" Dale asked. "Or Chinese? Your pick."

With a unanimous vote for pizza, they entered the house just as the phone began to ring. Charlie, who was ahead of the men, picked up the handset and could hear a ruckus on the other end. "Hey, Ramona," she said, laughing as Ramona yelled death threats at her brothers. "And don't you ever go in my room again!" Ramona finished with an exasperated huff. "Hey, Charlie. Sorry about that. The little shits went in my room and made away with my favorite giraffe stuffy. Turned him into Swiss cheese with their pellet guns!"

Charlie cringed at the image. "What's up?" she asked Ramona.

"Oh, yeah! I talked to Eric, and we're on for a double tomorrow. Leave from my house, say, five? Go grab some grub and maybe skate or go bowling?"

"Sounds like a plan! You're still coming over here in the daytime, though, right? Charlie asked.

"Sure am! I need some Charlie time without the hunk. I got lots to say about him behind his back," Ramona teased. They said their goodbyes and Charlie handed the phone off to her dad to place the pizza order.

Wanting to get cozy, as well as have a little one on one with Jared, Charlie excused themselves before heading up to her room. She shut the door behind them and said with a sigh, "Finally alone," leaning into Jared for a kiss.

"Yeah, what a day, huh?" he replied in between smooches.

Jared flopped down on the bed and made himself comfortable as Charlie dug through her dresser for her sweats. "So, your dad seems to be doing well with all of this," he said.

"Yeah, I guess. It's always hard to tell with him, as he's never been emotional. I mean, don't get me wrong, he was a wreck the first few months, but I think his *sensible shoes* personality has allowed him to approach this more analytically than I have," Charlie said as she slid out of her shirt and into a sweatshirt. "I think the move to Ohio, although hard on me, has helped with his compartmentalization, also." Stepping out of her shorts and into a pair of sweat cut-offs, she threw her hair up into a clip and joined Jared on the bed. Letting her head fall into the crook of Jared's arm, she informed him that they were on the books for tomorrow night with Ramona and Eric and that maybe after dinner, they could come back up here for a little movie watching. Pulling her in tighter, Jared gave her a kiss on top of her head. "Sounds great," he said. "Now let's get downstairs before your dad thinks I've taken advantage of you."

While Jared did a quick change himself, Charlie met her dad in the kitchen to help set up for pizza time in the family room. Looking at the clock, she knew that *Jeopardy!* would be on soon, so she gave the knob a turn to tune to the local ABC station. She slid the hassock up to the couch and centered her dad's chair on the end, allowing full access to the pizza as well as optimal Trebek viewing. With the sound of Jared coming down the stairs, Charlie simultaneously heard the engine of the delivery guy's car pull up. Headlights shadowed their way around the room, and a few seconds later, there was a knock at the door. "Money's on the landing table," Dale said from the kitchen. Snatching the bills off the glass top, Charlie opened the front door and traded them for the pizza. She wished the delivery guy a great night. He retorted with a "totally" as he spun on his heels to head to his next delivery.

Charlie set the pizza down on the hassock just in time for the intro to *Jeopardy!*. Calling out for her dad to join them, she and Jared cozied up on the couch and tore into their respective slices.

"Ah, couldn't wait for dear ole dad, huh?" Dale teased.

Nods and full-mouth mumbles were his answer as he sat down and settled in for a little trivia.

Jared and Dale took turns yelling their answers at the television in an attempt to beat the contestants. Charlie laughed at some of the ridiculous responses they came up with. *This is nice*, she thought. Any worries she had, however small, about Jared fitting in were gone for good. Looking up, she said a quick, "I know you're watching too, Mom," before shoving another slice of pizza into her mouth.

Jared assisted Charlie with the minimal clean-up duties. Dale had excused himself a few minutes prior, claiming he had a book with his name on it. Jared knew he was just being polite and giving him and Charlie some time alone.

With the trash secured, they turned off the lights and made their way up to Charlie's room. Jared followed Charlie over to her movie collection and stood beside her, arm around her waist, inhaling deeply. Charlie had the most intoxicating natural smell to her. If you didn't know better, you would swear it was the lingering scent from a shampoo or a fragrance, but it wasn't. He likened it to warm honey. He liked Charlie—a lot. He had come to believe that she was brought into his life by "fate," whatever or whomever fate was. He was glad that she had. He had enjoyed getting to know her. However, with everything surrounding the events earlier in the year, it had made getting to know her more *intimately* harder. Timing, distractions, and crashing at friends' places all summer made it hard. Hard, but thankfully, not impossible. He knew soon after they met that she had been a virgin, and he had been in no rush to pursue that aspect of their relationship, but he was also a young guy with needs, and with the knowledge of what it was like to be intimate with her, it took everything he had to not want to constantly be with her. Their first time was *WOW*, which made him crave her even more. But that was the one thing that was different about his relationship with Charlie; he was just as happy to lay in bed and cuddle in front of a movie. Like tonight. Lost in thought, he did not hear Charlie the first time she asked if her movie choice was ok. He quickly answered on the second ask, confirming that he was ok to delve into the world of John Hughes and see who this Jake Ryan was all about.

Hours later, the pair laid intertwined with each other. They had managed to make it to the scene with Farmer Ted panicking under the glass coffee table before the kissing had started. Honoring that they were in her family home, they had kept their time to a strict make-out and heavy petting session. The credits rolled, and their kisses slowed as Charlie leaned back on her elbows.

"I think I'm going to have to banish you for the night. Otherwise, I won't be able to stop. Up you go!" Charlie said, making a swift up motion with her hands.

Jared moaned and agreed that they probably should stop, but he made sure to let her know he didn't want to.

They said their goodnights, and Jared headed down the hall to the guest bedroom. Charlie brushed her teeth and splashed some water on her face before shuffling back to her room. She decided she was in no mood for more numbers and slid aside the leather-bound book from the night before. As she clicked off her lamp, she failed to notice a soft glow coming from the brooch on her dresser.

Cold air whipped around Charlie's head as she stood before the cottage. Looking down at where her feet should be, all she could see was a mound of snow almost up to her kneecaps. Before her was a door. Voices came from the other side—female voices. Whatever was being said had some emotion to it, however, it was not argumentative. Another swirl of cold air danced around her with such force that she sensed if she did not enter the home soon she would surely freeze to death. Reaching for the doorknob, she caught sight of her hands. These aren't my hands, *she thought. They were undeniably the hands of a man, with long slender fingers and wide knuckles. A ring on the left hand signified marriage.*

Charlie watched the hand push the door open, and she looked up to see a woman in period clothing greet her. She helped Charlie get comfortable and offered tea. Charlie could tell they were having a conversation, though she heard no words come from her own mouth. She also felt no emotions toward this woman. Who was she? The wife? Listening to the female speak, Charlie began to look around the room. It had a familiar feeling, yet different.

Returning her gaze to her immediate radius, she saw the woman place a cup of tea in front of her. They sat and drank. Out of the blue, Charlie felt an incredible pain and surge of nausea well up through her. She stood and doubled over. The woman was now standing, too. Her voice had changed. Gone was the loving tone, and in its place was hatred. Seething. Charlie doubled over at the next round of pains that came over her. Charlie fell to her knees and felt the intense heat from the fire before her. The woman had been joined by another, and now they were chanting. The pain! The pain was all Charlie could focus on, and then nothing at all.

CHAPTER SIXTEEN
DISCOMBOBULATED

CHARLIE WOKE TO DAYLIGHT, a soaked pillow, and a sense of dread. Nausea filled her throat. *Fuck,* she thought. *I've come down with something. Bad pizza, perhaps?* She attempted to lean up and saw the stack of books to her side and remembered her nightmare. It had been so vivid, yet she was struggling to remember what had happened. Barely able to stay in an upright position, the sense of vertigo and weakness overwhelmed her and she fell back to her pillow. Lying there for what seemed like an eternity, all she could do was focus on not puking. The smell emanating from her soaked pillow did not help. *Sour...so sour,* she thought as someone knocked on her door.

"Hey, you up?" she heard Jared say. Her bedroom door opened, and Jared walked in. "Good grief, Charlie, what's wrong? You look like shit. What can I get you?"

Using what little strength she had, Charlie let him know she needed a trash can, water, and a cold cloth. Quickly assembling the items, Jared made his way to her side. "What in the world happened?" Taking a sip of her water, Charlie fought back the nausea and motioned for him to apply the cold washcloth. Relief ran over her like a waterfall.

"Thank you," she said, sitting upright. "Was the weirdest thing." She took another small sip.

"What was?" Jared asked.

"I just woke up feeling like this. I remember dreaming. I was with those women from the other visions, I think. I wasn't me. I'm pretty sure I was in someone else's body. I remember feeling betrayed. Then I got sick. So, so sick," Charlie said.

"Can I bring you anything else?" Jared asked.

"No. Thank you, though. Think I should sit here for a few more minutes and see how I feel."

"Sure thing. I'm going to run down and see if your dad can delay our start time until I make sure you're ok."

"No! Please don't. You guys go. Have fun. If you can hand me the phone, I'll see if I can push Ramona off long enough for me to get myself together and shower," Charlie said.

Handing Charlie the phone, he resituated the washcloth on her forehead and gave her a kiss.

"I'll check in on you before we head out to see if you need anything," he said, pulling the door closed behind him.

Lying back and resting her head on the wall behind her, Charlie closed her eyes and fought back another small wave of nausea. When it passed, she picked up the funky handset and dialed Ramona.

"Lorenzano residence," a low, gruff voice said. Wow, Charlie thought, the rare Mr. Lorenzano answer. How did that happen?

"Hi, Mr. L. It's Charlie. Is Ramona there?"

"Hello, Charlie. Long time, no speak. Things going well, I hope?"

"Yeah, been a while, and yes they are, thank you," she replied, lying through her teeth.

"Good. Good. Ramona! Phone!" Charlie heard followed by the click of the other line and a chipper, "What's up, girlie!?"

"How did you know it was me?" Charlie asked, surprised.

"Only two people ever really call me, and Eric is working today over at Blockbuster; therefore, with my sleuthing deductions, I narrowed it down to you," she said, laughing maniacally. "Why the call? We're still on, right?" she asked, sounding concerned.

"Yeah, yeah. Of course," Charlie said. "I just woke up feeling a bit off and wanted to see if I could push it out an hour or so?"

"Oh, no! What's wrong?"

"I can fill you in when you get here, but basically, I woke up feeling like I'd been tossed around on a Tilt-A-Whirl," Charlie said.

"Was alcohol involved?" Ramona said in a teasing tone.

"No, no, nothing like that. Looking forward to hanging out. See you in a bit. Deal?"

"Deal," Ramona said, ending the call.

Charlie placed the handset back on the cradle and took a long chug of her water. Closing her eyes, flashes of her dream came back. She used some of the techniques Marcus had assisted her with and worked backward in an attempt to piece together what happened.

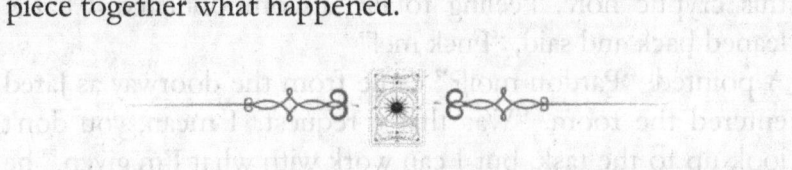

—❖—❖—✸—❖—❖—

The pieces lay disjointed in her brain. Charlie figured maybe the journal from last night might help trigger some memories. She leaned over to lift it from her bedside. The washcloth slipped off her forehead and to the floor. She attempted to catch it mid-fall and instead dropped the journal, which released a small piece of paper. *Odd,* she thought. She had fanned through the book pretty thoroughly and didn't find any loose paper then. Maybe it had been stuck between two pages? She reached down and picked up the paper and her washcloth, which she immediately tossed over to land with its friend, the pillowcase.

She read the note and immediately knew it was from Marcus. Physical communication like this was rare. Charlie had learned from Astrid's antics and writings that they had minute energies they could use for manipulation of actual physical objects. She knew the effort it took to write just this little bit. Charlie paid closer attention to the words, as they obviously must be important.

Charlie~ be cautious. An evil essence has arrived. Watch your steps. ~ Marcus

Her mind reeled from both her physical maladies and now this cryptic note. Feeling totally discombobulated, Charlie leaned back and said, "Fuck me!"
A pointed, "Pardon moi!?" came from the doorway as Jared entered the room. "Was that a request? I mean, you don't look up to the task, but I can work with what I'm given," he said with a shrug and a wink.

"Very funny," Charlie said. "It was most definitely not an invitation. It was a vocal expression of my current situation." She kept her answer vague as she did not want to explain the note or what was transpiring quite yet. She needed to get a firm grasp on some things before involving him. She needed to talk to Marcus.

Looking deflated, Jared said, "I was just checking in to see how you were doing. Anything I can get you before your dad and I head out? More water, perhaps?"

Charlie nodded, handing him the empty glass. "Thank you."

Jared went to the bathroom to retrieve her water. Charlie could hear him go on about the plans with her dad. "He's got us biking out to Fairport; said something about canals?"

"Yeah," Charlie said. "There's a whole canal system that runs throughout Rochester. It's a gorgeous ride. You'll love it. Make sure to have him treat you to an ice cream when you hit Fairport."

"Sure thing," he replied, handing her the glass. "Ramona still coming? I don't want you by yourself for too long."

Charlie nodded, taking a sip of her water. "We talked. She'll be here in about an hour or so. Thinking we'll just be hanging here today, given the circumstances."

"Good. Rest up. See you in a bit," he said, giving her a kiss on the forehead.

Charlie slid the note out from under the covers once he left. Folding it, she then tucked it in the journal, leaned back, and said, "Marcus, we need to talk." Closing her eyes, she waited and waited.

Feeling the vibration rise within her, Charlie knew Marcus was with her. *You know, Charlie, I'm not a genie. Rubbing the lamp and summoning me won't work ninety percent of the time. We are meant to guide and protect, not be on call. Luckily, the Master agreed that this indeed fell under the protection veil, so here I am. What concerns you today, Charlie?*

"What concerns me?" she thought. "Let's discuss what happened to me last night, why I woke up feeling like I had been run through a blender, and then we can discuss the note. I understand it's a warning, but I'm not sure of the context."

Charlie, what you're feeling this morning is the physical side effects of a postcognition experience. I must assume you have felt similar ailments before? Have you not? They will range in severity and coincide with your visions and dreams here on out. You will learn to balance the effects. I promise. With regards to the note, I cannot give you more at this time. My role here is to guide, not steer or interfere. You must go through your own trials and tribulations to learn the lessons you're meant to carry forward. Take the note and follow your instincts. Be aware. Take heed. If something feels off, it more than likely is. Learn how to use that technique again to your advantage.

Before Charlie could reply, he was gone. With a deep sigh, she finished her glass of water and sat the journal back on her nightstand. She swung her legs over and gave herself a quick pep talk before deciding she needed some sustenance.

CHAPTER SEVENTEEN
WHAT'S A BESTIE FOR

WITH THE HOUSE TO HERSELF, Charlie took her mug of coffee and box of Frosted Corn Flakes into the living room. "Who needs a bowl when you have hands," she said to herself, dropping a palm full of crunchy sweetness into her mouth. Maury was on, and it allowed her to temporarily escape from the dreams, visions, and Marcus. She took a sip of her coffee and thought about her mom. Was this what she went through growing up? Based on her mom's documentation, it seemed it may have been precisely what she had experienced since Astrid found her as a small child. Charlie wondered if Astrid had been good to her mom and helpful at first like Marcus. She knew from the journals Astrid had been a playmate of sorts, what most would label as an imaginary friend. How hard must that be to be so small and naive and not have the ability to share what was happening in your little world. To be placated and eventually scolded for something you never asked for. Charlie sort of knew why Astrid had chosen her mother. The Master had filled her in on that aspect of their world. But the piece she was missing was how it truly felt for her mom. These were questions she hoped to gain insight on through her studies in the upcoming year.

Another crunch or two and one final sip of coffee, and Charlie meandered up to shower to get ready for Ramona.

Charlie slid her T-shirt over her head and heard Ramona's familiar horn as she pulled up into the driveway. Giving herself a once-over in the mirror, Charlie acquiesced to the death-warmed-over look and headed down just in time to greet her bestie as she was entering the sunroom. Ramona eyed her up and down, tilting her head and asking if it was safe to hug.

"Yeah," Charlie said with a light chuckle. "What ailed me was more supernatural than natural, I found out." She finished the sentence just as Ramona swallowed her in a big bear hug.

"Good!" Ramona began. "Well, maybe not good for you, but good for me!" She flashed a huge, toothy grin.

"Before we go any further," Charlie said, "let's talk about how cute your hair looks! I know you said it was a whim, but I love it! Totally 'dorbs."

"Thank you," Ramona said, giving her dark hair a fluff.

"I've been wanting a change, too," Charlie said. "Just can't decide what, exactly. I'm not lucky enough to have those natural curls."

"Well, we can make that one of our goals for today! I've got *Teen Beat*, *Sassy*, *Seventeen*, and even a *Rolling Stone* in my backpack. I'm sure we can find you something!"

"Ok, but first get your butt in here and get settled," Charlie said. "Coke?" she offered, but then remembered the short supply of provisions. "Wait, before you answer, let me see if we even have any," Charlie said, opening the fridge. To her delight, there was still part of a six pack on the bottom shelf. Snapping two from the plastic rings, she handed one to Ramona. "I figured the answer was a yes," she said with a laugh. "Now let's get cozy in the family room."

Ramona flung her backpack down and cracked her Coke open. She perched herself half on, half off the arm of the sofa—one of her quirks. She loved sitting higher than everyone else and was banned from such shenanigans at her house. Since the Bauman household was pretty much a come as you are environment, all of Ramona's quirks were allowed and celebrated.

"Eric is working today, huh?" Charlie asked. "What time are we thinking for tonight?"

"He gets off at four o'clock, so we can meet at my house about five and go from there?" Ramona suggested.

"Sounds like a plan. Tell me how have things really been going with you two?" Charlie asked.

Conversation carried on effortlessly between the two for the next hour or so. Ramona spilled all the details on her relationship with Eric, and Charlie reminisced over the summer travels. The flow was interrupted by a low growl from Ramona's stomach. Ramona stood and announced she was raiding the snack closet. Ramona opened the pantry door and disappeared into its bowels. Charlie then heard a woeful, "Ummmmm, what did your dad do!? No Oreos, no Bugles, not even a Twinkie!"

Charlie got up and leaned to peer into the pantry. "Yeah, I guess without me around and with the impending move, he kind of went bare bones. We ate the Doritos last night, and I forgot to check earlier, sorry," she said.

"This is a snack emergency!" Ramona exclaimed, raising her fist into the air as if to charge the beaches of Normandy. Clicking her tongue, she exited the pantry and ordered Charlie to get some shoes on. They were outtie! "We have to get sustenance, stat."

Charlie did as she was instructed, slipping on her Keds and grabbing her crossbody off the newel post at the stairs' landing. The duo hopped into Ramona's well worn—very well worn—Dodge Daytona. The faded red paint looked even sadder against the matching crushed velvet interior. It had originally been Ramona's dad's car, but when his job gave him a company car, this one was gifted to Ramona. He, of course, explained that there was a price for this "gift," which came in the form of a built-in taxi service. The car took its beatings over the years as Ramona shuttled two sweaty, teen boys back and forth to soccer and baseball practices. It was a battle the crushed velvet would lose. *If this car could talk*, Charlie thought.

They were going to make the trip a quick one. The closest 7-11 made things easier. Charlie surmised that the decision was predetermined due to the fact it was pretty much next door to the Blockbuster Eric worked at. They sped down Monroe Avenue with the radio blasting. Ramona and Charlie sang along, adding their own flare as the songs faded into each other.

Pulling into the 7-11 parking lot, Ramona did exactly what Charlie predicted. "Hey, why don't you go snag us some snacks and I'll head over and grab a movie for us," Ramona said. "You got it, dude" Charlie chuckled. "Oreos, Doritos, and?"

"Bugles!" Ramona interjected as she made her way across the lot. "OH! And cherry Slurpees."

"Sure thing," Charlie said as she pulled open the door, the bell jingling above her head. The halogen lights assaulted her eyes upon entering the 7-11, the mecca of junk food and really bad hot dogs. She walked toward the chip section and took note of her surroundings. Something her dad had always instilled in her. Over by the Slurpee machine was a mom and her son arguing over what size he was allowed to get. At the register was a squirrely old man buying a pack of menthol cigarettes, flirting way too hard with the teen behind the counter. *Gross*, Charlie thought. *You could be her grandpa.* Shaking off the heebie-jeebies and overall ick factor, Charlie loaded her left arm with a bag of Doritos and Bugles, then made a U-turn at the end cap to go down the aisle that housed the candy and small array of cookies. She snatched a pack of Oreos and took them to the front counter where the flirtation was still in full swing.

Setting her items to the side, she gave a knowing look to the girl behind the counter—Tammy, if you believed her nametag. Charlie stifled a chuckle when the young girl quickly stuck her pointer finger toward her mouth symbolizing "gag me." With her hands now free to tackle the Slurpees, Charlie approached the machine. The boy had won the battle and was finishing up his custom mix of cherry and lime in the largest cup available. Stepping to the side, he grabbed a straw and followed his mom to the counter while beaming with happiness. Charlie slid two medium cups from their sleeve and began to pour the first cup full of cherry goodness. Pulling the lever, she felt dizzy, then...

Dust kicked up in front of Charlie's face. Waiting for it to clear, she shielded her eyes from the particles and noticed her hands were holding a cup of port. A woman's hands, but not hers. The dust cleared, and before her stood Elias. He was yelling at her. Something about how could she be so stupid as to get herself in this situation. He would not allow her to ruin his reputation. He demanded she figure something out or he would. She went to plead her case to him, but before she could say a word, he backhanded her across the face. She recoiled, then watched as the port fell...

"What's wrong with you!?" Charlie heard through the fog, followed by, "Come on! That's totally bogus! I'm the one who's gotta clean that shit up!"

As the last statement registered, Charlie felt something cold on her left hand, and she looked down to see a river of red ice flowing like lava over her hand, landing in a growing puddle at her feet. "My shoes!" she screamed, jumping back and almost slipping. Her favorite Keds were no longer white, but a shade of splotchy red.

Letting go of the dispenser handle, Charlie stepped back in disbelief as the girl who had previously been behind the counter wheeled a bright yellow institutional mop bucket in her direction. Charlie dropped the cup in the waste bin and profusely apologized to Tammy as she swirled the mop back and forth through the puddle.

"Yeah, yeah," Tammy said. "You ok? My uncle Tim has black-outs like that, but his are from Nam. Says they doused them with too much Agent Orange. I'm thinking that's not your case, so what's the deal?"

Charlie was mesmerized by the gray swirling muck water in the bucket and its corresponding stench that almost made her gag. She only really heard the last bit of what the clerk had said to her. *What's the deal?* Charlie honestly didn't know what the deal was. She was having a hard time remembering anything after the kid walked away. Apologizing again, she walked over to the register, her feet creating sticky wet footprints with every step. The girl cursed under her breath as she slid the mop over the footpath. Charlie waited for Tammy to finish up and wiped her hands on her jeans in an attempt to remove some of the sticky ick. Unable to make the stickiness go away, she looked down again at her shoes and let out a deep sigh as the girl rang her up.

"You giving up on the Slurpees then?" Tammy said, rolling her eyes. Charlie sheepishly nodded yes, handing the girl a ten. With her snacks and change in hand, Charlie walked back to Ramona's car. She tossed the bags in the open passenger-side window and leaned against the car to slide off her shoes. Her toes were a weird shade of pink, and their texture resembled that of mini raisins. Charlie looked up just in time to see Ramona walking toward her.

"Ummm, why are you barefoot? And where are the Slurpees?" she asked.

Charlie explained what had happened. Well, most of it. She white lied about the blackout, saying instead that the machine broke mid-pour and made a mess of her shoes. "Broken machine equals no Slurpees," she finished with a shrug. Charlie felt guilty for lying to Ramona. They always told each other everything, but Charlie just couldn't bring herself to try to explain something she didn't fully understand. She'd come clean later. She promised.

"Can I slip these in the trunk?" she asked Ramona, holding up her newly-dyed shoes.

"Sure thing," Ramona said, popping the trunk. "At least you got the goodies!" she added, sliding into the driver's seat. Charlie placed the shoes in the trunk, closed the hatch, and climbed barefoot into the passenger side. Ramona handed Charlie a Blockbuster case and said, "Here, one freshly rewound copy of *The Prince of Darkness* to bring up the mood a little!"

"Yes! I've been waiting to see this!" Charlie said. "I love John Carpenter! It's like you know me or something, huh?" she said with a smile. "I heard Alice Cooper makes a cameo!" And with that, they made their way back toward Charlie's.

They arrived back at the house, and the duo carried in their recently acquired items. Ramona divided the snacks on the hassock as Charlie made a quick change and washed her hands. Popping the tape in the VHS player, they spent the next hour and forty-five minutes watching Donald Pleasence portray yet another Loomis.

As the credits rolled, Charlie glanced over at Ramona who looked completely kerfuffled.

"What exactly happened just now at the 7-11?" Ramona asked.

"Yeah, um, I'm not quite sure. I'm still trying to wrap my head around it," Charlie answered.

Continuing their back and forth, the pair flipped through magazine after magazine in the search for Charlie's new look.

"Finding any inspiration?" Charlie asked Ramona.

"As a matter of fact, I believe I did," Ramon replied.

Lost in the pages of *Teen Beat* and *Rolling Stone*, Ramona and Charlie didn't hear Jared enter the room. Pair that with the already heightened fright they were experiencing from the movie, and they had quite a jump scare.

"Spooked much?" Jared asked them with a slight smirk.

Settling back into her skin, Charlie looked over at Ramona, who was wiping tears from her eyes, and said, "If you *must* know, we just finished watching *The Prince of Darkness* and may have still been in the zone."

"Ah," Jared said, walking over to plant a kiss on Charlie's cheek.

She picked up on Jared's odiferous scent. "P.U., you stink!" she said, waving her hand in front of her face. "Dad really gave you a solid workout. How many miles did you guys do and where's the parental unit?"

Jared plopped down across from the girls, grabbed the remains of Charlie's Coke, and took a swig. "We parked in Pittsford, then took the bikes down to Fairport and back. Stopped for lunch at the place you suggested. I passed on the ice cream, though. Your dad is out back unloading the bikes."

"Wow! You have to be worn out," Charlie replied.

"Not in a million years would I even attempt that," Ramona scoffed. "But I'm down for our activities tonight. Way more my speed. You gonna be able to participate, Jared?" she asked, eyeing him from top to bottom. "Doesn't look like anything's broken," she said with a wink.

"Nothing a hot shower won't fix," Jared replied "As a matter of fact, I think I'm going to head up and do just that. Catch you later, Ramona."

"Don't threaten me with a good time," Ramona piped up.

Charlie smiled. She was glad everyone got along well.

"K, girlie. I'm gonna high-tail it out of here and go prep *this*," she said, swirling her hand up and down her body, "for tonight's festivities."

"Bye, Ramona the terrible," Charlie said, giving her friend a hug. "See you guys in a bit."

Charlie placed the cans and empty bags in the trash, then heard her dad come in through the sunroom. In stark contrast to Jared, her dad looked no worse for the wear. She'd be concerned if he did, however, since this was pretty much his daily routine. Other than the outfit and slightly mussed hair from the helmet, she would never have known he just rode all those miles. Charlie definitely did not inherit the fitness genes from her dad, that was for sure.

"Heya, Charlie," he said, entering the kitchen. "Where'd Jared get to?"

"Well, it seems you did him in," Charlie said with a stern look. Unable to keep it going, she burst into laughter. "He's showering. But for real, you totally wore him out. Not sure if he'll be able to skate with us tonight."

"Who are you kidding?" Dale said "That young man has the stamina of ten of me. That shower will perk him right back up. He's got at least a decade before he'll feel any after effects from a ride like today's," he finished matter-of-factly. Grabbing a glass from one of the cabinets, he filled it with water.

"That's where you've been hiding them," Charlie said, nodding toward the glass. "You're busted!"

Taking his first gulp, Dale took a deep breath, then asked where the group was headed other than the rink.

"Not sure," Charlie said. "Kind of want Jared to experience a garbage plate, so maybe into the city. Visit Nick Tahou's, grab a beer or something nearby, then hit the rink."

Dale stared at his daughter. "It's so hard to believe my baby girl is old enough to drink now. Seems like just yesterday you were shoving your tiny toes in your mouth," he said with a sigh.

"Awww, Dad. I'm still your baby. But if you ever tell that toe anecdote to Jared, I'll disown you," she said and giggled.

"Yeah, yeah. My lips are sealed," he said, finishing his water and pouring another. "You seem to be feeling better."

"I am. Must have been my body catching up to itself from all the traveling," she lied, hoping her face didn't give her away.

"I was thinking we can sit in the morning and go over some things before you tackle your mom's studio?"

Charlie nodded. "Definitely. I want to do a finances review with you, too. Also, maybe check in with Grandma and Grandpa if we can? It's been a while."

"Sounds like a plan. Now I'm going to get my old tush in the shower. If I miss you guys heading out, have a wonderful time," Dale said, giving Charlie a peck on the cheek.

"Love ya, kiddo."

"Love you too, Dad," she replied.

CHAPTER EIGHTEEN
DOUBLE DATE

SHOWERED AND DRESSED, Jared and Charlie made their way to Ramona's. The ride was relatively quiet, the air a bit heavy with unspoken questions. Charlie knew Jared wanted to discuss the issues from this morning, and she also had the 7-11 incident she needed to somehow bring up. She did not, however, want to put a damper on their evening. Ramona was looking forward to tonight. This would be the last opportunity for them to do something like this before Charlie headed back to school. Honestly, it was really the last chance for the foreseeable future, since the house would theoretically be sold before the holidays. Her first, no, *their* first holiday without her mom, and now without a home, either. Charlie fought back the tears and turned her face to the passenger window so Jared wouldn't notice her ennui.

They parked in the same spot as before, but this time there was a Ford F150 in front of them. *That must be Eric's truck*, Charlie thought. Looking at it made her pause. There was no way four of them would fit in that truck or Juicy, which left Ramona's Dodge. Her knees began to hurt prematurely at the thought of being squished in the back of that car.

Just like the day before, Ramona greeted them at the door before they could even knock. Charlie amused herself with a vision of Ramona crouched at the front window like a puppy waiting for its owner to come home. Ramona turned to lead the way, and Charlie stifled a guffaw at the mental image of Ramona's tail wagging.

Spinning, Ramona gave Charlie a *what the fuck look*, then asked Jared if she had anything on her back.

"Um, no..." he stammered. "Should there be?"

"No, she's just paranoid cause I'm laughing," Charlie said. "We have a long history of mini pranks, don't we, Ramona?"

"Sure do. I once walked the whole school day, freshman year, with a 'honk if you love pizza' note taped to my back. Talk about thinking you're crazy. I felt like the whole school had been dosed with something. Couldn't figure out another viable reason for all the honks. That is, until I changed for gym class fifth period and saw the note. But anyhoo. Jared, meet Eric. Eric, Jared. You already know Charlie," she finished with a head bob.

"Heya," Eric said to Jared, sticking out his hand for a shake. As if there was some bro code, the pair immediately began talking about sports. Charlie and Ramona sat next to each other on the couch. The plastic released a tiny crackle.

"I saw he's got a new truck," Charlie whispered. "Are we really going to squeeze into your car tonight?" she asked, hoping the answer would be to drive separate vehicles.

"Ha! No!" Ramona exclaimed. "Actually, my mom said we can use Big Bertha tonight if we want. She isn't going anywhere, and since Dad's away on business, we can slide her in and out no problem."

Big Bertha was just that—big. She had been around for years. No. Decades. Charlie was surprised Mrs. Lorezano's Wagoneer still had a heartbeat. While all the leg space would be appreciated, Charlie couldn't help but wonder how in the world they'd maneuver the boat around the city.

The guys finally wrapped up with their sports stats, and Ramona wasted no time keeping the conversation going.

"So," Ramona began, "Jared, we were thinking of busting your cherry tonight." She smirked at her effective double entendre.

"Oh, how so?" Jared asked.

"I'm sure I've mentioned the famous Rochester delicacy to you before," Charlie said. "We think a good, greasy garbage plate is in store for you tonight. The original, to boot!"

"Garbage it is," he said, slapping his hand on his knee. "Wow! A phrase I never thought would ever come out of my mouth."

"I'll grab Bertha's keys and we can head out," Ramona announced, springing up from the plastic, peeling layers of epidermis with it.
The group piled into the paneled wagon and wove their way through the streets of Rochester until they came upon the silhouette of Nick's. Somehow, it never seemed to change over the years.

"So this is the amazing and infamous Nick's that you couldn't stop raving about?" Jared asked, aiming his question directly at Charlie.

"Sure is!" she answered with as much confidence and sass as she could muster. "Never judge a book by its cover, babe," she finished with a wink. Both Ramona and Eric nodded in agreement.

"Did you school him on how to order?" Ramona asked.

"School me?" Jared asked incredulously. "Since when do you need instructions on how to order?" But before he could finish the statement, Eric elbowed him and nodded to the person in front of them in line. "Just listen," he whispered.

Jared leaned in slightly and focused as the teen ordered. "I'll have a plate—one white hot, cheeseburg, mac-salad, and home-fries with hot sauce."

Seeing the perplexed look on Jared's face, Eric laughed. "Here are the basics. You'll want to choose your meat first, either white hot, red hot, or cheeseburg. Next, you'll pick your sides. You have mac salad, fries, home fries, and baked beans. You can get one or all, totally up to you. Then you need to decide if you want Nick's hot sauce. Think chili without the beans. Being your first time, I say go for it."

Jared listened as Ramona and Charlie ordered, then stepped in and made his choices. Eric brought up the rear and paid. "You get the rink, dude, I got this," he said to Jared.

"Cool beans," Jared said with a slight thumbs up.

Taking their seat at the window, Ramona filled the group in on her and Charlie making headway on Charlie's possible haircut decisions. "I think she should go Molly. Would look totally rad on her, don't you think, Jared?"

"You're cutting your hair?" Jared exclaimed. "Since when? Why? You have awesome hair. I'm a huge fan of how you have it now."

"Well, um, yeah," Charlie started. "But I'm kind of bored with it. It just seems to lay there," she said, lifting her hair up off her shoulders and letting it flop. "If it's not like this, then it ends up in a ponytail or banana clip."

"Hey, it's just hair, right? It'll grow back," Eric added.

"Exactly, she needs that new back to school 'do! Maybe we can go tomorrow and stop to grab a new pair of Keds, too," Ramona said before Charlie had a chance to stop her.

"New Keds?" Jared asked. "What's wrong with the ones you have?"

"Clumsy here spilled cherry Slurpee all over them today. They're totally tie-dyed!" Ramona finished with a laugh.

"You didn't say anything about that," Jared said, giving Charlie a concerned look.

"Huh, must have slipped my mind; I can tell you about it later," Charlie said firmly in an attempt to end the conversation.

"Well, ok. If you're sure," Jared said just as their order was up.

The boys got up to retrieve the trays, and Charlie shot Ramona a death glare.
"Whaaaaaat?" Ramona squealed. "How was I supposed to know it was a thing?"

"Not really a thing, really. Let's forget about it for now," Charlie said. Her tone dropped to a low whisper as her guilt for not including Ramona in on why it *was* a big deal set in.

CHAPTER NINETEEN
ODDS, ENDS AND KUCHEN

CHARLIE, EXHAUSTED FROM the night before, as well as the day's activities, closed her eyes and laid her head on Jared's shoulder. The melodic sounds of Simply Red filled the car's interior. Her breath slowed, and she reflected on what had transpired recently and how the pieces connected. Everything seemed to start after visiting Elias' old house. The dreams and visions were linked to items retrieved from the property. The most recent came after reading the ledgers and books. That's the key, Charlie concluded. She mentally made a goal to delve into the book more and get Jared to help her in some research.

"Hey! Charlie!"

"I don't think she heard you," Eric said.

"I heard you," Charlie grumbled. Looking around she saw they were approaching Ramona's street. "I must have dozed off is all."

"I'd say so," Jared teased.

"Sawing some serious logs there, girlie," Ramona interjected, smiling at her in the rearview mirror.

"Yeah, last night finally caught up with me. What'd I miss?"

"Nothing much," Ramona said. "Just Jared telling us what a monster you are in bed."

The last statement sent a rush of embarrassment through Charlie's brain and to her face. Turning, she glared at Jared.

"I did no such thing," he said. "Scout's honor."

Charlie relaxed back down as he held two fingers up in the air.

Ramona cackled at her own comedic prowess. Charlie gave Ramona's seat a firm kick, jolting her forward.

"Hey! Watch it!" she scolded. "Don't make me pull this car over."

The car's interior erupted with laughter as they pulled into the driveway.

Hugs, handshakes, and goodbyes were shared by all. Charlie reminded Ramona she would see what her schedule looked like tomorrow for the possible haircut, but she couldn't promise. "It hinges on how fast we can get Dad all set up for the sale."

"If you need another set of hands, just let me know," Ramona offered.

Jared walked ahead of Charlie and opened Juicy's door for her. Once she was in, he closed the door and made his way around to the driver's side.

"Hey, great night, huh?" Jared began.

Charlie nodded. "Sure was. I forgot how much I like skating."

"So, I was wondering; what was that whole thing about your shoes?" Jared asked.

Charlie took a deep breath. She had hoped he would have forgotten about that. "I, well, I lost a bit of time again." She paused to catch the reaction on his face. It didn't move. "I was pouring a Slurpee one moment, and the next, I was standing in a pool of red ice."

"You don't remember *anything*?" Jared asked.

Charlie shook her head. "It just happened. I've been trying to think if there were any precursors, but I can't come up with anything. It was almost identical to what happened in the shower, but this time, I wasn't trying to tap into a vision."

"Charlie, this worries me. What if you had been doing something a bit more precarious, like driving? This isn't good. Not good at all. Do you think you could reach out to Marcus for some help? Does it work like that?"

Charlie knew it didn't, but she also knew that they would not be able to sleep tonight if she didn't agree. "I'll see what he says," she replied.

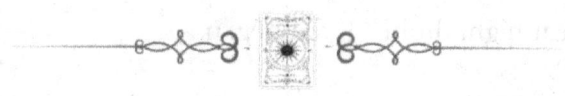

Charlie awoke to the smell of coffee. She sat up in her bed, looked out the window, and started to go through the plans for the day. Deep in thought, she heard the faintest of taps. Thinking it was Jared knocking softly so as not to startle her, she announced, "Come in." No response. While trying to pinpoint the source of the sound, it came again. Tap…tap, tap…tap. Then gone. This time, she was able to discern that the sound wasn't coming from one place; rather, it seemed to be coming from all places at once. *Gotta be a mouse or something in the ductwork or attic echoing*, she thought. She convinced herself it was nothing and pushed it out of her head. Swinging her legs to get out of bed, she was a bit shocked that Jared hadn't come to wake her. Her stomach growled. She slid on her robe and walked down the hall toward Jared's room. She could hear her dad shuffling about in the kitchen.

Softly knocking on the door, she turned the knob and looked in on Jared; still sound asleep. Charlie closed the door, deciding she would let him sleep in. Besides, she and her dad had some things to talk through, and this would be the perfect opportunity.

Charlie shut the door quietly and joined her dad, who was standing at the kitchen island perusing the morning paper.

"Morning, Charlie bear," Dale said without lifting his eyes from the front page. "Sleep well?"

"Yeah, actually, I did! I think the lack of sleep the night before mixed with the skating last night helped with that," Charlie answered, sliding to the counter to check on the coffee situation.

"I started that up earlier for you guys," he said, nodding in the direction of the coffee pot. "Figured it would lure you down sooner than later. You guys have fun last night?" he asked, taking a sip of his orange juice.

"Yeah! A ton! Ramona and Eric are definitely approaching the cute old couple phase. This guy may be in for the long haul," Charlie replied. "Jared had his first garbage plate."

"And?" Dale asked, raising an eyebrow.

"And…come on, Dad. Have we ever met anyone who can resist the power of the plate?" Charlie teased, grabbing the milk from the fridge.

"No, I guess not, kiddo." He chuckled. "Your mail's over at the table. You wanna go over some stuff before Jared joins us? I have a Wegmans' cheese kuchen warming up in the oven. We can take a slice over with us if you want."

"You don't have to ask me twice," Charlie said excitedly. "I can't remember the last time I had some."

Dale pulled out the tray and prepared a slice for each of them, then joined Charlie at the table. "It looks like we have you all set with the rental. You should be covered through the end of the second month. I can mail the payments for you or I can send you the check; whichever you prefer."

"Dad, I appreciate it, but you have the move and my tuition. I have plenty left from what Astrid pilfered over the years. I barely used any this summer thanks to friends and Jared's family accommodating us. Let me pay my rent," she said, looking her dad firmly in the eye.

"If you're sure…"

"I'm sure!"

"Ok," Dale said, taking a moment to bite into the kuchen. "Next would be the cell phone. Once I officially move, I'm going to look into a new plan. I'm going to ask that you leave yours here with me until I can ship you a new one. You comfortable with that?" he asked.

"No, Dad, are *you* comfortable with that? The cell phone was your doing," she reminded him. "I have a phone at the new place set up, and I have Jared now, so I won't be out alone as much. I'll be ok. I promise," Charlie finished, standing up to grab another slice. "Can I get you another?" she asked, pointing at the pastry.

"No, honey. My metabolism bit the big one a decade ago. One is plenty." He continued with his checklist. "Apartment.

Check. Phone. Check. U-Haul? Do you think you're going to need one to take anything up with you?"

Sitting back down with a full bite in her mouth, Charlie held up a finger to pause the convo. Taking a large sip of coffee, she swallowed and said, "I think so. Juicy has no room at all. Can we go through things today and assess later?"

"Definitely. I'm pretty sure Tony's is open late. We can hop over once we know more." Dale stood to refill his glass just as Jared shuffled in, wiping the sleep from his eyes.

"Morning," he said.

"Good morning to you, Jared. Can I get you juice? Coffee? Kuchen?" Dale asked, approaching the fridge.

"Coffee, please," Jared replied, then followed up with, "What's kuchen?"

"If I remember correctly, kuchen is the German word for cake, although this version is more of a crumb cake meets a Danish? This one is cheese and raspberry. It's all heated up," Dale explained.

"Well then, by all means, dish me up a slice," Jared replied, taking his coffee over to the table. Leaning down, he gave Charlie a kiss. "How's it going so far today? Any issues with your sleep or anything?"

"Nope! I woke up thinking I missed you. I was surprised to see you were still asleep. I decided to come down and go over a few things with Dad before we started with the studio. How are your legs feeling this morning? Between the bike ride and skating, they must be sore, huh?"

"As a matter of fact, they aren't that bad. Gave a stretch before coming down and right as rain now," Jared said.

"Jared," Dale chimed in. "What are your plans this year? It's your final one at Cornell, right?"

"Yes, sir. I'll be at the same place I was last year with my friend Gunther. I'm spending this year finishing up the last of my required classes and stepping in as a teacher's aide for one of my art history professors. Pretty sure I'm going to be slammed as soon as we set foot on campus," Jared said.

"Oh! Impressive, indeed," Dale said with an approving tone. "Well, I'm going to head up and change into my packing clothes. Meet y'all down in the studio in a bit?"

"Sure thing, Dad," Charlie replied, taking the last sip of her coffee.

"So, you going to be ok today?" Jared asked her.

"Yeah, I think I'll be fine. It's just stuff for the most part. Anything that has real memories, I'll keep. But my mom wasn't *things*. Besides, she'd totally want Dad and me to move on." Changing her tone in hopes that Jared would be cool with her next statement, Charlie said, "So, I was kind of hoping to get out with Ramona later today to go get my haircut."

"Oh, so you really wanna go through with that, huh?" Jared replied, sounding a bit deflated.

"Yeah. I do. I feel like this year has been full of changes, some not so good, some not by choice, and I kind of would like to have something that is both good and by choice. If that makes sense? Besides, it's hair. It'll grow back, and if it's that bad, I'll invest in some hats," she finished with a hearty laugh.

"It's totally cool as long as you don't go Sinead or Cyndi on me," Jared said, feigning a gag.

"Don't have to worry there, babe. So, plan of action then. Tackle the studio, and then you can help Dad with sorting out whatever he may have left while I get the snip and reconvene back here?"

"Sounds like a plan, Stan," Jared said as he followed Charlie up the stairs.

Charlie was the first back downstairs. With her boombox in hand, she grabbed some trash bags and made her way to her mom's studio. Walking over to the windows, she cracked them to let some fresh air in, set the boombox on the sill, and set the tuner to 106.7. Her dad, to the best of her knowledge, hadn't set foot in here since her mom passed.

Looking around, she quickly realized this might end up being harder than she thought. *Everything* reminded her of her mom. *Everything* was a memory. Taking a deep breath, Charlie assessed the room and made a plan of action. She would start on the far corner with the shelves containing books and knick-knacks. Then she and Jared could work clockwise around the room. This starting point seemed the most logical since she had already looked through most of it when she was looking for journals and clues in regards to her mom and Astrid. Grabbing a chair from beside the drafting table, Charlie slid a trash bag over its back and began to work from top to bottom. Since most of these items were personal, she would not be saving them to donate; however, she would need to make that decision soon.

She heard Jared humming as he came down the stairs and gave a quick bellow for him to grab a few boxes from the sunroom for donations. A succinct "Aye, aye!" echoed into the room, and a few seconds later, Jared appeared in the doorway. Looking over her shoulder as she grabbed a stack of books from the upper shelves, Charlie couldn't help but smile. She thought about her early teen years and how she and Ramona would "design" their perfect boyfriends. She smiled again at how skewed her ideas were back then. Maybe it was more that her reference points at the time came from teen magazines, but she couldn't have designed a better boyfriend than Jared. Even now, standing before her, with his hair pulled back with a bandana and wearing a pair of cutoffs and tank, he looked spectacular.

"Take a picture. It'll last longer," Jared teased.

Charlie blushed and began to lay out the plan of action she had come up with. Agreeing that he would be better off letting her make decisions, Jared offered to be the muscle behind the brains. The duo dove into their roles and worked their way around the room. Charlie surprised herself with how fast they were working through things and with how little she had set into their *keep* pile. When they got around to her mom's sketch-board, Jared said, "Hey, why don't you take some of those to Cornell and make yourself a collage of sorts? I can show you some examples from my art books when we get back if you want."

"I like that idea a lot," Charlie replied. Taking extra care not to tear or bend the sketches, she laid them flat on the drafting table. "I can sandwich these between some cardboard to protect them during transit." A few more childhood pottery pieces and a set of pillows she and her mom had made from scraps made it to the keep pile. They entered the final stretch, and Charlie heard an "ahem" from the doorway. She looked up to see her dad, wide-eyed at the progress she and Jared had made.

"How're things going in here, kiddo?" Dale asked.

"Almost done. Just have to get around that side of the room there. This here is my keep pile," she said, gesturing to the area on and around the drafting table. "The rest is either trash or donations, which are in those two boxes."

"You thinking of keeping any of the furniture?" Dale asked, wistfully looking around.

"I was going to assess that at the end. I want to look at some of the Polaroids Heather sent to get a sense of the rooms in the house," Charlie stated.

"Good idea. You may be able to avoid a U-Haul that way. Well, carry on. I'll be out in the garage if you need anything," Dale said, turning out of the doorway.

"Wait! Dad? I'm going to step out shortly to run an errand with Ramona. Jared is gonna stay and help you out if that's ok?"

"Yeah, definitely. I'm going to need some muscle on some things. Glad to have the help. See you out there shortly!" Dale said with a smile and a nod.

"Your dad is a trooper, Charlie," Jared stated. "He's definitely still hurting; you can tell. It's his eyes. But it's cool that he's got it leveled out for you," he finished, brushing a curl from Charlie's forehead.

With the motivational beat of Debarge's *Rhythm of the Night*, Charlie and Jared made quick work of the rest of the room. The pair then tackled the trash removal and took the donation boxes out to the sunroom for labeling. Sticking Jared with that task, Charlie made a beeline for her room, where she quickly snatched the envelope containing the Polaroids that Heather had mailed to her. Turning to exit, Charlie once again heard the noise from earlier in the morning. She stopped dead in her tracks and scanned the far side of the room from the ceiling to the vents. Holding her hand up, she confirmed that neither the heat or A/C were blowing. What was making that sound? It had to be mice, she thought, and made a mental note to check the attic out later with Jared.

Spreading the Polaroids before her, Charlie made visual notes on the perceived dimensions. Her room looked to be a smidge bigger than her dorm room last year, and it thankfully had an attached bath. Heather had the hall bath and Scarlett had a bath on the lower level. The trio would share the common space, so Charlie figured they would figure that room out when they got there.

Her dimensions in hand, Charlie made her way back to the studio to make some final decisions on which furniture pieces she would want. She looked at her list and took her pen and paper out to the garage where her dad and Jared were deep in sorting mode.

"Hey, guys! How's it going out here?" she asked.

"Jared's a godsend! Saving these poor old knees for sure," Dale said.

"I looked at the pictures and have my dimensions. I scoped out the studio again to think about what I want to take, but there still may be some things here I might want to consider before making final choices." Charlie said.

"Mostly boxes out here, hon," Dale said. "But you definitely have some decisions still left in the attic."
"Oh! That's right. Hey, Jared, wanna come with me?" Charlie encouraged.

Jared gave a nod, and the duo made their way up to the attic. They began to ascend the stairwell, and Charlie stopped abruptly to let Jared know that they had two goals to accomplish once they got up there. First, the furniture and stuff; second, the noise. She explained the noise that she had heard when she woke and then again when she went for the Polaroids.

"Could totally be some sort of animal based on that description." Jared agreed.

They got to the top of the stairs and pulled the string to illuminate the area. Charlie went to reach for the flashlights on the shelves out of habit and realized that her dad had pretty much packed everything in the space.

"Hey, do you mind running down and grabbing a flashlight from Dad?" Charlie asked Jared. "Looks like there's not much up here, but we'll need it for the one corner for sure."

Jared agreed and bopped down the stairs. Charlie glanced around. With the light provided by the tiny bulb, she scoped out the few boxes. Each was labeled with its general contents; she took a seat on the one to her immediate left marked "books" and took a deep breath. Having been in college, she was used to having her life packed and unpacked on the regular, but something about seeing these boxes made her heart heavy. This was more than just a utilitarian move. This was a chapter in her life coming to an end. She closed her eyes to fight back the tears and felt a warmth come over her.

Charlie, she heard from within. It was Marcus. *Charlie. Now is the time to keep your mind and your senses open. Be diligent in exploring what you're feeling. Do not dismiss what may come across as inconsequential. Malevolence presents in many forms. Trust your gut. Practice listening to your inner self. Your intuition will be your guiding light when I cannot be there for you. You're about to embark on some treacherous journeys. Do not let them frighten or discourage you. Your journey is one of guidance and revelation. These trials are part of your destiny. Embrace what you're about to go through and learn from it. Pleasant or not, you must go through the steps. We are here, but you must begin to learn self-awareness. Take care, Charlie, and peace be in your heart.*

With a final release of warmth, Charlie knew Marcus had left her. She really wished he could just explain things to her in a more direct way. She knew from what had transpired with Astrid that he could not, but Charlie still found herself lost and seeking a hand to hold. These cryptic messages sucked. Shaking her head, she heard Jared's footsteps coming up her way.

"Got it!" he said, holding the flashlight proudly as if it were a trophy. Stopping short when he reached Charlie, he cringed. "What happened? You ok?"

Charlie filled him in on what Marcus had relayed. Jared stood there, mouth agape. "Um, malevolent? Dangerous? Isn't he supposed to be like super positive and helpful? This totally seems more doom and gloom to me. And could he be any more vague? What are you supposed to do with that?" Jared spewed the questions rapid fire.

Charlie shrugged. "I don't know. I mean, weird stuff has been happening. We know that. Astrid is where she should be, so maybe it's the Dark Magician coming for me in retribution for taking his prize and setting his goals back? I really do want to research soon. Especially after this. Since we're sort of housebound tonight, you want to maybe take some time tonight and go through the books I have? Maybe you'll see something I don't."

Jared agreed and nudged Charlie to get a move on as she was quickly approaching her outing time with Ramona. She thanked him for keeping her on track. The pair took time to peruse the boxes, with Jared hauling them down as they separated church and state. The boxes Charlie wanted were set in her room and the rest were taken to Dale in the garage. Charlie chose to keep one of her mom's old dress forms and a few smaller items she found. She kept the boxes labeled with her name, figuring she could delve into those at some point at the house in Ithaca. With the last trip made, Charlie and Jared did a full walk around to see if they could find any signs of critters. Nothing. No nests, no droppings, no sawdust. Whatever that noise was could not be attributed to mice or squirrels. Giving the string one final pull, they descended the stairs, shut the door, and made their way down the hall, not noticing the soft glow of light sneaking through the cracks of the attic door.

CHAPTER TWENTY
NEW DO, NEW YOU

A QUICK CHANGE AND CHARLIE said her "see ya laters" to Jared and her dad, promising to come back a changed woman. Backing Juicy down the driveway, she gave a wave as she exited the cul-de-sac.

Once at Ramona's, she gave three quick honks to announce her arrival, something Mrs. Lorenzano hated. Ramona quickly appeared out the car-port-side of the house and bounced her way to the passenger door. Reaching over, Charlie flicked the button up to unlock the door.

"Heya, bestie Mcbesterson," Ramona said excitedly. "You ready for this!? I know I am! Can't wait! I've got the magazine right here! Punch it!" she finished with a full-fist thrust toward the windshield.

Cranking tunes, the pair sang along pretty much the whole way to Dead or Alive, Culture Club, and Human League. Delilah's Studio was just about twenty-five minutes from Ramona's. One of their old classmates' moms owned and ran the studio. Mrs. Lorenzano swore by her, and it's where Ramona got her latest look. As they turned the corner into the parking lot, Charlie felt her hands get a bit clammy and wiped them on her shorts. Noticing, Ramona said, "Uh oh, getting nervous?"

"Yes, but no," Charlie replied. "Does that even make sense?" she said, laughing out loud. Parked, she and Ramona made their way up the small path to the entrance. They stepped inside, and Charlie smelled that all too familiar perm smell. Back in the far-left corner, Charlie saw a woman with a "perm bonnet" secured on her head. A cheerful "Welcome to Delilah's" was heard coming from the back of the shop. "Have a seat; I'll be right up."

Charlie and Ramona did as they were asked, and a few moments later, Delilah appeared. Short in stature, Delilah was pear shaped and had a full head of blonde hair. Her apron was amply decorated with hair clips and pouches full of scissors. "How can I help you ladies?" she asked, wiping her hands on a towel at the check-in station.

"I would like a cut, please," Charlie said. "I have pictures of what I'm looking for here." Taking the magazine from Ramona's hands, she placed it on the counter and flipped through the pages until she got to the dog-eared page with the image.

"Oh! How cute! Have a seat over in that first chair for me. I'll take this with me if that's ok?" she asked with a nod to Ramona. "Your friend can slide up a stool next to you."

Ramona did like and promptly slid a small stool over, placing it just so. "I want to watch the full transformation! This spot is perfect," she firmly stated with a smirk. "It's not every day your bestie transforms into Molly Ringwald!"

Deliliah chuckled and set the magazine on the station top. She draped a cape over Charlie and secured it. "Let's see what we're working with here." Sliding the ponytail holder off Charlie's head, Delilah began running her fingers in and out of Charlie's hair. "Ok. It looks like you have some good waves in here somewhere. This cut will definitely help bring that out. With the weight gone, it should spring up nicely. We can mess with the bulk here on your crown as needed to bring in the shape. Now, where's your natural part at, honey?"

"Ummm. How do I know?" Charlie sheepishly asked.

"If you don't know, we can find out." Delilah spun Charlie around to face her, and lifted the front portion of her hair in the air. Giving it a shimmy shake, she released it, letting it fall naturally. She repeated the process and finished with an "Ah! There it is." She spun Charlie back to face the mirror. "See here? Where your hair falls off to the side? This is your natural part. This won't do for the cut you want, so we're going to have to train it to be more over...here!" she said, taking a comb and separating Charlie's hair to part a little further to the side. "Let's get you back to the washing station. Have a seat there while I check on Mrs. Fleishman. I'll be right over."

A few minutes later, Charlie was leaned back into the sink bowl and Delilah was running the most sublime hot water over her head. Charlie swore to herself that, if given enough time, she could actually fall asleep to this. Her thought was emphasized by the thorough shampoo and corresponding head massage Delilah was treating her to. With one final rinse, Delilah twisted the towel around Charlie's head and asked her to step up to the front station. Stopping to check again on Mrs. Fleishman, Delilah let her know that she was going to set the timer for another fifteen minutes and then she would be ready for her rinse. Mrs. Fleishman briefly looked up from her romance novel and gave a nod of acknowledgement.

Charlie sat for the next few minutes as Delilah ran a comb through her locks, separating and clipping sections up on her crown. Holding back laughter as she watched Ramona's expressions, Charlie took time to ask how Karrie had been doing. That question set Delilah into full mom brag mode. She gushed over her daughter's accomplishments as the scissors began their work. Charlie watched as Ramona's facial expressions continued to be pure entertainment. With the ding of the timer, Delilah spun Charlie so she faced away from the mirror. "No peeking! I'll be right back. Gotta rinse Mrs. Fleishman."

Ramona smiled hard and said, "I know you can't peek yet, but it's looking totally rad! Look down! You can see how much she's taken off so far." Charlie looked down at the floor in front of her and had an immediate wave of regret. Laying before her feet were piles of reddish hair. Ramona said, "It looks sooooo amazing! I promise. Besides, it's too late now, right? Can't go half-cocked," she finished with a shrug and a wink. Charlie took in a few deep breaths and agreed just as Delilah made her way back. "You ok there, honey? Looking a bit peaked." Charlie assured her she was ok, just surprised a bit by the amount of hair. "Good. Well, let's finish you up here," Delilah stated, picking a pair of shears back out of her smock. Ten minutes, some product, and a blow dry later, Delilah gave Charlie permission to "take a look."

"WOW!" was the only word that she could come up with upon seeing the finished product.

"Wow is right!" Ramona squealed. "Jared's gonna eat his words when he sees how hot you look!"

Charlie continued to eye the new cut from all angles, feeling and scrunching her tendrils. "Who knew my hair had this much curl to it!" Fighting back tears, she wistfully said, "I look like Mom."

"Boy, yeah, you do, Charlie," Ramona confirmed. "Totally do."

With a quick brush off, Delilah released Charlie from her capelette and sprayed a tiny mist of hairspray in a halo above her head. "All done!" she said with a huge smile. "I tell ya, very rarely do haircuts turn out like the pictures people show me, but dang if you aren't the spitting image of this one," she finished with a wink.

Swooping the magazine up, Charlie looked at it, then at herself, and concurred. She handed the magazine back to Ramona, who was in the middle of a full-on Snoopy dance. Charlie paid, and she and Ramona decided a celebratory snack was needed. They stopped at the Wegmans and each scarfed down a slice of pepperoni pizza and a Coke, then headed back to Charlie's, Ramona having graciously offered her services to the packing cause.

On the ride home, Charlie and Ramona agreed on how to present the new look. Charlie would park Juicy on the circle at the bottom of the driveway, just out of sight of the garage. Ramona would make her way up the driveway, faking tears. She would tell the men that something had gone *terribly wrong,* and instead of the sassy cut she had desired, Charlie had instead gotten a buzz cut due to major distractions from a perm mishap. Then, just before Jared and Dale completely lost their minds, Charlie would exit out the sunroom door and surprise them.

What they did not expect when they made their plans was the mail lady coming around the street, blocking the parking spot. Charlie stopped at the foot of the driveway, pulled down her visor to hide the "evidence," and Ramona walked up to the garage for phase two. Yet again they were thwarted as the men had decided to evidently take a break and were in the house. Ramona waved to Charlie to drive up the rest of the way. She leaned in the passenger window to inform her that the plan needed to be reworked just as Jared exited the back door.

"Heya, Ramona!" he said, waving. Crossing to the driver's side, he bent down to peek in at Charlie, who was laughing hysterically at Ramona and her failed plans. "Woah!" he exclaimed.

Unsure if that was a good woah or a bad woah, Charlie stepped out of the car and stood before Jared, hoping for a more definitive reaction.

"Isn't it rad?" Ramona squealed.

Jared made a complete circle around Charlie, expressing himself with a few hrms and huhs. Completing his orbit, Jared looked down, directly in the eyes, wrapped his hands around her newly bare neckline, and pulled her in for a kiss. Slowly releasing his lips from hers, he said, "I hope that clears things up."

"Boy, does it!" Ramona said. "I knew you'd love it!"

Charlie giggled as her heartbeat began to fade from her ears.

"Let's go show your dad!" Ramona said.

The trio entered the house, and the admiration continued.

"Charlie, honey. It looks great! I don't know if I've ever seen your hair so short! You look so much like your mom right now," Dale said softly.

Charlie gave her dad a smile and asked how the rest of their day had gone.

"Well, Jared and I got through most everything. I just wrapped up a call to the local church for them to come pick up the donations. I have my items tucked away in the far left corner of the garage. We just need to do a quick once over with you, load up my Jeep for a load to the dump, and I believe we are finito."

The group headed out to the garage and finished up what work was left. With everyone pitching in, Dale's Jeep was loaded up in no time.

"So, I was doing a quick inventory of the things you want to take to school with you, and it seems like one of those small tow behinds would work. I was going to give them a call to reserve one and stop by Tony's Auto to see about a hitch for Juicy. After talking it through with Jared, we think the best option would be for us to rent a small truck and have you and Jared drive separately," Dale said.

"Yeah, with the hiccups we've been having with Juicy this summer, I'd feel a lot better not putting any more pressure on her than we need to. You ok with that?" Jared asked.

Charlie took a deep breath in. "Well, if we go that route, I could take a few more boxes with us. This may work out better. Go ahead and make it happen, Dad, and I'll make sure what I want to bring won't put too much of a burden on the roomies' end. Worst case, I just take what I already had planned."

Clapping her hands on her shorts, Ramona blurted, "This means we're done!? Dinner time? All this hard work has me totally starved."

Charlie, Jared, and Dale all chuckled.

"Yeah, seems like this is it!" Dale said. "I believe there is a very large and yummy pot pie waiting for us inside. I'll pop it in the oven while you all do your thing. Jared, can you and Charlie close up shop?"

"Sure thing, Dale," Jared said with a nod.

With the garage closed up, the trio made their way into the house. Charlie grabbed a beer for each of them, and they collapsed in the sunroom.

Sipping his beer, Jared ran his fingers playfully through Charlie's hair and whispered softly in her ear what he was currently thinking of doing to her.

Charlie blushed hard.

"Hey now, you two! Save that for later," Ramona teased. "Besides, this is our last night together for a while. I was kind of hoping we could chill after dinner if that was ok."

Picking up on Ramona's sad tone, both Jared and Charlie nodded.

Ramona thanked Dale for a great dinner and patted her stomach.

"Don't thank me," he said, "I just heated it up. Irene was the chef."

"So, remind me again who Irene is?" Charlie asked her dad.

"Oh, you know. She's Tom Shea's widow. Tom and I worked together at Bausch and Lomb. He passed, gosh, I think it's been three years now. I'm pretty sure their son Steven went to school with you and Ramona. A year ahead of you two, I believe."

"Ah, ok," Charlie said. "Doesn't ring a bell, but there were a lot of kids in our school, so…"

"I think I remember him," Ramona said. "Tall skinny kid. He was in my algebra class."

"And she's making you dinners why?" Charlie asked, sounding a little too bratty.

Dale calmly stated, "Irene wanted to return the favor to our family. Your mom had done something similar when Tom passed. You get a lot of food and attention around the death and funeral, but the generosity fades as time goes on. It was very nice of her, honestly. With the impending move and everything, I wasn't cooking for myself at all. When she heard you were coming home, she wanted to make sure you had home-cooked meals for your visit."

Crossing her arms, Charlie let out an unimpressed, "Ok. I guess that's cool of her."

As if realizing a change of topic was needed, Ramona asked if everyone was up for a game or a movie.

With a resounding yes, they decided on the game of Life and began divvying up the tiny plastic cars and stick people.

Hours later, Ramona took her victory lap around the living room as Dale stretched and let out a yawn.

"This old man's hitting the hay. Congrats on the win, Ramona. It was a well fought game."

"Thanks, Mr. B.!" Ramona cheered. Turning to Jared and Charlie, she announced it was time for her to say adieu also. "Gonna give my mom a buzz to come get me since we've had a few tonight. Let you two stay put if that's ok?"

"Yeah, totally," Charlie said.

Ramona sashayed her way to the kitchen phone and called her mom.

"Ten minutes," she announced, hopping back onto the hassock across from Charlie and Jared. "I'm gonna miss you so much, Charlie," she continued. "Jared, you better be good to her, or else," she said, giving him a slap on the knee.

"I promise," Jared said, holding his hand up. "What are you doing with yourself this year?" he asked Ramona.

"Looks like community college. I had fun 'finding' myself the last two years, but I need to get serious now," she said with a jovial laugh.

Ramona came in for hugs all around just as a beep sounded from out front. "Gotta go before she gets a wild hair and comes in," Ramona said, giving Charlie one final bear hug. "Miss you already."

"Ditto," Charlie said, and the pair laughed at the *Ghost* reference.

"You may look like Molly, but you're still my Swayze," Ramona cackled, exiting the front door.

Charlie waved at Mrs. L., shut the front door, and turned to Jared. "How's about we have a little movie and one-on-one time upstairs?" Charlie said.

"Anything you want, Miss Ringwald," Jared said with a smirk.

CHAPTER TWENTY-ONE
NEW CHAPTERS

SOUNDS OF SNORING WOKE CHARLIE. Opening her eyes, she saw the TV across the room, its screen displaying static. She turned to see Jared next to her, smiled, then quickly realized she needed to get him out of there before her dad found them.

"Jared!" she said urgently. "Jared, babe, we fell asleep. You gotta wake up," she finished, softly shaking his shoulder.

"Huh, what?" Jared asked. "What's going on?"

"We fell asleep during the movie. It's almost dawn. My dad's gonna be up soon, and he can't find you in here," Charlie said in a slight panic.

"Oh, oh, ok," Jared said, rolling out of the bed. Placing her ear on the door, Charlie whispered, "Ok. Seems quiet. No coffee smell. I think we're good. Now go! I'll see you downstairs later," she finished with a peck to his cheek.

Jared slid out the door and tiptoed down the hall to the guest room.

Ensuring the coast was clear, Charlie shut her door and took a deep breath. Too wired to sleep, she went to her bathroom, peed, and took a few swigs of water via her hands before shuffling back to her bed, hitting the off button as she passed her TV. Settling down on her mattress, she flicked on her bedside light and picked up the ledger again.

Sliding her fingers through the pages in an attempt to start where she had left off, Charlie began to read.

Not wanting to alter the integrity of the journal, Charlie popped up from her bed and grabbed a notebook from her desk. She opened to the first page and took notes on words and ideas they would need to research. She was feverishly scribbling her ideas down when her nose caught a whiff of coffee. Looking at the clock, she saw the time and realized she and Jared had had plenty of time to spare to avoid confrontation with her dad. In fact, it was unlike him to sleep in so late. Charlie closed the book and set her notes aside before slipping on her robe and descending the stairs.

"Good morning!" Charlie said as she entered the kitchen. "Sleep well?"

"Hey there," Dale began. "As well as can be expected the day before your daughter leaves to head back to college," he finished with a wink. Handing her a mug of coffee, he continued. "So, today is going to be jam packed. I need to get Jared down to Tony's to pick up the U-Haul, and then pack it up. I was thinking you can work on centralizing the rest of the items in front of the garage, which will make it easier to load when we get back."

"Sure thing. Don't forget, we need to fit in an assessment of Juicy in there, too," Charlie reminded him.

"Why don't we do that before Jared and I head to Tony's? That way, if I need to get you anything, I can do it while we're out. Save a trip," Dale stated.

"Sounds like a plan," Charlie answered, taking a sip of her coffee just as her stomach gave a low rumble. "What's for breakfast?" she asked.

"Kiddo, to be honest, I'm not sure. I can whip up some sort of crazy omelet for you guys. We have bread, so I can make toast to go with it. Just missing a meat. Is that ok?"

"More than ok. As a matter of fact, I'll make the omelets. You just sit there and enjoy your orange juice and paper," Charlie said, turning to gather the ingredients from the fridge.

A few whisks and chops later, Charlie was busy flipping her creation when she heard Jared yawn a "morning" her way. Charlie turned to see Jared sit down at the island with her dad. "Got a coffee for me?" he asked.

Charlie poured a mug for Jared, popped a few slices of bread in the oven to toast since her dad packed the toaster, and finished her omelets with a handful of cheese. She handed out the plates and added a slice of "toast" to each one.

CHAPTER TWENTY-TWO
PREPARATIONS

CHARLIE KNELT BESIDE JUICY to check on her dad. "You ok down here?" she inquired. Happy with his answer, she stood up and relaxed into the crook of Jared's arm.

Giving her a peck, Jared said, "It's gonna be weird to be back to the norm, huh?"

"Sure is. Feels like forever ago since we headed out for the summer. We have so much to do when we get back." She sighed. "Way too much."

"It'll be fine," Jared said with a smile. "That's what lists are for," he joked, poking her in the side.

Dale emerged from inspecting Juicy with what he called "good news." "Everything seems ok, Charlie. Juicy's just getting on in age is all. We may have to think about alternatives soon. Especially with winter coming around the corner."

Charlie thanked her dad and gave both her men a hug as they headed out to retrieve the U-Haul. "See you in a bit!" she said, waving as they backed down the driveway.

Charlie stood in front of the open garage door and performed a count of boxes she was taking. She grabbed a Coke and a leftover piece of toast from the fridge, and proceeded to her mom's studio. She verified the contents she had marked and made sure nothing else was going to make the cut. She set her Coke on the small file cabinet, exited the doorway and made her way to her room to grab her space plan in order to ascertain what needed to be broken down and accounted for there.

Just inside her bedroom door, Charlie looked around her room at the enormity of what still needed to be accomplished. The dresser was going. She thought she may be able to transport it *as-is* with some well-placed tape to keep the drawers from sliding open. Her bed needed to be broken down and would require at least one more set of hands. The side table would go also. Unfortunately, she was going to have to give up her childhood desk in trade for her mom's drafting table. It just made more sense. She determined she could knock out the smaller items real quick, so she scuttled over to the attic door where her dad had placed the remaining boxes. She assembled two medium-size boxes and transferred half her window seat memorabilia to one and her side table and desk items into the other.

She then wrapped her TV with a blanket and set that on the floor and removed each of the dresser drawers for transporting to the garage area. She rolled up her decorative rug and carefully took down her wall and door art and placed them in the boxes. Charlie slipped her list into her back pocket along with a pen and carried items down to the garage. A few trips later, all that was left was the bed, mattress, and the dresser frame. Looking around for her Coke, she remembered she had left it down in the studio. With thirst conquering all her thoughts, she headed back down to retrieve her can.

To her dismay, it was not where she remembered leaving it. *Ok, I KNOW I definitely put it here. I'm sure...* And with every positive affirmation, her doubt grew. Maybe she hadn't left it there. Spinning around on her heels, she scanned the mostly empty room until she spied her can sitting over on the window-sill. *Whatever. Guess I was wrong.* She took a long sip, sat down with her paper, and looked at the sketch for her room and common space. With a plan in place, she finished her Coke and rolled the drafting table down the hallway to the sunroom. Back and forth she went with the items from the studio until only the items for the dump remained. Sliding those closer to the door for later, she decided a break was needed.

Charlie collapsed into a sun chair she found leaning just inside the garage door. Adjusting it back to a reclined position, she closed her eyes and let the summer sun beam down on her. Fair skin be damned. In these parts, sun was a luxury that would soon be taken from them. Get it while you can.

Jared approached the cul-de-sac and gave the horn a blast, startling Charlie upright. In the process, she felt like the chair had taken some of her skin with it. Shielding her eyes from the sun, she stood and saw Jared swing around to back into and up the driveway. Charlie plucked the chair back to give him more space to maneuver and stood to the side to help guide him to the center of the garage. Just as he came to a halt, Dale zipped up and parked to the left of the U-Haul.

"Hey, guys!" Charlie said. Jared exited the truck and came to the back to release the tailgate. He lifted it and exposed the open space. Charlie looked at her dad and asked why they needed something so big.

"Ah, that's not big." Dale laughed. "It just worked out better to get this one. Tony was able to give me the same pricing, so I figured why not."

"Won't my stuff slide around in there?" Charlie asked with concern.

"We'll make sure it doesn't. We have straps we can use behind the load once everything is in. It will help with any shifting issues. I promise," Dale assured her.

"Ok..." Charlie replied, not as confident in her dad's answer as he was. "I've everything down here with the exception of my bed, mattress, and dresser."

"Those should definitely go in first, don't you think, Dale?" Jared asked.

With a nod, Dale agreed, and the trio went up to Charlie's room. "You and Jared tackle the dresser, and I'll grab a tool to start on the bed frame."

Charlie and Jared decided the easiest way to get the dresser down the stairs would be to lay it on a quilt, then slide it down on its back where they could then right it and carry it to the garage. Charlie sacrificed her old tapestry blanket for the task. Jared took the upper stance with Charlie below to guide the bottom of the dresser over the steps. Working slowly, the pair successfully transported the dresser safely at the landing. Both gripping the upper edges, they maneuvered it out the sunroom and to the U-Haul.

"Let's lean it up and give it a push. I think we can get it against the back wall and lay it on its side for less momentum if there's a sudden stop on the trip," Jared said.

With the dresser in and secured, they went back up to check on the bed progress. Dale had made very quick work of the dismantling and was ready for the procession line to begin. Charlie grabbed the side rails while Jared took the headboard and Dale trailed with the footboard. Sliding them into place behind the dresser, the trio ascended the stairs one last time. Looking at the unruly mattress, Dale asked whether Charlie would prefer a new mattress to this one. "Heck no!" It took me years to get this just right. No way I'm starting over," she said with a laugh.

With unified grunts, Jared and Dale lifted the mattress and made their way down to the U-Haul. Charlie was left behind to tape up the slats and carry them down. Stacking the slats into two piles, she wrapped the packing tape around either end to keep them from coming loose. Charlie stood and took a quick bathroom break. She exited the bathroom and was greeted with the same creepy sound from earlier. Now that the room was empty, the knocks echoed off the four walls making it even more impossible to pinpoint. "Ok, whoever or whatever you are, get out here and show yourself so I can get you back out in the wild." Standing with her hands on her hips, she skimmed the room attempting to figure out the source of the noise. Stepping toward the closet, she stuck her head in. Nope. Turning to the window seat, she peered in the open confines. Nope. Closing her eyes, she focused and spun around with an, "Aha! Got ya!" She managed to throw herself off balance with the force. Catching herself with her left hand, Charlie immediately regretted the decision. Searing pain filled her palm, followed by the all too familiar feeling of hot, sticky liquid. Rolling onto her back, she lifted her hand in front of her face to see what she had fallen on. "God damnit," she screamed as she pulled the brooch, of all things, from her palm. *How the fuck did I manage this?* she thought, examining the hole the brooch had made in the fleshy part of her palm. Squeezing her hand closed in an attempt to stop the bleeding, Charlie swore she had placed the brooch with the books in her bag earlier when she packed up her room. "Guess I was wrong," she seethed to herself, opening her hand to assess the wound further. The bleeding seemed to have stopped, but the sting still lingered. Charlie stood and scooted back to the bathroom to give it a good wash up. The hot water helped with the sting. Turning the faucet off, she once again heard the pesky taps. Filled with rage from the injury, Charlie charged back out to the open space, and with renewed vigor, she stomped around the room, honing in on the sound.

"You okay in there?" Jared asked from the doorway. "What are you doing?"

"Don't you hear that?!" Charlie yelled, pointing up into the air above her.

Jared squinted, tilted his head, thought for a moment, then shook his head side to side. "Nope. Nothing. What do you hear?" he said, giving Charlie a curious look.

Standing still, Charlie pushed her palm against her shorts to help the pulsating pain and sighed when she realized the sound had seceded. "Of course it stops after you get up here. It was the same sound from earlier. I almost had it pinpointed, then I fell, and…and…" Fighting back tears of frustration, Charlie held out her hand to show Jared.

"What did you do?" he asked.

"I fell and landed on *that*!" Charlie screamed, pointing to the brooch on the opposite side of the room.

"Is that the brooch?" Jared questioned, walking over to pick it up. Lifting it between his fingers, he flipped the piece over and secured the pin behind the clip.

"Here," he said, walking toward Charlie. "Let's get that in your pocket before it does more damage." Sliding it into her pocket, he leaned in and lifted her hand up to his lips. Working his magic, Jared gave her palm a warm and soft kiss that sent electricity through her. Charlie felt her face get hot, and as the energy released through her toes, she wiggled them in her shoes.

"Better?" he asked.

"Better," she cooed.

"Let's get these down to the U-Haul, and if you're up for it, we'll finish loading up."

They turned to exit the room, and Dale appeared through the doorway.

"Wow!" he said, sounding flummoxed. "I think the last time your room was this empty was back in 1970. Your mom and I were just getting it set up as your nursery." Dale sauntered around the space as if taking in the totality of what this symbolized. He approached the window seat and chuckled to himself as he ran his fingers over the doodles Charlie had scrawled over the years. "My little doodlebug," he said wistfully.

Charlie felt the melancholia flowing off her dad. Funny how this had always been a thing. Ever since she was a little kid, she could feel people's emotions, whether they were obvious or pushed down and out of the way. "How about we dig out the Polaroid, if it's readily available, and document these before you have the painter come in?" she said gently.

"That would be wonderful, Charlie. Something your mom would have suggested. Let's do it! We can go around and capture all your little breadcrumbs. Maybe make myself a little piece of art for the new place," Dale said, his tone picking up slightly.

"How many more of these little gems do you have around the house?" Jared asked.

"Way too many for my liking," Dale joked. "Figured this one here was headed for a life of CSX trains and graffiti at the rate she was going for a while there. Birdie always encouraged her to keep going, though. That's just who she was. Why I love, erm, loved her so much," he finished, trailing off with a heavy sigh.

Charlie felt his pain on that last sentiment. Even now, months later, it was still difficult to speak about her mom in the past tense.

"Jared and I were going to head down and finish up the U-Haul if you want to go tackle that?" Charlie suggested.

"Better idea," Dale said, "How's about I help Jared, and you use your eye to capture them? Besides, you know better than I do where you left your indelible doodles," he said with a peck to her cheek.

"Ok. Can do," Charlie said. Exiting the room, she looked back over her shoulder and asked, "Camera is in your office, right?"

Dale answered her with a nod. "Should still be in a box on the couch. Fresh instant film should be in there, too, if you need more," he added.

Charlie was flabbergasted as she looked down at her Swatch. One o'clock already. Wow! She made her way to the kitchen with a handful of Polaroids she had taken, scattering them on the island to make sure she captured all the doodles. She remembered there were a few more here in the kitchen. Opening the pantry door, she knelt and peered up under the bottom shelf. There before her eyes was a whole wilderness scene she had doodled. With each snap of the camera, she reached with her opposite hand to collect the film as it ejected out of the camera's mouth. Giving each a quick shake, she repeated her steps three more times to make sure she captured the whole scene. Popping back up, she tossed the new photos with the others and saw her dad and Jared through the windows of the sunroom. They had made very quick work of the boxes, it seemed. Deciding to go take a closer look, she scooped up the Polaroids and stacked them neatly in an envelope. She would take them to Cornell and create something special for her dad. In doing so, she did not notice what she had captured in two of the photos.

Charlie, Jared, and Dale sat around the island and chugged down their beverages of choice.

"Job well done today, kids," Dale said, wiping his face on the sleeve of his shirt. "One last meal together before you head out?" he asked, bouncing his gaze between them. With their nods, he continued. "Perfect! Let me go clean up a bit and I'll get an order into Hunan Gourmet? Little bit of everything ok?" Another round of nods, and Dale took off.

"Do you wanna clean up, too?" Jared asked Charlie, giving his pits a whiff.

"Um, totally gross! Yeah, I guess we better. Might as well bring the bags with us when we come back down. I'd like to head out and beat the sunset, if possible."

Standing one final time in the center of her room, Charlie stripped down and hopped in for a quick shower. She decided to avoid getting her hair wet. Making quick work of it, she dried off and set her towel with the dirty clothes. Her choice for the drive back was a pair of acid wash jeans, a tank, and one of her recent flannel shirt purchases. She wanted to be home before dark, so leaving earlier meant layering. Even with the sun out in the summer, the temperatures were sure to drop after sunset. She stuffed the dirty clothes in her duffel, double checked her closet, looked out her window one final time, and exited, leaving her childhood behind with tears in her eyes.

All freshened up, Jared wandered out to Juicy to load the duffels for the road. He took a moment to reflect on the summer and all that had transpired. He couldn't help but smile at how much his life had changed since having Charlie in it. She brought excitement and comfort into his small world. She also brought something he hadn't had to deal with since his mother was sick, which was worry. He knew that going forward, Marcus and the whole paranormal craziness was a package deal. It still made him cringe to think what this could be inviting into her life in the long run.

He knew from stories in Tennessee, as well as anecdotes from Gunther and his dealings with his family history, that not all this stuff was pleasant or positive. The Dark Magician and Astrid showed them that for sure. He looked up to the sky and spoke to his mom. "Wherever you are, Mom, heck, maybe you're with Birdie, wouldn't that be a hoot? Please look over us, especially Charlie, Mom. I can't even fathom what I'd do if something bad happened." Taking a deep breath, he blew a kiss into the evening air and stepped back into the house just in time for the dinner bell.

The three ate their Asian feast while Dale tried his best to keep his feelings in check. This was the last meal they would have as a family here. When he and Birdie bought this house back in the sixties, he never thought there would be a last…anything, really. He was a predictable man. He wanted to live a predictable life, with a predictable job, and raise his family in this house until they were no longer afforded time on this earth. But as he had been told by his parents growing up, life will throw you curveballs. Some you'll be able to get a piece of, and some will fly by you and leave you in the dust. Birdie's death was the latter. It had set forth a series of events which unwound his tightly woven world like a loose stitch in a cable-knit sweater. He had tried hard to fight the move to Ohio. But he knew he would not be able to stay in their house without her. What panged his heart the most was what he feared it was doing to Charlie. She was strong, like her mom. Stoic, even, at times. But he knew she had to be distraught over her death. Even though she was pretty much an adult, and chances were would never live under this roof again, he still wanted the comfort and stability to be there for her should she ever need it. His little place in Ohio was just that—little. Utilitarian. Served its purpose. It would never be a home. Not truly. Taking bites of his food, he listened to the conversation bounce back and forth between her and Jared and smiled, knowing that she at least had *him* to rely on. And Ramona, of course. Little did he know she would be needing much more in the near future.

After one final check of the garage to ensure nothing was forgotten, Dale shut the rear door on the U-Haul. He gave it a solid slap.

"Ok, kids. Looks like it's time, huh?" Dale said, taking steps toward Charlie.

"Dad, I love you so much," Charlie said, throwing herself into the biggest of bear hugs.

"Now remember," Dale began, "you follow behind Jared and take your time. Call me as soon as you get back. Promise?" he asked, tilting his head.

"Promise," Charlie said.

"Dale, thank you so much for the stay. I promise to get her back safe and sound. Totally keep us posted on the Ohio front," Jared said, reaching for a handshake but quickly stunned by a fatherly hug. Even Uncle Arthur was limited to a one-armed pat.

"Now get going before I start crying," Dale insisted.

Watching as the vehicles left the cul-de-sac, Dale fought back tears.

CHAPTER TWENTY-THREE
ROAD WEARY AND PUT AWAY WET

ALTHOUGH THE TRIP WAS a short one, Charlie fought off the sleepy bug that threatened her ability to stay between the solid white lines. Forget the added monotony of staring at the same image letting her know that *Easy Tow Saves Dough*.

Her usual go-to for staying alert was limited to just the windows on this trip because, as she predicted, the air temps had dropped dramatically. Choosing the trusty sing-a-long-approach, she cranked tune after tune over the speakers. She was in the middle of belting out her best rendition of George Michael's *"Faith"* when the strangest noise interrupted the melody. It was brief, yet loud. Charlie knew it wasn't the test of the Emergency Broadcast System, so she shrugged it off and continued to sing along with a voice only a mother could love. Heck, she thought, better yet, a voice that could have only been given to her *by* her mom. The song neared its end and a second interruption came. This time, it resembled something a bit more…*familiar*. Back in elementary school, her friend's dad was a ham radio operator. This was one hundred percent reminiscent of that. Crackling and faded voices wove in and out of audible focus through the intermittent static. Someone must have picked up on this frequency, she thought, and she spun the dial to the next available station. She was greeted again with the voices and crackling. *Curious*. Maybe these stations were just too close on the dial, so she spun further, at least five scans. She passed each and every one and had the same issue. Before she could give it much more thought, she heard, clear as day, a loud, gruff male voice commanding her to *go away*. Then, just as abruptly as it had started, it ended, but not before creating a distraction that kept Charlie from noticing the bright red brake lights flash in front of her.

Confirming that Charlie was okay despite her chattering teeth, Jared stood beside her on the side of the highway and assessed any potential damage.

"What happened?" she stammered, trying to come to grips with the near accident.

"A deer!" Jared cursed. "Damn thing ran out right in front of me. Instincts kicked in, and I slammed on the brakes. Figured you were far enough behind to catch it. Guess I was wrong."

Charlie explained what had happened with the radio and apologized for letting it distract her. She decided to leave out the last bit about the male voice in an effort to continue their drive back without incident.

"Yeah," Jared said, "a lot of truckers on this stretch of the road. Probably got all mixed up in the airwaves. Everything looks good. Give me a hug, and let's see if we can settle your nerves a bit before we head out again."

Charlie accepted the warm and comforting hug. They separated, agreeing to no more drama until they got back. With an hour or so to go in her drive, Charlie hoped she wouldn't hear that voice again.

They timed their arrival perfectly. The sun had just begun to sink below the horizon, taking on the look of a giant bowl of sherbert. Jared pulled the U-Haul up to his driveway and saw his roommate Gunther's car. Jared joined Charlie at the base of the driveway and helped snag the duffels. They proceeded up the path to the front door. Jared fished for his keys and slid one into the lock.

"Almost forgot what this place looked like," Jared said, opening the door and gesturing for Charlie to proceed. Charlie scrambled past him and headed for the bathroom, pausing just long enough to deposit her duffel at the foot of the couch. Shutting the door, she quickly dropped trou. Jared asked her if she wanted a Dew or maybe something a little stronger. Stronger was her immediate answer. With a deep sigh of relief, Charlie finished and washed her hands. Not finding a towel handy, she exited the bathroom, dabbing her hands dry on her ass cheeks, and wandered over to the couch, where she collapsed into a puddle on Jared's lap.

"Hey now! Watch it!" he said. "No shoving the bladder." Jared patted her on the thighs as a signal to sit up and stood, giving her a quick peck, then made a straight shot to relieve himself.

Charlie wanted to take a long sip of her beer but waited for Jared to return instead. Moments later, he hurtled over the back of the couch and landed so hard Charlie swore she heard the couch groan. Jared snatched up their beers, handed one to Charlie, and made a toast: "We made it through the summer, alive!"

Charlie giggled as she clanked her bottle with his. "You thought I would kill you, huh?"

"You? Never," he said. "I was thinking more along the lines of random serial killers like Smitty or, say, a deer!"

The mention of their near-death experience made Charlie down her beer quicker than a fat kid eating a cupcake. Releasing a cacophonous belch, she held up her bottle and asked Jared if he needed another.

"Big time," Jared said. He followed Charlie's cue and downed his own beer. He could not, however, replicate the bellowing burp. He laughed and continued his conversation over his shoulder. "How does that tiny body produce such loud noises?"

"Dunno!" Charlie said excitedly, returning with their beers. "Natural talent, I guess. I could teach you, but it will cost you."

The pair spent the rest of the evening relaxing and cuddling in front of the TV. *This has to be the best part of having a boyfriend*, Charlie thought. She smiled, nestling deeper into the crook of his armpit. The beer, doing what it did best, started lulling her to sleep. Jared pulled the blanket from the armrest and covered her up. He leaned back to enjoy *SNL*, and soon enough, he was falling asleep too.

CHAPTER TWENTY-FOUR
A NEW DAWN, A NEW DAY

STARTLED AWAKE BY THE SOUND of a car backfiring, Charlie squinted to see through the darkness. The only illumination came from the static on the TV, so she knew it was after midnight. One thing she would miss with being off campus was the cable TV. She was notorious for falling asleep with the TV on, and this sound was a rude awakening for sure.

Carefully sitting upright, a small wave of embarrassment hit her as she saw the not-so-small drool spot she had left on Jared's T-shirt. *Oooops*. Stretching, she looked over at Jared, hating the thought of having to wake him. Slowly lifting the blanket, she leaned in and whispered his name. Nothing. She repeated her efforts with a little more oomph. This time her reward was a series of lip smacks and a groan. "Hey, babe. Let's go to bed," she said a little more firmly. With no movement, she teased, "I can try and carry you if you'd rather." That did it. With his eyes open the slightest sliver, Jared mumbled, "Ok, sure," and pretty much slept-walked down the hall. Charlie made a pit stop to pee and wash her face, then joined him under the piles of blankets. Sleep came fast.

With Gunther as a roommate, no alarms were needed. The sound of ABBA's *Dancing Queen* filled the air. Charlie rolled over to say good morning to Jared and saw he had already made his exit. She glanced over and saw the time. Eight forty-five. *Might as well get used to this,* she thought. Roommates and class schedules would be inhibiting her sleep soon. Padding down the hall, the music grew in intensity as the song faded and went into *Boogie Shoes*. Charlie groaned. It wasn't that she didn't like the songs, she just didn't particularly care for their exuberant beat before her coffee fix. She made a quick U-turn into the kitchen, where Jared and Gunther chatted over coffee.

"Morning, Charlie," Gunther greeted her. "It's been mad long since I've seen your pretty face, girlie," he finished with a smile. Standing for a hug, he offered to get her a coffee. Charlie graciously accepted and took a seat next to Jared.

"Mornin'," she said as Gunther slid a mug in front of her.

"Mornin', babe," Jared replied, moving the cream and sugar her way. "How'd you sleep?"

Charlie informed them she slept well and proceeded to scarf down her coffee, barely slowing at the scalding temps. Gunther's eyes grew as wide as saucers as he watched the feat performed before him.

"Whoa!" he exclaimed. "That was impressive!"

Charlie took a deep breath, lifted her pointer finger up, hiccupped, then gave Gunther a nod of thanks and a bow as she stood to retrieve cup number two.

"Did you even taste that first one?" Jared asked.

"A…doy…" Charlie said in a mocking tone, plopping down.

As Charlie settled in, Jared gave Gunther a knowing nod.

"So, Charlie, you won't believe what happened to me this summer," Gunther started.

"Oh?" Charlie said. "Do tell; I hope it's exciting!"

"Well, when I was in California, I got approached by, of all people, Stephen Spielberg!" Gunther continued.

Jared stifled a snicker.

"Wait, what? Who? Did you say Spielberg?" Charlie said, puzzled.

"Yup. Sure did," Gunther confirmed.

"Yeah," Jared said. "Gunther was just minding his own business and there Stephen was."

"Shut up!" Charlie exclaimed. "No way! That's totally bitchin," she squealed. "What did he want?"

"He asked if I wanted to be in his next film," Gunther said.

"Oh? What film?" Charlie said.

"*Goonies 2*! He said I would make a perfect Mikey," Gunther replied, unable to hold back a snicker.

"Ummm. You're joshin' me, aren't you? Not cool!" Charlie cried.

The table erupted in laughter.

"Sorry," Jared said. "I put him up to it."

Charlie gave Jared a small punch to his arm and declared more coffee was needed before shenanigans like that.

"One more cup to go, then we need to head out, Charlie," Jared said. Charlie agreed, took one final chug, and stood to go get dressed.

She reached in the duffel and pulled out a pair of jeans. Sticking her nose deep into the denim, she gave it a thorough whiff test. *Meh, I can go one more day,* she thought, slipping in one leg at a time. Choosing a shirt in the same manner, she gave her hair a fluff. She was really getting used to the new 'do. Much, much easier. She was about to splash her face with some water when she heard the jingling of keys. "Tik tok," Jared said from the living room. "Get a move on there."

Turning the corner, she grabbed her crossbody and said, "Let's bounce."

CHAPTER TWENTY-FIVE
ROOMIES

THE NEW PLACE WAS a very short drive away. Turning onto the street, Charlie saw Heather and Scarlett busy moving boxes from the back of an old pick up. Jared sidled up parallel on the road, and Charlie pulled in just behind him.

Standing at the bottom of the driveway, Charlie waved to the girls as they came out for their next round. "Perfect timing," Heather yelled. "Get your man up here to help us with this beast."

They walked over to the rear of the truck, joining Heather, who was instructing Scarlett on how to get the desk out of the truck's bed.

"What this thing lacks in size it makes up for in weight. There's no way to move it without the two of you," Heather said. "I'll hop in with Scarlett and we'll push it toward the edge of the tailgate. If you two could help steady it as we tip it up, that would be great! Watch your toes, though. We don't need some heinous toe severment."

Charlie and Jared nodded. With a one, two, three, the girls used their asses as leverage to slide the desk. Success! A few wiggles and they attempted the tip up but failed. Several tries later, nothing but sweat had moved. With defeat in their eyes, the girls jumped off the back of the truck. "Now what?" Heather asked.

"Let's think this through," Jared said. "Leverage seems like it will be our best ally here. Is there anything we can use as a fulcrum?" he asked the girls. "You know, like a metal bar or broom-stick?" Scarlett beamed and said, "We totally got something," and bolted into the house.

"Did he just dis her?" Heather asked Charlie. Charlie snickered in reply.

A few moments later, Scarlett returned with an old shower rod. "This guy came off when we did the walk through with the landlord. He put up a new one and left this for the trash pick-up. Quite fortuitous, dontcha think?"

"Def," Heather agreed.

"Hand me that when I get up in the bed," Jared said to Scarlett.

"Charlie, you take these drawers from me. We should have taken these out from the get go," Jared said.

With the drawers removed, Jared took the rod, and with Heather's help, slid it under the center section of the desk. He and Heather applied their body weight to the rod, lifting the desk slowly, allowing gravity to force slide it off the tailgate. Unfortunately, the speed of the falling desk freaked Charlie and Scarlett enough that they jumped back in fear of losing their toes, causing the desk to crash to the concrete below with an incredible *boom*.

"Well, we got it off the truck." Charlie shrugged. Jared jumped off the bed and inspected the piece for any damage.

"Surprisingly, it survived. Bonus of older furniture. Let's all grab and lift. Should be easy going now." The group made quick work of depositing the desk into Scarlett's room on the lower level. Each of them returned with a drawer.

"One down and about a bazillion to go," Heather said. "My stuff is mostly boxes. How 'bout we take a water break before tackling my car?"

All in agreement, they headed into the kitchen to get water, only to realize they had no glasses.

"Welp, I guess it's hose time." Heather chuckled as she exited the sliding door to the rear of the house. Charlie said she would hold off on the water for a few and asked Scarlett if she could give her and Jared a quick tour since she hadn't seen the place yet.

Taking the lead, Scarlett began. "Soooo this is the kitchen," she said, doing a spin. Charlie looked around to see the small space. The cabinets formed an "L" shape along the back of the house. Dark wood. Plenty of storage. What it seemed to lack was counter space. They could figure something out later, she thought. Gold appliances anchored both ends of the "L," a fridge and a freestanding dishwasher, something she had never seen before. A small area over by the slider would be enough for a small table and some chairs. Scarlett continued the tour, exiting the kitchen to the hallway. "Down this way is your room and Heather's. Yours has its own bath, and Heather has this hall bath," she said. Quickly peeking into her room, Charlie was beginning to question her measurements from earlier. The group turned and went back down a few steps to the landing, which took them to where they had just deposited the desk. Down on this level was Scarlett's room, bathroom, a utility room, and the largest room in the house—the common area they would be sharing. This space had plenty of room for any extras that she brought in the U-Haul.

Jared nudged them along, reminding them they needed to get the U-Haul unpacked so he could return it on time.

Traipsing out, they made quick work of switching out the truck for the car, and once the boxes were in place, Jared backed the U-Haul up the drive as Heather deposited her car in the grass to the side of the house. The group took turns maneuvering the furniture and boxes into the house. As the last bit made it in, Jared made the girls an offer they couldn't refuse, offering to return the U-Haul, and pick them up a pizza and wings from Dino's.

After Jared took off, Charlie returned to the house to join the chaos. Scarlett and Heather were in their respective rooms, tinkering with bed assembly and unpacking, so Charlie kept to her room. Standing at the door, she took in the totality of what she had to tackle. The bed couldn't go up until she made some headway on the floor space. With that, she began moving some of the boxes into the closet to get them out of the way. Most of her clothes never left the drawers they had been in, so not much was needed there. Deducing she would gain the most from dealing with the bookshelf, she began unloading various items and setting them on the shelves. One, two, three boxes down and she decided to check on the others. Heather's room was first, and with a quick peek, Charlie saw she was MIA. Kitchen, a ghost town. She found the pair on the lower level. Scarlett was in her room flitting around, and Heather was in the common area, elbow deep in a box of vinyl. Velvet Underground played in the background.

"Hey, guys," Charlie sang. "How's it going down here?"

"It's going!" Scarlett sounded from her room. "If I had known this was going to be so tedious, I would have donated half my junk to the Salvation Army."

"Oh my God, you have no idea," replied Heather. "When I was packing, everything seemed important, but a summer of your shit being boxed up can give you perspective for sure. What about you, Charlie? Getting unpacked ok?"

Charlie nodded. "So far just a bookshelf full. Still gotta ways to go."

"I say a mental break and girl talk are needed before Jared gets back," Scarlett offered.

In agreement, Heather ran to the fridge and grabbed a beer for each of them.

"So, Charlie, you start!" Scarlett said. "Yeah," Heather shouted. "We haven't really had a chance to regroup since combatting Astrid and the whole mess that went into that. I know it took several sage sessions and a few appointments with my therapist to deal with all of it."

Charlie filled them in briefly on the summer adventures but let them know they could wait for Jared for that. She was more interested in filling them in on the other stuff that happened over the summer—the visions, dreams, and so on since dealing with Astrid last spring. "Right after, it was pretty quiet," Charlie started. "The cosmic dust settling and all. Marcus popped in from time to time to check in on me. He wants to make sure I was copacetic with what we did and went through on a spiritual level. Things didn't get weird until we got to Jared's home-town."

"Oh?" Scarlett cooed, darting her eyes between them.

"Yeah. We went over to his best friend Benji's and got a crazy awesome tour of the house he inherited, which was cool and all. Old, rustic, but good energy. Then he took us on a hike to another house on the property. It belonged to his super-great-grandpa, Elias. Again, a super cool, old as fuck house. It was like they just abandoned the place. Like time stood still there. He took us up to the attic, and we got to rummage through a shit ton of stuff. I found a few really cool things. They're somewhere in a box upstairs. I promise to share as soon as I get them unearthed."

"What kind of stuff?" Heather asked.

"There was a cool button and some books," Charlie said.

"Oh no, not books," Heather inhaled.

Charlie snickered. "These are more ledgers and such. Although one seems to be a journal of some sort. I really haven't had time to delve into them too much." She paused. "Then there's a super creepy doll. She had this brooch attached to her dress, which looked way fancier than she was."

"What'd it look like?" Scarlett asked.

"Ummm, old? I'm not sure how to describe it, really. We took it to a historian in the town, and he said it was called a Luckenbooth…" As she finished the description, Scarlett's posture changed and her eyes grew wide. "What's wrong?" Charlie asked.

"Nothing *wrong*, it's just I know people who have had some experience with pieces like this, and they weren't always pleasant. We can—" Jared came in the front door, bellowing, "Pizza! Get it while it's hot."

The girls stood to go up, and Charlie stopped them briefly. "Hey guys, I have more I need to tell you, sooner rather than later, but just do me a favor and keep this on the hush hush for now. I wanna hash it out with you two before I involve Jared in the crazy."

Scarlett and Heather criss-crossed over their chests and gave a solidarity nod as the three ascended the stairs.

The group shared stories of their summer adventures over pizza, wings, and beer. When they were done, Jared assisted a bit longer on the heavier items before announcing he was going to head out for the night. He had a big day and needed to prepare for it. He plied Charlie with goodbye kisses, and no sooner did he step out the door than the girls insisted on Charlie finishing up her tales. They opted to lounge in Charlie's room since it was the most put together. Heather grabbed her bean bag chairs from the common area and tossed them at the foot of Charlie's newly-assembled bed. Scarlett joined them after snagging the last of the beer from the fridge. Charlie settled in on the edge of her bed and pulled out the items to share.

She handed the brooch to Scarlett and the doll and button to Heather, keeping the books on the bed with her. The girls inspected and got bored with the doll pretty quickly. The brooch, however, kept their interest.

"So, what you have here *is* a witch's heart." Scarlett began. "If I remember correctly, they were called Luckenbooths, originally. That's what the historian said, right?"

Charlie nodded.

"Well, these were definitely used in spells. Still are, but in more modern forms. What I started to say earlier was that while these were meant for protection against evil originally, they became much more throughout the years."

Heather interrupted. "Was the family this came from rich? Cause this looks fancy."

"I thought so, too. But the historian we met said it was basically just costume jewelry made to replicate an actual piece that was more expensive. I guess people were afraid of losing their nicer jewelry, so they had pieces like these made to wear instead," Charlie said, shrugging.

"And you said this was pinned to the doll when you found her?" Scarlett asked.

Again, Charlie confirmed.

"Interesting," Scarlett said, letting out a sigh. "Protection spells usually aren't placed on objects like a doll. Blankets, clothing, yes. But dolls…I'm going to have to confirm this for you if that's ok?"

"Yeah, sure!" Charlie said. "It's not that big of a deal, really, it's just that weird things have been happening since I found this stuff. Would be nice to know if it's this or maybe residual stuff from last year," she finished with a sigh.

Almost in unison, Heather and Scarlett asked, "What weird things?"

"Jinx! You owe me a Coke!" Heather said to Scarlett, who immediately rolled her eyes.

"Seriously, though, what weird stuff?" Scarlett asked.

"Well, the night we left the house, I had an experience with Marcus where he tried to show me something. We were in the family graveyard, and I found a stone off by itself. Turns out it was Elias' headstone. Marcus had me focus on the sounds, and he showed me two women. Olden times type stuff. You know, billowy skirts, bodices, big hair. I could see them like through a veil of smoke but couldn't hear them. I did hear a wail, though. Then I lost the connection. What was odd about that was that his headstone said the date he was born but not a date of death, just that he was presumed dead. Oh! I also found this button there, too! It matches the other one! Look!" she said excitedly, digging in her bag for the matching button.

"Wicked!" Heather said, taking the second button from Charlie. "What did you say these were from?"

Charlie filled them in on what the historian said about them possibly being waistcoat buttons. "Makes sense," Heather said. "Especially if you found this one near the dude's grave; could have come from him."

"Really?" Scarlett scoffed. "Heather, sometimes, I swear you don't think things through. How would a dead guy's button from a coat be on the outside of his grave?"

"Oh, yeah," Heather said bashfully. "Didn't think about that."

"Charlie, we can totally research this, too. It'll give us something to do until classes start next week."

"Well, if that's the case, I should keep going then," Charlie said.

"There's more!?" the two said in unison.

Charlie spent the next hour explaining the sequence of events to them: The shower vision, the dream about the house summoning her, the dream where she felt the intense pain, and Marcus' explanation of that whole mess, the loss of time at the 7-11, the weird noises at her house, and finally the near miss in the car on their drive back.

"Holy shit-balls!" Heather said, gawking at Charlie. "This is big time haunting stuff right here," she continued, looking over at Scarlett as if for confirmation.

"Haunting?" Charlie asked.

"Yeah, like, hey—something you brought out of that house is for sure attached to a spirit," Heather said, looking over the brooch and doll.

"Or maybe those!?" Scarlett said, pointing to the books stacked by Charlie's legs. "What are they again?"

Charlie lifted them onto her lap and began to sort through them. "This one seems to be a ledger of some sort. Like a business ledger/inventory book from Elias." She passed it down to Heather. "This one seems to be a journal," she said, handing it to Scarlett. "And this one, well, this one I haven't really looked at yet." She held it up and opened it to a random page. As she did, Scarlett looked up and exclaimed in a shrill, "Hey! Give me that now! Heather! This is a grimoire! I'd swear on it!" As she examined the cover, Heather looked over her shoulder. "Yep! Charlie, this here is a grimoire!"

Confused, Charlie asked, "And what's a grimware?"

"Not a grimware, a grim–war. It's a fancy word for a witch's book of spells. You found this in that house?" Charlie nodded, still a little confused. "Well then, that tells me that someone in that house was a witch. Let's see what we can figure out," Heather said, turning around so they could all see the pages at the same time.

"That's a grimoire for sure. Now where's that book you thought was a journal? I guarantee that's a book of spells. Also, I bet you anything that what's been happening to you is a result of a spell cast on one or more of the items you brought back with you," Scarlett said.

"Whoa, this is so cool," Heather cooed.

Having to pee, Charlie stood up and lost her balance as her right leg had fallen asleep while sitting. Righting herself, she said, "Hold on! Be back in a sec. Gotta pee!"

"Actually, me too," Heather said, standing and exiting Charlie's room.

With her face buried in the first few pages of the book, Scarlett popped up to pee as Charlie came out of the bathroom. "Here," she said, handing it to Charlie. "Look through the first few pages. I'll be right out."

Charlie did as Scarlett suggested. Turning each page, she noted how yellow and brittle the pages had become over time. Intricate illustrations and symbols accompanied each spell. The spells themselves were detailed and written in the most elegant, flowing script. One of the pages featured a diagram of circles, but most contained ingredients for potions and rituals. The margins, filled with handwritten notes and annotations, hinted at the journey the person went through as a witch. *Odd*, Charlie thought. *I would swear I'm feeling actual energy emitting from the pages.* As she reached page ten of the book, Scarlett returned, asking Charlie what she had found so far.

"Lots of spells and ingredients, but nothing that would be construed as evil. Seems to be simple potions and spells," Charlie said.

That last statement came out as mostly a yawn. Turning to look at her clock on the floor, she realized it was already two a.m.. "Guys, I have to crash. Gotta get up and get over to the campus for some check in stuff. Can we finish this later?"

"Hey, totally. Mind if we keep these here tomorrow to go through while you're out and about? Promise not to take them out of the house. Hopefully, we can have a few answers for you when you get back," Scarlett suggested.

"Sure thing," Charlie said, and as the girls said their goodnights, Charlie blurted, "And hey, thanks."

"No probs," Heather said, dragging the bean bags behind her. "See you tomorrow, roomie."

Not having it in her to bathe, Charlie brushed her teeth and gave a quick face wash before turning in. Turning off the light, she noticed the brooch and buttons were laying on the floor still. Charlie snatched them up and placed them in the drawer of her nightstand, and was out before she knew it.

CHAPTER TWENTY-SIX
HELL OF A DAY

THE ALARM SOUNDED way too early for Charlie's liking. Hitting the button to stop the assault on her ears, she rolled onto her back. Fearful she would fall asleep again if she closed her eyes, she sat up and reached for her backpack, sitting on the floor next to the bed.

Sliding out her trusty notebook, she quickly reviewed the list of to-do's she had compiled when she was at home. First, a shower, then coffee. Once that kicked in, she would head over to the main campus where she needed to check on the status of her classes and pick up any required materials from the bookstore. Happy that she wouldn't need to mess with a parking pass this year, she closed her notebook and laid it beside her. Looking around her room, she couldn't believe she wasn't in a dorm anymore. Although she had never had a bad experience in her dorm, there was something about living off campus that made her smile. She scored big time with Heather and Scarlett as roommates since they both seemed to be nocturnal beasts and slept in even later than she was prone to.

Swinging her legs off the bed, Charlie stretched her arms to the ceiling. Standing, she went to find a towel in the mess of boxes she still had to go through when she heard a thump. Stopping in her tracks, she stood still to figure out what direction the sound came from. *Thump*. Louder this time and from her closet. Tiptoeing over, she leaned forward to peer in. *Thump*. This one made her jump. *Ok,* she thought, *there's no way a mouse followed me from home, is there? A stowaway in my boxes? No. Stop being silly.* Turning to go to shower, a final *THUMP* rocked her closet. Peering in, she saw a small box had fallen off a stack of boxes in the corner. Remembering the conversation with Heather and Scarlett the night before, Charlie quietly said, "Go away, ghost! I'm not doing this with you. Now stop it!" And with that, she scurried into the bathroom, shutting the door behind her. Waiting for the water to reach temp, she stripped out of her jammies. *There's no way I have a ghost,* she thought. The part of her that came from her dad banished the idea from reality and she began to shower. Lathering up, she heard another *thump*, and the part of her that came from her mom said, "Fuck."

Dressed in summer layers, because, well, upstate New York, Charlie meandered down her street and stopped at the coffee shop a few blocks down. One black coffee, two sugars in hand, she continued her walk toward campus. *Going to be weird getting back to a schedule again,* she thought. That and not seeing Jared all the time. Definitely, going to be weird. Approaching the admin building, she downed the rest of her coffee and tossed the cup in the wastebasket. She headed down through the lobby to the registrar's office, a small line already forming. She signed in, took a seat in a chair against a wall, and gave a quick scan to see if she recognized anyone waiting. Nope. Pulling out a paperback copy of *The Shining*, she began to read. She had brought a stack of books with her on her trip this summer just in case, but didn't have much time to delve into them. She heard name after name being called back until she finally heard "Charlie" being called. Standing, she almost collided with a young man who had just signed the log book. "So sorry," she said, looking up to see a handsome face. Surprised at the energy he was putting off, she stammered, "They called my name; didn't see you." He nodded and smiled, and with a very British accent, said, "No worries, luv." Flummoxed, Charlie almost walked into the door as she followed the counselor back to her office.

"Ms. Bauman. Take a seat," the counselor said, pointing to a chair on the far side of her desk. "What can I help you with today?"

Help me? Charlie thought. "Oh! Yes! I wanted to make sure I was all set for the classes I signed up for," she clarified.

"Let's take a look, why don't we?" Ms. Bell said, opening Charlie's student file. "It looks here like you were heading toward a B.S. in biochemistry… and now you're…um, am I reading this correctly, Ms. Bauman?"

"Well, that depends on what it says," Charlie joked.

"It says you're enrolled in a few, well, non-traditional classes this semester." Charlie nodded.

"Yes, I believe I should be enrolled in Intro to Folklore; Magic, Science and the Occult-Medieval to Modern; General Psychology; and Death and Afterlife:Lessons in World Culture. Is that what you show?"

"Why, yes. But do you mind me asking why such a drastic veer off course, dear?"

"I'm not sure if my file shows it or not, but my mother passed away at the end of last year, and I had a lot of questions as a result. I know she would have wanted me to follow my curiosities, and my father, who, might I add, isn't the most open minded to these things, is ok with me taking this time to regroup and explore."

"I'm sorry for your loss, and how wonderful it is to have a family that supports you this way. It seems you're all set then. I'll print your schedule now with a list of the required textbooks and materials needed. Give me just a second, and I'll bring them back with me," she finished, turning to head toward the printer in the front room.

Charlie sat and thought about her discussions with the girls last night and wondered how they were coming along with their end of the research. How awesome that she may have found a spell book! *Mom would totally have been into that.*

The counselor returned with the papers she promised Charlie. Thanking her again, Charlie made her way out of the registrar's office and stepped out into the sunshine. Happy she had worn layers, the morning had already adjusted its temp, making Charlie shed the jacket she had on. Wrapping it around her waist, she gave the arms a tight cinch and strolled over to the bookstore. She made quick work of her selections, then approached the register with an arm full of textbooks. Second in line, she waited, only to see that guy from earlier enter. Her heart picked up its pace, and she felt her palms get sweaty. *What are you doing!?* she questioned herself, releasing a nervous giggle as she set the books down in front of the cashier.

"Cute, huh?" the blonde behind the register said.

Charlie looked up and said, "Who? That guy? Yeah, I guess."

"Mmmhmmm," was the snide response Charlie got back. "Student ID and bookstore number, please," the clerk finished.

Charlie handed her the ID and recited her bookstore account number. Glad her dad had put money on the account, she hoped it would cover what she was getting since there weren't any used options for these classes.

"You're all set," the clerk said to her. "Here's your receipt. Keep it. You have until the end of week one of classes to exchange or return if you decide to drop. Otherwise, all sales are final."

Charlie thanked her and gathered up her stack, wishing she had thought ahead and brought a sack of some sort with her. It was going to be a long walk back with these. She exited the bookstore, felt the rumble of her tummy, and realized it was just about lunch time. She figured she could make it up the hill to the little mart, get a bag, then head over to Dino's for some food.

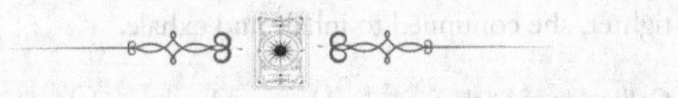

Scarlett woke up without the aid of an alarm. She had always been an early riser, and it was one of the main reasons she claimed the lower level room as hers when they had toured the house originally. This choice afforded her the flexibility of being an early mover and shaker without moving or shaking her roommates. No need to keep super quiet down here. Sneaking up to grab a Dew from the fridge, she quietly padded her way back down and sat deep into one of her bean bag chairs. She wanted to have some quiet time to peruse the books Charlie had presented them with the night before. She slid a box over, containing some of her more witchy items and pulled out a few of her ritual candles. She charged each one between her hands and then arranged them in a circle around her bean bag. Yellow for communication, purple for psychic power, white for protection, and finally, orange for success. Digging deep in her box, she felt around for her velvet pouch. Lifting it out, she unraveled the knot and pulled out a piece of jade and her favorite quartz crystal. She lit each of the candles and centered herself back on the bean bag, placing the two books in her lap. She closed her eyes and began to place herself in a meditative state. Her breathing slowed, and she began to focus on the energy coming from the objects in her lap. *Odd*. Mixed energies. Curious as to what could be causing this, Scarlett decided to play the elimination game. Plucking the book currently on top, she held it with one hand underneath and one on top. Sandwiching the book tighter, she continued to inhale and exhale.

Calling on Seshat for guidance, she honed in and quickly realized this book was emitting nothing but positive energy. She felt the love, care, and wisdom this particular book was built on. Words parted from the pages and made the spells within known. They swirled in and out of her focus. Images danced before her, simple sketches of both flora and fauna. Scarlett then saw a woman practicing the spells and mixing the ingredients she had gathered. Healing—that was the overwhelming vibe she got.

Satisfied with what the goddesses had shown her, she set the book aside and lifted the remaining book in her hands. Scarlett's brow furrowed in confusion. This book was emitting light but had an undeniable negative energy. Swirling through its pages in an attempt to hone in on what was causing the energy shifts, she pressed her palms tighter and immediately regretted doing so. The book discharged a heat so intense Scarlett swore she had burnt her hands. Releasing the book, it fell to her lap. She opened her eyes to check her hands. With both palms face up, she examined the skin for signs of blisters. Nothing. Not even a slight change in coloration. She shifted her weight on the bean bag, wiped her hands on her thighs, and snuffed out the candles. It was at that moment she heard Charlie leave through the front door, followed by a dark and resounding ***Bitch.*** The word was so gravelly, yet so clear, it caused Scarlett to spin out of her bean bag and onto all fours in anticipation of having to defend herself. Yet…nothing. No one. Not wanting to be "that girl," she quickly sprung up, grabbed the books, and ascended the stairs to take her party to the back patio. There she sat and read, waiting for Heather to wake up and join her.

Loading the books into her recently purchased tote, Charlie exited the drugstore and arrived at Dino's a few minutes before the doors were set to open for the day. She took a quick look up and down the street and spotted a bench two storefronts up. She made her way over, placed her bag down, and took a seat. Taking in the quiet, she realized that soon these streets would be full of students and local faculty. Deciding to take advantage of the quiet, Charlie closed her eyes to practice some of the mental exercises Marcus had shared with her over the summer. She took a deep breath in through her nose and slowly exhaled through her mouth. She let herself relax and freed her mind as best she could. Another breath in. Another out. She asked the universe to show her her mother's face. With each inhale and exhale she repeated her intent until small specks of light began to form from all corners of her mind's eye. Another breath in and the lights began to swirl in fluid movements, like the starling murmurations, until they began to take on color. Green at first, the color of her mother's eyes. Flickering orbs. Happy. Joyous. Then swirls of red began to appear as if they were bursting fireworks. Another breath in and out left her with a feeling of love and contentment. Charlie could *feel* her mother. She could actually ***feel*** her. Wanting more, she inhaled again…CLAP!   CRACK! Her thoughts were interrupted. A vibration sound followed. Then another CLAP! CRACK! And with that, Charlie lost her connection. A tear formed in her eye, followed by frustration as she opened her eyes to see a skateboarder coasting by her as he slapped another Ollie. Stunned at what had just transpired, Charlie wiped the tear which had rolled down to her chin, with the shoulder of her shirt. *We'll have to try that again soon, won't we, Mom?* Charlie waited for an answer she knew wouldn't come. Realizing the time, she stood up, grabbed her tote, and retraced her steps back to the now open door of the restaurant.

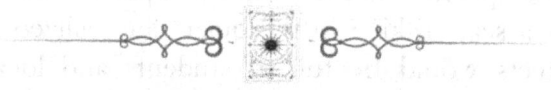

Heather awoke slowly to a weird noise coming from the hallway. In her morning haze, she thought it was perhaps Charlie. She sat up against her pillows, and rubbed her eyes in an attempt to adjust to her surroundings. She plucked her banana clip from the nightstand. Dipping her head forward, she secured her hair with a pinch. Heather peered over to her clock and was shocked to see she had slept in so late. She blamed the beers and physical labor from the day before. *Bump. Bump.* There it was again. Tilting her head like a puppy, Heather attempted to hone in on where the sound was coming from. The noise repeated itself a few more times, and each one seemed to resonate from a different spot, both inside and outside of her room. Closet; far left corner; far right corner; the hallway. *New house, new sounds,* she thought. She slid out of bed, stopped to pee, then entered the kitchen for coffee. Heather filled the carafe with water and noticed Scarlett out on the patio. She knew better than to ask Scarlett if she wanted any coffee. Scarlett was strictly a Dew girl. Heather loaded the filter with coffee grounds, pressed brew, and waited as the coffee slowly started to drip. While she did, she thought about how awesome this year was going to be. Living off campus, she felt she could finally spread her wings. Dorm life had not suited her at all. Too many people, too much drama. The only bonus that came from it had been meeting Scarlett. A random, well-placed flier promoting the Wicca group drew the pair together. They had been pretty much inseparable since.

Learning and expanding their craft, they had come a long way since. Then the chance meeting of Charlie. Heather giggled to herself at that. She had, in fact, predicted their paths meeting. A few days prior, she had a vision that she and Scarlett would intersect with a force that would alter their life paths. Thinking back to the whole Dark Magician/Astrid encounter, life altering was definitely the right term. The power those forces had held scared Heather to this day. You don't have encounters of that magnitude and not have it change you deep in your core. The residual energy that was left behind was palpable. She had some time to process it with Scarlett but never really had an opportunity to discuss the aftermath with Charlie. She and Jared had pretty much left right after. Charlie needed to know what Heather had foreseen. Soon. Promising herself it *would* be soon, she heard the click of the coffee maker as it released its final drops. Mug in hand, she joined Scarlett on the patio.

Charlie placed her order and pulled out the ledger, setting it on the table. Taking her time to fully examine it in daylight, she saw the same aged leather and button closure as before. She flipped it open and the cover released the faintest crackle. The blank, aged pages reminded her of a project she had done in summer camp with Ramona one year. They were studying the pilgrims and the colonies and were instructed to create their own journals documenting life as a colonist in a new land. To create the pages they would journal on, they had to first make them look authentic. Depositing tea bags into warm water would be the first step.

Working solely from a campfire, she remembered how long it took to just get the water above air temp. Then, using a cloth, they gingerly dabbed the tea solution onto the pages. This technique had amazed the group of eight-year-olds. *Magic.* They hung their stained pages with clothespins on a string they had tied between two branches and waited for them to dry. Charlie would put their tea paper up against these pages any day. Flipping through the next few pages, she saw the business name *Cobb Mercantile & Trades* with Elias Cobb—Founder underneath. A date was scrolled at the bottom center of the page—November 21, 1792. She continued to peruse the pages, remembering them from before. Rows and columns of the most perfect penmanship listing peoples' names, goods purveyed, cost and remuneration, whether it be cash or a credit account set up with Elias. She continued through the pages and could see where quite a few people had gotten themselves into severe debt with Elias. Notes written in the margins told the tales of Elias' conversations regarding debt collection attempts.

Her food arrived, and Charlie continued examining the book's contents. She was in awe at how well Elias had seemed to have been doing, but at a cost to the locals in the areas he did business in. She took notes for further research, documenting the date range and towns. Upon reaching the end of the first third of the book, the entries changed. No longer documenting transactions and inventory, Elias had begun to document new business ideas and meetings he had with fellow businessmen he met on his journeys. From what Charlie could tell, Elias was a somewhat greedy individual, unwilling to share or bend on what he wanted. This man made enemies; she was sure of it.

Heather pulled up one of the patio chairs next to Scarlett. The landlord had been *kind* enough to leave those for them. He made sure to emphasize his generosity. The prior tenants, in their rush to skip out on him, had left several items behind, the patio chairs being one of them. Sitting with her knees up, she took a long sip of her coffee and said a good morning to Scarlett, who was buried deep in one of the journals Charlie had left for them to research.

"Find out anything cool?" Heather asked. Not receiving an answer, she shoved her foot over and tapped Scarlett on the knee. "Earth to Scarlett...come in, Scarlett," she said, taunting her friend.

"Wha? Oh, sorry," Scarlett began. "I missed that. Totally spaced. Been reading these," she said, gesturing toward the journals. Handing the blue one to Heather, she continued. "Here, take this one. Before you get into it, let me tell you about my morning so far. You have to promise not to wig out though, 'K?"

Heather nodded, said, "'K," set the journal on her lap, and took another sip of her coffee. "Ready, set, go."

With both her wings and notes finished, Charlie paid her check and gathered her stuff. She couldn't wait to share this information with the girls, but she was missing Jared. Knowing he had a somewhat busy day, she hemmed and hawed as to whether she should take a shot he would be home. Silly, but she hadn't been apart from him this long since spring. She decided there was no harm in a quick pop by so she headed north on Main toward Jared's house.

Her short journey over, she slowly skipped up to the front door, gave it a rap, and waited. Nothing. Timing wasn't always her forte, so she sat on the stoop to write a little note.

She scrounged in her crossbody for a piece of paper and pen when she heard the doorknob twist behind her. Looking over her shoulder and hoping to see Jared, she was slightly disappointed when Gunther's face came into frame. Standing over her in his signature patterned shirt and crazy summer tanned body, he said, "Well, well, back again so soon, are we?" Gunther had a way of making her feel giddy. Smiling up at him, she felt guilty that she hadn't noticed his new look the morning before in the poorly-lit kitchen.

"Hey there, Gunther. Yeah, guilty. I was hoping to sneak a quick hello before I head home to meet with the girls. Guessing he's not around, huh?"

"Nope. Pretty sure he's gonna be out for a bit still. Rumor has it the skank of a teacher he got stuck TA'ing for is quite a slave driver. She's definitely going to be taking advantage of the free help. Wanna come in and hang for a bit? Have a Coke with me or something?" Gunther said, holding his hand down to assist her up.

"Uh, yeah, sure!" Charlie said, grabbing his hand and jumping up as her crossbody hit the stoop. "Shit," she said, bending down to stop the pen from making its great escape. She grabbed the rest of her stuff, followed Gunther into the living room, and made herself at home on the couch. Gunther appeared a few seconds later with two Cokes in hand.

"So, what were you up to today, missy?" Gunther quizzed in his super sassy tone.

Charlie filled him in on the boring details of her day so far, then placed the ball back in his court. "How about you? Senior year, huh? You have any grand plans? Or are you just gonna ride the easy train?"

Gunther let out the most righteous laugh Charlie had heard in a long time. "Honey," he said between giggles, "I plan on doing everything and nothing all at once. But, seriously, the few classes I'm taking are definitely off-plan. I have enough of the required stuff to get the degree. Now I'm going to have some fun with my brain."

Charlie nodded in solidarity with that last statement and finished telling him about her plans to take a little break to explore and why.

"Heck, yeah!" Gunther said, holding his hand up for a high five. Humoring him, Charlie reached up and gave it a slap.

"As a matter of fact, I think I'll have some pretty cool stuff to research while in these classes. Just waiting to meet with Heather and Scarlett to see what they came up with on their end of things. Remind me to share the cool stuff I found in Tennessee with you at some point. Actually, I'd love to maybe talk to your aunt Kezia again about two of the items if you think she'd be up for a phone call? She was such a help with the Astrid saga, maybe she could shed some light on what's happening here."

"Any chance to talk about spooky shit, she's down," Gunther said.

"Cool, I'll keep her in mind if her help's needed," Charlie said.

Heather sat across from Scarlett, sure her mouth was gaping at what she was being told. "Let me see your hands!" she exclaimed, leaning toward Scarlett. Peering down at her friend's unmarred palms, she continued. "So, you *felt* the heat? Like actually *felt* it?"

"Yeah, literally as if my hands were placed flat on the stove top," Scarlett replied. "That, mixed with the voice I heard when Charlie left, and I got totally spooked. The book you're holding, and this one here, are from the same witch, but her energy was totally in a different place between the two. I'd like to explore this more with the three of us together. Safety in numbers and all," she finished, looking to Heather for agreement.

CHAPTER TWENTY-SEVEN
MARGARET FUCKING COBB

ON HER WALK BACK from Jared's, Charlie thought about her experience earlier when she tapped into the energy that brought her mom, well, her mom's essence to her. A year ago, this wasn't even the tiniest possibility. She had just been a student, working hard, doing the things she was "supposed" to do, and not knowing there was much else in the world. Naïve—she was completely naive. Birdie should have pushed her harder to learn about this stuff. She wished she had. Marcus kept reminding her there was so much for her to learn. Shaking her head, she counted the dandelions popping up through the sidewalk cracks. Charlie couldn't imagine what was to come if this was truly only the beginning.

With a deep sigh, she lifted her head to see her street coming up on the left. She really hoped the girls were home. The desire to delve into the books more was eating at her. She had left a note for Jared to call, but if she didn't answer, it would be because they were deep in research mode. However, based on Gunther's statement about the slave driver teacher, she wasn't expecting a call.

Cutting across her yard, Charlie took two quick hops up the brick stairs and opened the door. She saw the girls sitting out back through the patio door. She gave a quick wave and scooted down the hall to drop off her texts and get a little more comfortable. A few moments later, now in super comfy sweats, she exited back down the hall with her ledger and notes.

Cracking the slider, she asked the girls if they needed anything. The replies came quick. "Dew me," Scarlett chirped. "Coke, please!" Heather chimed in. Carrying the sodas out, Charlie said her hellos for the day and passed out the goodies.

While they cracked open the cans, Charlie looked around to see they each had a book with them. Trying not to sound too overzealous, she said, "So, did you guys get a chance to peek through those today?"

Scarlett held her hand out and did a back-and-forth motion while she took a deep swig of her Dew. An over-the-top "Ooooh the burn," came from her lips shortly after exhaling. "I don't know if the bubbles are a different kind than the rest of the sodas, but man, nothing bites like a Dew. Anyhoo...I digress. I did have a chance to have some alone time with the books this morning..." she finished with a slow trail off.

"And?' Charlie pried.

"Well, let's just say, things got weird," Scarlett said with a click of her tongue, shifting her eyes to Heather.

"Charlie! Scarlett burned herself on the books!" Heather said way too emphatically.

"Huh? Burned her hands? How? Are you joshin' me?" Charlie replied.

"Nope. No joke. I got up really early this morning and was running an energy spell on the books. That one, in Heather's lap, great energy. This one here? Wicked crazy energy. Good at first, then baaaaaad," Scarlett explained. She continued to tell the whole tale, ending with the voice.

Mouth open, Charlie blinked a few times before verbalizing her thoughts. "So, you heard a man's voice call me a bitch?" she asked.

"More than that, Charlie," Heather said. "She heard 'bitch,' and I heard weird noises all over my room this morning. I thought it was you playing a joke, but you were already gone."

"Well, fuck a duck," Charlie said, feeling the color drain from her face. "I've been hearing weird thumps, too. At home, I thought it was mice or something, and here, well, I thought it may just be the noises a house makes, you know?"

The girls looked at each other and shrugged.

"Well, in addition to that, both Heather and I were able to go through the books and figured out we definitely have a book of spells and a book of shadows we're dealing with," Scarlett said. "This one, the one that had the good energy, is the book of spells. It holds all of…drum roll, please," she said, looking at Heather, who started her best snare drum imitation. Charlie sat on the edge of her chair with anticipation. "Margaret fucking Cobb!" Scarlett shouted, pausing for dramatic effect.

"No way!" Charlie said. "How do you know it's hers? Like for sure?"

"After Heather *finally* woke up," Scarlet said with a wink, "I gave her this one to look through while I worked on the more nefarious one. She found the first few pages were missing and-or damaged, and, well—Heather, you tell her," Scarlett urged as she took another sip from her can.

"So, yeah! This part here," Heather said, pointing to the clump of pages in front of the book. "These are useless, but see here, the next few pages? I figured, why not try the old pencil trick on it. Whoever was writing was using a pen that required pressure, and I remembered my dad teaching my sister and me how to use different techniques to leave each other secret messages. One was the lemon juice thing, and the other, the pencil trick." As if seeing the confused look on Charlie's face, she explained. "You know how writing leaves an impression on the pages below it? Well, you take a sheet of paper and place it over the page and lightly rub pencil lead over it to make the writing appear. Like this!" She flipped the page, performed the aforementioned steps, and there it was. The rubbing of the pencil had revealed several things sprawled across the page, one of them being Margaret's name.

"Wow!" Charlie said. "That's amazing! So you know it's Margaret, and now we know Elias was married to a witch. What else was there?"

Heather and Scarlet took turns explaining the various spells, recipes and incantations in the book. "There are spells for protection, love, finding lost items, and healing spells. This book is filled mainly with the latter and some recipes. It seems she was a local naturalist, and this is where she housed her most used and requested spells. Then there's this," Scarlet said, holding up the other.

"This one, I believe, is her book of shadows," Scarlett continued.

"Wait, isn't that what the other one was? I'm confused," Charlie said.

"Similar," Scarlett said. "The difference being the book of spells is just that—the recipes and incantations that make up the spells. The book of shadows is *also* a spell book, but the difference being this one also contains dreams, journals, and examples of when she would use a spell. Then why and how it turned out for her. This one she would keep to herself. The other, she would keep out on her shelves with her herbs and materials."

"Ok, I see, I think. Maybe a quick flip through will help me visually square it up," she said, taking the book of spells from Heather.

"Wow. So, I scanned through this before and just assumed these were journal entries. You guys really do have a spell for every occasion, huh?"

The girls chuckled. "Yeah, if you need something, anything, there's pretty much a spell for it. Not recommended, mind you, because spells can get you in trouble if you aren't pure and clear on your intent, but they're available," Scarlett said.

"Just because you *can* doesn't mean you *should*," Heather finished.

"Hey, hand me that one if you don't mind," Charlie asked Scarlett.

"Ok, I'm pretty sure you're going to find this one very interesting, especially toward the end."

Charlie opened the book and began to peruse its pages. She and Tilde had briefly looked it over, and then she had attempted to get into it the night she had that vision. Turning page after page, she saw spells and drawings. Just like Scarlett mentioned, there were journal entries. Lots of them. Skimming, she noticed that they almost all revolved around Elias and Margaret's life at the house. Charlie approached the halfway point when she started to see other names mentioned. Names Charlie recognized from the ledger. *Peculiar.* Then one name—Betsy—became more prevalent.

"You're almost there," Scarlett encouraged.

A few pages further, and some sketches and drawings revealed several images. One was of the house. "This! This is the house I found the books in. It's a little more simplistic here, but this is it! Benji told us it had been modified over the years. Wow! This is so wicked cool! And this, this is the…"

"That's your fucking brooch!" Heather interjected with the enthusiasm of a kid on Christmas morning.

"Woah," Charlie whispered. "And this must be Elias," she finished, staring into the eyes of Benji's ancestor's dark, soulless eyes. She shook off a chill, then took in the rest of his features—the lips, the sunken cheekbones. He seemed small. Small but menacing.

"Now turn the page," Scarlett instructed.

Charlie did, and as she read the title of the spell, she gasped.

"It seems that dear Margaret cast a spell that banished Elias' soul to be trapped here forever. Based on her journal entry two pages over, she used the help of Elias' mistress, Betsy, to invoke the spell. This, here, is real life drama!"

"This is so crazy, so…" Charlie stopped searching for the words to describe what was running through her mind.

"Yeah, totally," Heather said with a nod.

"There's a lot more," Scarlett said. "I think we need to sit together tonight and work through this. There's more to all of this than just some cool finds in an attic, and I want to see if we can pick up on it if you're okay with trying? I was telling Heather, safety in numbers and what not," Scarlett said, taking another gulp of her Dew.

"Yeah, I'm totally cool with that," Charlie responded.

The trio finished up their drinks and parted ways for a bit to tackle some more of the mundane moving stuff when Charlie realized she hadn't called her dad since getting back. She then remembered they hadn't even plugged any of the phones in yet. Digging through her box labeled side table, she found her phone. Placing it on the nightstand, she looked around the room for the jack. It was on the wall by her closet. Cursing the short cord she had brought with her, she walked over and slid the plug in. Lifting the handset, she set it to her ear in search of a dial tone. Success! She dialed her dad. He picked up and didn't even greet her.

"I hope this is my remiss daughter who isn't in a ditch or jail cell calling me to tell me so." Charlie fought back a giggle after hearing the sternness of his voice. He was never really ever good at feigning stern. She shyly replied, "Yes, this is her. Sorry, Dad. We had that long drive, crashed early at Jared's, then it's been non-stop this whole time. I literally just unpacked my phone two secs ago. Cross my heart."

"Mmmhmm," Dale said. "Well, ok. Glad you got there safe and everything's ok. Settling in a bit?"

"Sure am," Charlie answered. She spent the next fifteen minutes or so filling him in on her visit to the registrar and the unpacking. She conveniently left out the other stuff for now, especially the near rear ending on the drive over. He filled her in on the home updates. The house was officially on the market as of that day. He reserved a moving van for pick up the weekend, and he would be heading out to Ohio soon thereafter. He promised he would call with more updates as they happened.

"Charlie, have fun, honey. Take time to just have fun. Promise me that. Oh, and give a quick call to your grandparents when you can, please."

"Will do, Dad." Charlie replied.

CHAPTER TWENTY-EIGHT
FUN AND GAMES

LATER THAT DAY, as agreed, the trio congregated back together. Heather suggested the patio may be the best spot for later as they could utilize the concrete pad. They all scrounged around in the kitchen, looking for something to have for dinner. The realization that none of them had gone grocery shopping hit them. Standing with the fridge open, Scarlett announced there were only sodas and a handful of beer.

"Nothing here," Charlie sounded off, opening cabinet after cabinet.

"Ugh," Heather blurted. "We just had pizza last night. Any ideas?"

The three stood and looked at each other. It was too early in the evening—and the year, for that matter—for the food truck. "We could walk down to the deli and bring something back, I guess," Charlie offered. Consensus met, they left on a mission to gather sustenance.

Heather was the first to reach the front door. Both Charlie and Scarlett had their hands full of bags, so with her one free hand, she did the honor of unlocking and opening the door. The girls filed in one by one and headed to the kitchen. Immediately, they were stopped dead in their tracks by the spectacle that lay before them. Every cabinet door and drawer in the kitchen was wide open. Dropping the bags to the floor, they stood, mouths wide open in shock.

Scarlett was the first to speak. "Is everyone seeing what I'm seeing?"

"What the heck," Charlie said, walking over to close the fridge and some cabinets.

Heather closed the dishwasher and cabinets on the other end. Scarlett snuck in and grabbed a knife from one of the drawers.

Scarlett gave the other two a *come-on look*, and the three formed a tight circle, then shifted to check out the upstairs bedrooms. Heather's room, nothing. Charlie's, nothing. All exhaled sighs of relief and turned to head down to the common area. Nothing. Releasing the knife to her side, Scarlett said, "Well, it seems whoever did that has left."

"Maybe it was the old tenants," Heather suggested. "You know, coming back for something they left behind? Mr. Roach did say they left in a hurry."

"Maybe," Scarlett replied. "But Mr. Roach changed the locks, so odds are it wasn't them."

"Unless," Charlie began, "unless *we* left the slider unlocked."

They ascended back to the kitchen and tested the door. Sure enough, it was unlocked.

"We gotta get better at locking that," Heather said.

"Ok, so this could totally be a prank of some sort. Like someone getting their jollies freaking the *girls* out."

Charlie nodded, but she knew better. Her *gut* knew better.

With their minds settled a bit, they grabbed their bags and began to unpack them. Scarlett loaded the fridge with more beer and sodas while Charlie and Heather set out the subs on the table.

"You wanna go over this real quick in case there's something I'm missing with all this?" Charlie asked, lifting the ledger and her notes from her lap.

"Shoot," Scarlett said.

"Bang!" Heather popped with her classic giggle.

Charlie handed the ledger to Scarlett, who scooted closer to Heather so they could look at it together. Charlie guided them through the pages, explaining her thoughts on it.

"Do you agree that there seems to be something dark and nefarious about how Elias ran his business?"

"Yeah, he seems to not be on the up and up," Scarlett said.

"Was there even a mafia way back then?" Heather asked shyly.

The trio laughed at that mental image and quickly dispelled the idea of a mafia. But they all agreed more research needed to be done.

"Hey, before I forget! You weren't the only one who got to practice today. I had a bit of time earlier, and I used some stuff Marcus taught me to reach out to my mom. Well, her energy, at least. I had something going until a douche on wheels rolled by, killing my concentration." Charlie threw her hands in the air and continued to fill them in on what she had seen and experienced.

"Thatta girl!" Scarlett said. "Baby steps! We'll have you full Wicca in no time."

Dinner out of the way, the girls gathered the items to give their plan a go. Scarlett had gotten a head start on things by placing three mats down, just far enough apart that they could form a circle with their arms. She had laid out some candles in the center and placed the other items, including the books and some stones, to her left. The other items were set out. "We're almost ready," Scarlett said. "Anyone have to pee or anything before we start? We can't stop once we do."

"I think we're all set. Now what?" Charlie asked.

"Now we set up the circle," Scarlett answered.

Making a large circle on the concrete with a piece of chalk, Scarlett carefully paid attention to the circumference. As she did, she lightly murmured incantations under her breath. Once the circle was marked, Heather placed the crystals at regular intervals along the chalk line, also muttering incantations as she went. Scarlett instructed Charlie to place the candles in the center of the circle, handed her a book of matches, and said, "Now repeat after me." Charlie repeated the incantations word for word as she lit each candle. To her surprise, as she finished lighting the last one, the chalk line and crystals began to glow faintly.

"That's our cue to get started," Scarlett stated.

Each sat down in their spots, making sure they were close enough to form a circle with their arms. Scarlett placed an additional moonstone in front of Heather, an opal in front of Charlie, a zircon in front of herself, and her quartz centered with the candles.

Hands joined, their collective energy continued to flow as Scarlett stated their intentions and called forth the goddesses to aid in their truths.

Listening with her eyes closed, Charlie began to hear the voices of other women in the distance. Her mind then seemingly flew her over tree tops. Winding in and out between the plethora of trees, she swore the leaves were actually hitting her face. Cresting over the edge of the forest, she saw the pond that she, Jared, and Benji had gone swimming in; at least, she believed it was the same pond. The size, though, was much larger, and it was completely enveloped with trees. A quick dip in her trajectory and she was now hovering in front of the house from the sketch. From here, the voices were louder, clearer. She could hear the conversation forming in the air around her. Focusing harder, she heard,

"When did you decide that my husband was yours to claim?"

A timid voice began its reply. "I promise thee, I had no knowledge Elias was married. He filled my head and my heart with lies. Convenient lies. I had no reason to distrust him when he shared with me his world outside of his travels."

Wanting to see what was transpiring, Charlie attempted to force her body to descend closer to the windows. It did not budge. She continued to float, the words infiltrating her ears, but, without context. Completely flustered, she panicked and lost her connection.

Scarlett found herself in an unfamiliar place. She looked around and saw a narrow hallway, dimly lit with candles in wall sconces. She noticed half a dozen doors before her, each closed and fixed with a numbered plaque. *A hotel*, she thought. *I'm in a hotel.*

Concentrating, she picked up on ancillary sounds as they flowed down the hall toward her. Using her energy, she moved her vision slowly down the hall, and in doing so, was able to pick up on, and pinpoint, the sounds that were resonating. From one door, she could hear snoring. The next, she heard raucous male voices regaling others with their stories and placing bets. Honing in tighter, she finally heard what was undeniably a couple in the throes of passion. Moans of pleasure crescendoed over any and all sounds she had been hearing prior. Male. Female. Singularly and in unison. She felt her cheeks flush as a moment of guilt flowed over her. Realizing guilt had no place in a vision she focused in more as the pleasure spiked to screams. *Pleasure?* she wondered. *Pain?* She couldn't tell. Just as she was about to switch her focus, the door opened and a man peered up and down the hallway. She knew this face from the sketch—Elias Cobb!

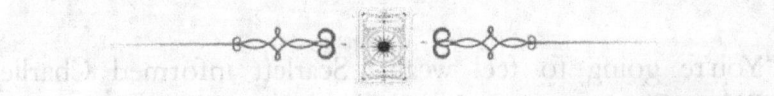

Heather allowed the energy to flow through her. Time stood still as she waited for her vision to reveal itself. Moments later, she heard crying. Were these tears of joy? Following the energy, Heather floated through the space, not knowing what to call it exactly. It wasn't dark, and it wasn't light. It reminded her of that weird in between. Kind of like the sky under a full moon. That was it. The crying continued as if it were surrounding her. Then a wail. Torment? Sorrow? Heather waited for the sound to repeat itself, and soon it did. This time, the wail was followed by a female voice. "You're doing well, my dear. Keep breathing. We want to control your breathing until…" Another wail, and another. Then silence. Heather waited for what seemed like an eternity. A smack, or perhaps a crack, echoed, and before it could complete, another cry resonated; this time it was a baby. Powerful, strong cries circled Heather, then a soft, "Congratulations, Ms. Cobb; it's a boy."

Calling their energies back to center, Scarlett thanked the goddesses for their assistance and guidance and closed the gateway.

Each of them released their hands and let their arms fall to their sides.

"You're going to feel weak," Scarlett informed Charlie. "Relax. Clear your mind, and chug some water if you need to."

Heather rolled her shoulders. "Man, you don't realize how tense you get. You'd think I'd know by now."

"Take your time. When we're ready, we can talk," Scarlett said as the trio laid back to reflect.

The girls took their time processing and coming to grips with what had transpired during the spell. Once settled back into her skin, Heather was ready to talk through her vision. She raised herself up onto her elbows and saw both Charlie and Scarlett lying toe to toe on their backs, staring up at the night sky. Unwilling to be the first to break the silence, Heather voraciously chugged water. She needed to know what the others experienced before making a final decision on what she had witnessed. Shaking off a chill, she laid back down to wait.

Lying still, Scarlett stared up at the night sky in an attempt to recenter herself. She knew from experience what spells like this could do to your life force and the tricks it could play on your mind. She felt bad for Heather, a relative newbie, and Charlie, a complete neophyte. They had to be whirling from what they just experienced. Scarlett, however, could not aid them until she, herself, got her mind and energy back to level. So she laid there. On her back. Staring into the night sky. Unable to shake Elias' image from her brain.

Wow was all she could think. Lying on her back, Charlie had started to mentally put some of the pieces together. She *knew* these were the same women from her prior visions. *How* to interpret what she saw, however, was a completely different story. Slowly releasing her brain from its fog, Charlie could see someone moving in her peripheral vision. She turned her head and saw Heather lean up, picking at her already way too short nails. "Hi," resonated from her dry throat. It was all she could manage to squeak out.

"Hey!" Heather replied. "I'm so glad you're back to reality!"

From the other side of Heather, Scarlett wriggled to an upright position and took a long swig of water. "Wow, what a trip, huh?" she said, exhaling. "You guys ok? This was way more in depth than I thought we would go. Surprised even me."

"I still feel like my brain is a bit Jello-y," Charlie replied. "I have a ton more questions than I do answers, that's for sure."

"You guys ready to talk about it?" Scarlett asked.

"I've never really done something quite like this before," Heather said, looking over to Scarlett as if for guidance. "Where do we start?"

"Well, I guess we can go around clockwise. I'll start. Charlie, can you take notes for now? I can take over when you go," Scarlett said, handing Charlie a small notepad and pencil.

With a nod, Charlie accepted the pencil and pad and flipped to a blank page. She took notes as Scarlett went through her vision in a very matter-of-fact and emotion-free manner. Heather was next. Charlie was completely flabbergasted at the emotional state Heather was in. Charlie wrote feverishly in an attempt to keep up with Heather and could tell

Heather was particularly spooked by what she saw. Charlie took a deep breath, knowing her turn was coming soon. Charlie took the last few notes from Heather, then handed off the pad and pencil to Scarlett to begin her tale.

Scarlett scribbled the last of Charlie's vision down, and a collective sigh rang through the night air.

"That was intense," Heather said. "I think I need a beer now. Can I get anyone else one?" she asked, standing to enter the house.

"Yes," was the response from both Scarlett and Charlie. Heather returned, beers in hand, and joined the girls, who had since migrated back to the table.

Charlie took a sip of her beer and suggested they each take a piece of paper to allow for any additional note taking. Divvying up the paper, Scarlett then dug in her satchel to scrounge up a few writing utensils. She began the conversation. "So, we had hoped to learn more. It seems we have. But in doing so, we have opened up an even bigger can of worms, so to speak."

"I'd say," Heather responded.

"So, here is what we know." Scarlett went through the timeline as Charlie had discussed it with them before. "Now, tack on what we each just experienced, and let's see if we can find anything that syncs up."

They each took their time writing their timelines and making connections between the journals, the visions and the other experiences. One by one, they read off their thoughts and ideas as to what could be going on. Frustrated, Charlie threw her hands up. "I can't make sense of any of this. We know, based on my visions, and now Scarlett's, that Elias was more than likely cheating on his wife. We also know that he seemed to be unscrupulous in his business dealings. So where does that leave us?"

"I think we need to research some more," Heather said. "See if we can find any actual information on Elias and Margaret. Do you think Jared's friend has had a chance to talk to his dad yet?"

Charlie shrugged. "Hopefully. I'll talk to Jared tonight. I can ask him then."

"Well, there's always the library," Scarlett said. "Worst case, we could try this again in a few days. I'd rather see what we can do without the magic first, though."

Draining the last of their beer, the girls decided to call it a night and parted ways, promising to think more on what had transpired that night and review the notes with a fresh mind.

Making sure to lock the slider, the trio headed their separate ways for the evening.

CHAPTER TWENTY-NINE
CHANCE ENCOUNTER

CHARLIE LOOKED AT THE CLOCK; it was too late to call her grandparents. She'd have to remember to try and give them a ring tomorrow. Instead, she chose to shower and get her jammies on. Tasks completed, she called Jared. On the fourth ring, she gave up, setting the handset down on the cradle, not knowing that she just missed the *hello* on the other end.

Too wired to sleep just yet, Charlie decided she'd watch something on the TV. She ambled over to turn on the set and grab her remote. Flicking through the channels, she attempted to find something to watch. With everything that had been going on, Charlie had lost track of what day it was. She replayed the last few days and deduced it must be Tuesday. Wishing she had picked up the *TV Guide* when she was out earlier, Charlie tried to remember what her normal Tuesday night show was and channel surfed her way into the end of an episode of *The Wonder Years*. She laid her head back to wait for *Roseanne* to start. The phone's ring startled her upright and triggered a few expletives.

"Hello," she answered.

"Heya, babe," Jared said from the other end. She smiled. "Did you just call and hang up on me?" he asked.

"Nooo, I let it ring and gave up right before the machine was set to pick up. How'd you know it was me?"

"Hey, you're not the only one with powers. Mine just happens to be *69," he finished with a healthy belly laugh.

Charlie snickered and said, "Such a wise guy. So, how was your first day with the new professor? Gunther mentioned she's kind of hard ass."

"Yeah, she is something, for sure. Younger. Trying to assert herself in a predominantly male field here. So, I guess she's decided she needs to work twice as hard to prove her worth. That means by default I have to work twice as hard to keep up. My guess is my weeknights for the foreseeable future are shot. I'm sorry," he said.

"Ugh. Well, that's bogus. The girls and I kind of had a thing tonight, and I was hoping we could team up for research like last time," Charlie said wistfully.

"What did you guys do, exactly?" Jared inquired.

"Scarlett set us up and we did an energy spell. She, Heather, and I. It was crazy! We each ended up in different places and saw a unique past event or what we think were past events. We aren't sure yet. Also, it all seems to tie to my past visions, and Elias, somehow. Hence the research. Since you won't be available, do you think you could spare a phone call to Benji to see if he's talked to his dad at all, or if he's planning to? We have some questions we would like to ask," Charlie said.

"I haven't, but I'm sure I could. If you want to drop off the questions in the next day or two, I can ask," Jared offered.

"That'd be great!" Charlie said with a smile.

"Just do me a favor, please," he began.

"What?" Charlie replied.

"Be careful. You don't know exactly what you're playing around with here. I know Scarlett is into all that stuff, but are either her or Heather truly experienced enough to make sure you're safe? There are so many things that could go wrong. We learned last year what levels of threats there are. I just don't want anything bad to happen to you. I know you have Marcus watching over you, but he's not always there, either. I'd feel much better if you promised to stick to traditional research for a bit and leave the hocus pocus alone," he finished.

"I promise to be careful. But I can't promise much more than that. Things are getting weirder and weirder," she said

"What? How so?" Jared asked.

Charlie filled him in on the noises increasing, the kitchen mishap, and the door being left unlocked.

"This is *exactly* what I mean, Charlie. Things are out there, and they aren't always pleasant," Jared scolded.

Charlie sighed deeply, then changed the subject. The pair talked for another hour about *this and that,* and then said their goodnights, promising to check in with each other soon.

Setting the phone on the cradle, Charlie realized she and Jared had talked their way completely through *Roseanne* and the late-night news. Charlie surfed the few options she had left this late at night and relinquished herself to sleep.

The next morning, Charlie surprised herself at how late she had slept in. For the first time in a while, she had no plans, and honestly, it felt good. Meandering out to the kitchen, she set coffee to brew and poked around in the fridge. Realizing that their quick run the night before had not really set them up for success in the breakfast department, Charlie decided to take some time today to stock up on some basics. The dining hall wouldn't be an option until Sunday, so they would need some provisions other than chips, cookies, subs, and beer. Charlie poured her coffee, set it on the table, and then went to her room to grab her notebook and pen. She enjoyed the silence and watched as the clouds rolled in from the West. *"Rain's on its way,"* she said to herself, continuing to make her shopping list.

Charlie took the last sip of her first cup and stood to pour another as Heather sleepily walked in with a mumbled, "Mornin'."

"Can I get you a cup?" Charlie asked, gesturing toward the coffee.

"Please," Heather said softly, taking a seat at the table. "What's this?" she asked, tapping the pad.

"Well, we have nothing real to eat here, so I started a list. Anything you wanna add? I figured I'd run to Wegmans before heading to the library for a bit."

Heather looked over the list. She was on a tight budget and this list was concerning her wallet. "Well, I would like some apple juice and some Rice Krispies for sure. I'll think about if I need anything else and get you some cash before you go," she said.

Charlie handed her the mug and said, "Got it."

"How'd you sleep?" Heather asked.

"Good. I was up a bit chatting with Jared, then crashed. Shocked I didn't end up having any dreams from what we did, though," Charlie said.

Heather looked deep into her mug. She took a few breaths and a long sip of her coffee. Charlie was just about to ask what was up when Scarlett entered the kitchen.

"Hey, guys," Scarlett said. "What's happenin'?"

Scarlett slipped a Dew out of the fridge, cracked it open, and took a swig. Charlie shuddered at the thought of drinking that shit so early in the day—to each their own.

They filled Scarlett in on what she missed, and Charlie took quick notes on Scarlett's request from Wegmans.

"So solid of you to do that," Scarlett said. "I'll throw you some cash before you head out. I'd go with, but I have to meet with one of my professors to review a few things she needs help with. I don't get credit for it, but hey, it is my favorite class this fall, so may as well set myself up as the teacher's pet early in the mix." She shrugged and gave a wink.

They laughed and continued small talk before separating off to go do their own things.

Heather plopped on her bed. Not being able to share the visions with Charlie was eating her up. She knew her visions were set in the future, but that was the thing about her visions—she could never tell if they would be today, tomorrow, or years from now. She also knew there was a chance her visions were wrong and could mean something different than what she was seeing. She laid back, slid her headphones on, and pressed play. The soothing sounds of Depeche Mode came through and settled her brain. As Dave Gahan's voice flowed, she released her worries by reminding herself that Charlie had Marcus and he wouldn't let anything bad happen. With that thought, she dozed off.

Charlie got dressed for the rainy day ahead—jeans, tank, flannel, and her raincoat. All the layers together were a tad steamy, but both Wegmans and the library would be colder, so she stuck with her instincts. Grabbing her crossbody, list, backpack, and the cash left on the table by the girls, she slipped out the door and hopped into Juicy. Wegmans was just outside of the walking comfort zone, especially with this large of a trip. Tuning to WVBR, Charlie hoped they had decided to migrate back to progressive rock, but she was disappointed when she heard Journey. She quickly flipped through the stations and landed on WICB, where Siouxsie sang *Dear Prudence*.

Charlie wound her way into the Wegmans parking lot just as the skies opened. Unable to find her umbrella under the seat, she flipped up the hood on her raincoat and made a run for it. Receiving a cold blast of air as she entered the main door, Charlie released a cart from its corral and began her shopping. While she was not a fan of grocery shopping in general, something about Wegmans put her in a happy place. Rounding the corner of the cereal aisle, Charlie almost collided with another shopper. She looked up; it was *him!* The guy from the registrar's office. She felt her cheeks flush yet again and smiled awkwardly at him. "Sorry 'bout that," she said.

"No worries, luv," he said, flashing another crooked smile her way. Again, his accent melted her.

Charlie was not sure if she giggled, snorted, or worse yet, became mute, but whatever she did, it caused a peculiar reaction on his part. Wide eyed, he nodded and rounded the corner, not taking his eyes off Charlie.

Odd, she thought. *If I didn't know better, I'd swear he was afraid of me.*

Charlie shook the feeling off and continued up and down the aisles until all the items were checked off her list. When she was ready to check out, Charlie slid into the shortest line. She paid for everything, then stopped short at the doors, noticing the rain was continuing its assault on the parking lot. With a sigh, she figured her best bet was to stay in the A/C and grab a fountain drink over at the café and try and wait it out. She didn't have anything super perishable in her bags, so she did just that. Not twenty minutes later, the coast was clear, and she took her haul back to the house to unload.

All unloaded, she tossed the bags in the bin and headed out to go to the library. The sky still threatened rain, so again, Charlie chose Juicy to get her there.

Charlie arrived in the library lot just as the sun was beginning to peek out behind the storm clouds. She looked out through the windshield and gauged the rainfall. *Looks like it's slowing down,* she thought. Charlie decided she didn't want to have to deal with her raincoat once inside, so she shed it and laid it on the front seat. She grabbed her crossbody and backpack, then headed in. There were several items she wanted to delve into, so she figured the first place to start would be the card catalog. Finding a quiet spot opposite the fishbowl, she placed her stuff down.

Plucking up a notepad and pen, she walked toward the catalog and inhaled deeply. This, the smell of books and knowledge; she would never get tired of this. Smiling, she arrived at the large wooden structure, set her notepad on top, her pen behind her ear, and slid open individual drawers in her search. Jotting down the information from the cards, she soon had a rather large list to start her treasure hunt. She closed the last of the drawers and made her way around the library in search of the books she would need. With her arms full, Charlie maneuvered back to her spot, set the books down with a loud plop, and sorted them into smaller, more approachable stacks.

Charlie settled in, opened her backpack, and pulled out her Walkman. She popped open the device to see what cassette she currently had in. Bananarama—**Wow!**. That was not the music she would need for research mode. Digging deeper in her bag, she felt the familiar shape of another cassette case and pulled it out. *Progressively Speaking* was written on the spine in Ramona's bubble letters. She had made this mixtape and played it for Charlie on her visit. Charlie loved it so much she asked for a copy. This was the mood she was going for. Sliding the cassette into the Walkman, she placed her headphones on and pressed play. The sounds of Echo and The Bunnymen filled her ears. She internally hummed along with *Bring on the Dancing Horses* as she set up the rest of her area.

Charlie looked at the stacks before her and chose to start with some history of the Jonesborough area to see if she could find any information on Elias himself. Nothing. Moving on to the next stack, she found some more in-depth information on the brooch. The documentation confirmed what Lowell and Scarlett had already told her. In addition, she found more examples of the varieties of witch's hearts. She was also able to do a deep dive into the folklore surrounding the Luckenbooth and the origins of the pieces. She was surprised to learn that they were named after the tenements that stood originally in the High Street of Edinburgh, Scotland. Booths were set up along these buildings where people would sell their goods, jewelry being one of the options. She read on to find that, just like Lowell had said, their purpose changed over time. With a grasp of the brooch complete, Charlie decided to take her research to the microfiche.

Charlie approached the librarian to ask for assistance. A few minutes later, she was set deep in the bowels of the library in front of a microfiche machine. A small stack of cases containing the cards she would need to research sat next to her. Listening to *West End Girls,* she scanned through card after card and unfortunately came up empty with regards to anything related to Elias Cobb. Frustrated, Charlie packed up the cases, turned off the machine, and returned to the main level of the library. While the day wasn't a total waste, she did feel defeated. Not one to accept defeat, however, she gave one final last-ditch effort to try and gain some information on Elias.

"I was wondering," she said to the librarian. "I need to research a particular family in Tennessee—lineage and their social contributions to the local commerce. Do you by chance know how I could go about doing that? I struck out here," she said, sliding the cases toward the librarian.

"Well, of course I can help you with that!" the librarian replied in a pleasant tone. "It will take a little bit of time, but I can reach out to the local college down there and do a university-to-university transfer of some items that may help you out. If you can leave me a list of the topics, I'll research our system and compile a list for you. Think you could swing back tomorrow to review the list before I request the transfer?" she finished, looking at Charlie.

"Oh! That'd be amazing!" Charlie answered. She grabbed the pen from behind her ear, jotted a few topics down, and slid the list over to the librarian. "Thank you so much!" Charlie said. "I'll see you tomorrow about the same time?"

"Perfect," the librarian said with a nod.

Charlie strutted over to her table and began to close up shop for the day. She looked at her watch and was surprised at the time. Something about a library made time seem to just disappear. Remembering her need for the *TV Guide*, Charlie made a pit stop at the local drugstore, then headed back to her house. It was the perfect time to give her grandparents a ring—after supper time but before *Jeopardy!*

Charlie made a grilled cheese and took it and her Coke to her room. Settling in on her bed, she dialed her grandparents' number. Two rings and Eleanor's voice greeted Charlie.

"Hello, Eleanor speaking."

"Hi, Grandma!" Charlie said.

"Walter! It's Charlie!" Eleanor called. A few shuffles of a handset and a clearing of the throat and Charlie heard her grandpa on the other end.

"Why Charlie, how's my favorite granddaughter?" he joked.

"Your *only* granddaughter is doing fine, Grandpa," Charlie replied.

"Why, yes, of course," Walter said. "So are you settled back in at college, dear?" he continued.

"Yep. Well, mostly. I still have a few boxes to unpack but thinking I can tackle that this weekend," Charlie said.

"How's that dear boy Jared?" Eleanor asked.

"He's fine, Grandma. He's been busy since we've been back. He's a teaching assistant to a very needy professor this semester," Charlie said.

"Isn't that nice," Eleanor replied. "And you? You're in a new place this year, if I understood your father correctly."

"Sure am. I'm sharing an off-campus house with Scarlett and Heather. I met them last year, and we kind of hit it off. So no more dorm life for me," she said.

"Well, that's wonderful," Walter replied. "When do classes actually start for you?"

"Monday. Hey, have you heard from Dad lately? I know he was loading up for his migration this weekend to Chagrin Falls."

"As a matter of fact, he called earlier. He should be here sometime Saturday. He'll stay with us that night, then we'll help him out Sunday when his truck arrives," Walter said.

They continued their back and forth for the next half hour or so, when in typical fashion Eleanor announced that this call must be costing Charlie an arm and a leg. Wishing her a great start on Monday, they said their goodbyes and hung up.

Charlie looked at the now cold cheese-filled bread in front of her and groaned. She took her cold sandwich back to the kitchen and gave it a quick toast-up on the stove. Sneaking a tube of Pringles to take back with her, she made herself cozy and planned her TV agenda with the aid of her recently acquired *TV Guide*.

As she waited for the local news to wrap up, Charlie nibbled on her snack and thought about how busy her life was about to get again. She was already feeling the effects of it through the limited time with Jared. Since they met earlier this year, they hadn't had much time apart as they were both wrapping up their academic years, then summer. Charlie pondered whether time apart would be good or bad for them. Heck, maybe it wouldn't even matter in the grand scheme of things, but she was missing being able to run to him with her theories or research questions. He had the most handsome and wonderfully smart brain to pick.

Realizing she couldn't do much without the research material and since her time was pretty much free until classes started, Charlie decided maybe it was time to embrace Marcus and his teachings a bit. Outside of the battle last spring, he hadn't given her too much to work with, but what he did, she hadn't really taken time to understand. He said he was limiting her because she needed to understand the whys and the importance of mastering one skill before moving onto the next.

Charlie concluded the best way to do this would be to treat his teachings as if they were one of her classes. With that light-bulb fully on, she stood and walked over to one of the boxes she still had left to unpack. She reached inside and pulled out a stack of spiral notebooks and assigned a color to each of her upcoming academic classes. In the end, she had two left over—one purple and one aqua. These lessons of Marcus' were definitely other-worldly, so she chose to go with the aqua, which was close to the ethereal blue she imagined when she thought of other realms. Charlie carried the chosen notebook back to her spot on the bed, flipped it open, grabbed her pencil case, and decorated the first page with doodles signifying what she envisioned was witchy and other-worldly. She wrote her name, the date, and the heading "The Education of Charlie."

Charlie proceeded to write down the few lessons and exercises that Marcus had shared with her so far, mostly meditation and reflection based. She also decided it could be helpful to mark down the dates, time, and mood she was in when she tried these practices. The list was coming to a close when she heard the knocking again. Just like before, it seemingly came from all directions at once. Soft at first, then progressively louder. Unlike before, however, it continued to escalate in volume until it caused items in her room to vibrate. Some of the vibrations were so strong they sent items around her room shimmying off the furniture and shelves. This auditory assault continued for another three minutes, finally ending in an abrupt boom across the room. That moment, staring at her TV, was when Charlie saw it. Gone was the face of Vanna, and in its place was the face she had come to know was Margaret Cobb's.

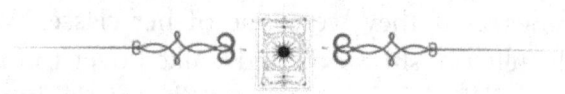

Ears buzzing and heart thumping, Charlie shivered, and minutes later, was still shaking from the experience. Her pen fell from her hand, hitting the floor next to her bed and bringing her back to a more alert state. She shook her head as if to swish the remaining buzz from her ears and looked back over at her TV to see Vanna. But that was not what she had just seen; she knew it. She had seen Margaret! But why? Was Margaret's spirit haunting her? Had this been what was going on the whole time? Had Margaret been with her since

Tennessee? Had the odd noises and visions been Margaret's way of communicating with Charlie?

With the urge to both quickly leave her room and discuss her theory with another human, Charlie tossed her notebook aside, grabbed her dishes, and proceeded to the kitchen. Not hearing any movement in Heather's room, Charlie lightly knocked to see if she could get a reply. None. Another knock, and again, nothing. *Heather must be out*, she thought. Charlie entered the kitchen and set her dishes in the sink. The event had left her parched. Smacking her lips, she reached into the fridge, pulled out a Coke, and proceeded to take an Olympic-size guzzle. Finally coming up for air, she thanked whoever came up with this glorious concoction. She wiped her mouth off on her shirt, took a second swig, and leaned back against the countertop, closing her eyes. Charlie took a few cleansing breaths and aimed in the direction of the stairs. Really hoping she would find Scarlett down in her room, Charlie descended to the lower level, relieved at the sight before her. Scarlett was sprawled on the couch, headphones on and eyeballs deep in Mary Shelley's *Frankenstein*. Charlie smiled and slowly walked over toward Scarlett, announcing her presence so as not to startle her. The last giant arm wave did the trick as Scarlett looked up from her book.

Scarlett slid the headphones down to her shoulders and greeted Charlie.

"Hey, how long have you been home? I didn't think anyone was here today."

"I got back about an hour or so ago. Gave my grandparents a call to check in with them, then worked on some other stuff. You got a minute?" Charlie said.

Scarlett said, "Sure, what's up?"

Charlie filled Scarlett in on the noise, the mini earthquake, and Margaret's image on the TV.

"Well, shit! I know I had headphones on, but that seems like something I would have heard!"

"Actually, I think it was meant just for me," Charlie said sheepishly.

"What? How so? Explain, please," Scarlett said.

Charlie explained her theory that the issues—noises, visions, black-outs, and other stuff that Scarlett and Heather had also experienced—was Margaret.

"I'm thinking she's a ghost or something. Back to haunt me for some reason. I think maybe she latched onto me in Tennessee and hasn't left. Like maybe there's something she needs to tell me. Something that's kept her around all these years. You said you're pretty sure she was a witch, right? Maybe she cast a spell on herself or something?" Charlie said.

"Could be," Scarlett agreed. "Definitely makes some sense. Kind of falls in line with what we all experienced last night, too. Were you able to research anything today?" she asked.

Charlie explained her strikeouts, ending with the positive information about finding some more on the Luckenbooth and the librarian who was willing to attempt a transfer for her. "I'm going back tomorrow to see what she came up with and what we can get sent here. I really want to find out more about Elias and Margaret. Especially now."

"Once it comes in, if you need any help, I'm here for you. I'm sure Heather will be, too," Scarlett offered.

Charlie thanked her and asked if she had any plans for dinner. Scarlett said she didn't.

"Well then, I'll make us something. I'm no chef, but I can whip it together like a fiend. Learned from the best," she said with a laugh.

"You got a deal then, cause I was planning on surviving off Vienna sausages and Dino's the whole year," Scarlett joked.

Charlie headed back up to her room to read more of the journals and ledger in hopes of finding more items that she would need to research. Carefully scanning through the books, she made some notes. She wanted to research the family tree, especially the birth of Elias' child. There was also Elias' business. She had a few bullet points underneath that topic:

a. Articles on his standing within the communities he served
b. Articles on any wrong doings or business-related misconduct

c.   Articles on any disappearances or untimely deaths of his employees, suppliers, or any other folks he would have come in contact with.

She also wanted to research this other woman, Betsy. She didn't have a last name, but maybe, since the town was so small, she could find something in the records. Charlie finished perusing the ledger and the book of spells. She looked down to her side at the book of shadows. Just as she was about to pick it up, her phone rang.

"Hello?" she answered.

"Heya!" Ramona sang. "How's settling in coming along? How's that scrumptious boyfriend of yours?" she said, letting the questions flow like water.

"Hey, Ramona," Charlie said. "I'm ok. Settled in pretty good. Jared's been busy with his new T.A. position. How's it going there? You all registered and ready to start your classes?" she asked.

"Yep, went and took those stupid placement tests. They make you take them when you don't matriculate straight from high school. Had to prove I could write and do basic math," she said, laughing. "I *passed*," she continued. "I'm all set for English, computer science, and psych 101. Figured that's all I wanted to take on to start."

The two continued the conversation, going back and forth on silly things like who was doing what with who, and of course the Lorenzo family drama. Charlie let Ramona know her dad would be on his way to Ohio officially.

"Yup," Ramona said. "I went down and drove by the house. It was really really weird," she finished sadly.

"Yeah, going to take some getting used to, that's for sure," Charlie replied. "So, you wanna hear something kind of cool and super creepy?" Charlie asked.

"Ummmm always!" Ramona said.

Charlie filled her in on the spell session she had with Scarlett and Heather and the subsequent scare she had that night.

"Holy shitballs!" Ramona said. "That's straight-up horror! Please tell me you have your TV unplugged and covered up now!?"

"Well, it's off. But now that you mention it, maybe I should do that, at least for tonight. I don't know if I could get any sleep if I didn't," Charlie said. "I was just about to read Margaret's book of shadows when you rang. If you don't mind the charges, you want to stay on the line with me while I read through? Maybe you can help me out," Charlie suggested.

"Sure thing, girlie. My dad writes off most of these charges anyway. Let's do this!"

Charlie lifted the book to her lap and began to turn the pages. She described the writings and sketches to Ramona as they went through.

"Like Scarlett said, it seems like she was a *good* witch. Most of these spells were for her own use and seem to be helpful in some way, shape, or form. I'm not getting any evil vibes from any of this. Which is why I don't understand why she would be haunting me."

"Well, my cousin Tanya's best friend's brother's girlfriend, is into all the ghost stuff. I know she told Tanya there's all kinds of ghosts. You should look into that when you get stuff from the library. Maybe she has unsettled business or something? Or maybe she's like Astrid and wants to take over your life!? Oh my God Charlie! Do you think that's it?" Ramona cried.

"I don't know, Ramona. That's pretty far-fetched. I mean, it's true, I never would have thought any of this stuff was *really* possible, but look at where I was last year. I can't definitively say no, but it just seems different, you know?"

"Ok, well, maybe sleep with some garlic or a cross or something. Make your bestie feel better," Ramona suggested.

Charlie laughed. "Ramona, that's for vampires, not ghosts," she said, continuing to laugh.

"Oh, yeah," Ramona said, giggling. "I guess it is."

The duo continued to bounce through the pages of the book, reading the diary entries that went along with the spells.

"So she would do a spell, then write about it? Like we used to do in bio or chemistry class?" Ramona said quizzically.

"Yeah, great analogy," Charlie said. "I can see where she would modify the spells, too. Like she would write one, do it, assess it, then make adjustments. Pretty cool, actually."

Charlie and Ramona giggled and commented on the various spells and what they were used for. Ramona wondered out loud if Margaret had turned anyone into a toad or a mouse.

Charlie laughed at the questions because she had thought them herself earlier with Heather and Scarlett.

"No, no toads, no mice. But here's the big spell. The one she used against Elias. It's the last entry in this book." Charlie read the spell and reminded Ramona of her visions.

"So, Margaret and this Betsy chick killed Elias with this spell?"

"From what I saw and felt, that's my assumption. I felt his pain. I saw blood. There are just key pieces missing, you know. Hard to come to a real conclusion on this."

"Totally rad and frustrating," Ramona said. "You think you're going to try that spell thing again with your roomies?" she asked.

"I don't think so. I forgot to tell you—Marcus left me a warning of sorts, also. I think maybe it was his not-so-subtle way of telling me to chill with the magic," Charlie said with a sigh. "Besides, doing this stuff totally leaves you messed up for a bit. Like riding a roller coaster, but not the fun ones."

"Hey!" Ramona said. "My mom's beckoning. Gotta bounce. Miss you already! And because I know we won't catch each other beforehand, have a great first day of school. Be sure to dress all pretty," she said in a sarcastic tone.

"Will do. You too! I'll try and check in once I have the research on this pinned down," Charlie said, followed by a goodbye. She hung up the phone and was about to set the book down when she realized there was something odd going on. Just like the other book, this one's last few pages were stuck together. Lifting it to the light, Charlie could see it was about four pages. She grabbed the plastic cap off her pen and attempted to slide it between the pages, but they weren't giving, and she was afraid they would tear. Just as she was about to call it quits, she had an idea. She jumped off her bed and went to the kitchen.

Charlie filled the tea kettle with water, set it on the burner, and waited. A few minutes later, the steam started to flow, and Charlie lifted the book high enough above the mist so as not to get the pages too wet and also to avoid scalding herself. She rocked the pages back and forth, letting the steam work its magic. It was working! Charlie laid the book on the countertop and began to peel apart the pages one by one. With her mission a success, she gave thanks to her many years of reading Nancy Drew, turned off the kettle, and took the book back to her room.

Sitting back on her bed, she crossed her legs, slid her notebook closer, and looked at the newly released pages. Like the spells before, this last one had a journal entry, too! This was gold! Charlie's eyes widened as she read the words before her. This spell was definitely meant to kill Elias, no doubt about it. The reasons were also revealed. Elias had been having an affair with someone in town. Margaret had found out and began to plot her revenge. This spell—*this* spell would end her husband's miserable, cheating life. Charlie continued to read how the spell had worked as planned. *But wait*, Charlie thought. She reread the pages; again, she felt confusion. The spell didn't kill Elias; the poison in the tea Margaret gave him did. Charlie let out a gasp. She would never know what the spell was actually for because someone had torn the page out from the end of the book.

Charlie threw her head back in frustration, then looked at her watch. She needed to get a move on if she was going to throw dinner together. She carried the book to the kitchen in hopes Scarlett would want to scope it out.

Charlie stood at the kitchen counter, chopping up a package of Oscar Meyer wieners as the sizzle of oil filled the kitchen.

"So are you going to tell me what you're making?" Scarlett asked from atop a stool she had dragged from the common room.

"It's an ancient Bauman secret," Charlie said. "Hey, can you do me a quick favor? Go in the freezer and grab the O'Brien potatoes out for me."

Scarlett looked at Charlie like she was speaking a foreign language, but abided and tossed the bag of frozen potatoes on the counter next to Charlie.

"Can I get you a drink while I'm over this way?" Scarlett asked.

"Coke, please," Charlie said.

Scarlett set the can down on the counter and watched Charlie splash a few fingertips of water into the scalding pan. Steam rose as insanely loud crackles and pops sounded off.

"I'm not even going to pretend to understand what that was for," Scarlett joked.

"It's supposed to let you know if the pan is hot enough," Charlie said with a shrug. "I'm assuming it is," she said, dumping the bag of frozen potato pieces on top of the oil.

Charlie placed a lid on it and turned to lean against the counter. She took a swig of her Coke and explained that the tiny amount of cooking knowledge she had could fill a small cup, but she knew enough to not starve.

"I know nothing about nothing when it comes to the kitchen. Other than how to use a microwave. My parents got one of those two years back and it was a godsend," she said as she laughed.

"Hey, you want, I can go grab my radio and get some tunes up in here," Scarlett offered.

"Heck, yeah. Do it!" Charlie said, turning back to break up the potato chunks.

As Scarlett returned and set the station, they caught the tail end of Blondie's *Rapture* which led into Bowie's *Space Oddity*.

"Perfect," Scarlett said, sighing contently "The coolest place in town, right here."

Charlie chuckled and returned to her cooking. A comfortable silence settled over them just in time for when Taco's *Putting on the Ritz* blasted.

The two sang in unison, well, mostly in unison, to the lyrics while Charlie added the hot dog chunks to the pan. She gave a quick stir and slid over to the fridge to acquire a few eggs. Back at her station she cracked them into a bowl, tossing the shells into the sink-erator. She rapidly whipped the eggs and poured them over the now crispy potatoes and meat chunks. Stirring, she threw in some salt, pepper, and celery seed, then placed the lid back on it.

"Hey, five minute countdown. Wanna get our plates ready?" Charlie asked.

"Aye, aye," Scarlett said, reaching up and pulling down two plates. She grabbed a couple of forks and sat back down to finish her beer.

"Smells intriguing," Scarlett said.

"Oh, just you wait," Charlie taunted.

Charlie and Scarlett gathered their plates and carried them to the common area. They both wanted to watch TV but gave each other a knowing glance before turning it on. Soft, nervous giggles filled the room as *Unsolved Mysteries* came on and they settled in on the bean bags. They continued to watch TV and converse between bites.

"Charlie, girl, you can throw shit together! It's like you know what you're doing," Scarlett said.

"Thanks, but really, it's my mom's influence. I just watched her. It's as simple as knowing your three groups—meat, starch, and vegetables. Once you have one of those picked, it's like spinning the roulette wheel for the rest," she said. "Wait until you have my Spam noodle surprise," she finished. Taking a huge bite of her dinner, she heard the front door open.

"Hey!" Charlie called. "We're down here!"

Heather made her way down, her Doc Martens clumping on the stairs.

"Hey guys, what smells so good?" she asked.

Scarlett filled her in on their roommate's talents and gestured for her to go grab a plate. A few minutes later, Heather was seated next to them with a plate of her own.

"So," Scarlett said. "Charlie here had an encounter today…"

"An encounter?" Heather asked.

"Yep! Tell her, Charlie!" Scarlett prodded.

Charlie told the tale of the noises and seeing Margaret's face. She watched as Heather's face contorted into sheer horror, then stopped. "You ok? I was the one who saw a ghost, but you sure look like you did," Charlie said.

Heather shook her head. "Yeah, I'm ok," she said. "So, what do you think is going on?" she asked.

Charlie explained her theory and added the recently discovered information from the book. "I'm thinking maybe Margaret feels guilty for what she did and hasn't been able to move on. Maybe she was tied to the books since they were hers."

Heather nodded, but kept her mouth shut. She wouldn't swear that Charlie's theory was wrong, but she knew that whatever was coming Charlie's way could not be Margaret.

The evening had gone well, despite not hearing from Jared. The sleep that followed was pleasant and undisturbed. Charlie woke up on Thursday morning ready to take on the library. But first, coffee. She decided to take her mug out onto the patio so as to not wake her roommates. She sat and slowly sipped it, running scenarios through her head. Something felt off. She couldn't pinpoint it. Heather's reaction. It wasn't bad, per se. But it wasn't Heather, either. Heather usually had a lot more to say and contribute. *Don't be silly*, Charlie thought. *She probably just had a long day, and you went and threw a bunch of weird and heavy shit her way.* Charlie finished her coffee, wondering if she should take a moment to practice one of Marcus' little lessons, when she heard what she thought was her phone ringing. She skittered down the hall just as the last ring sounded. Knowing she missed whomever had called, she lifted the handset and dialed *69. The phone rang twice and "Bauman Residence" came through the line.

"Dad?" Charlie asked.

"Hey, Charlie! When you didn't pick up, I figured maybe you were still sleeping. Did I wake you?" Dale said.

With her phone call to her dad complete, Charlie went ahead and got dressed for the day. Not wanting to relinquish summer just yet, she slid on a pair of flip flops, took her empty mug to the kitchen, and quietly slid out the front door. The day, shaping up to be another beauty, allowed her the freedom to once again walk to her destination.

She arrived at the library just as the doors were being unlocked for its approaching visitors. Taking a shortcut through to the circulation desk over by the fishbowl, she took in the extreme quiet and serenity that was the library. Charlie saw the librarian she had spoken with prior and approached.

"Good morning," Charlie said.

"Well, good morning to you, too. I've good news!" the librarian announced. "I was able to confirm that ETSU is in our lending tree, so based on your list, we can go ahead and get those ordered. Did you have any additional items?"

Utterly relieved at the news, Charlie proceeded to give the librarian the new list. The librarian warned Charlie they had approached the possible limit of what she could request. Running through the list again, they decided to drop two of the requests, thinking some of the other items would very likely have what Charlie was looking for. With the amended list completed, the librarian took Charlie's ID card and wrote out the lending slip. She had Charlie sign and promised these would be faxed over momentarily to get the transfer started. The librarian let Charlie know she was estimating about a week's lead time, but that Charlie could feel free to check back in mid-week just to be sure a miracle hadn't happened.

"This early in the year, anything is possible," the librarian said with a wink.

"So, I noticed there was a lot of information directly related to residents of that area, but you also have some items on here that I may be able to assist in getting a leg up on. Follow me over to the occult section."

Charlie followed the librarian quietly through the aisles until they reached a small section tucked away from the hustle and bustle of the main part of the library. Charlie looked at what the librarian was offering. There were probably a hundred or so books covering all things occult related, including witchcraft.

"I think there is a possibility you may find some answers in some of these," the librarian said with a smile. "There's a table right there you can sit at if you like. It should be pretty quiet back here." And with that, she left Charlie to her perusing.

Charlie decided she would start at the upper shelf on the far end and work her way across, kind of like eating corn off the cob. Using her finger, she let it guide her eyes from one book binding to the next. Charlie took books she felt would be of interest from the shelves and carried them over to the table. Surprised that she had already found so many on the first row, she sat down to look them over before continuing.

Taking her Walkman out of her crossbody, she set it on the table and grabbed a pen and paper for note taking. She placed the headphones on and pushed the play button. Luckily, it was the same mixtape from before. The sounds of The Cure's *Fascination Street* flowed through the headphones. Plucking up the book closest to her, she looked at the title—*Witchcraft in the Middle Ages*—and decided to start there. Taking her time at first, she flipped through page after page, skimming to see if anything matched what she was seeking. As her tape clicked to a stop, she realized that if she kept going at this rate, she would be there all day. Charlie refocused and decided to tackle the books with a different approach. She began to utilize the book's index to find keywords. As *Punk Rock Girl* began to play in her ear, Charlie fast forwarded to the more mood-appropriate *Charlotte Anne*. Turning her attention back to the task at hand, she continued with her new way of doing things.

Plucking the last book from the stack, she was amazed at how much faster she was going. She was now able to narrow down a book solely on its blurb and had passed up about a third of what she had already pulled. Charlie stood, stretched, and carried the books over to the return cart at the end of the aisle. A twinge of guilt hit her from knowing that someone was going to have to put them all back up. The guilt assisted her in being a bit more choosy with the next collection. Placing the latest haul on the table, she realized how thirsty she was and made her way to the water fountain around the corner. Several gulps later, her thirst was satiated. She took a moment to look around and was surprised to see how much busier the library had gotten since she had been held up in her little corner. Sauntering back she sat and continued her expeditious research. Two mix tapes, dozens of books, pages of notes, and a very inhuman stomach growl later, Charlie looked at her watch in disbelief at how much time had gone by. She decided enough was enough for this day, packed up, and let her stomach begin to lead her out of the library. With her head down, Charlie fumbled to put her notebook back in her crossbody.

As she collided with someone in front of her, she looked up, ready to fight, when she noticed who it was. *Wow! The universe really wants me to notice this guy.* She felt her cheeks warm and she stammered to apologize.

"Totally my fault," she began. "I wasn't…"

"I wasn't, either," he said with a smile.

Charlie looked up at him and swore he had theme music playing as he spoke.

"Well, I guess we both need to keep our heads up then, huh?" she asked.

"Indeed," he agreed. "My name is Finn," he continued, sticking his hand out for a shake. "And you are?"

"Charlie," she said.

"Nice to run into you, Charlie," he said coyly. "Did I just see you come from the occult niche?" he asked.

"The...what?" Charlie said.

He chuckled and continued with that accent that was currently sending little lightning bolts down to Charlie's toes. "I said the occult niche. That little pathetic hole they allow for those of us who dare to dabble in things other-worldly," he finished with a dramatic flare.

"Oh, yeah," Charlie said. "I was trying to do a bit of research on something. Kind of got a bit overwhelmed, honestly."

"Oh? Do tell," he pried.

"It's nothing, really. I just found a few things on a recent trip that had me questioning witchcraft and spells. I found some stuff, but what I'm really looking for will be coming later this week."

"Where are you headed to now? Would you like a second opinion? Not to boast, but I come from a rather unique household. Plus there's the 'British' of it all, you know," he said, laughing at himself.

"I was going to see if I could find some lunch. I got so caught up in this I lost track of time," Charlie said.

"Mind if I join you?" Finn asked.

Thinking for what seemed like an eternity, Charlie finally replied, "Um, well, yeah, sure, why not."

The duo turned and headed out in search of someplace to eat.

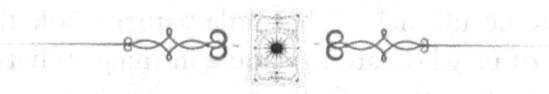

Finding a seat at the small sandwich cafe on campus, the two took turns going up to order. Settling in with their sandwiches and chips, Charlie began the conversation.

"So, you mentioned you're British; that would explain the accent," she said. "But what brought you here to Cornell?"

"Well, I was tired of living in my small little world, in my small little house, in my very small little town, and decided that anyone who is anyone heads to the United States for some adventure," he said in the most horrible fake American accent imaginable.

Charlie groaned as she took a bite of her sandwich. "So, you've been here for how long? I don't remember seeing you around campus before."

"Ah! See, there you go! American's hear what they want to hear and don't listen," he teased. "I came to the United States for an adventure! And I found it. First in California, then Texas, then in DC, where a friend of mine was attending Georgetown University. I hung with her a bit at her flat, observed, and eventually chose to attend myself. I finished my BA there, then decided I wanted to continue. She recommended Cornell as a place to hunker down for my MA So, here I am."

Charlie took another bite of her sandwich. *That means he's older than he looks.*

"So, that makes you..." Charlie began to ask.

"Oh, no, not math!" Finn teased. "That makes me twenty-four this past June. Tell me, why are you researching the occult? You mentioned you happened upon some items that steered you in that direction?"

Charlie crumpled up her sandwich paper and shoved it in her empty chip bag. "Yeah," she began but stopped herself. How was she going to skirt around Jared? Wait, *why* would she skirt around Jared? *Jesus.* "So, my boyfriend, Jared, and I spent the summer traveling and ended up in the town he grew up in." She paused, looking to see if there was any reaction to the boyfriend news. She couldn't quite tell. There may have been an eyebrow raise, but his hair fell perfectly above his green eyes. Charlie shook her head and continued. "We visited his best friend and got a tour of an old family home. I got to take some stuff from the attic home with me."

"What were the items?" Finn asked, completely ignoring the mention of a boyfriend.

Charlie continued to tell the story behind the doll, the books, and the brooch. She mentioned some of her dreams and that the woman who owned two of the books was actually a witch. Finn listened intently and was about to chime in when a small chirp sounded from his wrist.

"Shite!" he exclaimed. "Charlie, I hate to eat and run, but I forgot I have to get to this orientation of sorts. Can we pick this up later? Maybe another day? Can we exchange numbers?" he asked.

"Oh! Of course," Charlie said, not knowing how to react to the sudden stop. Finn jotted down his number on a piece of paper, tore the paper in half, and slid it over to Charlie so she could write her number down.

"Again, so sorry to have to bolt. It was great talking," he finished as he turned and exited the cafe.

Not sure what had just happened, and even more unsure why she was feeling guilty, Charlie turned to head home. As she walked through campus the guilt grew, so she decided to see if she could maybe catch Jared at home by some chance. No luck. Several knocks and not even Gunther answered. She wrote a quick note and slid it under the door, remembering to add the questions for Benji, and promised to try him later that night. Charlie sighed and knew right then and there why she had felt guilty. Finn had intrigued her. They had flirted. She had been so quick to forget Jared, if only for an hour. *Fuck*, she thought. This didn't mean anything. She was with Jared; Finn was an acquaintance. A research tool. A distraction. *"Damn straight,"* she said to herself out loud as she headed up the hill toward home.

Charlie entered the front door and found it quiet and dark. One thing the house lacked was natural light. She made her way down the hall to her room, dropped her crossbody on the bed, and headed to the kitchen to grab a Coke. She wanted to curl up in bed and lose herself in a movie since she knew her free time was about to disappear as classes started. She couldn't, however, shake the fear from the night before. Would she see Margaret again? With a deep sigh, she carried her Coke down the hall, rummaged through her videos, and ultimately chose to get lost in a little Keith and Watts drama. Charlie slid in the cassette and retreated to her bed as Watts furiously played the drums. She let her mind relax, took a large swig of her Coke, and flipped her pillow down to the foot of the bed for optimum movie viewing.

Charlie, wrapped up in the Amanda Jones of it all, snapped out of movie mode thanks to her stomach demanding food yet again. Letting out a sigh, she slid off her bed and made her way over to the VHS player. She pressed pause, took a long stretch, then shuffled her way to the kitchen. The house, still dark and quiet, felt extra eerie. Something she was going to have to get used to. "One of the benefits of not being in a dorm," she said to herself. Charlie riffled through the cupboards and found her target meal for the night. Slipping the blue box of Kraft Mac and Cheese from the second shelf, she placed it to the side of the stove. She leaned down and grabbed a saucepan from its confines, then followed the instructions on the package. A few taste tests and a Coke later, she spooned the cheesy goodness into a monster-sized bowl, grabbed a spoon and her Coke, and padded back to her room. She pressed play on the machine, climbed back on her bed, and finished watching as true love prevailed yet again. Not really feeling a second movie was in her future, Charlie flipped the channels until she found something suitable. As she spooned the last bit of her mac and cheese into her mouth, she heard one of the girls coming through the front door. Charlie let out a "Hey" and heard the all too familiar sound of Heather clumping down the hallway. She giggled. Heather had to have the heaviest walk for someone under a hundred pounds she'd ever met. A few seconds later, she saw Heather's face pop in through her bedroom doorway.

"Heya," Heather said "How's it going?"

"Chill," Charlie replied. "I just finished up dinner. But there's leftovers from before if you want some."

"Cool," Heather replied. "Appreciate the gesture, but I just snagged something on the run. Had my orientation over at the bookstore on Main today. Seems like a pretty copacetic workplace as long as I remember that I can't spend all my money on books," she said as she laughed.

Charlie nodded in agreement.

"Well, I'll chat more later," Heather said. "I gotta fill out a bunch of paperwork and stuff." She said a quick "bye" then headed back down the hall.

Alone again, Charlie peeked at the clock and decided to try Jared. Three rings and no pick up. She sighed, set the handset down on the cradle, just about to release it when it rang. Assuming it was Jared and his *69, she picked up and said, "Hey, babe. Glad you're home."

"Well thanks, babe," a voice with a sultry British accent said back, causing Charlie to almost drop the handset.

"You there?" she heard.

"Uh, oh, um, yeah! Sorry," Charlie answered. "I was expecting someone else."

"Obviously," Finn replied in a teasing tone. "Am I catching you at a bad time?"

"No, really, not at all. What's up?" Charlie asked, trying to sound a bit more civil.

"Well, I was thinking about you after we split this afternoon," he said. Charlie asked, a little too enthusiastically, "You were?" Silence. Awkward silence. Then a clearing of the throat.

"Um, as I was saying. I was thinking after we split up this afternoon. I have some more stories that may help you, as well as a few texts on hauntings. Would you happen to be free at all tomorrow?" he asked.

Charlie said yes, and in order to keep the call more business-like, she immediately went into schedule mode and agreed they could meet for coffee around nine-ish if that worked for him.

Finn agreed and said his goodbyes.

Charlie set the phone down, missing the cradle completely.

Jared trudged up his walkway and let himself into the house. What a week this has been, he thought. Stepping inside, he almost slipped on a piece of paper lying on the floor. He picked it up and recognized the handwriting. It was from Charlie. He smiled. He really missed her. Like, all of her. Odd how she had that effect on him. Flipping open the folded legal paper, he read her note, which wished him a great day and returned her feeling of separation anxiety. He continued to read and saw the reminder questions for Benji. Jared had flopped on his couch by this point. Reaching for the phone on the side table, he dialed Charlie's number. Busy. Never had he wished for call waiting as much as he was wishing for it now. He set the phone on the cradle, sighed, and forced himself up to grab a beer and a half-eaten container of chicken fried rice. Taking his finds back to the couch, he clicked the TV and quickly found a movie to fill the silence. Again, he attempted to call Charlie. Again, busy. *She must be on with Ramona or her dad,* he thought. Tapping the switch, he waited for the dial tone and punched in Benji's number.

"Hello," Benji answered.

"Hey, what's up, dawg," Jared said.

"Jared, dude! Not much, what's up with you? I'm assuming you made it back ok?" he asked

"Yep, a few days back. Been inundated with the new TA position. You back at it, too?" Jared asked.

The two continued catching up until Jared got around to the reason for his call.

"Hey, so, Charlie's been having some really spooky shit happen since we got back. She thinks it's related to your ancestors and that stuff she got from the attic. You aren't going to see your dad anytime soon, are you?" Jared asked.

"Ah, damn, dude. No. I guess I should have led with the bad news. Found out through the grapevine that my pop died earlier this week. Nothing super crazy. I mean, it wasn't a prison riot or a shanking or what not. Just poor health."

"Well, fuck," Jared said. "I'm sorry 'bout that, Benji. Anything I can do for you?" he asked.

"Nope, it sucks, I guess, but it's not like we were close or nothin'. I gotta find a way to let my mom know, though. The prison is taking care of the cremation. I gotta go pick him up. He wanted to be buried in the family graveyard, next to Maw Maw and Pop Pop," Benji said with a slight hitch in his voice.

"Well hey, if you need to talk at all, please call. I'm not around a bunch, but leave a message and I'll get back to you for sure," Jared said.

"Yeah. Righteous. Thanks, bro," Benji said.

And with that, they wrapped up the call, saying they would keep in touch.

Jared placed the handset on the cradle and set the phone back on the side table. Focusing what energy he had left on snarfing down his rice, he finished it off with a long swig of his beer. Eyes heavy, he laid across the couch and shut his eyes. Soon, he was asleep.

Charlie awoke to her alarm and let out a groan. Peeking over at her clock, she gave herself a little pep talk to get moving. The coffee house wasn't too far of a walk, so she had time, but she wanted to be sure to take time to get ready. Why? Who knew. Wrong. She knew. She wanted to leave a more positive impression on Finn. Ugh. *It's got to be the accent,* she told herself. Charlie sat up and decided to pre-game, and headed for the kitchen. To her surprise, there was already a carafe half full waiting for her. Heather must have gotten up before her. Filling a mug, Charlie carried it back to her room and began to choose the outfit for the day. Lifting her window sill, she stuck her hand out and found a chill in the air. *Jeans it is,* she thought. She chose a peach cotton polo to go with it and a pair of flip flops. Slinking into the bathroom, she looked in the mirror. Her skin was looking pretty rad today, so no makeup was needed. She was, however, going to have to run her hair under the faucet to perk the shorter do back up. Turning the faucet to hot, she waited for the temp to catch up to the command. She leaned her head down and ran the water through her locks. Wrapping them with a towel, she turned off the water and strolled back into her room to find her Caboodle with her mousse. Three boxes later, she found it and scrunched the foamy goodness through her tendrils. She gave her head a heave-ho flip up and shook her head from side to side in a way that must have made her look like the Shaggy D.A. Grabbing her Swatch, she realized that she had lost track of time and was borderline running late. Scrambling for her crossbody, she made sure it contained a notebook and pen and scurried out the front door, just missing the ring of her phone.

Jared listened as the phone rang. *She's probably still sleeping*, he thought and hung up. Stretching his neck from side to side, he cursed his couch and his ability to fall asleep anywhere. He needed to be more careful or he'd end up permanently crooked.

Charlie walked briskly down to Cafe Luna, entering the front door, hoping she was first. She was. With a sense of relief, she found a two top at the far end, set her stuff down, and ordered her Americano and a Danish.

CHAPTER THIRTY
WHO'S THE NEW GUY

CHARLIE TOOK A SIZEABLE BITE of her Danish as she waited for her coffee to cool down a bit. She looked at her watch; she still had another few minutes, and well, she had forgotten how good a Danish tasted. Quickly chewing, she popped the rest of the initial one in her mouth, stood, still chewing, and ordered a second. *What happens in the coffee house, stays in the coffee house*, she joked with herself. Charlie carried her newly acquired Danish back to her seat, took a swig of her scalding hot coffee, regretting the act immediately, and began to set up shop. She pulled out her notebook and pen as she saw movement from the corner of her eye. Finn was here. She pushed down a smile and gave him a small wave.

Finn made his way over to the table and said his good morning, then excused himself to go fetch a beverage. He returned, set his tea on the table, and properly greeted Charlie.

Taking a seat, he looked Charlie in the eye and said with a smile "So, you're one of those, huh?"

"One of...?" Charlie asked

"*Those* people who believe early is twenty minutes before, on time is ten minutes prior, and anything else is actually late," he stated, using his fingers as visual aids in his counting points.

"Ahhhh. Well, yes, I guess I am," Charlie said. "I can thank my dad for that one." She smiled.

"Oh, yes, the parental units. Are yours still together?" he asked.

"Well, actually, no."

"Aha! Another child of divorce, like so many these days, eh?" Finn said.

"Not exactly. It was more the death-do-us part thing that separated them," she finished, hanging her head.

"Well, I've gone and stepped in it, haven't I? Bollocks, I'm so sorry. I tend to do this, you know, open mouth, insert foot," Finn said.

"It's ok. You didn't know; you *couldn't* have known. There was no time for it to come up before," Charlie said.

"Do you mind me being a total wanker and asking how?" Finn said.

"Well, see, I wouldn't say you're a *wanker*, exactly. It's just complicated. A crazy long story that leads into this other long story. I don't know if you have that much time," Charlie said.

"If need be, I'm all yours most of today. I purposefully kept myself somewhat free to give myself a break before classes tomorrow," Finn explained.

"Ok. I'm only open to it because you mentioned you come from a *unique* household. Don't say I didn't warn you," Charlie said with a smirk.

Finn sat and stared at Charlie in somewhat disbelief as she ran through her life events from the prior school year. Only stopping to sip her coffee, she kept the tale informative; but vague, so as not to totally spook him.

"Wow!" Finn responded. "That's almost unbelievable. Spectacular, in a tragic way. I know my mum would love to have been here for this one," he finished.

"Yeah, it was beyond, for sure. A lot to take in. Even more to absorb, and now I've gotten myself knee deep in this other situation. The one I needed your help with. But how about we get some refills first and then I'd like to hear more about your unique upbringing," Charlie said.

"Sounds spectacular," Finn said.

Glad she had chosen this spot, Charlie watched as Finn messed with his tea in an attempt to get it to cool down. He was the first person she met who put cream in hot tea.

Bizarre, she thought. She continued to watch him as he began to speak.

"So, as you know," Finn began, his accent giving his words a melodic quality, "I was raised in a rather unique household. In addition to my parents, who were always dabbling in the supernatural, my *granny* could see the future. Living with her was like having your own personal oracle at home. She was always hinting at your future, disguising it as helpful advice. You know, *Don't you think it would be better for your health if you walked to school today?* Knowing that if I took the bus, some nutter on it was going to bully me."

Charlie leaned forward, sipped her coffee, and said, "Really? That sounds so cool! I wish my grandma had been like that. My mom's mom, Dorothy, was a bit of a religious nut and would never acknowledge anything out of the ordinary. On the rare occasion she did, it was because *God* had a hand in it," Charlie said.

"It was definitely interesting. Top that with my mum's ability to interpret dreams, and I was always in the know. You know?" He laughed. "But seriously, she'd spend hours discussing what my dreams meant, trying to piece together the messages they held. By the time I was ten, I was pretty good at it. Used it to my advantage at parties. Girls ate it up," he said with a smile.

"Continue," Charlie urged, her fingers playing with the edge of her cup. "Do you still interpret dreams for random strangers?" she asked.

"Only if they're cute." He winked. "Hey, that's right! You mentioned at lunch that you were having some dreams. You want a consultation, miss?"

"Yeah, I guess I did, didn't I? Well, sure, if you're up for it," she said. "I mean, I have time today, so sure." Why was she coming across like a nincompoop? *You're intelligent, Charlie, so act like it!*

"I'd be glad to help. Tell me about the dreams. Are they recurring? When do you have them, like are they at a specific time? Are you in the dreams?" he asked.

"I guess I want to be upfront here," Charlie started. "These aren't really *dreams*, you see; they're more like visions. A few on my own, never at a specific time of day, and one just the other night brought on by a spell."

"Well then, that sort of changes the scope of things, now, doesn't it," Finn said, looking quizzically into Charlie's eyes. "So, let's start this over. Are these *visions* something you have been prone to your whole life?"

"Nope. They started after my mother's death," Charlie said.

"Oh, ok. So they were triggered by a traumatic event then," Finn replied. "What brings them on? Stress? Sorrow over your mom?"

"This is beginning to sound like more of a therapy session here," Charlie joked.

Finn smiled. Charlie melted.

"No, no therapy here. Trust me. Just trying to get to the core of what's bringing these on."

"At first, they were *implanted*. When I was trying to figure out what had happened to my mom, there were the external forces, the ones I talked about before, helping me. Feeding me the things I needed to see and know to solve the mystery of it all." She paused, waiting for Finn to react. All she got was a nod, letting her know to continue. "I hadn't really had any other visions or issues until I found this stuff in the attic. The stuff I mentioned at lunch. Then I was having what seemed to be vignettes surrounding the items. Like the button. I also had one at a graveyard after seeing a headstone. That vision led me to a matching button from the attic," she said.

"I see," Finn said. "Ok. Let's start with that one then. You were at a graveyard and you say the headstone triggered the vision. What did you see?"

"There were two women, and they were fussing about something. I couldn't really make it out," Charlie said. "I heard a wail, then nothing. Just as quickly as it had started, it ended."

"I can't really help you with this one. You're right, though. This was definitely more of a vision than a dream. Are you psychic, Charlie?" he asked.

"Huh? No. Not at all. All this stuff I've been experiencing is because of Marcus. Not me."

"Marcus?" Finn asked. "I thought your boyfriend's name was Jared?"

"It is." Charlie giggled. "Remember my mentioning of the external forces earlier? Well, once we defeated the Dark Magician, I was assigned my own *guardian angel* of sorts. His name is Marcus. He's omnipresent, is my understanding. Always watching over me. Stepping in as needed. He's been helping me hone in on certain skills. There's some chatter in his realm that I'm *special, whatever* that means," she said with a sigh.

"Whoa, whoa, whoa!" Finn exclaimed "Take that back a moment, please. You seem to have left out a few key points in your story before. Dark Magician? What, pardon my English, the fuck is that?" he said with a gasp.

"Ugh," Charlie said. "See, this is why I wasn't sure we should get into this. It's all so complicated. Ok, this is another long story. You have enough tea there?"

Finn nodded, and Charlie began to amend the story, this time with more details.

Charlie sat back and waited for Finn's response. He hadn't laughed; that was good. He hadn't moved or blinked; that was bad. Picking up her cup, Charlie felt that it was empty. *I really need more,* she thought. *But I don't know if I should get up or not. Will he bolt?*

Finn must have noticed Charlie's tension. He cleared his throat, lifted his cup, and offered to go get them a refill.

That's a good sign, Charlie thought. She nervously waited for him to return, watching his body language as he asked for the refills. He seemed cool. Charlie felt a bit of relief.

Finn returned, set the cups down, and said, "Ok, now *that* was crazy! Sorry, wrong word; that was amazing. So you, Jared, and your current roommates did this? You defeated an evil entity from another, what? Universe?" he asked.

Charlie nodded. "More like a realm is my understanding. I'm still trying to understand it all, which is one of the reasons I switched my classes up this year."

"So, now I know there's more here than psychic abilities. You have verifiable other *realm* help here. I would love to know more about this Dark Magician at some point, but let's work some more on what's going on with your current visions," he said. "What was another that you had?"

Charlie thought. "Soon after that, I had one in the shower."

Finn smirked. Charlie felt herself blush.

Charlie continued. "This one was on me. I was attempting to practice recalling the past vision. I used some of the techniques Marcus had shown me and took myself right back to where the vision had left off. What was cool was I could pivot my vision around. It was like I had a video camera and was looking through the lens. I was able to see more than just the women this time. I saw snow and blood. Then I lost the vision."

Finn sat in silence. Charlie couldn't tell if he was spooked or just thinking things through. She lifted her coffee, sucked down about half its contents, and waited.

Finn began to speak, then paused. He lifted a finger as if he had a thought, then paused again. He took a sip of his tea, cleared his throat, and finally spoke.

"Ok. Wow. So, I truly don't know what to say here to help. This is way beyond my experiences, even with practicing witches for parents and a clairvoyant granny. You mentioned switching up your classes. What are you taking?"

Charlie named off the list.

"Well, well, well, it seems that we will be classmates in a few of those. If you want, we can learn about this together," he said.

Charlie was just about to answer him when, to her shock, she saw Jared come through the door, followed by a look of bewilderment on his face. Jared made his way over to the table.

"Hey, Charlie," he said. "Who's the new guy?"

CHAPTER THIRTY-ONE
THE FASCINATING WORLD OF GHOSTS

UNSURE HOW MUCH TIME had passed since Jared asked his question, Charlie began to panic, thinking she was taking too long to answer. Her eyes bounced back and forth between Jared and Finn when she heard a voice.

"Finn's the name," Finn said, extending his hand to Jared. "You must be Jared, I presume?"

"You got it," Jared said, releasing Finn's hand, then bending down to give Charlie a kiss. "Nice to meet you," Jared finished.

"Finn was helping me interpret the visions I've been having," Charlie said sheepishly. "He has a family history of spooky stuff." *Spooky stuff? Really? That's what you come up with?* Charlie thought, looking over at Finn in an attempt to apologize with her eyes.

"Is that so?" Jared asked.

"My parents and my granny," Finn replied. "They have the gifts."

Awkward silence, then, "Well, don't let me interrupt you two. I just needed to grab some caffeine for the professor here; looks like it's going to be another long day. I'll be glad when classes start tomorrow. Maybe things will slow down a bit then," Jared said.

"Yeah, Jared is a teaching assistant this year for one of his professors. He's been slammed since we got back," Charlie said.

"It was nice to meet you, Finn," Jared said.

"Likewise," Finn said.

Jared leaned to give Charlie a farewell kiss, whispered, *Call me,* and was soon out the door, coffees in hand.

"Well, that was awkward," Finn said, looking over at Charlie. "Now, where were we?"

With a deep inhale, Charlie said, "I think we were talking about our classes."

"Ah, yes. Should be fun, don't you think?" he asked, looking at his watch.

"So, do you want to get into what we really came here for?"

Charlie, puzzled at first, paused. As the lightswitch turned on in her brain, she nodded and opened her notebook.

"I have a theory that all of what has been happening is because of a spell. My roommates and I determined that two of the books belonged to a witch. I've figured out that the spell I saw her cast in one of my visions, was the one she documented in her book of shadows. It seems that she found out her husband, Elias, was cheating on her. She got angry, and with the help of another woman, cast a spell that took her husband's life. I have some research texts coming later this week that should shed some light on the people and their roles in the town, but I'm thinking what's really been happening around me is the workings of a ghost. I think Margaret is not at rest because of her guilt."

"I see," Finn said. "Let's start with that then. I have a few texts here we can go through. I can leave them with you to look at, also. But when we're done, I have a few more questions for you."

Charlie nodded. "Got it." she said.

Finn slid the first book in the center of the small table, opened it, read through the first page or two, then spun it around for Charlie to see.

"Let's dive into the fascinating world of ghosts. There are quite a few types, each with their own unique characteristics and meaning in the paranormal world. Shall we start with a classic?" He paused. Charlie nodded. "Feel free to ask questions as we go," Finn added.

"To start with, we have the most commonly reported type, the 'residual ghost.' These buggers are essentially imprints of past events, playing over and over again. They don't interact with the living, a.k.a. us, and seem to be stuck in a loop, repeating the same actions."

Charlie nodded. "I've heard of these. They're like trapped in time. Unable to register anything around them or acknowledge their surroundings, right?"

Finn nodded, leaning forward. "Precisely. Next we have intelligent ghosts. Aware of their surroundings and will interact with us. They will attempt to communicate, move stuff around, and even respond to questions."

Charlie took in what he had just said and thought, *This sounds like what I've been experiencing*. Not wanting to make assumptions, she asked Finn if there were more on the list.

He nodded. "Next we have shadow people. There's a lot of debate as to whether these are classified as ghosts, but they're usually visual apparitions and don't typically interact. Moving on, we have doppelgangers, which I honestly thought was what you had dealt with regarding your mom until you explained the Dark Magician and the Master. These are ghostly doubles of those who are still living. They are considered to be ominous, a sign of bad luck or impending tragedy. My granny thoroughly believed in doppelgangers. They terrified her. She and my mum had crystals and religious trinkets all over the house to protect us from them. The next one has a horrible name but is quite the opposite—the crisis apparition. They are ghosts of loved ones who, at the moment of their death, or during a *crisis*, find a way to convey a final message or a goodbye," Finn finished, his expression growing a bit more serious. "Finally, we have geists, tormenter ghosts, and poltergeists, noisy ghosts. Most of us have adopted the poltergeist as the term of choice, but there is a difference between them and geists.

Geists are perhaps the most frightening of all. They are known to move objects, make loud noises, and even cause physical harm to people. Poltergeists typically stay on the more pranking side of things. They make noises, move stuff around, but rarely get physical. No one is quite sure how these come to be."

"The only thing I know about poltergeists is what I saw in the movie," Charlie admitted. "But based on what you just explained, the movie probably should have been named geist."

"You got it!"

"So that's the nuts and bolts of the ghost world. There are a lot of opinions, believe me, on what I just shared, but that's the basics. Any questions?"

Charlie sat back and stared at her notes. She tapped her pen, then circled a few words. "Wow. This is a lot. I thought for sure that Margaret was just guilt ridden and wasn't at rest, but this gives me a lot more to think about."

"Ok. I've a few questions for you, then. What makes you think the spell killed the husband? Did you see anything specific that made you think that?" Finn asked.

Charlie sat still, thinking.

"How about this—tell me what you saw. As much as you can remember, that is," Finn guided.

Charlie explained she saw it happen through what she assumed was Elias' eyes. She saw him come in, be greeted, and loved on. She explained the tea and then the pains, followed by the chanting. She also retold what had been written in the book of shadows, including the pages that were torn out.

Finn listened, gave some thought, and was about to speak when his stomach rumbled loud enough to be heard over the din of the coffee shop. He chuckled and said, "Would you mind if we picked this up again another time? Maybe bring the book with you? I hate to cut this short, but I have to eat."

Charlie looked at her watch and gasped. "Oh my God," she exclaimed. "No wonder you're hungry—it's after three!" She apologized again and agreed they could meet another time. "Maybe later this week after I get some of my research stuff in," she said.

"Right. Well, we will touch base in class, then," he said, closing the books and standing. "Hey, Charlie, twas a pleasure today, you know? You're one ok bird," he finished with a smile. "Bye now, luv."

"Bye," Charlie replied and watched as he exited the cafe.

Charlie sat for a moment longer, then gathered up her items and headed out. She, too, was ravenous, but she had things to get done at home. Turning so as not to be tempted by Dino's, she took the longer path home and enjoyed the weather.

She arrived home to an empty house-yet again, with Heather working, and Scarlett out with her school stuff. Charlie set her things down on the kitchen table and headed directly for the fridge. *Do I go for it now, or just snack and wait for dinner,* she asked herself. Standing center with the fridge door open, Charlie perused the contents. She decided easier was better and pulled out a pack of bologna, a container of mustard, and her loaf of Wonder bread. Closing the fridge door with a kick, she unloaded her arms onto the counter, grabbed a butter knife, and began to assemble two bologna sandwiches. Realizing she had forgotten the cheese, she slid back to the fridge and pulled out two slices of American. Sandwiches complete, she took a large bite out of one and set it and the second on a plate. Returning the unused items back to their cold nest, she pulled a Coke out and a bag of Ruffles. Ramona had taught her that trick. "Keep your chips in the fridge and they'll stay crisp longer," she had told Charlie. Her dad never let her do this as it was considered chip heresy, but now, with her own place, she dared to buck the system.

Charlie carried her lunch back to her room and set everything down on her desk. She returned to the kitchen to grab her stuff off the table and saw that everything was now scattered across the kitchen floor.

Tears formed in her eyes as she bent down to collect her things. Things were escalating. Based on what Finn had told her, Charlie was almost positive she was dealing with a poltergeist.

Charlie spent the next hour or so calming herself down, eating her sandwiches, and thinking back on the day. She also took some time to pick out her clothing for her first day. Anything that would distract her from what had happened in the kitchen. Taking her last bite, she decided she was not ready to go back into the kitchen, especially since no one else was home. Instead, she pulled out a deck of cards and began to play Solitaire to help distract her. The quiet of the house was deafening, so she flicked on her TV and found *60 Minutes* was on. *Perfect,* she thought; nothing like a little Harry and Morely to bring someone down to earth. She continued to place card after card in her quest to empty the deck when the phone rang.

"Hello," she answered.

"Hey, babe," Jared said. "I have a small window before I have to dive back into the lesson plan for tomorrow, so I figured I'd give you a ring. What are you up to tonight?"

"Oh, just the most amazing game of Solitaire," she teased. "And it looks like I'm losing."

"Totally rigged," Jared said.

"Totally," Charlie agreed. "So, not to weird you out, but the stuff here at the house is escalating."

"Escalating? How so?" Jared asked.

Charlie filled him in on things since they last talked and included the incident in the kitchen.

"Oh, damn," Jared said.

"Yeah. Finn educated me on some of the types of ghosts today, and I'm beginning to believe I've a poltergeist courtesy of Margaret," Charlie said.

"Ah, oh, yes, Finn," Jared said wryly. "How is it you two know each other, exactly?"

"We literally bumped into each other at the library when I was researching over in the occult section. We got to talking, and I quickly found out that he came from a paranormal family, like I mentioned earlier. His mom and dad are sort of witches and his grandma is a seer."

"Ah, mmhmm," Jared replied. "I'm glad you found someone who can help with all this. Especially since I've fallen short on being able to. Things should slow down a tiny bit, I'm hoping, and I'll be back to being the boyfriend/research assistant extraordinaire." He chuckled, sounding a bit nervous.

"I miss you," Charlie sighed.

"Me too. Me too," Jared agreed.

Jared filled her in on Benji's dad, explaining that avenue of research opportunity was closed. Charlie empathized and let Jared know to extend her condolences. Charlie heard what sounded like a timer go off on Jared's end of the phone.

"What was that?" she asked.

"Oh, sorry. I set an old egg timer so I wouldn't get lost talking to you. I'm sorry, I've to go. Hey, have a great first day! Let's try and talk tomorrow at some point if we can," he said, sounding a bit sad.

"Will do. Don't let her crush your soul too much," Charlie teased.

"Deal," Jared said, and they hung up.

Realizing she needed to check in on her dad, she picked up the handset and dialed her grandparents.

"Bauman residence," Dale answered.

A feeling of relief hit Charlie, as she had worried she might be cutting into knitting/puzzle time. "Hey, Dad," Charlie said. "I was hoping to catch you there. How'd the move go?"

"Hey there, kiddo. Everything is in and waiting for me to unpack. I decided to stay one more night here so I didn't have to subject this old back to the floor," he said with a chuckle.

"Gotcha." Charlie smiled. The two chatted for a bit about the new place, plans for painting at some point, and Charlie's upcoming first day. Charlie kept her day and Finn to herself for now. Her dad didn't need to worry with everything he was going through. She inquired about her grandparents, and Dale confirmed they were in the family room, Eleanor knitting and Walter puzzling. They laughed in unison when Dale reminded her to keep this short. "Costs and all." They said their goodbyes and promised to check in again soon.

Charlie placed the phone back on the bedside table, leaned back, and saw that it was almost eight thirty, which meant *My Two Dads*. She stood and changed the channel. Turning to brave the kitchen, she gathered up her trash and headed down the hallway.

Snacks and Sunday night comedies kept her busy for the rest of the night. She even leveled the playing field with her Solitaire, finishing the night with a win. A yawn and sugar crash were her signals to call it a night. *I'll shower in the morning,* she told herself, and slid between the covers, making sure her alarm was set for the correct time.

Charlie was startled awake by her alarm and flung her arm over to quiet the buzz. She had slept well. No dreams, no visions, just a good night's sleep. Sitting up, she let her eyes adjust to the light coming through the window. Flinging her legs over the side of the bed, her feet searched the floor for her slippers. Sliding them on, she stood, stretched, and shuffled her way to the kitchen to make coffee. This time, there was no sign of a coffee fairy.

Charlie knew from talking with her roomies that she was the only glutton for punishment when it came to class schedules. She quietly prepared the maker, pulled out a mug, and walked over to the slider to take in the morning. As the coffee pushed its way through to the carafe, the kitchen began to smell like what Charlie imagined heaven would smell like. Well, that and maybe pizza. She watched as birds flitted their way from one tree to another, occasionally swooping down to the ground to grab some breakfast. She smiled. She missed her mom. Birdie had a way of knowing every bird in the Rochester area. She knew their mating habits, their chirps, and their migration patterns. *Birdie knew birdies*. Charlie chucked to herself. As the last few dribbles emptied into the carafe, Charlie poured the heavenly hot beverage into her mug, doctored it up a bit, then went back to her room to shower.

Not wanting to risk being late, Charlie chose to take Juicy down to campus. She parked, gathered up her backpack, and headed into the small lecture hall for her first day of classes. Immediately, she could tell this first was not going to be like other classes she had taken before. Gone was the formality of structured seating and in its place was a small semi-circle of desks with bean bags chairs dotted about. Charlie picked a desk front and center; some habits were impossible to break. She set herself up for the class, pulled out her nutritious breakfast, and sat back to take in the room. The space was about one-third the size of her previous lecture halls, and counting the chairs, she figured out why. As she was about to take a quick nibble on her Hostess Donnettes, she heard a few people come in the room behind her. Popping two Donettes in, she chewed before she recognized one of the voices. Finn. Chewing faster, Charlie swallowed just in time to hear him greet her.

"Mornin' there, Charlie girl," he said, laughing.

"Morning, Finn," Charlie replied, clearing her throat.

She looked up at him just as his finger motioned around the corners of his mouth. She must have looked befuddled, because he whispered, "You got a little somethin' there, darlin'."

Complete embarrassment hit Charlie. She turned her head and gave a quick wipe to free her mouth of the powdered sugar that had settled in the corners. Turning back around, she saw Finn take a seat next to hers. They sat in silence while he prepped his notebook and other items for class. The desks and bean bags filled up with a very eclectic group of students. Moments later, the professor came in, announced herself and the class details, then began her lecture.

"I have to skedaddle," Finn said after class wrapped up. "My next lecture is way across campus. It was a pleasure assisting you this morning," he said with a smirk, turning to head out the lecture hall.

Not quite sure what had just happened, Charlie slowly made her way out into the hallway, stopping briefly at the water fountain nearby. Several gulps later, she hitched her back-pack up and bee-lined her way to class number two.

The rest of her day went spectacularly, and very happily, was uneventful. Having stopped for a quick bite between her morning and afternoon classes, Charlie was now free to pop over to the bookstore to grab another suggested textbook.

Entering, she was pleasantly surprised to see Jared at the counter, chatting with the student behind the register.

Charlie waved and walked over to him. He came in for a long bear hug, sending Charlie's backpack crashing to the floor. A kiss, or two, or three later and he released her. She giggled at seeing the clerk behind the register roll her eyes at the rather large display of PDA.

"I was *not* expecting to see you here," Charlie said. "But I'm glad I did."

"Yeah, I had a break between lectures and needed to grab a text for one of my other classes. Thankful to just be a student for a change," he said with a heavy sigh.

Charlie picked up her backpack and headed over to the section she was looking for. Jared joined her, and the two conversed, holding hands as they did. *Man, I've missed this,* Charlie thought. Since they both had a few minutes, they sat at a small table in the corner and caught up, filling each other in on their days so far and what was ahead. Realizing he had to get going if he was to be on time, Jared stood, gave Charlie a quick peck, and promised to call later.

Charlie took her book to the register, paid, and headed out toward Juicy.

The next few days went by quickly and were wonderfully uneventful. No new ghost issues, great lectures, and late-night chats with Jared were all a welcome relief to Charlie. When she got home Wednesday night, she had a message from the librarian that her items had arrived a day early. Not wanting to make her way back down to campus, Charlie opted to wait and grab them after her morning lectures. She'd have plenty of time Thursday and Friday to research as she would have no other distractions.

Charlie woke Thursday excited and ready to get through her class. Taking her seat, Finn soon joined to her right. She filled him in on the items being ready at the library and asked if he had time to join her after class.

"Unfortunately, I have another lecture right after this one," he said. "But if you'll be there for a bit, I can come check in on you?"

Charlie sighed. "I was going to take the books and treat myself to wings while I submerged myself in all things Jonesborough."

"Well, wings do sound amazing!" Finn said. "You go ahead; treat yourself. I should be done about noon and will pop in for a visit if that's ok."

Charlie nodded just as the professor began the day's lecture.

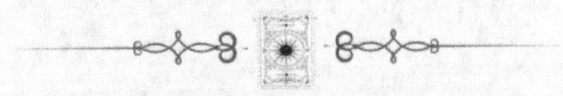

Practically skipping to the library, Charlie entered the front doors with an air of excitement. She smiled as she approached the research desk and saw the librarian assisting another student. Stepping forward when it was her turn, Charlie said her greetings and thanked the librarian for the phone call.

"You're quite welcome," she said "I was rather surprised at how fast we got these," she said as she finished placing a stack of media in front of Charlie. She went through each item, explaining the first two were for the microfiche machines, so they had to stay within the walls of the library, but the books and articles were hers to check out.

Charlie looked at her watch to see if she had time to run through the microfiche and determined that she didn't. "Would there be a way to hold these here for me until tomorrow? I have to be somewhere soon and won't have time to do the deep dive I need to."

"Of course," the librarian said. "I'll keep them here in our cubby. I'll be here tomorrow, so just come get me and we can get you set up at a machine."

Charlie thanked her, grabbed the books, and headed out to Dino's.

A dozen wings, a Coke, and some french fries later, Charlie had her nose deep in the first of the books she had borrowed. Making sure she didn't get wing sauce on the pages, she wiped her fingers before each page turn. For the next hour, she took notes, and with the answers came more questions. Sliding her plate of wing carcasses over to the edge of the table, Charlie saw Finn make his way over to the table. He said his hellos, slid in across from Charlie, and ordered himself a root beer and burger.

"So, how's it going?" he asked.

"Slow and a tad aggravating," Charlie answered. She explained that she was finding good information, but that it was leading her down a rabbit hole she wasn't prepared for.

The two looked over her notes, Finn commiserating with her frustrations.

"What if we approached this in smaller bites," he suggested.

"Smaller bites?" Charlie asked

"Yeah. It seems like you're trying to gain answers to very broad questions. What if we broke them down into, how do you Americans say…bite-size pieces," he said, tilting his head.

"Ohhhhhh! Duh, smaller bites," she said with a laugh.

They worked on breaking the research down into smaller chunks to help make the puzzle come together a bit more clearly. By the time Finn was done with his burger, they had a pretty good picture before them.

"So, what do we know now?" Finn asked.

Charlie went through the bullet points, starting with how witches were perceived in that part of the country in that time period. She learned that Margaret wouldn't have had to hide her abilities too much, as she truly would have been a helpful citizen with her healing balms and potions. They learned more about how Elias' business worked and found several articles that had been printed for Charlie on big events and news surrounding his accomplishments. He was successful, but definitely at the expense of the less fortunate in the areas he covered. They found that while he tended to keep the local folks more appeased, he was not so cordial in other states. He had several run-ins with the law in Kentucky and West Virginia over some land purchases and that he had gained in some rather unscrupulous manners. The two continued through a few more refills when Charlie looked at her watch and decided she needed to call it a day.

"I have to get some actual classwork done tonight if I'm going to be at the library tomorrow," she said, signaling to the waitress to bring the checks.

"Let me get this," Finn offered.

"That's nice of you, Finn, but…" Charlie started to object.

"No buts," he said. "It's my pleasure." He smiled. The waitress came, delivered the check, and rang in Finn's cash payment at the register as he continued. "So what are you hoping to find on the microfiche?"

"I'm hoping it will have some information on Margaret, Betsy, Elias and the baby. I need to know more about the baby and what transpired between them all that made Margaret snap," Charlie said.

"Ah, ok. Have you given any thought to our ghost talk?" he asked.

"Yeah, I hate to say it, but after yet another experience the other night, I think I may have myself a poltergeist. It's died down the past few days, so maybe it's gone," she said hopefully.

"Hate to break it to you, but they don't just go. You have only experienced the first few levels of that particular haunting style, if it is indeed a poltergeist," he warned.
"What do you mean the first few levels?" she asked.

"I mean, if it is *truly* a poltergeist, things are going to get much worse before they get better. You'll need to work on a plan to get rid of it. To pacify or settle whatever is causing it to haunt you," he said, lowering his head. "Did you have a chance to read the books I gave you?"

Charlie shook her head. "I honestly haven't."

"If you have a few more moments, we can discuss the steps and what you may come to expect."

Charlie nodded, a knot forming in her stomach. She leaned in and listened as Finn listed off the stages.

"First," he said, "are what they call the beginnings—faint sounds and scratches you may have thought were mice or something. Yes?"

Charlie nodded.

"Stage two is the noises. Knocking, cracking sounds, or bangs. I know you mentioned those. So that leads to three—moving objects. Again, you have mentioned you experienced this, too, just the other night."

Charlie nodded again, trying hard not to whimper.

"Four—you may start to see objects appear or disappear." He waited. "Ok, so we aren't there yet. Four may get skipped all together and go straight to five—communication. This will not be communication as you and I know it; it will be a rudimentary communication. Think one knock for yes, two for no type of thing." He paused and let that statement settle in.

"Next will be the climax—you will experience all the previous stages at an increasing rate, and if the poltergeist has the ability to talk, this may be when you begin to hear them. This is a crucial stage, Charlie. If it is truly a poltergeist, then the activity will begin to decline. It will gradually become weaker, and the activity will slowly creep to an end. If it is *not*, however, just a poltergeist, then you will be moving on to a stage of physical contact and possible harm. This will be a geist, Charlie, and extreme steps will have to be taken. I'm not trying to scare you; I just want you to be prepared. To keep an ear and eye out and not let anything slide by as unimportant. Please read the books I gave you," he finished, laying his hand on top of hers.

Charlie loosened the grip her teeth had on her lower lip and felt the blood rush back to it.

She took a deep breath and thanked Finn. She knew what she had to do in addition to reading the books; she had to reach out to Marcus.

Feeling drained, Charlie entered the house and made her way to her room. She could hear sounds coming from Heather's room but chose not to engage her. Charlie's head was still whirling from what Finn had dumped on her. She placed her backpack down, stripped out of her clothes, and chose her cozies for the night.

Stepping into the bathroom, she turned the hot water on and waited for the steam to rise. Leaning down, she splashed her face half a dozen times before reaching over to grab a towel. She took a few deep breaths, closed her eyes, and asked Marcus for some guidance. No answer. She asked again; this time, tears formed in her eyes and rolled down her cheeks. Nothing. Not wanting to come to grips with the silence, she leaned down and splashed her face a few more times, lifting her head up to see an "M" written in the steam that had formed on the mirror. She let out a sigh of relief and said, "Thank you." She then began to exposition dump into the air that surrounded her, finishing with "I hope you heard all of that." Silence. Just the water rushing out of the faucet. She knew he couldn't always communicate the way she wanted him to, so she turned off the faucet, dried her hands, and made her way back to the bed, picking up the two books Finn had given her during their coffee shop meeting. She placed them on the bed and sat. She really needed to focus on her school stuff, but her head just wasn't in it. Promising herself she would tackle it over the weekend, she leaned back against the headboard and picked up the first book.

The information in the book confirmed everything Finn had told her. It went on to discuss the various types of hauntings and had a small section on poltergeists, which left Charlie wanting to know more. What she did gather from it, however, was that she needed to understand the source. Done. Margaret. Once that was done, setting boundaries would be the best way to calm down the entity. Because they were considered an intelligent haunt, they could and sometimes did respond to assertiveness from the person they were taunting. Firmly stating that they were not welcome, or that they needed to leave had been shown to be surprisingly effective. *Interesting,* Charlie thought.

Deciding she needed a break, Charlie headed out to the kitchen for a snack. Noticing the time, she realized she should think about a real meal. Digging around, she pulled out some ground beef, a can of Hunts sauce, and a box of spaghetti. She browned the beef and added the can of sauce. She filled the pot with enough water to boil the whole box of spaghetti. She stood and waited for the water to boil. The steam began to form, dancing lightly above the surface of the water. Mesmerized, she got lost in her thoughts when she heard him. *Marcus.* He was here with her. He was communicating with her, but, not like people talk. He was somehow filling her head with information without sound. It was like she was absorbing his words somehow. She listened and took it all in. His concerns for her; his warnings; his suggestions to keep learning and that the truth would show itself to her. He fed her mind with the names of who would be key in conquering the days, weeks, and yes, months to come. He informed her this would not be quick. Nor would it be easy. Then, as quickly as it began, it stopped. Before her was a raging pot of water. She shook her head, opened the box of spaghetti, and dumped it in, giving it a quick whirl.

Taking her dinner back to her room, she sat and ate as *Jeopardy!* played in the background. Chewing her food, yet not really tasting it, she ran through the thoughts that Marcus had planted in her mind. Grabbing her notebook, she decided to capture what she could remember for future reference, then she settled in with a swig of her Coke and opened the second book.

This particular book took the time to spell out "geist.". While the word itself meant many things, the definition of ghost or spirit seemed to be the most accepted. It seemed the majority of what people dealt with were poltergeists, a.k.a. noisy ghosts. But there were other variations of these entities: weltgeist, world spirit; volksgeist, national spirit; and zeitgeist, spirit of the age.

Charlie perused through the text, fascinated with what she was reading, centuries of people and their tales of poltergeist activity. Some things were similar to what she was experiencing, but others, such as showers of stones or even small animals being thrown, were quite disconcerting. She was glad at that moment she did not have pets. More benign pranks such as items levitating or sheets and curtains being moved or torn were another set of signs she was glad she had not experienced. Yet. As she read, that single word became the thought that prevailed in her mind. *Yet.* Every one of these stories began innocently and escalated just as Finn had explained to her. Every one heightened to more terrifying states to include physicality in the form of slaps, shoves, teeth marks, and scratches. Geists, she read on, would use anything at their disposal to make their desires known. That once you figured out the desires, you could then come to grips that there would be demands. Sometimes the demands only needed to be acknowledged; other times, they would demand action. Charlie sat back and thought about this last statement. This was what she needed to figure out! She needed to find Margaret's desires, and then, and only then, could she put her to rest.

Deciding enough was enough for the night, Charlie closed the book and settled in between her sheets, hopeful for some sleep.

Charlie looked around her bedroom. Gone was the comfort she normally felt, and in its place was a sinister vibe, shadows creeping along the walls. An unnatural chill swirled around her. She moved her eyes around the dimly lit space. The poltergeist's presence was palpable, a heavy and oppressive force that made the hairs on the back of her neck stand on end.

Continuing to scan the room for any clues as to what was going on, objects in the bedroom began to move of their own accord, floating and flying. Books hurled themselves off shelves, and picture frames shattered against the walls with increasing violence. The poltergeist's actions had never been this intense, this aggressive. Finn was right! The stages were coming at a more rapid pace. Fear surged through Charlie as she witnessed the chaos unfolding around her.

Desperate to find some semblance of safety, she rushed out of her room to the common area, where she hoped to find Heather and Scarlett. She found them there, talking, animated, completely unaware of the terror she was experiencing. Charlie tried to scream, to call out to them, but no sound emerged from her lips. It was as if an invisible force had stolen her voice.

Panicking, she reached out to shake them, to make them see and hear her. Her hands passed through their bodies as if they were made of mist. They continued obliviously, laughing and chatting as though nothing was wrong. The disconnect was terrifying. It was as if she were trapped, close enough to see them but forever out of reach.

Tears of frustration and fear welled up in her eyes. The poltergeist's malevolence seemed to amplify, feeding off her helplessness. She could feel its cold breath on the back of her neck, hear its mocking whispers in her ear. It was a nightmare in every sense, and the more she struggled, the deeper her sense of isolation became. Suddenly, a particularly violent tremor shook the bedroom, and she cried out for help, surprised at whose name came from her lips—Finn's.

Charlie jolted awake. She sat up in bed, drenched in sweat, her heart racing. The room was quiet, the shadows benign once more. But the sense of unease lingered. The dream had felt too real, too vivid. She couldn't shake the feeling that things were about to get bad, very bad.

She looked at the clock—three fifteen. Too early to get up, so she curled back up under her sheets and laid there until the sun rose.

Completely exhausted, Charlie sat up slowly, fighting off the dizziness and disorientation. She carefully made her way to the bathroom and splashed her face with cold water, grabbing a washcloth to remove the residue from her night sweats. Coffee. She needed coffee. With a pot made, she carried her mug back to her room and clicked on the television. *Morning news. Great,* she thought. She really could go for some Bugs and Wile E. Coyote right about then. The coffee slowly took hold, and she decided another cup was needed. Entering the kitchen, she saw Heather helping herself to her morning pick-me-up.

"Mornin'," Charlie groaned.

"Morning, Charlie," Heather said, looking at her from over her shoulder. "Oooof, you look like hell. Long night?" she asked

"Something like that," Charlie said, not wanting to get into anything this early in the morning. Still too fresh.

"Gotta jet," Heather said, taking a swig of her coffee before heading out the front door.

Charlie refilled her mug and took it back to her room to get her day started.

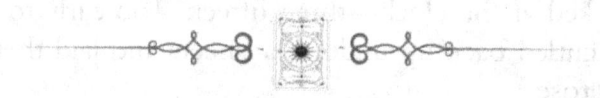

Charlie peeked out the curtains and saw that it was a somewhat cloudy morning. Between her lack of sleep, the weather, and the known temperatures that would be down in the microfiche pit, she opted for a pair of Cavaricci's, a T-shirt, and her flannel. Still too early to head out to the library, Charlie sat back and ran over the dream. Since all of this started last year, she was never sure anymore if her dreams were dreams or some sort of vision of the future, of things to come. She hoped in this instance it was just a dream. Watching the local news, she waited patiently for the clock to read nine. She wondered if Jared was awake, or better yet, home. Sleep hit Charlie hard, and she dozed off, waking to find it was ten a.m.

Feeling a bit more rested, Charlie headed out to the library, gathering her backpack and a banana for the road.

"Good morning," Charlie said, noticing that it was a different librarian today.

"Good morning; how may I help you?" she asked.

"I have some microfiche cards being held for me. I was wondering if I could pick them up and head down to the machines," Charlie said. The woman opened and closed several cubbies before finding the cards.

"Here we go," she announced, handing the small stack over to Charlie. "Please don't hesitate to ask if you need any help with the machines," she finished with a smile.

Charlie was at a machine in no time flat. Taking out her notebook, she inserted the card and began her research. Tedious was going to be the word of the day; she could feel it.

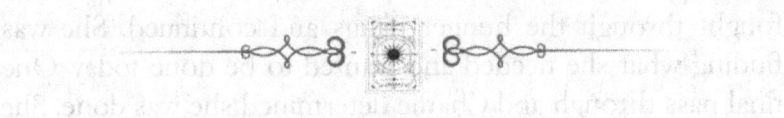

Charlie slid through the screens to find Elias' birth record first, then Margaret's, confirming that their ages at the time would have likely made her too old to truthfully conceive a baby. Continuing her deep dive into the birth records, Charlie chose to span a few years around that date. No child was born to Margaret Cobb. Curious. Wheels turning, Charlie then looked up records of anyone in the area named Betsy. Not too many Betsys, so it shouldn't be hard to deduce. Voila! Betsy was a solid twenty years younger than Margaret and, holy shit, *she* gave birth to a boy a few months after Elias' presumed death. Charlie scoffed at the presumed part because she knew he had indeed died. She saw it. The boy, named Thomas, had school records that placed him in Piney Flats. His residence was listed as Elias' home. Charlie continued digging in the records and came across that Betsy had been an employee of Elias'.

She then found a few photographs of what seemed to be Elias' funeral. There, standing before the headstone that Charlie recognized from her visions, were Margaret's and Betsy's heads, bowed with smiles? Yes! Those were definitely smiles, ever so slight, but both Betsy's and Margaret's lips curled in the corners. *This doesn't feel right*, Charlie thought. She marked the spot for printing later, along with the birth records, and continued.

Hours passed. Her stomach let her know as much, but she fought through the hunger pangs and continued. She was finding what she needed and wanted to be done today. One final pass through and Charlie determined she was done. She left the machine in search of a librarian to assist her with the printing.

With all her documentation, she closed the cards back in their cases and carried them back to the media desk. A quick "thank you" and Charlie decided to take a food break, then come back to look at more of the other information.

Finishing up her food, she scooted back over to the library to finish researching. Her mind drifted to the list of stages Finn had told her about. She was definitely in stage three and wanted to keep it that way for a bit. She hoped Jared would be available to help her review everything she was finding.

The rest of the day flew by as Charlie kept her head deep in the research. Taking the last of her notes, she closed up shop for the day and headed out to see if Jared was home.

Seeing that there was movement through the front windows, Charlie was hopeful that she was going to get to see and spend some time with Jared. A quick knock and her hopes were confirmed. Jared opened the door, and a huge smile came across his face.

"Have time for some company?" Charlie asked.

"Boy, do I!" Jared said, stepping aside to let Charlie in. "What's with the haul there?" he asked, pointing to her overly full backpack.

"I was over at the library today, diving into all the items I got from the ETSU library. Have a bunch of stuff to share and talk about, if you're interested," Charlie said in a hopeful tone.

"You actually caught me at a good spot. With the first week of classes done and past us, my professor has eased up a bit, so I do have time but I was thinking…" Jared leaned in to kiss Charlie. It was one of those heel kick kisses, the kind that leads to distractions…

The pair laid with Charlie's arm in the crook of Jared's shoulder, one leg sprawled across his body and the other twisted up in his top sheet.

"Penny for your thoughts," Jared said.

"Well, young man, the amount of thoughts I've going on, it's going to be way more than a penny," she said with a snicker. "But seriously, I have a bunch of stuff that I would ideally like you to help me with, but if it's not a good time, we can figure out another."

Jared sighed. "I would like nothing more than to help you. But even though things have eased up, I still have a ton of work to do in addition to my other classes. You want to give me a quick run-down?" he asked.

Charlie gave him some bullet points and how she thought she'd be able to just tell Margaret to go away.

"You think it will be that simple?" Jared asked.

"Well, it can't hurt," Charlie replied.

The two continued to chit chat for a bit before Jared insisted he had to get moving or he would surely never leave the bed. Charlie chuckled, got dressed, and gave a kiss goodbye. A short walk later, she was back in her house which, for once, had some life and activity in it. Charlie opened the front door and could hear about half a dozen or so voices down in the common area as the Bangles' *Eternal Flame* played in the background. *Odd choice,* Charlie thought. Making a quick jaunt to her room to set her bags down, she slowly made her way down the stairs to say hello. Scarlett, Heather, and a few faces Charlie remembered from the group last year were sitting around talking.

Charlie said "hi" and decided she wasn't in a group mood. She walked over to Scarlett and whispered, "When you guys are done, I've got some news."

Scarlett nodded, and Charlie excused herself. Feeling a bit hungry, she made herself a peanut butter sandwich, reminding herself that she had spaghetti leftovers for dinner. She took the sandwich to her room, turned on the TV, and flipped through the channels until she found something that would suffice.

It was a few hours later before Charlie heard a knock on her door. Scarlett and Heather came in.

"So, tell us what's been going on. I haven't seen you for a couple of days," Scarlett said.

"I've only seen you long enough to make a coffee," Heather followed.

"It's been a busy week for sure," Charlie answered. "I was able to get the items from the other library sent and had a chat with someone with some background on this type of stuff, and I wanted to share it with you both and let you know what I came up with."

Charlie ended with her decision to ask, no, tell Margaret to leave them alone. "I believe that she will. Based on everything I've found, it seems she killed Elias in a fit of rage and jealousy over Betsy and the baby, then regretted her decision after."

"But why would she raise Betsy's kid if she were so enraged?" Heather asked.

"That's the only part that doesn't make sense. Maybe out of that guilt? I still think I need to give the statement a shot. Once she knows she isn't welcome, there's a really good chance she'll back down. That's what the research I've done tells me, at least."

"I say do it," Scarlett said. "I can help with some sage. I'll burn it right after you express your intent."

Charlie accepted and thanked them for their support.

"Now, who's hungry? I made enough spaghetti last night for an army."

The next few days flew by with very few disturbances. Charlie made sure she had everything prepared for her declaration. Finn had helped her determine she should have the journals and the doll present in the room, since it seemed they were the cause of the attachment. Scarlett secured the sage needed for burning. It was now the time and day for the act itself. Jared had blocked out time to be there with her, and with Scarlett and Heather on deck for after. With the items centered in Charlie's room, she and Jared held hands and Charlie called forth Margaret.

"Margaret Cobb, I call on you to listen to the words I'm saying to you. I wish, no, I *command* you to leave me alone. You're no longer wanted here. Return to a place where you're welcomed, for you're not welcome here," Charlie stated firmly. She and Jared waited. Nothing. No noises, no answer back, no movement of the items, just silence.

"Is that how it was supposed to go?" Jared asked. "That simple?"

"I believe that was it," Charlie said, shrugging. She opened her door and let Scarlett sage her room, then watched as she continued through the rest of the house.

Charlie laid back in Jared's arms as they watched TV. She was so happy to have this sense of normalcy back after having dealt with Margaret. Taking a deep breath, she shifted toward Jared's face and said, "I can't believe it worked! It's been, what, a month or so and no signs of anything?"

"You and me both! I'm so glad you got rid of that annoyance. I'm even more glad that my schedule freed up like I had hoped and we've been able to get back to this stuff on a regular basis again. It's insane how fast September has flown by," Jared replied.

"So, Scarlett, Heather and I were thinking of having a Halloween party. What do you think?"

"I think that'd be fun!" He paused. "That doesn't mean we have to do a couples costume, does it?" He looked at Charlie with slight fear in his eyes.

"No, no couples costume. I promise." She laughed. "I have an idea for mine, but it's a secret," Charlie teased.

"Well, don't expect much from me," Jared said. "I have no creativity at all. Let me know if you guys need any help planning or putting it together; I know two weeks isn't a lot of time."

"Can do," Charlie said, nuzzling in closer as they began to watch their next show.

Marcus watched solemnly over Charlie and Jared. He was proud of her for taking her *calling* more seriously. Content knowing she had an inner circle in the human realm to help her and protect her when needed. He was proud of himself for his ability to force fate a bit with regards to Finn, but still nervous, very nervous as to how Charlie would handle this next series of events.

Charlie sat at her desk, studying. She looked up at the calendar on her wall and sighed. Less than two weeks until Halloween, even less until their party. With the actual date falling on a Tuesday, they decided to have the party on the twenty-eighth. This left them with just about ten days to get ready. Unable to focus on her work, Charlie worked on her party list instead. The food was going to be easy, and Heather had that covered. Scarlett was working on the beer. They had already pulled their collection of records together for the music. All that was left was Charlie's end—the decorations. Since they were on a budget, Charlie would be frugal and come up with some ways to decorate creatively. But Charlie did have some funds, so she was going to surprise them with a few really cool props. She'd head out later to see if she could snag them.

Still having no clue what Jared was wearing, Charlie turned her attention to her costume. She and Ramona had a long talk over the ideas and came up with one of Charlie's icons—the Bride of Frankenstein. The Bride had been one of Charlie's first introductions into the horror genre, and, well, she was cool as shit. Using her mother's sewing form and the rudimentary techniques she had picked up from her mom, Charlie had managed to create a really cool piece. The hair would be the tricky part, but she figured she could find something while she was scoping out the props later. Charlie tried to bring her focus back around to her homework, when she heard something that sent a chill down her spine. Three knocks. Three knocks that seemed to come from everywhere and nowhere at the same time. Charlie turned around in her chair, her heart pounding, small beads of sweat forming along her hairline. She took a deep breath and scanned the room. Nothing. Silence—until there wasn't. All at once, every item on her bookshelf came flying off in all directions across her room. Charlie panicked, jumped up, and ran from her room, tears rolling down her face.

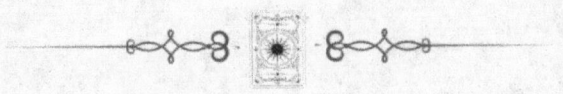

She found herself out on the patio a few minutes later, unsure how she had gotten there. All she knew was that she must have created a ruckus because she looked up to see Heather staring at her from the sliding glass door.

"Charlie? You ok? What was that? I heard a bunch of bangs and thuds then you screaming and running past my door," Heather said.

Just as Heather finished her statement, Scarlett appeared next to her, wiping the sleep from her eyes.

"What's going on?" she asked.

Charlie lifted her head out of her hands and looked up at her friends. "She's back."

CHAPTER THIRTY-TWO
THE BITCH IS BACK

"WHAT DO YOU MEAN, she's back??" Scarlett asked, her voice crescendoing to a squeak.

"Margaret. She's back. She just knocked, and...and..." Charlie began to cry again.

Heather looked at Scarlett and said, "And what? Charlie? What happened?"

Charlie fought through a hitch in her breath and said, "And she emptied my bookshelf in one fell swoop. Go! Look! Books everywhere! All around my room. That's the thuds you heard, Heather."

Heather nodded to Scarlett for her to go check it out. Heather stayed with Charlie. "Head down," she began. "Deep breaths in and out. Go ahead. It's ok."

Charlie did as she was instructed and was able to control her breathing after a few moments. Scarlett returned, her face even paler than usual, and said, "She's right. Her room looks like a bomb went off. Shit everywhere. One thing's for sure—Margaret's a total bitch!"

"How can she be back?" Heather asked. "I—we watched you banish her. Didn't Finn say that would work?"

Charlie nodded and attempted to not start crying again as she spoke. "Yeah, he and the books I read said that it should have worked. And it did! She was gone. So why is she back?" Charlie whined.

The three sat and hypothesized over the reasons until Scarlett offered a suggestion. "Maybe more than just her spirit was the issue. Maybe her will, like Heather suggested, is strong, and with what we know about her being a witch, she very well could be more than a poltergeist. Maybe she's even tied to one of those objects. So, you'll try again. *We* will try again, and this time, try and determine what object she seems to be clinging to," Scarlett finished.

Charlie sat, taking in what Scarlett had just suggested. "Can we try that spell again? The one we did? But with a variation?" Charlie asked.

"Variation, how?" Scarlett replied.

"You're the stronger one, and you've been doing this the longest. Maybe *you* lead Heather and I through it instead of going off on your own? Kind of like a guide? Is there a way you can use the facts we know about Margaret to steer us around?" Charlie asked.

Scarlett looked at Heather, then Charlie, and nodded. "I can, but we'll need a third to anchor the two of you. Can we ask Finn?" she asked.

Charlie, startled by that suggestion, looked at Scarlett quizzically.

"Finn, because he comes from a solid background in this. He has knowledge and experience that will help me. Something I'm thinking Jared just isn't able to provide," Scarlett explained.

Charlie nodded. "I'll give him a call. When should I tell him we'll need his help?" she asked.

"Tonight, if he can. Otherwise, tomorrow night. You can't sit too long on this. If she came back this forceful, then she'll only continue to get stronger with her taunts," Scarlett said.

Charlie agreed and asked them if they could come back and help her clean up a bit. They agreed.

Once the room was back to normal, well, as normal as a room could be with a taunting ghost lurking, Charlie gave Finn a ring.

"Finn here," Charlie heard.

"Hey Finn," she replied.

"Charlie! Well, isn't this a surprise!" Finn said. "What could possibly bring you to give me a call so randomly?"

Charlie filled him in on what had transpired and what their plans were. She asked if he would be able to help them out.

"Oh," Finn said, sounding a bit surprised. "Sure, I guess. Not sure what help I'll be other than providing you with another body, but I'll chat with Scarlett to get more info on what she thinks I'm capable of. When would you like my services?" he asked.

Something about the way he said the last part made Charlie's head go a bit woozy. It wasn't until she heard him repeat himself that she answered. "Tonight. We would like to do this tonight."

Charlie hung up after they confirmed the time and turned back to her homework. Knowing there was no way she could focus on it, she gathered up her crossbody and her list and headed out to Juicy.

Sliding into Juicy, Charlie sat for a moment to think. She would definitely be able to secure the Halloween props at Chase Pitkins. It was where to find the wig that was the problem. Giving Juicy some juice, Charlie remembered a store in Syracuse that may help her with both. She looked at her watch and figured she had just enough time to run out there and back before the spell was to take place that evening.

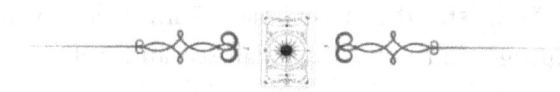

The weather cooperated on the drive up to Syracuse, and although the wind would be too intense to have her top down on the highway, she at least enjoyed the windows being down. Her favorite playlists aided in keeping her mind off what had transpired earlier and allowed her to focus on the drive and not trying to find stations. An hour or so later, she pulled up to the Costume Castle, ironically housed in a building that resembled an actual castle. Ramona had mentioned this place years ago when her mom had decided that the Lorenzano's would '*do Halloween right*' this time and dressed them all as characters from the Addams Family. Ramona had come back with tales of this castle that had everything you could ever want for Halloween. Glad she had a great memory, Charlie entered. A few moments later, a small, spritely woman came from behind a curtain.

"How may I assist you today?" she asked with what Charlie swore was a curtsy.

"Hi, I was hoping to find some props for our house party and also a wig for my Bride of Frankenstein costume. Do you by chance have something?" Charlie asked, hope in her voice.

"Why, of course we do," the woman said, smiling. "Follow me."

Charlie did and was astonished at how large the store actually was. It seemed to go on forever, shelf after shelf, rack after rack.

"Let's start back this way for those props you had mentioned," the tiny woman said, leading the way.

Pushing through one final curtain, Charlie saw before her an array of props that made her mouth drop. Everything from headstones, to large Jack-in-the-Boxes, to horse-drawn carriages.

"Are all of these for sale?" Charlie asked incredulously.

"Most are, my dear. Some are for rent. A few for just show," she stated matter-of-factly. "Tell me, what are you looking for?"

Charlie filled her in on the needs and they began their hunt. They loaded up a small flat cart then made their way out of the prop section and into the wig and makeup wing. Yes, *wing*. There were at least fifteen aisles of just wigs. Cher, Madonna, Einstein, Elvis, Shirley Temple, and on and on. Charlie was guided down an aisle housing some more unique wigs when she saw what she was looking for—an almost exact replica of the Bride's hair. Other than it being synthetic, it was a perfect match.

The owner rang Charlie up. Charlie paid and rolled the cart out to Juicy. This would be the hard part—to fit this stuff in a car that truly had no room! For the next twenty minutes, she played Tetris in her mind in an attempt to figure out the best configuration. Once the vision was there, Charlie began to replicate it, and in moments, Juicy was loaded up and Charlie was on her way out of Syracuse. Just as she was about to head out of *civilization* for a bit, Charlie's stomach halted her. There weren't many options, so Charlie chose McDonalds. Parking Juicy, she got out, went in, and ordered her food. Unable to decide, she ended up with a Big Mac, nuggets, cheeseburger, fries, and two apple pies. Oh, and a Coke, of course.

Realizing there was no way she would be able to eat and maneuver Juicy safely, Charlie chose to sit in Juicy, top down, music playing while she ate. Enjoying the sun on her face, she nibbled through a little of this and a little of that, excited over the Halloween items she just acquired. She knew the girls were going to love them. The tape Charlie currently had in the player ended, ejecting itself. Charlie fingered through her case to find another to take its place. Inserting the new cassette, she listened as the beginning of Wham!'s *I'm Your Man* started.

Taking a large bite of her Big Mac, a shuffling sound interrupted the song, followed by a woman's voice. Not just any woman. Her mom, Birdie's, voice. Stunned, Charlie stopped mid-chew and set her burger down as tears welled up in her eyes. She heard her mom talking to herself, cursing the technology and wondering if the thing was even on. *Yes, Mom, it's on,* Charlie thought. She continued to listen as her mom presumably flitted around her studio. It hit Charlie that her mom had thought she was listening to this tape. She had no clue she was recording. Charlie spent the next twenty minutes or so listening in on a day in the life of Birdie. She missed her so much. She had begun to forget some of her little idiosyncrasies and phrases. This tape was a find. A jewel. The tape flipped to its other side, and soon Cyndie Lauper was singing *Time After Time*. Gone was her mother.

Not wanting to damage the tape, Charlie ejected it and placed it back in its case, taking a pen from her bag and marking it MOM. Charlie found a replacement tape and slid it in. She finished her food, thankful for what the universe had just provided her. What a fabulous end to the day. She hoped it would continue into the night.

Later that evening, the three roommates gathered out on the patio once again. All prepped for the spell, they waited on Finn to arrive. Charlie looked at the drawn circle and asked Scarlett why it looked slightly different. "I will not be part of the circle, so I had to amend the setup to include both an inner circle and a central spell point. That space in the center will be where I'll reside for the duration. The three of you will do exactly what we did prior," Scarlett explained. Just as Charlie was set to ask another question, they heard a knock at the door. The knock alarmed Charlie a bit until she realized where it had come from.

"I got it," she said, and let Finn in.

"Well, hello there, Charlie. Your knight in shining armor has arrived," he said, taking a bow.

Charlie snickered and let him in. The duo went up the stairs and out to the patio, where Finn stood in awe over the prepped area.

"Wow! So we're going full on out here!? Bitchin'," he said in a mock surfer accent.

The three girls turned their heads in shock at what they had just heard.

"Alright, then, no surfer dude in the witch circle. Got it," he said with a laugh.

Scarlett explained how the evening would be going. Finn listened, suddenly serious, and took his place on the circle with the others. "Remember," Scarlett said, "we are going in with the purpose of finding out what was special about the boy, and what, if any, significance he was to Margaret's choosing to haunt Charlie."

Soon, the air around them shimmered, as if a fold in time was taking place. The world seemed to tilt, and only Scarlett's voice could be heard. They all watched as the space formed before them—a small room in a house, and a woman laying on a bed, another pacing by her side. The fireplace glowed with warmth, a small basket with linens close by. The woman in the bed moaned. Beads of sweat trickled down the plump young woman's face. "I cannot do this. 'Tis too much to bear," she cried. The second woman, the one pacing, turned and immediately was shown to be Margaret Cobb. "You can, and you must! Your baby's life, as well as yours, depends on it! Now, I'll bring back the nursemaid and we will go again." An older woman, heavyset, all in white, fluttered through the curtain, hands dripping with water. She made her way to the foot of the bed and commanded the plump woman to push. Again. As she did,

Margaret was seen standing to the side with what looked like both worry and anger on her face. She wrung her hands as the young woman gave a final push and…now they were seemingly in the same house but a different room. Charlie knew this room. She knew it well from her visions. This was the room where Elias died. She was certain of it. As she looked around, Margaret prepared for what seemed to be a visitor. She gathered herbs for a tea as well as two place settings on the table. She paced back and forth in front of the fire and nervously peeked out her window. Moments later, Betsy arrived. Communication between them ensued, and the three listened in awe…then they were back to the prior room. The woman, having given birth, was now in some sort of distress. Margaret stood, holding the newborn. She watched as the heavyset nursemaid attempted to save the young woman. Margaret clung to the baby as the woman softly announced, "I'm sorry, ma'am. She could not be saved." A door shut, and they found they were back in the front room. Elias was removing his outer clothes and boots. He accepted tea from Margaret and began to tell her of his day. Margaret, obviously upset, spewed her concerns over his latest issues that were arising. "Do you not know what your deceptions are doing to this family, our family, not to mention your business and reputation!? Your bad land deals are coming back upon you, Elias! The towns you're swindling are growing wise to your bait-and-switch tactics. The townspeople here are through with your promises of fortune while they suffer and starve. This has to stop!" she commanded. Elias, enraged by his wife's words, slapped her. How dare she speak against him and all he had done and built. They continued back and forth until the scene Charlie knew all too well played out before them. Elias, doubled over, retching, asking his wife what was going on. They continued to watch as Betsy showed herself and the spell was read. Elias collapsed, and…the three were pulled back with a force that was unexplainable. Their worlds went dark.

They laid in silence, Scarlett watching over them. Once balance was restored, they sat up and looked at each other.

Finn was the first to speak. "Well, that was a fine ride. A fine ride indeed!"

The group discussed the vision and confirmed they had all seen the same things. Scarlett sat back and listened, as she was not able to bear witness to anything they had seen.

"That totally answers why Margaret ended up raising the kid," Heather said.

"Totally," Finn agreed. "Charlie, that vision with Elias. That is the same one you have seen?"

"Yep. I hadn't seen it all as one continuous vision, though. It was nice to see the pieces fit together and to finally confirm that Elias was the scumbag we all thought he was."

"Cool. Cool. But something about that spell bothered me. I can't put my finger on it," Finn said with a bit of worry in his tone.

"Is it something bad?" Heather asked.

"I don't know," he said. "Just something off. Gonna need a bit of reflection on it, I guess," he finished. "Hey, I'm cream crackered. Gonna have to head out, ladies."

"You're what!?" Heather asked.

"Uh, cream crackered. You know. Tired. Exhausted," Finn replied.

The girls all in unison said "Ohhhhhhhh" and laughed.

With the mystery solved, at least for now, life went on. Classes were attended. Charlie and the others planned and began to set up for the party. Jared and Charlie had more time for each other. Instances continued and escalated for Charlie, who confided in Ramona, yet kept her family in the dark. Time moved on until...

CHAPTER THIRTY-THREE
HALLOWEEN

CHARLIE, BUSY IN HER ROOM hand-cutting ghosts and bats and stringing spiderwebs together, gazed at Saturday morning cartoons to keep her mind busy. The past ten days had gone by pretty quickly. It was hard to believe that the Halloween party was tonight. The exterior was fully spooked out and only the finishing touches were needed inside. Despite several dozen instances of Margaret's tauntings, they had been able to carry on with their lives, even if interrupted. Taking her completed crafts to the kitchen, Charlie smiled at the spread they had accomplished. No Julia Childs, but it would feed a bunch of hungry and drunk college students, no problem.

Heather came in through the slider with a huge smile on her face.

"I think we're going to pull this off, Charlie!" she squealed.

Charlie nodded. "Can you help me hang these around the house?"

"Sure can," Heather said, running to her room. She returned with some Scotch tape and got busy hanging Charlie's creations.

Scarlett arrived with a friend and a few kegs of beer.

"Going to get these set up out back," Scarlett said, making her way out the slider.

The day continued into the afternoon, and it was soon time for Charlie to get ready. She still had no clue what Jared was coming as, and since this was their first Halloween together, she had no reference point to even guess.

Charlie spent the next few hours meticulously assembling and transforming herself into the wonderful and spooky Bride. Time had flown by, and she was surprised to look out her window and see the sun setting. In addition to how well they had done planning and setting up this party, Charlie was extra happy that the weather was cooperating. There had been snow on Halloween in prior years, and that had been lingering in the back of her mind as the temps had begun to drop. But thankfully, not tonight. Clear, and chilly for sure, but otherwise a great night for a party.

A knock at her door startled Charlie. Even with the instances picking up pace, she had not grown used to them, making simple life noises startling by default. Again, a knock.

"Come in," Charlie said, turning to see who was coming through her door.

Jared peeked his head in first, giving her a huge smile. "Hey, girlie," he said. "Need any help with any of that?" he asked, walking in the rest of the way.

"Nope, I've got…" And at that moment, Charlie saw his costume. Puzzled at first, she stared. "What in the…?" she began.

"Here, let me help you out," Jared said, performing a slow turn.

It was then that Charlie got it. "Mr. Springsteen! I mean, Bruce!!"

Nodding, Jared smiled. "I know, I know. Easy way out. But with everything going on with classes and midterms and the professor, I was lucky I had time to even come up with this. Luckily, I had this red cap and the rest fell into place," he said with a chuckle, pointing to his ass that held said hat.

Charlie giggled, then got serious. "I need one more minute," she said.

Sliding her feet into a pair of chunky black boots, she turned, held her arms up to expose the full costume, and slowly turned for Jared. "Whatcha think?"

"Totally boss!" he said. "No pun intended." They both laughed.

Guests began to arrive, and soon the party was in full swing. People meandered in and out of the house. Small groups gathered upstairs and down. Charlie was in the kitchen admiring the variety of costumes. Scarlett was a witch—what else. Heather was a vampire. Finn, who had shown up fashionably late, was Sherlock Holmes. Gunther came as Dolly Parton, herself. Everyone was in high spirits and high on spirits. Someone had set up a horror movie marathon on the common room TV. Upstairs, music was playing. *Everyday is Halloween* was currently on its fourth rotation.

Charlie took a sip of her beer when a chilling breeze suddenly swept through the room. At first, it didn't phase her since the slider was open and a breeze or two was to be expected. Another blew through, this time causing the candles in the jack 'o lanterns to flicker and the music to warble and distort. Charlie looked over and saw Jared looking back at her. Before he could form a word, the lights flickered and went out, plunging the room into darkness. A crash of thunder sounded. Again, Charlie looked at Jared. No storms had been in the forecast for tonight. The room fell silent, and screams were heard from downstairs. A deafening roar filled the house, causing everyone to cover their ears. Just as suddenly as it had started, it stopped, and the room filled with an oppressive silence. A low, guttural growl echoed through the house, seeming to come from the walls themselves. Charlie heard some guy yell, "Heck, yeah!

Killer sound effects, guys!" Charlie knew this was not the case. Jared had made it to her side, eyes wide with fear.

"What's happening?" he asked, grabbing Charlie's hand.

The growl grew louder and louder as objects around the room began to move on their own. Books flew off shelves, chairs tipped over, curtains swayed and twirled ominously. A cold, malevolent vibe took over the room, making it hard to breathe. A flash of light came from the corner, revealing a shadowy figure. Its eyes glowed a fierce blue, then red. Charlie heard several screams and what she assumed were people fainting. She could not be sure, however, of any of this. The figure began to float around the room, its presence exuding darkness. It let out a bone-chilling laugh. Charlie tried to move, but her feet felt glued to the floor, rooted in terror. "You will help me! I shall prevail!" the entity hissed, its voice echoing with an otherworldly resonance. "I shall be freed!"

No one moved. Charlie turned to Jared and mouthed to find Scarlett or Finn. *They have to know what to do,* she thought. Jared nodded and looked around. Scarlett was coming up the stairs and had something in her hands. As the entity advanced, everyone watched in horror. Just as it had made its way over toward Charlie, it stopped a foot short. The air grew colder and the shadows seemed to close in. Then Charlie saw a face forming in the blob that was the entity. The mist that made it up was forming together. Charlie looked up and saw a face she had seen before. Elias! She was pinned with fear. It wasn't Margaret!! It was Elias! Charlie began to cry as she heard Scarlett say, "Charlie, close your eyes!" Moments later, Charlie felt a splash of something grainy hit her face. She kept her eyes closed and heard a rumble, followed by a vacuum of air and then silence. Blinking, Charlie opened her eyes to see the lights had returned. Everyone in the room stood either stunned or crying.

"What the fuck was that!?" she heard someone across the room yell.

Reeling from what had just transpired, Charlie, Jared, Heather, Scarlett, and Finn were the last remaining partiers. The rest of the party made a mass exodus soon after the entity vanished. The gang all sat outside on the patio, trying to make sense of what just happened.

Charlie confirmed that she had seen Elias's face.

Scarlett explained how she got rid of it.

Finn sat forward and cleared his throat. "I'm so sorry. Tonight is all my fault. I reached out to my mum after we did the spell. Remember, I said something felt off about it? Well, I was right. And I was set to tell you but figured it could wait until after the party. I'm so sorry, Charlie. My mum said that the spell we saw in the vision was not a spell to kill someone at all! Based on Elias' actions after drinking the tea, he was poisoned. Mum thinks maybe arsenic or something comparable. Besides that, the spell, well, it had nothing to do with killing him; it was one to trap a soul. They used that spell to affix Elias' soul and spirit to an item. My granny confirmed and added that it wouldn't have been the dolly. It would have been the brooch. Something personal to both parties."

The room went silent.

"All this time, I thought it was Margaret. I'm so stupid," Charlie began. "This is why I should be training more with Marcus. I thought Margaret was angry for having to raise his love child and lingered because of it *and* the guilt of killing him. But in fact it was Margaret's vengeance to make Elias pay for his evil ways. I couldn't see what was being shown to me. I was assuming," Charlie said angrily.

"Don't blame yourself, babe. We all had the same information, and we all thought it was Margaret. It made sense," Jared said.

"So what does Charlie do now?" Heather asked.

"My mum said the answer was in the books that I gave Charlie," Finn said.

"I...I still have them," Charlie said, standing to go to her room.

"Stay put," Scarlett said. "Where are they? I'll grab them for you."

A moment later, Scarlett was back. Finn took the book in question and searched for the text that explained what they needed to do.

"Ok," he said. "It says Charlie needs to get the cursed item back to its original location and reverse the curse to release the soul," Finn read. "Well, clearly, there is not a spell here, so we'll need to research that."

"No, we won't," Charlie said, looking around at everyone. This time, she stood and went to her room. She returned with the book of shadows, a piece of paper, and a pencil. "I knew something had to have been on this missing page prior to this one; the patterns in the pages didn't make sense. See up top here," she said, pointing to the delicate patterns that adorned the tops of each page. Charlie began to rub the pencil lead over the paper. As she did, words began to form. Everyone watched as Charlie handed the paper to Scarlett.

"Yep, this will do it," Scarlett said. "She must have torn it out to prevent anyone from doing what we're going to have to do."

"We?" Charlie said. "No, this is my mess; I'll do it. Besides, the location is down in Tennessee! There's no way I'm going to ask you to go with me that far."

"You?" Jared said. "You mean us?"

"And me," Heather said.

"And me," Finn added.

Charlie began to cry. "Ok. Well, then, it's settled, I guess. *We* will go to Tennessee. But *we* will need a plan."

The group worked together over the next few hours to put together their plan. They would each spend the week working on their individual parts in preparation for their departure on Friday morning. Finn was sure he could borrow a van from a friend that would hold all of them for the trip. Jared would work on the route, timing, and make sure Benji knew what was going on and when to expect them. Scarlett, Charlie, and Heather would work on copying the spell, making sure it was indeed complete, then gather any items needed. This, of course, would all happen on top of their normal daily lives.

Completely exhausted, the group said their goodnights.

What the group had not anticipated when formulating their plan was how the events at the party would affect their guests and the community. They forgot how good news travels fast but bad news travels faster. Their little party had spawned a media frenzy. While the day after had been a quiet one, by day two, they had started seeing local news stations recording along the street, and by day three, they had a complete news monstrosity on their hands.

"Jesus," Charlie said to Scarlett as she peered through the front curtains. "I never expected this."

"We should have known there was going to be some upheaval, given the amount of people we had here that night. I have a feeling it's going to get worse before it gets better," Scarlett said.

"What are we going to do?" Heather asked. "You know as soon as we step out they'll be all over us like white on rice."

"We have to spin this, and quickly," Scarlett answered.

"But how?" Charlie asked.

"By giving them a nicely wrapped little present," Scarlett said.

"Present?" Heather asked.

"Yeah. No one but us knows what really happened. We stick together and feed them a story that will explain everything," Scarlett said. "Let me show you."

With Scarlett's plan laid out, Charlie called both Jared and Finn to come over, letting them know to come to the back gate if possible.

Later, the group exited the house, and as a unified front, told their story to the media crowds that had continued to grow throughout the day.

As the microphones were forced toward their faces, Charlie stepped forward and spoke for them all. "We know there have been rumors about a party we held to celebrate Halloween. We apologize for the panic and inconvenience our party and our little prank had on both our guests and the campus community as a whole. We want to take this time to set the record straight." Charlie took a deep breath and continued. "As part of our Halloween set-up, we thought, at the time, it would be a phenomenal idea to make the party more than just a party. We wanted to make it an experience. With the help of a friend of ours, we were able to rig the props to create a one-of-a-kind haunting. What we accomplished was beyond our expectations and, well, was truly amazing. We regret any harm it caused our guests, both physically and mentally. We have learned from our experience with this and can only ask for forgiveness." Stepping back from the microphones, Charlie let the others handle the onslaught of questions.

The next few days leading up to their departure were some of the longest any of them would have to endure.

Although busy, each of them was terrified Elias would come back even harder at them, especially if he sensed their plan. Unlike the prior year, there was no spell to hide behind. Their only hope had been that Elias' energy had been tapped completely after his last display, rendering him too weak and unable to "listen" in on their plans.

Each of them proceeded through their days as normally as they could while also tending to the tasks they had laid out after the party.

They gathered one final time at Jared's house. The only one missing would be Charlie. Finn had made a great point in suggesting that she not be present as it seemed Elias was bound to her through the brooch and may be able to sense what they were up to. Charlie put up a fuss at first but relinquished in the end, knowing Finn was right. Meeting one final time with their completed assignments, they performed a practice run of sorts to make sure nothing was missing. Having agreed that all seemed in order, they confirmed they would meet in the morning at Jared's. Finn would pick everyone up in the van he was able to secure. The girls suggested that they and Charlie stay there for the night to ease both the morning exodus and to allow for a somewhat good night's sleep.

"Power in numbers," Scarlett joked.

Jared agreed; and gave Charlie a ring to see if she was ready to head over.

Not more than an hour later, Charlie was lying next to Jared in his bed, staring up at the ceiling. She wanted nothing more than to talk about the plan and her fears, but she knew she had to stay silent. Curling up against Jared, she sighed and drifted off to sleep.

CHAPTER THIRTY-FOUR
CHANNELING THEIR INNER SCOOBIES

THEY TOOK TURNS DRIVING to Piney Flats, stopping only a few times to stretch, eat, and relieve themselves. Jared had given Benji a call to let him know a firmer estimated time of arrival. Benji promised he'd be ready.

As the van pulled up to the familiar red mailbox, Charlie and Jared looked at each other and smiled. It was a knowing smile. One filled with a lot of context and feelings that could not be vocalized at the moment. They were stunned out of the lull as Heather said, "Whoa! That place is creepy!"

"That's not it," Jared said. "This is Benji's place. We'll meet here and walk to where we need to go."

Charlie took a deep breath, hoping that Elias' spirit was not picking up on what was happening. She had tried to keep her mind on other things for the ride. She had also asked Marcus for help before she headed out. He could not offer much, but what he did do was suggest she wrap the brooch in an item of hers in hopes to trick the spirit, then place it in a box surrounded by several of Scarlett's crystals. The final step was to draw a protection symbol on the inside of the lid. Charlie did as she had been instructed. Now as they exited the vehicle, she clenched her jaw, hoping it would continue to work until they reached their destination.

Benji stood outside on his porch, armed with several flashlights, jackets, and his trusty boombox. The rest of the gang double checked their items and gave a nod that they were ready to proceed. Benji clicked the play button on his box and "*Highway to Hell*" resounded from the speakers.

"Benji, dude! You always have a song for everything," Jared said, chuckling.

Benji, leading the way, moved confidently but quietly, his footsteps barely leaving a trace on the soft forest floor. Behind him, the gang whispered nervously to each other, their eyes darting to every rustling bush and shadow. Scarlett stayed close to Heather, who occasionally let out an anxious giggle. Finn brought up the rear, glancing over his shoulder every few steps as if he was expecting to see something—or someone—following them.

The deeper they went, the more the woods seemed to close in on them. Charlie didn't remember it being quite this ominous on their original walk out. Strange sounds echoed in the distance: the hoot of an owl, the snap of a twig, the rustle of unseen creatures living their nocturnal lives. They finally approached the pond, and Benji stopped to ask everyone if they were ok. With nods all around, Benji continued. The group followed him over the footbridge, and it wasn't long before they were looking up at the dilapidated house.

"Holy shit!" Scarlett said.

"Uh huh," Heather agreed.

"Charming," Finn tossed in.

They continued their approach, the windows looking like dark eyes watching them. The sense of anticipation and dread hung heavy in the night air as they stood before the front porch.

"Are we ready?" Benji asked.

A unanimous but soft *yes* resounded.

"Ok," he continued. "Jared and Charlie here know the layout and where we're going. The rest of you stick close to one of us. The floors aren't very stable, and I don't want anyone's leg, or entire body for that matter, falling through the boards."

Again, everyone agreed.

Benji headed in. They made their way through the front door and over to the room that was once the kitchen/main living area.

"Here is where I believe you want to be," Benji said. "At least based on what Jared here told me. Do you agree, Charlie?" he asked.

Charlie nodded, then said, "Ok. Let's get this started."

CHAPTER THIRTY-FIVE
SUCK IT, MR. COBB

USING THEIR FLASHLIGHTS to set up the space, Scarlett began to light the candles they would need. She instructed the others to start their portion of the set up. Everyone worked together quickly.

Charlie was the first to stand back and assess their progress. She looked at the now dimly lit space, candles flickering and casting shadows across the room. The scent of incense filled the air, yet somehow was unable to cut through the thick and heavy tension. She thought about what their plan was going to mean for Elias. While he had not asked to be trapped for eternity, she wasn't sure that where he was going to end up would be much better. The decision Margaret and Betsy had made for him may have saved him from a life of eternal damnation for the pain and suffering he had caused so many through the years. Her empathy was short lived, though. He deserved whatever he got. She knew this needed to be done and truly hoped the plan would work. The critical part would be the mirror. The timing had to be perfect, and they only had one shot. If anything went wrong, or the mirror broke before it was time, then they would fail. She didn't know what failure would mean in the grand scheme of things, but she did know it was not an option. Scarlett finished the circle of protection while instructing the rest where to sit for the ritual.

Charlie took her place in the middle. She sat criss-cross with the box in her lap. Jared, Heather, Benji, and Finn sat at key points around her, but still within the circle's protection. Each of them, as with the other spells, had been given their own crystals to protect them from what may transpire. Scarlett, who would lead the incantation, stood just outside the larger circle in her own ring of salt for protection.

Scarlett began to chant arcane words that resonated with power and intensity as the others waited for their cues. Minutes seemed like hours. The anticipation was palpable. With the roar growing exponentially in the room, Scarlett shouted to Charlie who would be the first to perform her task. Opening the box, she removed the brooch and placed it before her on the mark Scarlett had laid out. The room grew colder and louder. Somehow, though she wasn't sure how, there was wind. Charlie looked up as Heather was given her cue. Leaning forward, Heather sprinkled a mixture of herbs and salt around the brooch. The room got even colder. The brooch started to glow with an ethereal light. It flickered with shades of blues. Jared, who was sitting directly in front of Charlie on the outer circle, watched in abject horror while waiting for his crucial cue. Scarlett, barely able to catch her breath, finally screamed, "NOW, JARED!" Jared held up an antique mirror and shouted, "Elias! We command you to show yourself!"

The room began to hum, low at first, then growing to a roar. Scarlett continued to chant. Finn and Benji, reciting a protection spell, looked on edge as they concentrated on their words. The brooch began to shift from the blues to a series of brights as it reached the most beautiful and pure white light Charlie had ever seen. It was her turn yet again.

"Elias, come forth! Let us undo the awful deed Margaret set upon you! We command you to leave this realm. We insist you make your journey to whatever plane you're meant to reside in. This, this plane is not yours! I'm not yours to torment any longer. You have done your damage here on earth; now you must go and pay for your transgressions. Elias, we command you!"

At that moment, Charlie looked up to see Elias' face forming, and the temperature dropped to dangerous levels, so low their breath crystallized before them. Scarlett was still deep in her incantation. Even though the room was as cold as it was, beads of sweat formed and rolled down Scarlett's face. Heather broke her watch over Scarlett as Elias loomed over Charlie, who was stunned in his presence. "DO IT NOW, JARED!" Heather screamed.

Jared stood and yelled, "Elias, I demand you face me!"

Elias' misty form slowly turned its gaze from Charlie to Jared, and with a final incantation from Scarlett, Elias let out a wail of intense pain and anguish, then entered the mirror with a deafening crack. Jared quickly took his chance, throwing the mirror to the ground and smashing his foot upon it with a triumphant, "Suck it, Mr. Cobb," sending a sudden rush of wind over the room, knocking over everything in its path. Then silence. Pure silence. Scarlett collapsed as Heather went to her aid. Jared, avoiding the glass surrounding him, made his way to Charlie. The group sat in silence; they had seen the last of Elias Cobb.

EPILOGUE

WITH THE GANG ALL BACK at Cornell, life carried on like normal. Classes were attended, dates were had, and everything was peaceful.

Charlie had finally called her dad to communicate what they had just gone through and received the exact response she knew she would get. Dale was mad. She knew he would be, however, the extent of his anger was softened slightly by the news he had for Charlie. The house had sold. The new owners would be taking possession by Thanksgiving. He offered for her and Jared to stop by on their way to see him for the holiday. He had asked a final favor from his real estate agent, who had agreed she would meet them if they needed to say a final goodbye. Charlie had thanked her dad for the gesture and said she would need to think about it. It had been hard enough to say goodbye before; this time, it might be impossible. With her plans to visit all set, Charlie had said her goodbyes to her dad and went on with college life for the next few weeks.

Now that they were back, Heather knew she had to express her concerns to Charlie sooner than later. It was going to be hard. How do you tell someone who just went through a horrible ordeal that more was coming? She shook her head. *Just do it.* She *has* to know, Heather told herself.

Scarlett was the first to head out for the break; she had a flight to catch to California. Finn was next. He was off to visit his mum and granny in England. Heather would be staying behind to hold down the fort and was the final man standing when Charlie and Jared packed up Juicy for the drive to Ohio.

"Hey, Charlie," Heather said from the front stoop. "Can I've a quick minute?"

"Be right back, Jared," Charlie said. "Heather needs me."

Leaping over the stones, Charlie did a final foot plant in front of Heather. "What's up? I thought we had covered all the goodbyes."

Heather took a deep breath and began. "Charlie, um, I'm not sure how to say this, but, well, I guess I just have to now, huh? Ok, here it goes. I have visions. Not like yours. Mine are not dreams of past events; mine are premonitions of what's to come." She paused, waiting for Charlie to acknowledge that she understood.

"Ok…" Charlie answered.

"They've been getting clearer, and it seems from the most recent, that a very powerful and malevolent entity will be entering your life at some point. I saw shadows around you and Jared, and it seems like this force will challenge you and force you to face some terrible things. Fuck, Charlie, something bad is going to happen. I can feel it. I don't know exactly when it will happen, but I can't shake the feeling that it's coming soon. I know it involves you and Jared, and there seem to be others involved as well. I know you've been practicing with Marcus and have the knowledge from both Astrid and Elias in your wheelhouse, but you need to be careful. You need to prepare. Danger is lurking, and it feels like it's waiting for the right moment to strike. Please be careful," she finished, giving her friend a long hug for what might be the final time.

THE AUTHOR

C.L. Merklinger the author of the Realms and Realities Series, grew up with an insatiable appetite for reading and all things scary. Inspired by Horror Authors such as Ray Bradbury; Stephen King; Dean Koontz; and Edgar Allan Poe, she was also deeply influenced by great Mystery Character Authors such as Lawrence Sanders, Agatha Christie and Mary Higgins Clark. Following her passions for Horror and the Paranormal she pulls from her experiences as an Empath which inspired her to write this series. C.L. resides in the Chesapeake Bay area of Maryland where she dabbles in photography.

GEIST

COMPANION PLAYLIST